FATIMA BALA

Hafsatu Bebi

A story about identity and loss

First edition

ISBN: 9798398236361

This book was professionally typeset on Reedsy.
Find out more at reedsy.com

Dedicated to my mother, Ummita.

Absence diminishes mediocre passions and increases great ones, as the wind extinguishes candles and fans fires.

FRANCOIS DE LA ROCHEFOUCAULD

Acknowledgement

Many amazing women -whether they know it or not, helped me write this book, including my mother, Hajiya Hauwa Mohammed, the bravest and kindest woman ever to grace the face of this earth. My mother-in-law, for her stories and her passion for education.

For her patience, honesty, and persistence, my wonderful editor turned friend, Khadija Yusra Sanusi, who spent countless long nights and days painstakingly going through every single word on these pages even through changing time zones and her numerous other deliverables, she always prioritized "Z's story."

Dr. Fatima Mana, my tweeny, for always starting my day with twenty memes, for a friendship that redefined what friendship should look like for me at a turning point in my life, for your family that's mine as well, and for answering all my "how would a doctor" questions while I was writing the character Ibrahim.

Ummi Yakubu, Creative Director at Griot Studios, and her love of authentic art and expression from all over the globe, especially from Arewa girls, thank you for your feedback and for being an inspiration.

Pamela Bhe, who listened to me every morning, helped me through my winter blues and constantly gave me the most wholesome advice, muffins, and recipes.

Aisha Abubakar - my beauty, Sa'ada Abdulmalik -my sister from another mother, Mofe Popo - mother of my daughter; and Rabi Ahmadu-Ali - my yar uwa. Thank you all for being my trusted pillars and family. My support system since college days: Angelina Acheampong, Grace Eke, and Judy Kallaghe; all your very different personalities were condensed into the friendship that Ilham represented.

i

And the men too.

I would like to thank my husband, Kabir, for patiently listening to my story ideas, for reading the drafts, and for your screenshots with big red circles on things you think I should revisit.

My brother Ya Adamu. Allah blessed me immensely by giving me a supportive, caring, and loving big brother.

Professor Merv Jefferies who has taught me to find a sense of wonderment in every new piece of information.

For my father and for daddy, I miss you both dearly.

Ibrahim

Kaduna, 1998

I still remember the first day I met her. It was a Saturday afternoon and the sun was scorching hot. She was outside, drying clothes on the cloth line by the abandoned water tank, the one with the peeling paint and the barely legible letters 'G' and 'P'. The tank had since been replaced by a well in the middle of the compound, which served all the ten tenants in the three flats since water stopped running through the pipes and taps years ago. The three flats were built side by side with no space in between them, thin walls meant you could hear when pots fell in your neighbor's kitchen.

I dropped the metal bucket I was holding to the ground and grabbed the small yellow pail tied to meters of rope. Then I positioned myself by the well so I could watch her, while fetching my water. She had her back to me, in a black T-shirt over a yellow and black wrapper tied around her waist, and was bending over a repurposed white paint bucket to pick up wrung pieces of clothes, unroll them and flap them into the air, expelling droplets of water with a force that was hard to believe her tiny frame could conjure. I watched as her hands spread a navy blue fabric on the line, her henna-stained fingertips moving it until it was symmetrical on both sides. It was a hijab. She reached for two wooden pegs and clipped it in place, while humming quietly. She might have heard the burbling of the water in the well, because, she stopped humming but she didn't turn around; she continued drying her clothes on the line, as I continued fetching water from the well.

I wouldn't have known her name if not for Hajiya Tani, the tenant who lived in Flat 3 with her four children and a husband who visited once a week. Her husband, Alhaji Sani, was a civil servant in Zaria, where his other wife resided. "Zuwaira, don't sleep there *o*. Somebody cannot even ask you to do something and expect you to finish on time," she said in Hausa from inside her flat.

Zuwaira.

I looked up at her as she slowly wiped her hands on the wrapper tied around her waist and she walked away from the drying line; the T-shirt she was wearing gently hinted at the curves beneath.

I looked away, filling up my bucket. At the same time, she placed her now-empty white bucket on the ground next to the well and grabbed the second pail used to fetch water from the well. Her movements were gentle as she lowered the pail with her hands wrapped around the black ropes, gently letting go of one hand as the pail hit the water at the same time I pulled mine out. Without looking at her, I emptied the full pail into her bucket, filling it up completely.

I almost lost my balance after I dropped the pail on the ground because that was the first time I looked up at her face. Beneath her haphazardly tied yellow scarf, her jet-black hair was tightly braided into plaits that fell over her shoulders. Her skin was a deep shade of brown, like her eyes, and the black lashes surrounding them flickered upwards as she looked up at me. I watched as her lips parted as if to thank me, but that never happened because at the same time, Hajiya Tani's voice came bellowing towards us again.

"Zuwaira? Are you deaf?" The verandah door to Flat 3 opened as Hajiya Tani's robust figure stepped out of the barricade that held up the mosquito net. "So you can hear me, but you didn't answer?" she spoke in Hausa as she walked closer to us, in a black long dress with one end of her black veil draped over her shoulder and trailing the floor.

"I've finished. I'm just about to bring the water inside," Zuwaira said. Her voice was soft, yet devoid of emotion – no fear and definitely no respect for Hajiya Tani.

I cleared my throat, and Hajiya Tani's features softened as she saw me behind the hijabs on the cloth line by the well. *"Likita,* is that you?" she smiled.

All the other tenants referred to me by my name Ibro, except Hajiya Tani. She called me *"likita,"* the Hausa word for 'doctor', even though I was only in my 4th year in Medical school. I secretly suspected that she didn't remember my name. After all, I only visited my older brother, Ya Isa, the tenant in Flat 1, once every few weeks from my university, ABU Zaria. Visiting him in Kaduna was much more convenient and cost-effective than traveling all the way to our family house in Kano.

"Hajiya, good evening," I greeted her. Through the corner of my eye, I watched as the girl, Zuwaira, quietly picked up the bucket of water and moved away, obscured by all the wrappers and hijabs on the line.

"How much longer will this strike go on for?" Hajiya Tani asked as she inspected the clothes Zuwaira had washed, as though she were looking for an unwashed stain; she didn't find any.

"Hopefully, the authorities can reach a middle ground and call us back to school soon," I answered, wondering if I would see the girl again. Was she visiting a relative, or was she here because of the strike, too? She looked a bit young so if she was at the university, she would be in her first year.

"Anyway, it's a good thing you're here," Hajiya Tani said. "Jamil has been struggling with further maths. Aisha told me you had aced your WAEC exams. Can you help him with his? His exams start in a few months."

I knew my brother's wife, Ya Aisha, and Hajiya Tani were friends. I just didn't know that along with what I was studying, my exam results from five years ago were also gossip fodder.

I opened my mouth to speak, but before I could get a word out, the main gate opened with its loud, squeaky sound. It was an old gate with rusty red paint, and like every other thing in the building that was falling apart, the landlord, Alhaji Wada, refused to fix it. Five months ago, when Ya Aisha

3

complained about snakes making their way to her verandah because of the unkempt grass, Alhaji Wada shrugged and said there was nothing he could do, that snakes move about in the rainy season. It was I who ended up cutting the grass around the compound.

When the gate stopped creaking, Jamil – a tall and lanky teenager – entered the compound in his jersey, sweat dripping from his face as he kicked a ball towards us.

"Wash your feet before you enter the house; don't drag all that dirt inside," his mother said before he even had a chance to greet her. "Zuwaira made *tuwo*. You can ask her to warm it up for you when you're ready to eat." She walked away from the well towards my brother's flat and I heard her call for my sister-in-law, her loud voice resounding behind me.

Zuwaira. Was she the maid, then? I could have sworn there was a slight resemblance between her and Hajiya Tani's daughters. Maybe it was just the ebony complexion.

"Ya Ibro," Jamil called out to me playfully, as he dragged down the pail to fetch water with the deftness of a sixteen-year-old kid. "Did you watch the Liverpool match?"

"Yes, 2 - 0," I answered and started making my way into the house with my metal bucket as he washed his face and legs. As I walked, I looked back towards Flat 3 to see if I would catch another glimpse of Zuwaira, but to no avail.

* * *

I didn't see Zuwaira for a whole week. In fact, I was partially convinced that she had already left the compound until one Saturday evening. I was sitting under the mango tree with Jamil, helping him with maths homework. The tree was planted opposite their flat and from my spot, I could see the ins and outs of their flat.

"Jamil, you got everything right," I announced, mildly surprised as I marked all the questions. There were two other kids I tutored for WAEC who lived down the street and they never got all the homework questions right. Nobody ever did, except this one time that Jamil answered them all correctly.

Tutoring him was something I was prepared to do without pay, but when his father insisted on paying me every month, I couldn't refuse. I already felt like a burden to Ya Isa; apart from sending money to our extended family in Kano and paying for my University tuition, the ASUU strike had forced me to temporarily relocate to his house, forcing him to feed me too. Ya Aisha was kind enough never to make me feel like I was crowding their space; she would not say it, but my sleeping in their living room for the past week had been quite inconvenient for their family, especially because she had to walk through the living room to get to the bathroom.

"Zuwaira went over them for me and she corrected the last three," Jamil said, now pointing at the scribble on the notebook. It suddenly became obvious to me that there was a change in writing over the crossed-off wrongly-answered probability questions.

Zuwaira. I stiffened as I wrote down his grade on the paper and circled it with my red pen.

"Who's Zuwaira?" I asked nonchalantly, managing to suppress the interest in my question.

"My cousin. Her father is Baba's brother," he answered, scowling as he saw his grade. "90 percent?"

"I'm taking off ten marks, since you had help." *His cousin. His Uncle's daughter. Does that mean her family lives in Zaria, like his father? How long is she here for? When will I see her again?*

"Jamil!" We heard Hajiya Tani's voice bellow from the flat.

"*Na'am?* Yes, Mama?" he called back, as he stood up to go into the house. I looked at the windows, hoping to catch another glimpse of Zuwaira, but the lack of electricity made it hard to see much beyond the front door. I saw movement around the kitchen window, but maybe I imagined it because I blinked and nobody was there.

5

"Ya Ibro, Mama said I should call you." Jamil came back and started packing up his notebooks.

Did Hajiya Tani see me stealing glances at their window? Is she worried that I was ogling at her or planning to steal from her house? Or did she know I set up the designated lesson spot so I could catch a glimpse of Zuwaira? I thought, moving my gaze to the brown, dying grass by the tree.

"What happened?" I asked as I followed him into the house, my palms sweaty, even though I didn't do anything wrong.

"I don't know," he shrugged.

"Assalamu alaikum," I called as I stood by the door, waiting to be called in.

"Ah! *Likita*, please come in."

I followed her voice inside, raising the curtain and ducking as I entered the small living room. I found her seated on a three-seater couch with three white crotched dollies arranged on the headrest. Her three preteen daughters were sprawled on the carpet, lip-singing a song from the Hausa movie playing on the TV. It was the same song Zuwaira was humming by the well a week earlier, but there was no sign of her anywhere.

Behind Hajiya Tani, a framed picture of her and her husband took up the space between the doors that led to the rooms and the kitchen. Their flat was small just like ours, except for its white landline rotary telephone, the only one in our compound, and a brown ceiling fan that had light bulbs attached to it – an upgrade from the simple white ones the flats came with.

"Good evening," I greeted her, still standing by the door.

"Good evening, *likita*," she smiled at me before turning her attention to her daughters. "Can't you girls greet?" she barked at the startled girls who hurriedly mumbled 'salam' to me. I answered in kind.

"Can you help us look at the lightbulb in the kitchen? It just went off. The low and high current keep eating up all our bulbs in this house." She pointed at the door to the right of the picture frame with her right hand.

There was a clatter in the kitchen, and I got excited at the possibility of seeing Zuwaira in the kitchen. "Can I go and check it?"

Hajiya Tani nodded absentmindedly as her attention returned to the television. With measured steps, I made my way across the carpet and was in the kitchen in no time. There she was – between the stainless-steel sink that was scoured clean and two kerosine stoves on a table. She was sitting on a wooden stool and picking stones out of beans in a tray. Behind her was an uncovered pan with chopped onions, peppers, and tomatoes.

"As-assalamu alaikum,"

She stood up the moment she saw me, placed the pot on the sink, and wiped her hands on her wrapper. She was still wearing the black short-sleeved T-shirt I saw her in the previous week; I knew it was the same one because of the round neck.

"Good evening," she pulled the black scarf that was falling off her head, making sure it covered the visible part of her hair.

"I'm just going to check the light bulb," I explained, glancing up at the ceiling and back to the kitchen, looking around for something I could climb on. There was an empty gas cylinder by the corner; I reached for it, placing it in the middle of the kitchen as I reached for the bulb and unscrewed it. I glanced down at her, but she had her back to me. She was now fetching water from a drum in the corner and adding it to the pot.

I looked back at the bulb. "It's burnt out," I muttered, but she did not acknowledge me. I came down from the cylinder and out of the kitchen to find Hajiya Tani looking up at me expectantly as though she had been staring at the door, waiting for me. "The bulb is dead," I said. "I think we might have a spare one at our place. Let me check."

"I hope you have a spare one because Mallam Abu's kiosk is closed already, and that's where we normally get bulbs from."

I went into Ya Isa's flat and met Ya Aisha with my nieces. She was braiding three-year-old Salma's hair while five-year-old Bilkisu ate rice from her plate. I went straight to the cassette player to check for the extra bulb I hid behind it when I changed the one on the verandah three weeks earlier. It was right there.

"Uncle Ibro, where are you going?" Bilkisu asked.

"Somewhere five-year-olds aren't allowed," I laughed and playfully ruffled her hair as she heaped rice on her spoon. "Eat your food."

I hurried back to Hajiya Tani's flat, relieved that Zuwaira was still in the kitchen. She was standing by the stove, watching as the pot of beans boiled. I climbed the cylinder again, and as I screwed the bulb on, I must have leaned too far to the right because I felt the cylinder wobble beneath my feet. Before I could steady myself, Zuwaira crouched and held the cylinder in place.

"Thank you." I said, my hands spreading open as I regained my balance on the cylinder. If it hadn't been for her, I would have fallen into the hot pot of beans.

I looked down at her, and her eyes met mine. She nodded.

Hafsatu

Abuja, 2021

I'm in front of the double mirrors that also serve as doors to my closet, or more accurately, the messy excuse of white-walled space I call a closet. Honestly, Mariya, one of the maids, is getting on the last bit of my nerves these few days; all the clothes I tried on before going for Ilham's dinner last night are still on the navy blue accent chair in front of my shoe wall. She also keeps putting my shoes back in the wrong cubes. I've told her several times that the browns and nudes stay together, and the pumps go a level beneath the stilettos. Flats and my running shoes stay at the bottom, and for goodness sake, all shoes face outward! How hard is it for her to follow my simple instructions?

I hold a black-and-white swimsuit against my body, turning slightly to the left. *I'm not sure about the horizontal stripes, but the ruched midriff is flattering,* I think to myself just as the intercom in my bedroom starts ringing. I walk out of the closet towards the queen-sized upholstered platform bed that matches the deep brown and gold drapes and shag carpet. The floral wallflower on opposite ends of the room highlights the glossy white paneled walls and minimizes the monstrosity of having faux plants – the tall orchids by the window next to my reading nook and the white pots that house the big green elephant-ear plants. To be honest, you can't really tell that they are artificial plants; that is their only redeeming factor.

9

"Ma'am, your friend Ilham just arrived," Joe's familiar voice came through the speakers after I answered the phone. Joe is the head of security. He has been the head now for more years than I care to remember. Other security men come and go, but Joe remains the head of security.

"Has my dad gone out?"

"No, not yet."

I drop the receiver without saying another word, returning to the mirror. *It's 2021,* I think to myself; there's *no reason why security should call to announce visitors. We all have mobile phones now.* I knew Ilham was coming because, at 5:16 pm, she sent me a text: *'on my way.'* The doors to my room swing open, interrupting my thoughts.

"Remind me never to have that many caffeinated drinks at night. I couldn't sleep until 4 am," Ilham says, as she walks into my room slowly and lazily, using the least effort to close the door behind her. She's wearing a red sundress with bell sleeves, her shoulders hiding under her scarf, exposing her curly hair that is tied into a tight knot at her nape. She is tall and slim, features that are partially thanks to her religious habit of counting her calories. "You're not wearing that, are you?" She removes her dark cat-eye sunglasses and widens her eyes.

"What's wrong with it?" I look back at the mirror as she stands behind me.

"*Bebi,* horizontal stripes? Not slimming at all," she walks into my closet and looks around. "What about that Balmain you got at Saks?"

"The pink one?" I walk in with her and open the top-shelf drawers that had the new clothes I got over the summer holiday in California; most of them still had their price tags on them. I pull out the one-piece swimsuit, undressing as she checks a message on her phone. "What are you wearing?" I ask her as I squeeze into the figure-hugging polyester with a low plunge back. I fish for my silicon nipple covers and press them over my breasts, looking up as she returns, holding a red one-shoulder swimsuit with cutouts on the side.

"Wow, Bashir will go crazy!" She laughs as her eyes go over me.

I sigh out loud at the thought of Bashir, who has been distant these days.

I don't even know what is worse: the calls he doesn't pick up or the sorry excuses he always comes up with.

"I feel like it's a bit over the top," I say as I adjust the white edge of the straps on my shoulder, my left-hand resting over the stitched B logo just between my breasts.

"And so? It's your boyfriend's birthday! And it's just gonna be us."

* * *

Ilham and I meet my dad in the garden on our way to my car. He's playing a round of mini golf alone on the artificial grass turf that Umm'Hafsa paid a contractor to install for him on his last birthday. This was after he hurt his knee and couldn't go to the golf course in Garki for three months due to the slight limp. My siblings, Saratu, Aishatu (who we call Shatu to set her apart from our other cousin, Aisha), and Mohammed all call our mother 'mum' when we're talking to her, but daddy calls her Umm'Hafsa. Well, really, he calls her 'my love' when he's talking to her, but when he's talking about her in her absence, he refers to her as Umm'Hafsa; somehow, everyone calls her that too – even me.

"Daddy, why are you playing alone? Where's Moh?" I wonder where my 12-year-old brother was. He is our youngest and still at the age when things like mini-golf excite him. My sisters and I? Not so much, although when daddy had the injury, I always came down here to play with him – just because.

Daddy is holding his silver putter in a Tiger Woods stance, concentrating hard as he eyeballs the golf ball. "I told him he had to practice his pendulum swing before he can play with me again," he swings the putter forward, and the dimpled white ball rolls silently into the hole.

"Nicely done," Ilham claps as my dad looks up, noticing her presence. "Good evening uncle." she greets him in Hausa.

"How are you, Ilham?" He looks at me. "Where are you going?"

"Just going back to Ilham's house; we're going to finish the sketches for the Eid collection." I adjust the blue kimono I'm wearing over my swimsuit. The lie comes out easily because it is half true; we have sketches to work on, just not tonight. We design for our brand, a clothing store that we both manage, *H&I*. The Kimono I'm wearing is one of our bestsellers. "I'll be back in a few hours."

"Make sure you're back before the security lights come on," he looks down at another ball about a meter away from the hole, *"Hmm, Hafsatu bebi?"*

My dad has called me 'Hafsatu Bebi' or 'Bebi' for short, as early as my memory can recall, so much that everyone at the house started calling me that. I'm glad 'Hafsatu Bebi' stuck with me; I am his baby, even though I had three younger siblings. No one else has the suffix 'bebi' to their name.

I learned very early on that daddy and mum were very different. When my parents got called to school for something I'd done (or even not done), my father would remind the school to do their jobs right and let kids be kids. But not Umm'Hafsa; the one day she turned up for a PTA meeting, she gave the teachers the green light to discipline me however they saw fit. That's why I always took excursion slips to daddy to sign. He never asked questions; if it was safe and I wanted it, I would get it. And he's still like that today.

Umm'Hafsa says when I was born, I was a colicky baby who cried a lot. The only person who could calm me was daddy when he held me in his arms singing 'Hafsatu bebi. *Bebin babanta*, her father's baby.' As I grew older and started playing outdoors, tripping over my feet and getting injuries, I would run to him with grazed knees and elbows. "Hafsatu Bebi," he would coo to distract me from the sting as Umm'Hafsa applied iodine with cotton balls. Or, if she was not home, he would apply the blue GV on my wound – which I always thought was a better alternative, as it didn't sting.

"Yes, daddy," I say as I give him a light hug.

* * *

The white Mercedes-Benz coupe daddy got me as a Uni grad gift – which Umm'Hafsa thought was too extravagant – quietens down as I turn off the ignition. We're now at Bellanova, Maitama, a huge block of serviced apartments with two restaurants, a café and a lounge on the main floor. I check my phone for Bashir's text, which reads: *Roof-top.*

"Good evening, Hajiya," the guard greets us, smiling with all his teeth open as we make our way into the elevators.

"Haven't seen this one before, have we?" I ask her when the guard was out of sight and start dialing Bashir's number for the third time today. The call goes to voicemail.

"No idea. Why?"

"Just the way he greeted us, he was looking at you," I reply absent-mindedly, as I sent Bashir a message instead: We*'re here...*

"That's how they greet everyone so that when we're leaving, we can give them something."

I chuckle as we leave the elevator that opens to the open rooftop; a placard reading 'private event' sits right by the doors, which are opened by a female hostess. I don't bother looking at her name tag as she ushers us to the beautiful rooftop swimming pool with white loungers on opposite ends of the pool and five other people.

"Finally," Bashir says. He's in a white unbuttoned shirt over black swim trunks. He stands up from the lounge chair as soon as we walk in. "African time, even on my birthday." He is shouting so that we can hear him over the massive speakers blasting Afrobeat. He walks towards me, and Ilham goes over to the edge of the pool to meet his friends, Sadiq and Usman; she unzips her sundress, slips out of it, and enters the pool legs first. At the other end of the pool, I see two girls rubbing sunscreen on each other.

Bashir gives me a kiss on my cheek, and he has a sly smile on his face as he reaches for my hand. He is two or three shades lighter than me and stands at 5'8, only a few inches taller than I am.

"Why weren't you picking up my calls?" I watch his brows furrow into the familiar frown that always comes before an excuse.

He turns to the pool and calls out to Usman. "Hey, Baba! Where's my phone?" He asks in Hausa. He repeats himself again above the voices of the girls who are now in the pool singing along to the music. Girls that I had never seen before. Usman shrugged off the question before turning his attention to the waitress that brought out more drinks.

"You don't know where your phone is?" I find that hard to believe that because I know how protective Bashir is about his phone; he even prays with it in his pocket and carries it to the restroom.

"Ohhhh," he feigns remembrance, "it's connected to the Bluetooth speakers."

Just what I thought, another sorry-ass excuse. "And who are these girls? Thought it was going to be just the four of us?"

"Babe, Sadiq invited them. He posted his location on Snapchat when he got here and they showed up a few minutes later," he says, playing with my hand. "What do you want me to do? He's my friend."

Yes, your worst friend. Why is he even invited? I look towards the gang; Ilham and Usman are laughing at something on his phone, and the girls are making videos on their phones. "I hope they know not to put anything about me or Ilham on social media," I finally say. "No pictures at all."

"They won't. We told them as soon as they came in," Bashir replies, almost defensively. "Are you upset? C'mon babe, it's my birthday. Let's not do this, please."

I sigh, look at him, and my lips pull into a wide smile almost on their own accord. It's hard to stay mad at him. "Happy birthday, babe."

The waitress returns with more mocktails. I take a glass and she returns to the buffet spread by the wall. Ladipoe and Buju's *Feeling* starts playing over the speakers, and Bashir peels his shirt off and jumps into the pool, his friends hailing him. I take off my kimono and walk over to lounge on the pool chair next to Ilham, who now had her sunshades back on.

"Is that a *Fashion Nova* swimsuit? So tacky." Ilham scoffs, and I follow her eyes to one of the girls in a black crochet two-piece. The girl can't hear us as her and her friend are sitting so close to the big JBL speakers, chatting animatedly. This particular girl was sitting by the deep end of the pool on the white lounger with Sadiq's head on her thigh as he plays with his phone. Almost as if he could tell we were looking in their direction, he turns his head and fixes his stare on me.

On a normal day, I would stare him down, but I feel exposed in this tiny swimsuit, and there is always something about Sadiq and his constant frown and his aloof attitude that makes me uneasy.

"Don't be mean," I say to Ilham as I drag my eyes away from him and gulp down my virgin pina colada.

Ibrahim

1998

I had been in Kaduna for four weeks, and ASUU had not called off the strike. I had so much time on my hands that I had Zuwaira's morning routine memorized in my head. My days usually started the same way. As soon as the *athan*, call for the morning prayer rang, I took my pillow into the small store where foodstuff was kept, which also doubled as my closet. From my Ghana-must-go, I would fish out my toothbrush and leave the house before Ya Isa, or Ya Aisha came out of their room to use the shared bathroom.

When I returned from the mosque, I would then fill up the kitchen drum that Ya Aisha used for cooking and washing plates during the day. I timed myself perfectly so that by the time I was filling the drum, Zuwaira would be out with four white buckets – to fetch bathing water for Hajiya Tani and her children. She came out at the same time every day. The barely audible 'thank you' she said every time I filled the buckets for her, seemed like a reward, even as I tried not to stare when she carried the buckets of water on her head back into the house one after the other.

While she got her cousins ready for school and made their breakfast, I washed Ya Isa's car, lathering the blue Honda Civic hatchback with so much gusto one would think I was getting paid to do it. I was usually back at the well to get water to rinse the car by the time Zuwaira came out to fetch more water to wash plates. As usual, I would fill up her buckets while replying to her 'thank you' with a head shake. *It's nothing.*

Our near-silent routine continued like that until Ya Isa – who was usually the first to drive out of the compound with the children – left for work. He taught chemistry in Capital School and had to be out of the gate by 7:30 am.

Hajiya Tani was usually the second person to leave the compound. She drove out at about 7:45 am with all her children in the car. Jamil – who was always surprisingly cheerful in the morning –would wave at me from the front seat, while his sisters would be arguing in the backseat. Their departure would be closely followed by Tanko, the Landlord's son, a quiet man in his late twenties who moved into Flat 2 a few weeks prior.

As soon as the gate was closed, I would go into our flat and ask Ya Aisha if there was anything she needed help with. She would say no, but I would insist on doing the laundry. Once I gathered all the dirty clothes, I would head out to the well. Almost at the same time, Zuwaira would be closing the door to their flat, carrying a round pail filled with Hajiya Tani and her cousins' clothes to wash.

One day, I finally summoned the courage to talk to Zuwaira. Normally, when she reached the well, she would mumble a quiet "As-sallamu Alaikum," and I answer her with the standard 'Wa'alaikumus Salam.' I would then start fetching water for the clothes I would be washing and use the opportunity to fill up her bucket. She would thank me, and I would say, 'no problem.' When I went to the clothing line to spread the first batch of clothes – Ya Isa's work shirts – I would catch a glimpse of her sitting by the big tree stump, emptying a small pack of blue detergent into the bucket of water and using her hands to wave on the surface of the water until big foams covered the bucket. We would do our chores quietly, occasionally stealing timid glances at each other for an hour or two until she finished her chore and went back into Flat 3. But on that day, I decided to break this silent routine and engage in a conversation with her.

"How are the holidays?" I asked her in Hausa, as she scrubbed a yellow bedsheet. The ASUU strike counted as a holiday for us.

She did not answer. Instead, she continued scrubbing what looked like a coffee stain from the bedsheet, dipping the stain into the soapy water and pulling it out to scrub harder.

I'd just opened my mouth to repeat the question louder when she looked up at me with a questioning look.

"Were you talking to me?" she widened her eyes as her wet hand touched her chest.

I nodded.

"Fine," she answered, her voice soft and melodious. I wanted to keep her talking so I could listen to it.

"Which school do you go to?" I asked. I imagined she went to ABU and smiled at the thought. Maybe we would be on the same bus back to Zaria if ASUU ever stopped the strike, and I could help her with her luggage. Girls usually had a lot of luggage. I imagined her Uncle, Alhaji Sani, telling me to take care of her at the University. "Don't let all those boys distract her from her studies," he would caution with that stern voice of his. Maybe on weekends, we could go to the motor park together and get on the bus back to Kaduna.

"I finished from GGSS Zaria," she replied.

Oh, not yet in University, then. There goes my little motor-park scenario. "When did you finish?" I tried not to sound disappointed.

"In June."

About seven months ago, I thought. *That means she'll be starting her first year as soon as the strike is called off.* "What Universities did you apply to?" I asked. *Please say ABU. Please say ABU. Please say ABU.*

"I'm not going to the University," she said as-a-matter-of-factly.

"Why not?" I asked, remembering the further maths questions she solved for Jamil. Why wouldn't a brilliant girl like herself continue her education beyond secondary school?

She sighed as she dunked the bedsheet in a different bucket with clean water, rising off the soap suds. "I didn't pass English," she finally said, her downcast eyes avoiding mine.

A passing grade in Maths and English was a pre-requisite for Nigerian

Universities. So maybe numbers were her forte but not so much letter writing and composition. "You can study, take lessons and rewrite the exams; it's just a one-year delay. I'll even coach you, if you want," I offered, already imagining spending time with her. We could sit in Jamil's designated learning spot – under the tree opposite Hajiya Tani's flat – and I could go over her multiple-choice answers and practice essay writing with her. I looked up and caught her glance before she looked away, slowly shaking her head. "Why not?" I asked again. "Your parents don't want you to retake the exam?"

"My parents are dead," she bit her lower lip as a distracted look clouded her face.

"I'm so sorry. I didn't – *Allah ya jikan su*; May their souls rest in peace." I wanted to ask how and when they died, but she looked like she was fighting tears, so I held my tongue.

"Ameen," she answered silently, standing up to spread the bedsheet on the drying line, securing the ends with pegs like she always did. But she didn't return to the well. I looked up to find her tiny frame closing the door into their flat quietly.

Later that evening, as I marked Jamil's homework, I noticed that he got all the questions right. Without asking, I knew Zuwaira had a hand in it. As I gave him more questions to solve, I found myself looking up some more to see if she was by the kitchen window. She wasn't.

* * *

Two days later, on my way home from the mosque, I saw her walking down the street holding a small, covered bucket. She was wearing a black hijab that stopped halfway down her thighs and a green wrapper underneath. I thought against calling out to her as there were a few men on the street, as they usually were after the congregational prayer was dispersed. I was about to push the gate open when I changed my mind and went back outside, catching a glimpse of her black hijab as she made a left turn. I walked quietly behind her and watched as she entered a house known for *markade*, large-scale blending, and grinding, usually of beans and tomatoes. I peeped through the gate and watched her exchange pleasantries with the woman who operated the blending machines, and within seconds, the loud, mechanical whir drowned their conversation.

I walked to Mallam Abu's kiosk, which was opposite the *markade* house, and decided to wait there for her, wondering what to buy with the small change in my pocket. I looked over the display he had on the table outside the small rectangular store: newspapers, bread, biscuits, and several brands of cigarettes.

"Should I give you Benson and Hedges, Ibro?" he asked as he pointed to the popular cigarette brand in a brown pack with his chewing stick. His Hausa was accented with Fulani intonation.

"May God never give me a reason to smoke one in my life," I answered jovially.

"You say that as if it's something bad," he laughed as he spat and returned his chewing stick to his mouth.

"It has the word 'dangerous' written on the pack," I said to him as I read out the warnings on all the cigarette boxes in English slowly, pointing as I read. "Smo-king is dan-ge-rous to health. Smo-kers are li-a-ble to die yo-ung."

"All this is English. Life and death is in the hands of Allah alone," he stopped talking as a brand new Peugeot 404 stalled in front of his kiosk, and the windows rolled down. "*Ranka ya dade*, Alhaji; May you live long." He crouched in respect as he greeted the man.

It was Alhaji Ringim, the wealthiest man in the neighborhood. No one knew where his wealth was from – maybe it was inherited, or maybe it was from his many businesses; but Alhaji Ringim, his four wives, and eleven children all lived in the biggest house at the end of the street. His mansion had a Mosque where most men from our street and the next go to pray, myself included.

20

"Give me *Daily Times* and *Vanguard*," he said, even though Mallam Abu had already picked them up and was already halfway to the rolled-down window.

"Good evening, Alhaji," I greeted him. He replied with a curt nod as his driver pulled away. The gate to the *markade* house opened and Zuwaira came out, walking quickly towards our compound.

"Mallam Abu, give me matches," I said hurriedly, dropping a five naira note on the table. I carried two and left the kiosk without saying goodbye.

"Zuwaira," I called out, as I crossed the now deserted road.

She turned around, the confused look on her face replaced by a surprised one. "Where are you coming from?" she asked when I closed the distance between us.

"I went to get some matches," I said, showing her the boxes I was holding. "What about you?"

"I went to grind millet." There was a shy smile on her face, and for the first time, I noticed that she had a dimple on her right cheek.

"Sorry if I upset you the other day we were talking. I noticed you went back indoors without carrying your buckets."

"No, it's not that. It's just – it's just that – I was –" she cleared her throat. "I had left food on the fire."

"What happened to your parents, if you don't mind me asking?" We were less than two minutes away from the compound now.

"Um... an accident," she sniffed. "Two years ago."

"May their souls rest in peace."

"I was staying with my grandmother in Sabon Gari. When she died, *Kawu* Sani became my only living relative so I moved in with his first wife in Zaria. But she – she –" She shook her head. "He decided to bring me here to stay with Hajiya Tani instead."

But she what? What did your Uncle's wife in Zaria do that made him bring you to his youngest wife, who, from the look of things, treats you as her personal maid? I wondered, but I knew I couldn't ask; we were already at the rusty red gate. The loud squeak as I pushed it open for her to walk in before me echoed in my head as she looked at me to say goodbye. Walking silently away from me.

"Goodnight, Zuwaira." I said, watching the distance between us get wider and wider.

Hafsatu

2021

The pool party is in full swing now that it's completely dark outside. The rooftop pool at Bellanova is closed to other customers, as it usually is when we were hanging outside the guest houses of our respective mansions. The underwater LED pool lights cast a bluish glow on us. Sadiq and Bashir are now in charge of the poolside bar by the dark-green shrub wall lit with flashing bulbs that spell out the words: 'Happy Birthday Bashir.' They keep passing drinks around, trying to mix as many mocktails as they possibly can with the bottles of premium non-alcoholic spirits they ordered in from Qatar. The music is non-stop, and the two girls are now dancing on table tops, dripping wet from the water gun Usman keeps shooting at them.

"Between the one with the fake hair and that one with the questionable taste in fashion, I wonder who he's sleeping with." Ilham blows out cloudy rings of smoke before returning the mouthpiece of the hookah hose to her mouth, inhaling again as the water in the tank bubbles.

"I don't think he's sleeping with any of them. Usman isn't the sleeping-with-random-girls kind; he just likes to have a good time," I say, already feeling lightheaded from all the shisha I smoked in the past hour.

"Good for him. But I was talking about Sadiq."

The hostess from earlier comes by to change the coal in our hookahs. I look up at the bar to find Bashir taking a video with his phone. Videos we take on nights like these are seen by only a close-knit set of friends, the ones on our Instagram 'close friends' list. And even at that, Ilham and my faces are never visible in the videos. Next to him, Sadiq is jiggling a silver shaker with both hands as he sings along to Burna's '*Ye.*' As I watch, he opens it and pours its contents into more martini glasses, and the hostess brings them our way.

"I have no idea," I say to Ilham. I don't know anything about Sadiq except that he always has different girls around him – some from within our circle and others we never ever see again. He was the kind of guy who knew he was good-looking and acted like it. It didn't help that a year ago when he moved back to Abuja after grad school, he had many brands reaching out to him for partnerships; his pictures kept popping up on social media, constantly trending due the comments and likes that got. He loves the attention as well, constantly fueling articles on gossip websites by posting shirtless pictures in the name of working out to promote his gym. The gym is one of the few businesses he owns that wasn't handed down to him or his brothers from their late father. I suspect that's why it's important to him that it succeeds. Bashir tells me that both their fathers own prime real estate in Abuja, and that's why they became friends. Eventually, the joint ventures and shared profit interests made them business partners.

I feel hands around my waist and stubble around my neck as I take another drag of the cappuccino-orange-flavored shisha, exhaling into the dark sky.

"Bebi?" It was Bashir. He has barely spoken to me all evening, but now that the party is winding down, he is by my side. "Are you having fun?" He kisses me.

I nod as I use my right thumb to remove the burgundy stain my lipstick leaves from his lips. From the corner of my eye, I notice that Sadiq, who's sitting across us, has a sour expression on his face. When the lipstick is all gone, Bashir takes my hookah hose and drags from it.

"*Kai buzu!* Hey, nomad," he calls out to Usman, who raises both middle fingers at him as he walks towards us. Ilham watches the exchange and bursts out laughing.

"You all need to stop calling him that," I say, even though it's harder to stop laughing as Usman tackles Bashir.

A few weeks ago, the boys brought back *DNA Ancestry* tests from one of their trips abroad as a joke to find out what parts of the world their ancestors originated from. Bashir is 78 percent Nigerian and has some North African and Arab mix in there, which is not surprising. However, Usman, whose family is based in Sokoto, is only 17 percent Nigerian; his ancestors mainly originated from Niger Republic, and about 2 percent were from Mali. They've called him 'Buzu' since that day and even offer him chai when everyone else is having regular drinks.

"Maybe we should take the test too," I say to Ilham. "Imagine if our great grandparents are from Ghana or something too."

"Yes! From my maternal grandmom's side, I know there's definitely some mix there."

"Bashir, do you have any of those kits left?" I ask, collecting the hookah hose from him.

"Sadiq should have a few left. Baba, you still have the kits?"

At the mention of his name, his sharp jawline jerks away from my direction, but not before I notice the deep burning embers in his eyes as they glint with something that looks like boredom or disdain.

"I'll take two," I say just to piss him off even further as I lean into Bashir's chest.

* * *

It's already past 9 pm, and before we leave the Nova restaurant on the main floor, I go into Bashir's apartment on the 16th floor to use the restroom. It's a two-bedroom suite that all his friends have keys to and where they come to run away from the restrictions of being in their fathers' houses –

mostly partying, weed, and girls. I look at my reflection in the restroom as I call my sister Saratu. "Sara, are you home?" I ask, even though I know the answer. My siblings have a strict curfew, even Saratu, who is already in her third year at the University of Edinburgh and is just home for the holidays.

"Yup, Umm'Hafsa has asked about you twice already."

"And what did you tell her?" I dab some powder on my nose and apply more lip gloss.

"I told her you were at Ilham's place."

"I'm on my way back," I say and start making my way out of the apartment to join everyone on the main floor. When the elevator finally arrives, the doors open and Sadiq is leaning on the wall with one hand in his pocket. He looks up from his phone, and his eyes sweep over me, from my stilettos to my eyes.

Maybe I should just wait for the next elevator, I think, but my feet move on their accord. I step into the elevator car that's filled with his cologne.

"Hafsat," he says my name slowly, as he looks back at his phone.

"Abubakar-Sadiq," I say, as slowly as he did mine.

He scoffs and shakes his head, two mannerisms I find tediously irksome.

Once the elevators start to descend, I ask, "where are your girlfriends?" I haven't seen them since we left the pool to go have dinner in the lounge downstairs.

He looks at me, raising his eyebrows impossibly high and a frown settles between them. "Girlfriends?" The rich baritone of his voice is almost as annoying as how his towering over me in his six-foot frame.

"The ones you invited to a *private* party," I say as I glance at my wristwatch.

"Oh, *I* invited them? Really?" He chuckles as he puts his phone in his pocket.

The elevator beeps as we get to the main floor, and as the doors open, we see Ilham, Usman, and Bashir waiting for us.

"My *girlfriends* are where I want them to be, Hafsat. Worry about yourself." He walks out of the doors before I have the chance to ask what it means.

26

Sadiq

I lean back into the brown leather swivel chair in my office, thinking about how little I use this home office – the black oak executive desk in front of me is bordered by two white conference chairs, which are currently occupied by bank officials. Past them are monochromatic art pieces on the wall framed by black wall-to-wall cabinets. Everything in the room was gotten on the recommendation of the interior designer, except for the art pieces, which I bought at an exhibition in the UK years ago. Bello's voice brings me back to him; the stocky account manager is reading out clauses for beneficiaries. Having done this several times, I find the process to be not just time-wasting, but unnecessary. Next to the manager is a lady in a red pantsuit, her lips blood red and her hair in a cropped short hairstyle, who has been stealing glances at me since she walked in.

I glance at the Movado on my wrist. It is 3:34 pm. This has gone on for over an hour, an hour I can never get back. I look up to see the red lady giving me a slow and practiced smile, looking away for about a second and then back at me. Her fingers all-too-casually played with the top buttons of her shirt, which open to reveal more than one would expect in a business meeting. I scoff quietly as she slowly moves the tip of her pen into her mouth in a move I think she believes to be seductive, but I make it a rule not to mix business with pleasure.

"Okay," I cut the manager short. "I'll have my lawyer go over this and the signed documents will be sent to your office before the week ends." I stand up, bringing the meeting to an end. I did not need my lawyer to go through any of the documents as I have the affidavit signed by a Shari'ah judge, stating that the inheritance on the newly discovered account has been shared according to the stipulations of our religion. Like the prior ones that flowed into my accounts since my father died, this transaction is also handled by Bello, who my uncle got to manage my finances since I was sixteen. When my father passed away, most of my other siblings were older than me, and they already had their finances in order. The ones who were younger had their mothers recommend account managers who would act in their best interest. I still remember the day it happened. I was in the sixth form at Stonar School. The look on my houseparent's face when he came to get me from the common room, gave it away, even before my uncle's voice came through the receiver as I picked up the phone.

"Okay, sir," Bello says, breaking into my thoughts as he returns the documents into the brown envelope. "If you like, Linda here can always come by your office to pick them up."

"I'll be in touch," I say as I shake his hand, immediately reaching to adjust the silver cufflink on my left wrist in a bid to avoid Linda's outstretched arm.

"Mr. Sadiq, I have always wanted to meet you," she says, putting the strap of the handbag on her shoulder. It is a calculated move, one that pulls her shirt downward by an inch, slightly exposing a hit of red lace underneath. I raise my eyebrow, looking past her and towards the door to speed up their exit. "Well, to thank you," she continues, "you and your family, really. My four years in university were completely sponsored by your father's Trust for orphans."

"Oh." Being told that your father had a Trust that helped hundreds of people is one thing; actually seeing one of the people who benefited from his kindness is another.

"And it's great that even after his death, you and your siblings still support the Trust to continue what he started in his lifetime. God bless you and

28

may his soul continue to rest in peace."

"Ameen, thank you," I say before I usher them out of the office, watching as the door closes behind them. It's been twelve years, and he's still around me, in every corner. Every damn day. In many forms – his framed pictures among other former members of the state government in government organizations and parastatals; the family members who can't seem to shut up about the resemblance between him and me; and worst of all, my presence at weddings and events which are heralded by the sounds of local musicians singing praise songs about his kindness and legacy. Everywhere I look, I am constantly reminded that I am my father's son – the son of a man they think to be righteous, God-fearing, and inspiring. In reality, the father I remember was nothing like they describe. The man I knew for the first sixteen years of my life was far from what everyone says about him today. I still remember the red welts on my back from being beaten with his belt when I didn't do well in school. Worse still, the sounds of Hajiya Amina's cries on days she fell out of favor with him. I remember the oversized sunglasses she wore to hide the bruises he left around her eyes all too well and the turtle-neck long-sleeved shirts beneath her regular clothes she was fond of wearing to cover the marks on her neck and body.

* * *

Hajiya Amina still lives in the Asokoro house my father died in and left her in. I visit her there a few times a week. The recently renovated house has been restructured to remove a section now hidden behind a gate and flower hedge as part of my younger sister's inheritance. Of all the women my father married, she is the closest I have ever known to a mother.

"I heard the account manager finally got a hold of you today. If you just move back to the house, it'll be easier to find you when these issues come up." Hajiya Amina says.

We both know that I can't ever stay in this house. Not only is it now hers and to be passed on to her own children, and even though so much work has gone into burying my father, who once lived here, the walls still carry many horrible memories for us – memories of the man who connected us, even in his death.

I look away from the vice president's address on the television as her maid carefully balances a tray of drinks and snacks on the side table. She crouches next to me as she unscrews the cap from the bottled water.

"Thank you," I say, covering the glass cup with my palm to stop her. I collect the bottle from her and pour the water into the glass. As I place the bottle next to a bottle of juice with pink designs on it. I recognize the shade of pink, and it reminds me of the swimsuit Hafsat had on two days ago.

Hafsat. There has to be a reason someone I dislike so much keeps being in my thoughts. I was not going to go to the pool party, but when Bashir let it slip on the phone that it would be just us – us being the guys, Ilham and her – I postponed my meeting with Bello and headed to Bellanova.

There is a certain *je ne sais quoi* about twenty-two-year-old Hafsatu Gaya – perhaps it was the smooth sweep of her high cheekbones or the full lips that look like they were made for sin. There's just something about the way she manages to look unimpressed even by the most glamorous things and how she looks both innocent and worldly at the same time. She and I have never gotten along. The first time Bashir introduced us, she didn't do as much as spare a glance in my direction. She only had eyes for him. That in itself is as admirable as it was mind-boggling – not because I was slighted by her unanticipated dismissal but because it was hard to imagine someone with such grace and impeccable taste being with someone like Bashir. She has to know that he's seeing other girls. If all his friends know, that just tells me that he isn't exactly a man who cares enough to be discreet.

Hafsatu initially did not strike me as a doormat or the kind of girl who would turn a blind eye to what he does. But they have been together for about a year now, and that only makes me lose respect for her. Or at least, that's what I told myself when I saw her on the rooftop that evening with

Ilham. *The untouchables* - that is what I call them. Both of them seem to have an impenetrable and invisible shell around them that even Bashir and Usman – who have been friends with them for close to two decades – can't seem to break.

I watched from the pool as she gravitated towards Bashir, who had his tongue down the throat of one of the girls he brought along just a few minutes prior.

As I changed the playlist to something more upbeat from the romantic songs Bashir had on repeat the past hour, I watched, behind my dark sunglasses, as she took the belt off the long, white and blue dress she wore, holding my breath as she slipped it off her shoulders. It was hard not to stare at the way the light danced over her smooth brown skin, the Balmain swimsuit she had on emphasizing her tiny waist. She has a body that makes anything look good. She is not skinny like Ilham; she is curvy with hips and legs that seem to continue forever as she walked over to the white lounge chair she gracefully sinks into.

Everything about her is practically daring me to act against my better judgment – asking me to break a code, to tell her that a man like Bashir does not deserve her.

Ibrahim

1999

Over the next three months, I got some English WAEC and NECO past question papers that I gave Zuwaira. I told her to answer the questions to the best of her ability and give them back to me to mark. She did that diligently, leaving the answered sheets under the GP tank so I could pick them up when I went to the well in the morning.

After our regular chores, when only Ya Aisha was left in the compound, we would sit under the mango tree, and I would correct the ones she got wrong.

"63 percent! At this rate, you'll have a B by the time the exam comes around," I said one day, giving the papers I had finished marking back to her. She seemed very pleased with the progress that she was making.

Throughout my stay in Kaduna, I was always on high alert whenever Zuwaira was headed out of the compound. On Wednesdays, before *Maghrib*, the evening prayer, she went to grind millet or tomatoes. On Saturday mornings, just before noon, she took her cousins to braid their hair, and on Sundays, she went to the market alone.

I would usually wait until she was a little far ahead then I would follow her, ensuring that no one from the compound saw me. When I finally caught up to her, she would cover her face with her hands to hide a smile. During these long walks, we talked about everything, learning more about each other as we navigated the dusty unpaved roads. She was her parents' only surviving child; her younger sister died in the accident that claimed her parents' lives. Her family used to live in Bauchi, not Zaria, as I had wrongly assumed. Alhaji Sani, Hajiya Tani's husband, was her father's older brother. When their mother, Hajiya Tabawa, who was taking care of Zuwaira, died, he brought her to live with his first wife. Strange as it was, even with Hajiya Tani's horrible behavior towards Zuwaira, the seventeen-year-old was always the last to go to bed and first to wake up; she washed all their clothes and cooked all their meals, Yet the girl never complained. She even told me she preferred Kaduna to Zaria.

"His first wife accused me of stealing her jewellery," she said on one of our walks to the market on a particularly cloudy day.

"Accused you?"

"Yes, she told Kawu Sani that I went into her room, opened her jewellery kit and stole her gold. *Wallahi*, I swear, I have never stolen a thing in my life. And where would I even take her gold to? I was never even allowed to leave the house."

"What did your uncle say?" from my observations, Alhaji Sani cared about his niece. Whenever he was around, I noticed that Zuwaira's chores were shared amongst her and her cousins, but as soon as he left, it returned to the way it was.

"I don't think he believed her, but he didn't stop her from beating me. The following day, he said that he was bringing me to Kaduna. I was so relieved."

Once we got to the crowded stalls of the market, I slowed down my steps and walked behind her again – far enough so that people didn't suspect we were together but close enough for her to know that I was there if she needed me. We continued this way, weaving our way through the lanes that smelled of chicken shit and grilled fish. As we walked, I jumped over open gutters and greeted meat vendors as she priced mounds of tomatoes and chose dried fish from other vendors. I watched her, never interrupting her, as she worked down Hajiya Tani's shopping list. Occasionally, she glanced over her shoulder, searching until she saw me leaning against a tree or electric pole across the street, waiting for her.

When she was done, we walked back with grocery bags in both hands; no one questioned me when they saw me helping with her bags. They always assumed that we met on the way back from the market and I was being a gentleman.

I always looked forward to the trips to and from the market. Surrounded by strangers in the busy Ungwan Rimi market was even more liberating than being alone at the well in the middle of the compound.

One day – as we dried clothes on the drying line as we usually did after washing together – Zuwaira said, "Last night, she told Kawu Sani I shouldn't be registered for the upcoming exams."

"Hajiya Tani? Why would she do that?"

"She says when I get married, if my husband wants me to continue studying, I can do it from his house," she sniffed.

We had spent months studying for the exams that I knew she would pass this time. Should I use the money I had saved up to register her? I thought. But even if I did that, how would she explain her absence to Hajiya Tani on the days of the exams, when the woman depended on Zuwaira for everything in the house, from cooking to cleaning? Twice daily – at random times between 10 am and 1 pm – Hajiya Tani would call the landline in their flat from the Secretariat, where she worked as a clerk twice to give Zuwaira orders on what to cook and chores to do. But it also served as a security measure – to make sure that Zuwaira was at home all the time.

"What did your uncle say?"

"He agreed with her."

"Do you want to go the University, though?" We were back to the well. She arranged our buckets, and I grabbed the small yellow pail.

"Yes. Yes, I do," she looked away, almost as if she didn't want me to see the tears forming in her eyes.

My pail hit the surface of the water as I drowned in my thoughts. If I wasn't studying Medicine by now, I would have graduated and would be at liberty to ask her uncle for her hand in marriage and register her for the exams.

A few days later, Hajiya Tani sent for me to help adjust the antenna so that she could get a clearer signal to the program she was watching on TV. When I fixed it, she invited me to a meal. Of course, I declined, knowing that the invitation was merely out of courtesy – as was common in our culture. When I returned to the house to return the stick I used to balance the antenna, I noticed that she and her children ate their rice and beans in the living room under the ceiling fan, while Zuwaira was eating hers in the kitchen, sweating in the heat.

* * *

On one quiet evening a few weeks later, I quietly walked to the window of Hajiya Tani's kitchen just after *Isha*, the late evening prayer. I knew that only Zuwaira would be in there at that time, washing the plates, pots, and pans from their dinner.

"Can you come out for a bit?" I whispered, startling her as I spoke through the window.

She held her chest with one hand and covered her mouth with the other, laughing quietly as she recovered from the shock of seeing me peeping in. "What are you doing? What if someone sees you?" she whispered back. The full moon was high up in the sky, and as she looked at me, a shy smile took over her features, highlighting her dimples.

"Just come to the well," I implored. At this point, I was already head over heels for Zuwaira, and most of my actions towards her were never the product of well-thought-out decisions. I just went with my feelings, and that evening proved to me that it was the same for her.

I was back at the well waiting under the GP tank with peeling letters, wondering if she would come or not, when I heard her faint voice seeking permission from Hajiya Tani. *"Zan je in zubar da shara*; I'm going to take the garbage out."

When she pushed open the door with the mosquito net, she had on a long black hijab that covered her body entirely except for her blue rubber slippers that peeked out under. I could not look anywhere else as she hurriedly walked toward me.

"What is it?" She asked, her voice heavy with worry.

I reached into my pocket and brought out a portable walkman. "I want you to listen to something," I said. She looked confused, but she took the earphones I held out from me and tucked them in her ears, covering them with the fabric of her hijab. When it was securely placed, she looked up at me and nodded. I pressed play. It was *As long as you love me* by Backstreet Boys.

Her eyes were downcast as she listened quietly. I watched her measured breaths. Her form was so still that it was almost statue-like, just concentrating on the words. I inhaled when she did and exhaled only when she did, wondering what she thought of me asking her to listen to the song by five unknown strangers.

At one point in the chorus, she looked up at me and smiled. It was a shy smile, but it was a smile. I felt on top of the world. When the song ended 3 minutes 20 seconds later, she removed the earpiece and timidly handed it back to me, the smile never leaving her face.

"You can keep listening to it," I said as I folded the earpiece around the walkman and gave it to her. I wanted this to be the song she would always associate with me. I started walking back to Ya Isa's flat, walking backward just to keep looking at her.

"Ibrahim," she called out just loud enough for me to hear. I loved the way she called my name, how it sounded when she said it – almost sacred. Ibrahim. Not Ibro like everyone else did.

"Na'am," I answered. The smile on my face was not going anywhere. Not that night, at least.

"Throw this away for me," she handed me the garbage she said she was taking out, and our fingers slightly grazed as I collected the polythene bag from her, our eyes never leaving each other. I stood and watched as she went back silently into Flat 3, turning around to look at me one more time with the walkman tucked under her hijab.

I still play that night in my head over and over.

* * *

"I have to leave for Zaria tomorrow," I said, my heart aching in a way I did not know how to describe as I watched the tears fill her eyes. "Hey, hey. Don't cry. I will be back for *babban sallah*, for Eid."

ASUU had called off the strike after 5 months, and students were expected back to the federal universities. It was strange to think that when I came back to Kaduna, I couldn't wait to go back to campus, but suddenly, I was not looking forward to my fifth year in medical school.

"*Ka ce wallahi*, swear by Allah."

"Wallahi, I'll come back in a few months. Even if I have to go to Kano, I'll come here first to see you." It was a promise I intended to keep. "Do you know the number for the landline at your flat?" I asked her

"I don't," she said, using the back of her hands to wipe her cheeks, "but I can ask Jamil."

I had to leave for the motor park very early the next day. I checked under the GP tank, and there was a piece of paper. I picked it up, and it was the landline number: 062 217865.

The stolen moments in innocent relationships are the ones lovers never talk about but reminisce about day after day. I called Zuwaira every Friday at 9 am unfailingly. I would head to the phone booth armed with a NITEL calling card and would dial the seven digits I soon memorized on the rotary phone, waiting with bated breath until I heard her soft voice on the other end.

Time didn't seem to exist when we spoke. I listened as she told me about her chores, her lone trips to the market, the heavy rain that Hajiya Tani slipped in, and the heavy wind that brought down the drying lines.

For weeks, we spoke for hours on the landline when she was alone, and counted down the weeks until my return to Kaduna for Eid.

Until one fateful Friday, I called and heard Alhaji Sani's voice on the other end. I panicked and hung up, afraid that I might get her in trouble. Since then, she never picked up. I would keep trying, holding the phone until the call rang out and went unanswered. There was no way to contact Ya Aisha or Ya Isa to find out if she was okay.

When I returned for Eid two weeks later, Zuwaira was nowhere to be found. I was met with the news that she had been married off to Alhaji Ringim.

Hafsatu

2021

Since Bashir's birthday two weeks ago, he has become even more distant. He was completely MIA yesterday, and when he finally reached out after Isha, he came up with an excuse about coming down with a bad flu. A few minutes ago, just after we prayed Maghrib, he called to say he wanted to come by the house, and I asked him to meet me in the game room downstairs.

The game room is what we call our in-house theatre because that's where daddy watches Premier League and golf tournaments. It's a soundproof circular room with a large drop-down screen, high ceilings, curved walls with framed posters of popular classics like *Casablanca, The Godfather, Gone with the Wind,* and a black-and-white poster of Marilyn Monroe biting her nails.

My sisters and I just finished watching the last episode of *You,* where serial killer Joe escapes the vault and kills Beck. We are about to start the next episode when Bashir comes in. He sits next to me on a leather recliner and makes small talk with my sisters, asking about school and whatnot.

"Did you enjoy your session?" I ask him when my sisters leave us to get more popcorn and board games. For his birthday, I got him a Gucci *G-Timeless* wristwatch and a prepaid deluxe spa day at the *Escape House*; today was the only available slot to fit in the massage and cupping session, but he didn't even stay for the mani-pedi.

"Yes, but it would have been better if you were there," he says as he types on his phone and puts the phone screen down on the armrest.

"I was there two days ago for my Hamman appointment. Besides, it was supposed to be a you thing. I know how busy you've been."

"Well… that wasn't the gift I was hoping to get from you," he smirks, his hand on my cheek, as he turns my face towards his. His phone vibrates, and he picks it up to type a reply.

"Can you put your phone away? You literally just got here."

"Chill, madam. It's just the shipment from the warehouse I'm coordinating," he laughs. Bashir and Sadiq have a joint venture called *The Waffle Drop* that is being relaunched; the location in Wuse was being renovated, and most of the new furniture they ordered from Turkey has finally made it into Abuja. "Anyway, back to what I was saying. You know what I *really* want as a gift…"

"And what would that be, Bashir?" *Not this conversation again.*

"*Kin sani ai*; you know what."

"Nope, no idea." I stretch my hands out in front of me, inspecting my painted nails. "You're going to have to spell it out, mister."

"Bebi, c'mon. Haven't I tried? Haven't I been patient enough? We've been together for like a year –"

"Nine months," I interrupt calmly.

"What?" He looks at me with a puzzled expression on his face.

"Nine months. We've been together for nine months."

"Whatever," he exhales loudly, and the back of his head hits the headrest. "Nine months, twelve months – no difference."

"I'm not going to have sex with you just because you think you deserve it after being with me for so long," I say.

"Why are you making it such a big deal? We're going to get married, anyway. So what difference does it make?" He looks at me as if I am being unreasonable before the chime from his phone takes away his attention.

"I've told you – I am not ready." I won't be exaggerating if I say he brings up the subject monthly.

"Everyone's doing it," he scoffs as he picks up his phone again and starts typing furiously. "Besides, everyone already thinks we're doing it anyway, so I don't know why you're acting like –"

"I don't care what people think I'm doing or not doing." This conversation is getting on the last of my nerves. I pick up my phone and open Instagram. The first post on my feed is the latest exposé by *Bujgist,* a notorious gossip blogger in Abuja. It's mostly news that usually carries no weight, but sometimes the anonymous blogger has evidence, untastefully referred to as 'receipts.' Today, they claim they have proof that a senator was caught pants down with his son's ex-girlfriend.

"Hey, where are you?" I look up at Bashir, speaking into his phone. "Can you come in ten minutes?" Pause. "Okay, I'll tell security to let you in."

It's weird that the whole conversation is in English – a bit too formal for someone he's asking to meet at his house at 7:00 pm. Except the person at the other end is female, and speaking in Hausa will make that obvious because of the gender-based pronouns. But would he really...? I don't think so.

"Bebi, the contractor is going back to Lagos tomorrow. They have some papers for me to sign, so I need to head back home," he kisses my forehead. "Enjoy your sisters' night in."

"Goodnight." I say without looking up.

He heads towards the sliding door, which opens as my sister Aisha comes in with a big bag of popcorn and four packs of Maltesers. Her oval-shaped eyeglasses give her an owlish look underneath the dim lights. All of my siblings wear reading glasses, just like daddy, even Mohammed, who is not even a teen yet.

"Shatu, all this for you?"

"No, it's for all of us. Oh, you're leaving already?" she asks Bashir as she flops on the leather recliner, accidentally pouring some popcorn on the couch I was on.

"Watch what you're doing!" I snap, misdirecting my pent-up anger, as the one who riled me up says bye to her and leaves.

I return my attention to Instagram, scrolling until I come across a picture of Sadiq. He's shirtless, sitting on an exercise training bench with a dumbbell in his right hand, exposing his biceps. The caption is a photo credit to a Lilybeth. I click on the profile and recognize her from a photoshoot Ilham commissioned for *H&I* about six months ago. Halima Adam, a model. *Is she his latest conquest?*

I go back into his profile and scroll down his pictures, taking extra care not to mistakenly click the like button on any of them. There's one with a groom at a recent high-profile wedding, another at a polo tournament where he's riding a dark brown horse, and yet another on a busy street in Amsterdam. I sigh and close out of the app as the door slides open again. This time, Saratu comes in with two board games. She closes the door with her hips, managing to look cute even in her oversized sweater and baggy trousers.

"I wasn't sure if we're feeling like Charades tonight or something more competitive like King of Tokyo, so I brought both," she announces as she enters the room.

"You guys will have to play alone," I say, standing up. The popcorn Aisha poured earlier fell on the grey-carpeted floor. I pat my jeans to get popcorn dust off and tuck my phone into my pocket.

"You're bailing out *again*?" shrieks Aisha. "You always do this."

"Charades then. King of Tokyo isn't much of a game with just two people," Saratu rolls her eyes like she's not surprised. She throws a dirty glance my way as I close the door behind me and climb the winding staircase, bumping into one of the house helps who is mopping the stair landing.

"This late? Can't you do it in the morning?" I ask, annoyed that my socks are getting wet as I walk on the damp floor. I peel off my socks and give them to her as I hop on the carpet on the next flight of stairs, towards the living room upstairs.

"There was water on the floor," she explains.

The TV is the first sound I hear, followed by my mother's laughter. I look up as I enter the living room and find my parents sitting on the loveseat. She is wearing a simple pink boubou, and he is in one of the jallabiyas I got for him from a friend's store a few months back. A navy blue velvet pillow is sitting on Umm'Hafsa's laps as she reads an excerpt from a book to daddy, and in front of them are half-empty tea mugs with a half-eaten platter of fruits.

"Bebi, somebody dropped an early Eid hamper for me today and it has those nuts you like – pistachios," he smiles and adjusts his glass as he talks to me. "I asked Mariya to drop them in your room."

"Thank you, daddy," I flash him my biggest smile. As Umm'Hafsa looks up at me, I realize it's Thursday and ask her about her regular biweekly fast. "Mummy, *an sha ruwa lafiya?* Hope your *iftar* went well?"

"*Alhmadulillah;* thank God," she answers. "You've read this book, haven't you?" She holds up *Born a Crime* by Trevor Noah, and I shake my head no. "I was just telling your dad about this funny part but I messed up the punchline, so I have to read it out to him for him to get it."

As she speaks, daddy doesn't stop looking at her. "Those are two entirely different stories, my love."

"I just skipped a small part," she laughs as she reaches for his hand. "Just wait till I finish this page."

I walk to the tray and help myself to a slice of watermelon as I sit down on the sectional opposite them, listening as Umm'Hafsa's voice fills the room. My parents have been best friends for as long as I can remember. The mirrored console under our family portrait is lined with pictures from their adventures through the years: pottery classes in London, basket weaving with strangers in Amsterdam, Opèra in Paris. We have never taken a family trip abroad without them planning something to do together. Even here in Abuja, they go for evening walks together at least twice a week.

Growing up, it was a regular sight to see my mum cooking up a buffet of his favorite dishes, complete with candlelights and light music in the background for no reason at all. He has never come back from a trip without her accompanying the driver to go pick him up at the airport. I have walked into this living room hundreds of times to find them sitting quietly, holding hands with her head on his shoulder while the television droned away as background noise.

I grew up hoping for a love like theirs, praying for someone like my father. I used to think Bashir could be that guy. I imagined us living in a house I have already redecorated three times in my mind, raising kids I have already picked middle names for, and drinking tea together at odd hours of the night together. That dream is, unfortunately, drifting away as I begin to think he won't be a part of my future – not with the way things have been going in the past months.

Umm'Hafsa continues to read to daddy, detailing Trevor Noah's dreaded bus rides to church, their family's Sunday routine and how his mother always reminded him that she beats him only out of love because the world is a cruel place. My mother's shoulder-length hair is piled atop of her head, and the few strands of grey just above her forehead catch the light in the yellow glow of the living room. As I watch, I see mannerisms that mirror mine – the way she raises her index finger and places it on her upper lip looking up at my dad with a wide smile as she reaches the punchline at the end of the chapter.

I might be my father's favorite, but I am my mom's look-alike; maybe that is the reason he dotes on me so much.

Sadiq

The luxury apartment I have called home for the past year is always spotless, thanks to the serviced cleaners on a regular rotation. It has an office, a den I made into a prayer room, and a second bedroom I converted into a home gym. In the living room, the 70-inch television mounted on the paneled wall adjacent to the abstract black-and-gold paintings, the sleek white leather couch, and the white lacquered center table with a decorative chess board, Leila, the interior decorator insisted would complete the overall look; it was polished and well-put together. The boys are at my place after *Juma'ah*, the congregational Friday prayer we attended at the Central Mosque, and we're eating lunch at the dining table as we watch a football match between Man City and Arsenal.

"Bash, I'm thinking of a possible buy-out with *Ranchers* and *The Waffle Drop*." *Ranchers*, an outdoor gaming and entertainment lounge, was our first project together. Its immediate success prompted us to start a second business, *The Waffle Drop*.

Bashir slows his movement as he takes another chicken thigh to his plate. In front of us are food warmers with fried rice, jollof rice, peppered chicken, and shredded beef delivered from a popular restaurant down the street.

"So," he drops his cutlery as he ponders over what I just said. "Are we talking about you buying me out, or me buying you out?"

"Well, there's that, or a handover of assets for the principal holding companies – say maybe 60-40 in favor of whoever ends up with *Ranchers*, since its valuation is currently lower than *The Drop*?" I've spent all week with my lawyers, discussing the implications of a contract infraction before our initial two-year term is up.

I watch as he quietly goes over the numbers in his head, working out the valuation gap and wondering if the trade-in will be profitable for him. Our contract states that in the event that one partner wants out, the other can buy them out at the current market estimate. Next to him, Usman is concentrating on the football match, and from the way he kept berating the referees, I can tell his team was losing. Usman was very happy filling his father's shoes at their family-managed energy business; it generates so much profit he never bothers about new investments. It is something I both admire and envy, but I've always known that I have to create a name for myself; it's a defiance of sorts, something I hope my father can see from wherever he is.

When I met Bashir, we quickly fell into business. We were both interested in taking advantage of the real estate boom and the subsequent market for entertainment, so we started buying and flipping properties together. The profits from the sales led us to where we are now, except that now I wanted out. Even though the businesses are currently profitable, spending time with Bashir has shown me that a long-term business contract with him is bound to get complicated somewhere down the line. As a matter of fact, it is already complicated; he just doesn't know it yet. And it was all triggered by *her*.

Four days ago, we were at Bashir's family house, indulging in the usual evening shenanigans. A mutual friend was getting married, and Abuja was unusually busy that weekend, so it was a full house. We were having a loud night with over a dozen friends, and whoever else they brought along until it was time for us to head out to the airport to Lagos for boys' night out, the final party for the groom as a single guy – the plan was for us to pull an all-nighter and fly back to Abuja the following morning. That way, the groom will be well rested by the time he was due to attend an event the bride's family will be hosting in the evening to kick off the festivities.

Somehow, during the pre-party, the conversation turned to the hardest-to-get girls in town. Instagram profiles were displayed, DMs leaked, and voice notes were played.

"Baba, all these girls they're talking about, none of them is as hot as my babe. Wait, let me show you." He pulled out his phone, scrolls through his gallery, and passes it to me.

I looked at the screen and find a picture of Hafsat. She was half-naked in the picture, on rumpled sheets, wearing red lace that barely covered her voluptuous breasts, as they threatened to spill out, but not quite; it was just enough to tease.

"What's this?" My temple started pulsing hard. It was a rhetorical question. I knew exactly what the picture was.

His finger scrolled to the next picture. This was a selfie; she was in a strappy kind of lingerie that revealed more than it covered. The white lace against her skin was the definition of naughty and nice; it accentuated her devilish curves. Her hair, which was usually covered, was straightened, covering her shoulders. She looked into the camera with her smokey eyes and those luscious red lips. I had never seen her like this. It wasn't just the outfit; it was the look, the confidence, everything.

His finger was about to scroll to another one when I stopped him. "Bash, this is messed up. Why would you show someone pictures she sent to you in private?" I tried to keep my voice even as I did not want to attract attention to the pictures, but the anger in my voice increased with every word at the same rate my trousers tightened. I was filled with a wave of inexplicable anger that he had seen her like that. I wanted to smash something.

"*Haba*, it's just you," he said, raising his hands innocently.

"In a room full of guys?" I asked, wondering how long he'd had the pictures and what he had done while looking at them.

"I – I – No, I – I wasn't going to show them," he stammered. I could tell that was a lie; he was the kind of guy who needed to feel like the most important person in the room at any time, even if it meant throwing a loved one under the bus. Discretion meant nothing to him, and at that moment, I was faced with two realizations: One, he did not care about Hafsat, and two, I was fucking attracted to his girlfriend; the growing bulge in my trousers was a telltale sign I knew I had to hide. I reached for a can of coke, amidst the loud chatter and music, chugging the whole thing in two gulps. A scowl forms on my face as I watched Bashir scroll through pictures of multiple girls; he had a whole gallery of semi-nude to nude pictures of different girls. The empty can crumbled silently into an unrecognizable mess between my palms. *Maybe some codes are meant to be broken.*

Hafsatu

I just got back home from *H&I*. I've been there all day, talking to the manager about the inventory for the restocked kimonos. As I enter my room, the maid comes in with two boxes of the DNA Ancestry kits that Bashir's driver dropped off earlier. I call Ilham.

"Are you coming over today?" I ask as I drop my veil on my bed, catching my reflection in the mirror. It is a Friday, and I am appropriately overdressed in a black Abaya with wide green flower appliques on the bottom half. The decoration had stones that glimmered when I walked. I am also wearing more makeup than I have all week – false lashes and all.

"I don't know. Why?"

"I have your box of the DNA thingy we said we were gonna do." I pop my lips silently as I inspect the matte lipstick I put on two hours ago; it still looks flawless. *Fenty, Baby.*

"Oh, I already got mine. Sadiq gave me one when we met at the gym yesterday. Oh, by the way, you should join me tomorrow; they have a women only section at the top floor."

"Hmm," I murmur non-committedly, "I'll think about it." *A member at Sadiq's gym, like one of his groupies? No, thanks.*

"They have Zumba classes. It was so much fun yesterday, I even met…" she goes on, talking about mutual friends who have also joined Sadiq's gym. It's not even like he's always there; I've overheard him talking about how he prefers to work out at his place and only goes to the gym for cardio and on chest days.

"I'll just stick to my Pilates in our garden," I say before saying bye. I hang up as Saratu walks into my room in a brown Abaya, her tall frame prancing around in giant steps as she looks at her wrist.

"I'm just trying to get my five thousand steps in before the day ends," she announces as she keeps marching on one spot.

"So this fitness app is pretty much the boss of you."

Maybe I should take her to go get registered in Sadiq's gym.

"What's this?" she asks, glancing at the green and white boxes on my bed that Mariya brought.

"Try putting the letters together, see if they form words you can pronounce."

She hisses at my sarcasm and picks up one of the boxes. "Wait, is this one of those tests that tell you what you're mixed with?"

I smile as I nod. Our apartment in California had running advertisements on the TV for the DNA Ancestry tests all summer. Emotional stories about families getting reunited with lost loved ones as they spoke to an unseen interviewer.

"Bebi, I want one," she says louder than necessary. "I could use it for my summer project."

Sara is a biomedical science student, so I can see how this would interest her. "It's yours," I say, "but you must credit me in your acknowledgments or something."

"Calm down, it's not a thesis. It's just a paper."

After we pray *Asr,* the late afternoon prayer, we use the spatula to scratch the inside of our cheeks as directed in the YouTube instructional video and insert it in the blue fluid provided. Sara proudly explains – in a nerd spiel – to me that it's a stabilizing solution that inactivates bacteria and minimizes hydrolysis of the DNA we provided. We put our samples in collection bags, and she calls for Mariya to have a driver take the pre-addressed box to the courier office.

Mariya comes back with another package for me, "someone just dropped this at the gate for you," she says in Hausa as she hands me an envelope.

I'm not expecting any delivery today. I turn it around, expecting to see a name, but it's blank. I rip it open, and a white keycard with the *Bellanova* logo falls onto my bed.

I turn the card around and see a number scribbled on it. 1601. That's Bashir's apartment. *Why will Bashir send me his key when he's away in Lagos for three days?* He called me from the airport this morning just before he boarded his flight because he said he felt bad about an argument we had the previous evening. *Is he giving me the key to his apartment as an appeasement? Will he do that?*

The one time I asked him for an extra key, he turned me down, and I never bothered to ask again. It was during one of the photo shoots we had late last year for a new line of shift dresses Ilham, and I designed. The model and photographer were at the Nova restaurant on the main floor, taking pictures, and I asked Bashir for the key to his apartment so that my model could change there in between shoots, but he refused, saying we could be invading his friends' privacy and it wouldn't be right for me to have the key and barge in on them. His argument made no sense to me because we all hang out in that apartment or on the rooftop by the poolside, and they all had keys except Ilham and I. And *I'm* his girlfriend. If anyone should get a key, it should be me, right? But I was in no mood to argue, so I just paid for a one-bedroom suite for one night for my model to use. But he's sending me a key now? When he's away in Lagos? Is there an errand he needs me to run? Is there a surprise waiting for me?

I look up to find Sara still reading the instruction leaflet from the kit. I wrap my veil around my head and pick up my clutch bag. "Hey, I'll be back soon," I say, and she nods distractedly.

I pick up the keys to my car and head downstairs, happy that this is happening at a time when both my parents are out. I'm trying to get back into Umm'Hafsa's good books by not being out late since the night I came back after 10 pm on Bashir's birthday and met her waiting in my room when I walked in, her face a mask of sheer disappointment.

I hope this is not some silly game, I think to myself as my phone automatically connects to my car's Bluetooth system.

"Hey, Siri. Call Bashir," I say out loud as I drive past the gates and out of the house.

The number dials, and I hear an engaged tone before the automated voice: "The number you've dialled is not reachable at the moment. Please try again later."

This is stupid. Should I go alone or get Ilham to come with me? I decide against calling her as she lives 12 minutes away and off the route to Bellanova.

When I get to the highrise building, I park on the street and walk through the gates. The guards greet me, and I walk past the crowded restaurants into the elevators. *It's always so crowded on Fridays and Saturdays, I miss the days when this corner of Abuja was a hidden gem,* I think to myself as the elevator beeps and the doors open. I enter and press the button for the 16th floor. When I step out, my heels click as I walk towards the apartment that Bashir has had on standing reservation in his name for the past 6 months.

I use the keycard to open the door and push it open. The apartment isn't as quiet as I expected it to be. The TV in the living space was on the music channel, and there were take-out boxes in the sink in the kitchen. I start walking towards his bedroom, wondering if he got back from Lagos earlier than scheduled, and then I hear it – a sound I can't quite place. I slow my steps, listen harder, and I hear it again. It was a moan. It was quiet, almost inaudible, but it was definitely a moan.

Then I hear grunting and the sound of something banging against the wall. Or was it… someone? The grunting comes through again, and then a female voice laughs: "Hmm, you like that, don't you?"

I am already at the door. My stomach is in knots, and I hold my breath as I push the door open. On the king-sized bed is Bashir, naked, with his head buried in the white pillows and his hands tightly grabbing a naked girl's hair as her head bobbed up and down between his legs. *This is Lagos, huh?*

The door behind me closes with a thud, and they both look up at me.

* * *

I watch as they scramble out of bed, trying to find pieces of their clothing thrown all over the room – a pair of panties on the armchair, a black shirt on the floor, and something that looks like a really short red skirt or a bandeau on the lamp. My movements are slow as I drop my green clutch on the dresser that's just a few steps from the door. The girl was sweating, and the coolness of the air-conditioned room did little to hide the smell of perspiration, latex, and sex. Bashir is stumbling as he hurriedly pulls up his jeans. His mouth is moving, but I can't quite hear him over the blood rushing to my head. I look at the black dustbin by his leg; a used condom is sticking out of it.

The girl, wearing only panties now, knocks down the lamp as she takes the short skirt or bandeau over it. I see that it's a skirt now. Her hands are over her breasts, covering herself as she gathers her clothes with the other hand, and she makes her way towards the bathroom, tiptoeing like she wasn't the elephant in the room.

"Um," I clear my throat, "you need to leave." I point at the door behind me.

The girl looks up at Bashir with her eyes wide and questioning; the glittery eye shadow she has on is smudged in her sweat. Bashir, now in *Calvin Klein* briefs, gives her a slight nod before his eyes return to my face; he looked apologetic, almost fearful. I don't take my eyes off him, even for a second. At this moment, he looks so mediocre; nothing about him appeals to me now – not his physique, not the smile that creeps at the corner of his mouth, not the soft curly hair I used to enjoy running my fingers through. How did I fall for this guy? – with his pudgy stomach and, in this light, his arms look flabby. I'm almost repulsed.

"It's not what it looks like," he starts walking towards me.

I raise my hand to shut him up; I'm not going to have a discussion with a stranger in the room. The last thing I need right now is a video of me screaming at him going viral on *Bujgist*.

As she heads for the door, she leans away from me like she's scared I will lay a finger on her, as if I will intentionally taint myself with whatever filth she has been rolling around in. Once she reaches the door, she makes a dive for it, still covering her breasts with one hand and carrying her clothes with the other. As Bashir and I stare at each other in silence, I imagine the girl slipping into her clothes in the sitting room before I hear the main door open and close with a bang. I remain quiet as I listen to the sound of her unmistakable footsteps running down the hallway, a loud cry from *"hmm, you like that, don't you?"*

"I can expla –" he moves forward as his hand reaches for me.

"I don't want your explanation," I chuckle bitterly. "It's over."

"You're joking, right? Bebi, you know that she means nothing to me. This was –"

"I don't care," I reach for my clutch, turn around and walk out of the room just as he reaches for the shirt on the floor, wearing it as he catches me by the exit door leading out of the apartment.

"Are you seriously breaking up with me?"

I walk past the sitting room and towards the front door, ignoring him.

"But you do know this was all your fault, *ko?*" his voice raises with every word.

I turn around to look at him. He is now wearing the black shirt that was on the floor earlier, the buttons open so the *Calvin Klein* briefs are still visible. "Oh yeah?" I'm surprised at how cool and unbothered my voice sounds.

"I'm a guy," he explains. "I have needs."

I raise my eyebrow as I look at him.

"And you – I tried to talk to you, but you're – you're so stubborn."

"Lose my number, Bashir," I say, then begin to walk towards the door and down the hallway. As I press the elevator button, I realize I'm shaking; my fingers tremble as I bring out my phone. How long has he been sleeping around? I feel so stupid because all the signs were there – the missed calls, the ghosting for hours at a time, the random girls showing up at his events. A few weeks before his birthday, I remember finding a brown, lacy bra in his apartment. When I confronted him, he swore he knew nothing about it, that it belonged to one of the girls Sadiq had over that weekend. *How long has he been lying to me?*

I can't get the smell of the room out of my head, and it was numbing. I have been so stupidly blind. I really thought this man was in love with me – with his extravagant displays of affection and the gifts and flowers he sent to *H&I* for me whenever he knew we had photoshoots with models. During the summer, he went to the US to surprise me on my birthday and took me on a helicopter ride, hiring a videographer to document the experience, even though he knows that I hate all that publicity. The pictures and videos somehow made it to Instagram, where they trended for days. Now I realize that it was never about me; those were publicity reels for him to portray himself as desirable. And there I was, playing the role of the naive girlfriend who claimed a cheat publicly.

I have been so stupid. My mind keeps going to the pictures I sent him over the summer, an apology for not having sex with him. I was half-naked in those pictures, in lingerie I bought just for him. Now I am so mad at myself. I wish I could undo that particular moment.

As I step out of the elevator, I notice even more people in the lobby. Some drinking, others eating, and lounging with soft music blowing through the speakers. I had just taken a few steps when I hear a familiar voice.

"Hafsat." *Of course, just my luck.* It's the voice of the last person I want to see.

I glance over my shoulder and see Sadiq catching up to me. I look behind him and see Halima Adam or Lilybeth or whatever her name is sitting in the restaurant with another guy and giving their orders to a waiter.

"Sadiq," I say, still walking. I open my mouth to tell him I have to go, but no words come out. As I continue walking towards the gate, his words begin to echo in my head: *Worry about yourself, Hafsat. Worry about yourself, Hafsat. Worry about yourself, Hafsat.* Did he know about the girl that Bashir had upstairs? If yes, then Usman knew as well. Usman tells Ilham everything. Does that mean that she knows too? This is all too much. Can I even drive right now? I might be trying to keep it together, but I am still shaking.

"Hey, are you okay?" He asks, matching my steps.

I roll my eyes as I look up to him just as I reach my car. "Yup, everything's peachy." The doors automatically unlock, but as I reach for the handle, his hands reach out in front of me, stopping me from opening the door.

"You don't seem okay," he says.

I look up at him expecting to see a smug look. I don't see the usual disdain in his eyes; I see concern. I follow his eyes as they look down at my trembling hands. I look up at him again, and from his forlorn expression, my unasked question is answered. He knows. My mouth slowly falls open, but I regain my composure quickly.

He looks towards the gate as if to see if someone's watching and then back at me, lowering his voice as he speaks. "I know this is out of place, but please let me drive you home. I can't let you drive like this." His hands raise as if to reach for mine, but they drop quickly, almost on their own accord.

"I'm per –perfectly capable of driving myself. Thanks," my voice breaks a little as I speak.

"Yeah, I don't doubt that, but I do *need* you to get home safe." He stretches his palm out, silently asking for my keys.

I stare at his hands in front of me for a while, then sigh out loud as I give him the keychain with the black fob. I walk round to the passenger side, open the door, get in, and recline the seat all the way down. I hear him talking to someone, and a few seconds later, he opens the door, and he adjusts the driver's seat. As he adjusts the rearview mirror, he looks at me. "Are you o-"

"Please don't ask if I'm okay."

"Got it," he mutters under his breath, just when the car starts moving. Almost immediately, my phone starts ringing, and from the display unit on the dashboard, we can both see that it is Bashir. I reject the call from my phone, and a message comes in, then another and a third. The phone starts ringing again, so I switch it off, ignoring the unread messages.

I feel Sadiq's eyes glancing at me in the reclined seat before turning back to the road. I turn and stare out the window – at the top of buildings and the grey skies, seeing everything yet looking at nothing. I must have been quiet for five minutes before I break the silence. "I can't believe I actually thought he was really busy working. All those times, all those ignored calls… I actually believed him," I finally say out loud. Sadiq says nothing. "I've been so blind," I chuckle to myself bitterly.

We are now at our gate. I bring my seat upward and wave at the security man, who was looking for a familiar face. When he sees me, he pushes the gate open and allows Sadiq to drive in.

"I thought you knew about them," he says as we drive through the gates.

"Them?" I say, mostly to myself. Then I whirl my head towards him, eyes and mouth wide open, "Did you say 'them'? There's more than one?"

He doesn't look at me. All I see is a slight twitch in his jaw as the car gradually comes to a halt. I watch as his fingers lightly touch the ignition button to turn the car off, the screen displaying the time before going black; it's a few minutes to Maghrib. My parents will be driving in any moment now.

I look up to thank him for driving me back, but the words fail me, as it dawns on me that he and I have never been alone before. The blue T-shirt he had on and his blue denim trousers make him seem very approachable for the first time ever.

"Are you going to be okay?" His eyes pierce into mine, and my mouth becomes dry. "If you need anything, just let me know."

"Sure," I nod as I reach to open the door. How am I supposed to do that? We don't have each other's numbers. Besides, what would I possibly need that would warrant Sadiq leaving his numerous commitments to show up for me? "Let me get the driver to drop you." I say as I glance toward the gate.

He shakes his head as he brings out his phone. "That won't be necessary. I told my driver to drive behind us. He's parked outside your gate."

My second phone starts ringing from my clutch. I bring it out and see Bashir's name. I reject the call. I look up to see Sadiq looking at my phone with a frown on his face. "See you around, I guess," I say.

He nods slowly. "Good night, Hafsat."

Ibrahim

If anyone had asked me if I had ever had my heart broken, the answer would be no, I hadn't. Growing up, people would talk about their hearts breaking, and as an aspiring doctor, I would joke that it could be fixed with a cast or splint; I used to even take it further and say that since the heart was a muscle, a suture should put it back in its previous state.

The loss of a loved one was very abstract; you couldn't quite define how you feel. When our father died, I was only eleven years old, and there was a sense of dreadful emptiness all around our family house in Kano. For days, I would stand outside our gate, expecting to see him coming back from the Mosque pulling his dark brown *tasbeeh*, rosary. There were moments I turned around, expecting to see him behind me. Except he never was. On the mornings that followed his death, I would get up from the bed I shared with my brother once I heard the call for *Fajr* prayer and pick up one of the rubber kettles in the compound fill up with water for his ablution. Somewhere between *zauren gida*, the thatched space leading into our family house where visitors would usually wait, and the tap, I would suddenly remember that the person I was fetching water for was gone. That realization would usually stop me in my tracks, the rubber kettle falling to the cemented ground under the tap as I watched the tap fill it up and overflow. Sometimes Ya Isa would knock me on my head before turning off the tap, prompting me to start my ablution and run to the mosque with him so we didn't miss the morning prayer.

After my return to Kaduna for Eid, the emptiness I felt in Ya Isa's house was the same – it was abstract. First came the many symptoms of malaria: I couldn't sleep, I was feverish, I had a raging headache, and loss of appetite. I had to go to the chemist to get medication. Three days later, I had finished all six doses, and the symptoms still persisted. So, I concluded it wasn't malaria in the first place. Was this the heartbreak people talk about?

On Saturday evening, five days after my return, I had just helped Ya Aisha fetch some water from the well, and when I entered the kitchen, she was peeling yam that she was going to boil for dinner. I took a rubber cup from a tray that had washed cups and utensils and got myself some water to drink. The cup was new – it was a bright purple one I had never seen before. For some reason, I turned the cup around when I finished drinking the water, and the words on the white sticker seemed like a jumble of alphabet letters to me. I kept reading the words repeatedly, but they seemed to lag every time my brain made sense of the words.

Congratulations!!!
Alhaji Mohammed Ringim weds Zuwaira.
Cutsey: Hajiya Tani and co

A wedding souvenir. I read the wrong spelling of the word *courtesy* over and over as I inattentively peeled the white sticker from the cup. It was like picking at the scab of an old wound; you don't know when to stop until you see blood.

"I think it all started with Tanko. You know Tanko *ko*?" Ya Aisha asked me unexpectedly.

Tanko?

"From the middle flat? The landlord's son," She looked at me worriedly as I stood against the kitchen sink. She had stopped peeling the yam.

"Oh yes, I remember him – the one who never smiles," I said, as I rinsed the cup and dropped it back on the tray.

She nodded as she continued. "Yes. So, apparently, he went to Alhaji Sani and said that he wanted to marry *her*."

The whispered tone Ya Aisha used to tell me that Zuwaira had gotten married when I came back from Zaria makes me wonder if she knew that I liked Zuwaira, if she knew that I was in love with her. Sometimes when she came to take dried clothes off the line, she would see us washing side by side on some afternoons, but we were usually quiet, and she might have just assumed there was nothing there.

"Really? He did?" This was news to me. I remembered him giving us an odd look one day as we returned from the market, Zuwaira might not have noticed because her eyes were usually downcast, but when I said Assalamu Alaikum to him, he didn't take his eyes off her, even as he answered me.

"That was when Alhaji Sani told Tani that *ai* Alhaji Ringim wanted to marry her as his fourth wife. So they rejected Tanko and accepted the Alhaji's proposal," she came to the sink, and I moved away to give her space as she washed the pieces of yam.

"Didn't he already have four wives?" I asked as I dissembled the green stove, taking out the black inner casket and lighting the cream-colored wicks with a lit broomstick.

"His third wife died during child birth some months ago. Tani and I even went to do *ta'aziya,* to offer our condolences to the family when it happened. It was sad." she said.

"Allah sarki, and Alhaji Sani just gave her to him as replacement?"

"No, they said he gave her to him in exchange for becoming a manager at the textile mill."

"Really?"

"*Toh,* that's what I heard the women in Islammiya saying oh. Apparently, he bought the big textile mill in Zaria and made Alhaji Sani manager. Some say it was in exchange for Zuwaira," she paused. "Whatever the case, he *is* a very rich man. People say he has at least one house from Daura to Suleja, and most of them are even empty. They just have guards outside them day and night. Some people think he's hiding money; others think he literally has skeletons in his closet," she put the pot of yam on the fire, salting it before covering the pot. "During the wedding, he sent a bag of rice to every house on this street. Can you imagine what that must have cost? Well, if the rumors are true, he has a farm on the outskirts of town, so he could very well afford it."

I remembered seeing a sack of rice that wedged the door open when I went to drop my bag in the store upon my return; it had the words *Ringim Farms* written over the white woven sac. How could one even compete with a man like that – a man who created jobs for his in-laws, who had empty houses, and gave away sacs of rice as souvenirs for attending his wedding? There was no way I stood a chance. Zuwaira was never going to end up with a struggling man like me – me and all my belongings that fit in a blue *Ghana-must-go* bag. Granted, we still have the family house in Kano, but the rent from most of that house supplemented what Ya Isa paid for our younger twin sisters and me to go to school. Even if by some fluke in kismat, I was able to ask for her hand in marriage and I got to marry her, where would I keep her? I was currently crashing on the couch in my brother's house, and my clothes were kept in a store next to their foodstuff. I did not have any income and would not for another few years, at least.

I thought back to all the quiet plans I had made for us both – registering her for the exams, and encouraging her to go to University after we got married. I thought we had more time.

The day I understood why it was called heartbreak was a few months later. On a sunny Tuesday afternoon. Whenever I was back in Kaduna, I used to go to a different mosque that was a ten-minute walk away from the compound; it just seemed like avoiding Alhaji Ringim's house was the right thing to do. But on that day, Ya Isa waited for me to finish my ablution, and we headed out of the compound towards the mosque together. I followed his lead to the mosque in Alhaji Ringim's house.

That was the first time I saw Zuwaira ever since she got married. She was wearing a light pink lace made into one of those long gowns women wore and a white veil over the scarf wrapped around her head, covering her arms and the top half of her body. She looked so different, but I couldn't quite place what was so different about her; the only word that came to my head was... *rich*. With a black bag over her shoulders, gold around her neck and on her earlobes, four bangles on each wrist, and lipstick – she looked rich. I had never seen her with makeup on, and she looked even more beautiful than I had ever seen her.

Astagfirullah. I found myself silently asking for Allah's forgiveness as I stared at her much longer than I should have. She was a married woman now, I reminded myself as I lowered my gaze and continued listening to Ya Isa; he was telling me about the issues he was having with the tenant in our family house in Kano.

Luckily for me, she didn't notice me. She opened the door to a Toyota Pathfinder jeep, and I noticed that she was with a much older woman. The driver drove off with them just as we got close to the Mosque.

The way my heart dropped when I saw her that day finally made me understand why it was called a heartbreak. It felt like my heart dropped out of my chest and shattered into a thousand pieces with her name written on every single one. It was not something that could be fixed with a suture or a cast; this was an irreversible kind of loss. I knew I would live with this loss for the rest of my life, the loss of someone my heart had taken as mine, but that person that was never actually mine; the loss of a dream I dared to nurture except, in reality, a woman like Zuwaira was never meant for a man like me, not while men like Alhaji Ringim still had wife spots and empty houses to be filled.

The feeling of loss continued for months; sometimes, I would be fine, and then I'd see a young patient with their wife gazing at their newborn baby; or while I was at a store getting some provisions, I would hear backstreet boys on an FM channel, and I would think of her. I would be taken back to the days Zuwaira, and I used to talk for hours in front of the drying line by the well in the compound. Even during my housemanship, when I was working in the hospital in Lere, on the outskirts of Kaduna, the long hours and being on call for 24 hours would sometimes be punctuated by the sight of someone who wore a black hijab or had a dimple. My heart was dealing with a part of it that was gone forever.

Hafsatu

S hatu is the first person I tell about my break up. I open the door to her room on the way to mine and meet her bouncing her head as she types away on her laptop, listening to the same album on repeat.

She looks up at me as I stand by the door. The inviting nature of her room's purple and white interior fails to help me make a sarcastic comment about her *Taylor Swift* obsession. "I just broke up with Bashir." I hear myself say.

She pushes her glasses into her face, a twitch she often does. The music stops playing as she shuts her laptop. "Are you okay?" That is the first question she asks: am I okay? Not 'what happened' or 'why', like my friends would have. I think it's her concern for my well-being that makes me tear up a little. I enter the room, rolling my eyes at the single tear that rolls down my cheek. I wipe it off with the sleeve of my abaya. These are not tears for Bashir. I'm mostly mourning the relationship – everything I thought it signified – not the man. I step into the cold room and make my way under her bed covers; she always has the air conditioner cranked to the lowest, it feels like the Artic here. She silently joins me in bed.

"I'll be fine," I say, smiling at the way she's peering at my face like I am fragile. When Ilham comes over after Maghrib, she finds us laughing at Tik-Tok videos on Aisha's phone. We both look up as the door opens; she is holding a tub of ice cream and two spoons she must have gotten from the kitchen downstairs.

"I thought this was going to be an intervention, but it looks like you're

63

over it already," she smiles as she comes in.

"Not yet. *Chocolate Therapy* will help, though," I stretch my hand for the Ben and Jerry's tub and my sister laughs.

I spend the next few hours tucked between my best friend and my sister, eating ice cream as we watch episodes of *Money Heist* on the small screen of Aisha's laptop.

The days that follow the break-up are a drag. Between rejecting Bashir's phone calls and signing contracts for the upcoming fashion show *H&I* is participating in, I have no time to think of my ex.

Two weeks later, I'm still managing to keep myself busy, even more so now because I'm working to distract myself from this stupid blind item that Bujgist put out on Instagram:

Bujgist Blind item

What is on the table, my people?
Breakfast!
HOT, hot breakfast.
It has been confirmed that one over-sabi but good-looking couple has reached Splitsville.
While the damsel, a 'designer' was waiting for the bling, she found her beau pants down in the act!
I guess waffles are not the only thing on this breakfast table ;)
This is the same beau that Bujgist told you months ago was caught in a compromising position with a music video vixen at an after-party during his brother's wedding.
Don't forget you read it here first!

"Why the heck did they put designer in quotes?!" I yell into the phone as soon as Ilham's call comes through.

"Ah, I guess you have seen it. I was calling to tell you to avoid Instagram today."

"No, really. What does designer in quotes mean? Like, I'm a fake designer, or something."

"Bebi, I doubt anyone even knows it's you. It's a vague description – pitiful, at best. Just ignore it."

I roll my eyes. I don't care if people clue in that the post is about me; the Instagrammer just needs to get my job title right. "How far with the plus-sized models?" We have a line-up of 10 models for the fashion event coming up, and since *H&I* is all about inclusivity, four of them were plus-sized models. Ilham and I go over some details, and I make notes on calls to make before the end of the day.

As I end the call, I make my way upstairs, where it is freezing in the dining room. Daddy usually gets back from his practice earlier than usual on Wednesdays and once he is home, the first thing he does is make the AC even cooler – a constant battle between him and Umm'Hafsa. When I enter, I find him sitting at the head of the dining table still in the white kaftan and trousers he wore for work. His daily newspapers are folded in front of him and the television is on a news channel displaying the Paris Climate Pact.

"These glasses don't change anything for me, Bebi," he says, as I sit next to him. He pulls the offending spectacles he got three months ago down the bridge of his nose and squints at the newspaper in front of him with and without them. Next to the papers, his phone, with a picture of Umm'Hafsa as the screensaver, lights up as he receives a message.

"Really? Let me see," I say, taking the glasses from him and I look through them; everything immediately seems bigger around me. "I'll book another consultation with Dr. Ifeanyi for you." I dial the family optometrist's office number and talk to his receptionist, as daddy studies the CCTV footage of the main gate. The obscured security screen is placed strategically to the left of the television so that it doesn't distract him at mealtimes, while giving him the opportunity to see the comings and goings of people in the house.

"That car has been waiting there for a while now," he finally says.

I look at the security screen and see Bashir's black Lexus still parked just outside the gate. He has been here every day since the break-up. I gave Joe, the head of security, strict instructions to revoke his access to the house and even when they called to tell me that he was outside, I told them to tell him that I was unavailable. It's funny to think that when I was his girlfriend, he didn't spend this much time coming to our house.

"When he's tired he'll leave." My parents knew Bashir because he had greeted them on a few occasions when he dropped by. I take the blue cleaning cloth from the *Ray-Ban* case next to daddy's phone and clean the lenses of his glasses. When it's smudge-free, I lean closer to him and put them on his face. "Is that better?"

"A little," he shrugs as he looks around the room, then returns his eyes to me, as if contemplating on whether to speak.

"What, daddy?"

"You know I'm never going to meddle in your relationship, but you have to remember that fights are part of life. *Amma ko fadan ma, a dinga yi da mutunci*; even when you're fighting, there should be respect. Is leaving him out there the right thing to do?"

I try to think back to the times I've witnessed my parents fighting. Most times, when Umm'Hafsa was angry at daddy like, when he keeps her waiting or forgets something important – he would make sure she didn't go to bed angry; he would apologize in as many ways as she needed. The same thing with her – she would rush to the couch and sit next to him, holding his hands in hers: "My love, when you said Monday, I thought you meant next week. *Wallahi* I didn't realize... I am sorry." Despite his foiled plans or whatever the case, he would move his head to the side and say: "It's no problem."

She would tease him and say that since he wasn't smiling, it was not okay and he would repeat himself, telling her that it was. But she would keep going on until he finally smiled, then she would hug him or kiss his cheek.

Fights in relationships are not new to me. I grew up watching my parents settle their fights and arguments amicably. This, however, cannot be solved amicably.

"It's over between us," I tell daddy. "I don't know how else he wants me to tell him. But if he chooses to spend his free time outside the gate, who am I to stop him?"

My dad looks at me quietly, his left thumb and index finger rubbing his moustache and beard, something he always does when he's paying attention or thinking of a solution.

"There's no chance of reconciliation?"

"No way, daddy. I can never trust him again."

Umm'Hafsa comes in with Ladidi, the second househelp, following closely behind her with a trolley of food warmers. As Ladidi puts the food warmers on the table, Umm'Hafsa sets a plate in front of daddy. "Patience, Hafsat. Patience is everything," she says as she serves him the *tuwon shinkafa* and uses a ladle to dish the dried okro soup and chicken stew into a different bowl.

I've always wondered why even though we have a cook, Umm' Hafsa always supervises my dad's meals. If he's having tuwo or pounded yam, she'll always be the one to make his soup for him. Some years ago, when she travelled for a one-week education seminar in South Africa, daddy kept complaining about the soups the cook made: "too salty", "too spicy", "*kuka* doesn't need all these things he put inside.." To be honest, there was nothing wrong with what the cook made; he's just used to eating Umm'Hafsa's food that everything else tastes wrong when someone else cooks.

Personally, I'll never relieve the cook of his or her duties when I get married. In fact, I'm okay not having a driver in my own house, but a cook? That's non-negotiable for me.

"But you heard her *ai*; he broke her trust. What you forgive in a relationship only increases after marriage, and you cannot marry someone you do not trust."

"Trust is everything," Umm'Hafsa agrees. "Do you want zobo or water, my love?" On the table is a clear pitcher with the red drink and another with iced water.

"*Zauna*; sit down. Let's eat," a smile forms on his face as he looks up at her. "I'll pour some water for us." As he says it, he fills two glass cups with water and sets one in front of her as she sits down next to him, opposite me.

The help is almost at the door when Umm'Hafsa stops her. "Ladidi," she calls, "before you leave, reduce the AC," she rubs her hand together as she looks from daddy's face to mine. "Isn't it too cold in here?" I shrug as I smile at them both. If Umm'Hafsa and I agree on anything, it's that daddy liked the room too cold.

* * *

Later that night, as I'm scrolling through my Instagram, I see a picture of Sadiq. His pictures are always on my Explore page. This is a new one. I click on it and scroll down his profile, something I do more times than I care to admit. I avoid his stories because I don't want to be among his viewers, but the reels he posts? Those are my favorite.

Sometimes, I watch them on a loop, even though they are mostly brand endorsements. After I watch a 30-second black and white video that was an obvious ad for men's wristwatches from an upcoming African brand, I scroll to another picture of him next to his car. He has his hands in his pocket as he looks into the camera, his brown trousers snug against him and the sleeves of his shirt molded over his toned arms. As I stare at the picture, his dark full eyebrows, his chiseled face, a DM comes in and I am taken aback by the sender. Sadiq: *Hello stranger...*

It's the first message he has ever sent to me. It has been three weeks and a day – not that I'm counting – since he dropped me home since that day in Bellanova. From his pictures, I knew he had gone to London and returned.

While I'm thinking of what to type, another message comes in: *Or should I say, stalker?* There's a smirking emoji at the end of the message.

I immediately type *back: What?*

Stalker? What does he mean? He doesn't know, does he? Can he?

Sadiq: *I find it interesting that you never followed me back, yet you're on my profile multiple times a day, Hafsat.*

He knows. I stare at my phone, reading his message over and over again.

I type back slowly: *Sorry, don't know what you're talking about.*

Sadiq: *For brand engagement insights, I have an app that tells me how often someone checks my profile. Guess who's at the very top?*

Is there really an app for that, or is he bluffing? Does he know how many times I look at his pictures? Since when? Even when I checked his profile while Bashir and I were together? *Shikenan*, it's all over. Hafsatu-Bebi in the mud. Someone needs to burn down the Instagram headquarters, if they have one, then throw my phone in the Nile.

Sadiq*: Hey, I'm just teasing. How have you been?*

Is he, though? I'm not sure what to think, but I also want to talk to him so I reply: *Fine and you?*

I immediately open Google and type: "Can people tell when you check their Instagram profile?" A long list of paid apps appears on the page. I scroll through them, hoping he's joking. These apps should be illegal.

He messages again: *I'm good. Hey, just about to start driving. What's your number?*

I send him my number without even thinking twice about it then my finger hovers over the follow button on his Instagram profile, wondering if I should wait a few days before following him back.

What's the point? We just chatted and if he really knows how often I'm on his profile, I might as well follow him. I click the blue follow-back button just as a call from an unsaved number comes through. Even before I pick up, I know it's him.

"Hello?"

Hafsatu

I'm at *H&I* finishing up the alterations to the collection that the models will display on the ramp. In front of me is a white table that is cluttered with pictures, sketches, and fabrics. I bend in front of a shiny black mannequin, using pin tacks to fasten the material where the tailor would shorten and tuck in. I'm almost done with the last one when my phone buzzes. Ilham is sending me her DNA Ancestry test results.

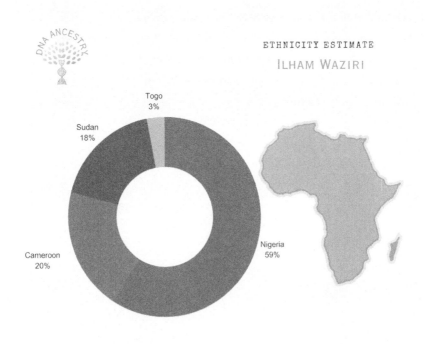

DNA ANCESTRY

ETHNICITY ESTIMATE
ILHAM WAZIRI

Togo
3%

Sudan
18%

Cameroon
20%

Nigeria
59%

She sends another message: *No surprise here, if we're being honest.*

I type back: *Really? Why?* then drop the phone on the table as I remove another pin tack from between my lips and begin to secure the final pleat on the bodice of the mannequin in place. As I pick up my phone again, Ilham's name flashes on the screen.

"*Kinsan*, none of Gwaggo's sisters speak Hausa," she says as soon as I pick up. Gwaggo, Ilham's paternal grandmother, is a decade or less away from becoming a centenarian but she's surprisingly agile for her age. Rumor has it that her sons – who are in their sixties and seventies – never make important decisions without consulting her. "Out of all her sisters, she's the only one who speaks Hausa. They all speak French and Arabic."

That makes sense. There are so many inter-tribal marriages in Nigeria and between Nigerians and Africans from neighboring countries. And because these are primarily patriarchal communities, a woman's language and tradition usually get overshadowed when she marries a man from a different tribe. In this case, she adopts her husband's culture as her own. In northern Nigeria especially, when you marry into our culture, you become one of us. Growing up, I went to school with people who had Efik, Urhobo, Igbo, and Edo mothers but whose fathers were Hausa, so they only identify as Hausa. I think Yoruba wives are the only ones who sometimes hold onto their language and culture even after marriage.

Other times, the other side of their heritage gradually disappears into obscurity. It's no surprise that Ilham identifies as Hausa; when she is part Fulbe, French, Arabic, and God knows what else.

"Yeah, I remember. You told me," I say, as I look at my phone. Sadiq had called few minutes ago and said he wanted to drop by to say hi. I wonder if he's close now. This is the third time I'll be seeing him this week.

"I wonder if I have extended family in all these other countries. It'll be nice to have distant cousins who speak foreign languages," she muses out loud.

"Yeah, I guess," I say. With DNA testing becoming so common in the

21st century, I reckon even a feat that seemed hard some years ago can be quickly done now, like finding distant relations.

"Anyways, the stage manager for tomorrow is asking for a playlist. We decided Afrobeat instrumentals, right?"

"Yup. Oh, did you see my text? The technician came by after the rehearsal. The projection display has finally been fixed."

"Ah, finally!" she screams. "What were your results, by the way? Have you received it yet?"

"I haven't seen it. I'll check my email and send you a screenshot."

We say our goodbyes and I start packing up. As I step into the parking lot, I see a black Mercedes parked right next to my car and Sadiq comes out from the passenger's seat and walks towards me. He's wearing a well-tailored kaftan made out of a blue patterned material. I notice that his car is still running. "I figured you wouldn't want to be disturbed less than 24 hours to your show."

When he bought a dozen front-row tickets to my show, I didn't bother asking him who they were for. I was not sure that I was ready to hear the answer.

"So you've been waiting here?" The parking lot is usually deserted at this time of the evening. Most of the boutiques in the plaza close at 6 pm, only a few are open until 8 pm. It's 7:50 pm now and even those are getting ready to close.

"Not for long. I tried calling you, but it went straight to voicemail." He reaches for a piece of lint on my arm and removes it, flicking it into the air away from us.

"Yes, I was on the phone with Ilham," I explain, as we move towards the cars.

"Do you always work this late?" He glances at his wristwatch and back at me.

"No, not really. I usually check in around noon for inventory or at closing for a meeting with the manager, I say as I approach my car.

"You must be hungry," he offers. "Wanna grab a bite?"

A part of me is still finding it hard to believe that I'm talking to Sadiq.

Speaking without rude comebacks or sarcastic comments and when he looks at me, I don't feel his eyes burning with hatred and disdain. Our phone calls are becoming frequent too and we talk on the phone most nights till close to midnight. "Nah, I already ate. Ilham ordered us pizza before she left."

"Cool," he puts one hand in his pocket and points towards his car. "Can I drive you home?"

I click a button on my fob and my car unlocks. "My car is right here," I point.

"Yea, I know," he laughs. "I brought my driver along to drive yours – if you don't mind, of course." He looks through the dark-tinted windscreen and a short guy in his late twenties comes out of the driver's seat.

"Fine. If you insist on being my chauffeur again," I laugh as I give him the keys. Bits of his conversation to the driver drift past me as I get into the car, welcomed by the sleek deep brown and black interior. He joins me in minutes, one hand settling on the steering wheel and the other tapping chrome knobs between us on the dark dashboard as music fills the car.

We wait for a woman walking in front of his car with a child. She raises her hand to thank him for stopping and walks faster to the other side of the parking lot as we exit the open gates of the plaza.

"Your dad owns this place, right?" he asks me.

It catches me off-guard because not a lot of people know that, but maybe Bashir told him. "Uh yeah, he does. Good thing I don't have to pay rent for *H&I*," I laugh, and he joins me.

"What does ATUM mean?" He points towards the name of the Plaza on the brightly lit signboard. ATUM Plaza.

"Oh, it's my siblings and me," I explain, "Hafsatu, Saratu and Aishatu."

He starts driving and is quiet for a few seconds, like he's pondering on my reply. "Ah, gotcha, all your names end in 'atu,'" He smiles, nodding like he just learnt something interesting. "And the M?"

"My brother Mohammed."

"Are you the oldest?"

"Yes. Sara is turning 20, Shatu is 17 and Moh is 12, well almost thirteen, his birthday is next month."

"And you – how old are you?" He gives me a roguish smile as he asks.

"A lady never tells," I bite my lip to stop the smile forming on my face. "Hey, can I ask you something?" It's something I've been meaning to ask.

"Sure, what's up?" The smile isn't on his face anymore .

"Did you send that Bellanova keycard to me?" I've been wondering about the person who did – who among Bashir's friends would actually risk their friendship so badly for me? I've been assuming it's Sadiq, but I want to make sure.

He's quiet for a few seconds and the car is filled with Tem's sexy drawl on the song *Essence*, which is currently one of the most played songs across the country. I watch him as he turns the steering wheel to the left and we join a long traffic. Finally, he shakes his head. "No, I didn't." The traffic moves a bit but as we approach the junction, we are stopped by a red light. He looks back at me.

Then who did? I sigh, leaning into the seat, inhaling his cologne and the scent of new leather. Apart from him and Usman, I know some of Bashir's cousins have extra keys to the apartment, but would they send it to me? It seems unlikely.

"Are you okay?"

I nod, feigning a smile as I change the topic. "So, where's your friend?" I pretend to think of her name, "Billy, or is it Lily?"

He frowns as his head tilts. "Lily? Do you mean Halima? Lilybeth?" The light turns green and we begin to move.

"Oh, that's her name?"

He shrugs. "She's fine, I think. I haven't seen her in weeks."

"Isn't she your girlfriend?"

"Girlfriend? God no." He signals to the left as he changes lanes, driving faster than the other cars.

"What do you mean 'God no'?"

He looks at me as we stop at another traffic light. "She's not my type, We work out together sometimes because she's into fitness and our gym times coincide often."

"So, what's your type then?"

Amusement flickers in his eyes and he looks back at the light turns green. The car is silent once again before Chike's *Running to you* starts playing.

"I love this song," I say, then start humming quietly to Chike's verse. Sadiq watches me as he makes the left turn that leads to our street. When we get to the gate, security steps up to his window and Sadiq rolls the glass down, and I lean towards it and wave. As soon as he see me, he signals for the gate to open.

We pull up the driveway and park behind my parents' cars. His driver parks my car in the available covered parking spot and brings the keys to him. I hear them talk for a bit, then he gives the driver some cash and the driver walks out of the compound just as the song ends.

"Lily is not my girlfriend," he pauses, "I actually haven't had a girlfriend since I moved back to Nigeria."

"Oh c'mon, now you're lying." I have seen him with so many girls on different occasions – girls who would touch his arm as they laughed, girls who would lean into him as they posed for pictures, pretend to clean something from the corner of his lips at lunch, or hug him for much longer than necessary.

"*Wallahi*. My last relationship was three years ago."

"That's hard to believe."

"Because your resident blogger has named me a Casanova?" He's referring to the many blind items *Bujgist* has put out in the past year about his different girlfriends and the many hearts he broke.

I raise my brow at him, "you tell me."

"The easiest way to stay unattached is to be surrounded by many women," he says quietly.

"Why do you talk in riddles, Sadiq?"

* * *

75

When he leaves, I go straight to the living room upstairs and right at the door, I hear daddy and Umm'Hafsa talking quietly in the living room. They know how hard I work before these shows but still, Umm'Hafsa will use my not-so-late return as another admonishment opportunity, so I quietly turn around to head to my room.

"Hafsatu," I hear her voice just as I take the first step.

Ugh. So close. "Na'am?"

I make my way into the living room. Umm'Hafsa is wearing a maroon and silver brocade grown with her hair in a low ponytail and hands intertwined in daddy's, who is in a blue jallabiya, another gift from me. We all get him gifts, but he wears mine the most because I actually buy him things that he likes, things that look good on him. On his last birthday, Shatu got him an expensive Swiss Army pocket knife with 40 tiny tools. I almost asked what exactly she thought our father would *ever* use that for. Sara's gift was better: she took him out for a movie. But Umm'Hafsa invited herself to their movie date. Later that evening, we all went to a restaurant for Indian food. The family picture I asked a waiter to take of us that day after dinner is still my screen-saver.

"Assalamu-alaikum," I say as I enter.

"Ameen, wa'alaikumus salam," they answer in unison.

"Daddy, how did your appointment with Dr. Ifeanyi go?" His second eye-test was earlier today.

"It was fine. I was just telling your mum that he's recommending surgery."

"I thought he said the cataract was non-progressive?" I ask as look over to Umm'Hafsa, and she looks unhappy.

"Its a minor procedure," he shrugs.

"When is it? I'll come with you," I pull up the calendar on my phone to add it to my reminders.

"It's tomorrow morning, and you have nothing to worry about, Bebi." He smiles as Umm'Hafsa squeezes his fingers. "I'll be with my love."

"No, I'll come. I want to."

Umm'Hafsa finally looks in my direction. "Don't you have the fashion show tomorrow?"

"It's in the evening."

"Oh, okay," she is quiet for a bit and then: "*Ya shirye shirye?* How are the preparations going?"

"Fine, *Alhamdulillah*. We're expecting a sold-out show." I'm a bit surprised she asked me about my show; she usually steers away from conversations about *H&I*. She wanted me to put my Economics degree to better use and has never hidden her disappointment that daddy supported me to follow my passion instead.

* * *

I've been home for three hours now. I've prayed, showered, changed into my pyjamas and have gotten into bed when I go through my email for the DNA Ancestry results. I follow the link, open my results and take a screenshot for Ilham.

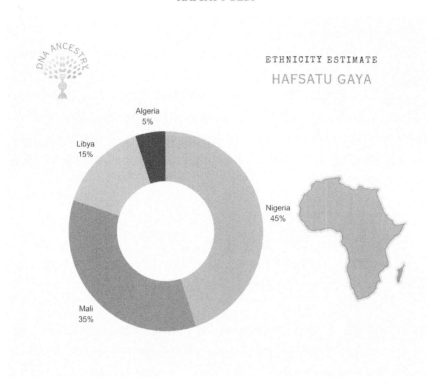

I caption the picture: *Maybe I should leave Nigeria for you guys and tell the Malian president to give me a passport.*

Her cheeky reply comes in immediately: *Haha, you wish. We die here.*

I spend the next few minutes reading the notes on the website detailing migration in the 1900s, and the pre-independence influx of North Africans into West Africa. The pages gave historical insights into what branches of our family lived outside our current geographical region. I look up as Saratu enters the room in her lilac hijab; she must have just finished praying Isha.

"Did you get your results?" she asks excitedly. "I spent the whole day finishing up my paper. I can't wait to hear my professor's feedback!"

"You're welcome," I say dryly as she stands in front of my vanity, no doubt looking for a perfume she's going to eventually take and make hers. "Don't take anything from there," I warn her, even though that never stops her.

"I'm just returning this," she brings out her hand from the hijab and raise the blue shoe-like bottle of my *Carolina Herrera* perfume I didn't even know it was missing from my collection. Then she picks up an *Armani* lip stain and uses the applicator lightly on her lips. "Senegal and Gambia – who would have thought? It's so interesting how bloodlines mix over hundreds of years," she rubs her lips together, still looking in the mirror.

"Senegal and Gambia?" Our eyes meet as I look at her reflection in the mirror.

"Yeah, I know it's just twenty something percent but in genetics, that's a huge part of our DNA."

"What are you talking about?" I sit up on my bed, "there's no Senegal or Gambia in the results." I show her my screen and moves towards me, looking through her glasses as a frown forms on her face.

"This doesn't make sense," she pulls up her results on her phone and gives it to me.

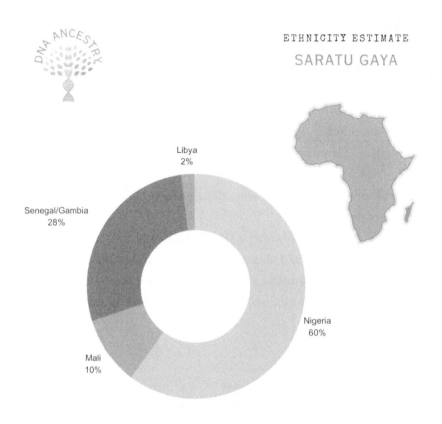

I stare at the screen, reading the details out loud, surprised at the obvious difference between her result and mine. "There has to be a mistake somewhere," I look up to her for answers; she is the Biomedical Sciences student, after all. But from the way she's looking at me, I can tell that something is wrong.

"Yeah, I mean," she hesitates, looks at my phone again and then looks at hers. "siblings should have the same DNA breakdown," she says, her words slow, like she's thinking.

"Yeah, I thought so…" my voice trails off.

The furrow between her brows only increases as she keeps reading the breakdown of the results, moving from my phone to hers. "Yeah, our estimate should be the exact same thing –because same ancestors and all that." She looks up at me, her eyes mirroring the question I had in mine: Or don't we have the same ancestors?

"They made a mistake *kenan*," I say, getting up from my bed and opening the drawers by my bedside table, trying to find the one I put the empty *DNA Ancestry* kit in, "Did they mix up our samples with some random person?"

Sara is quiet for a little bit before she answers. "For a company as reputable as that, this can be a major problem for them if that's the case; their whole business model is based on accuracy."

I turn the box around, looking for a customer service contact information. I find an email address and a 1-800 phone number, but I don't want to spend days waiting for a reply, so I dial the number immediately.

"What are you doing?" she asks me.

"Calling somebody. We need an explanation."

She nods as the number links me with an automated answering bot. After five minutes of transfers and waiting, I finally reach a human representative.

"Good morning," a cheery voice says. I open my mouth to correct him, then remember there's a time difference. "My name is Kris. Thank you for calling *DNA Ancestry*. How may I direct your call today?"

"Hi. My name is Hafsatu. My sister and I just got our results back and it seems there's a mix up or something."

Short pause.

"Oh, I'm sorry to hear that. Can I get your reference code to access your account?"

"Sure," I read the numbers off the box I'm holding. As I read, I hear a keyboard clanking on the other end.

"Miss Gaya, I have your profile in front of me, what seems to be the problem?"

"We think there's a mistake with the results you sent us."

This time around the pause is longer.

"Hmm, may I keep you on hold while I send your query to the lab? I apologize for the wait."

"That's okay," I tap my feet impatiently as I paced up and down the room, the phone on speaker. Saratu is now three pages deep in the result analysis, reading about our ethnicity and genealogy and comparing them. The more she reads, the more deeply worried she looks.

"Miss Gaya, are you there?" the voice returns and I leave it on speaker so that Sara can listen in. "Thank you for your patience. As for your query, unless estimates have been confirmed by our lab and double-checked by the in-house biologists, our clients do not receive their results."

"So there was no mistake?" I rub my forehead. "Can I ask for a re-test?"

"The lab just ran another quick one while you were on hold. Both tests under your account have been re-verified; they are accurate based on the samples you sent."

Saratu looks up at me and signals for me to hang up.

"Okay, thanks," I click the red button on my phone and look up at my sister.

"What does this mean?" I join her on the bed, looking at our analysis side by side.

She is quiet for a while, then she starts laughing nervously, she does that in high-stress situations. When she finally speaks, her voice a tiny little whisper: "Maybe one of us is adopted."

"Well, there's only one way to find out," I say as I open my laptop, go to the DNA Ancestry website and scroll down to the page where you can order kits. Each one cost $199. I add two to my cart, put in my credit card details and our address, I am about to complete the order when Sara brings my attention to the shipping time, the earliest it can get to me is in two months.

I can't wait that long to find out if an adoption is the key to this big confusion or not, so I pick up my phone and I type a message to Sadiq: *Hey, I need a favor.*

A minute later, my phone beeps: *For you, anything.*

I smile at his reply despite the turn this evening has taken, as I type: *Do you have any of those DNA kits remaining?*

A ten-second wait and then: *Yeah, a couple.*

Can I buy two from you?

This time the wait is shorter and my phone beeps twice. The first message reads: *Why would you buy them from me?* Then a second: *I can bring them to you now if you want.*

Yes, please. Thanks!

See you in a bit.

By the time he arrives, it is about 10:30 pm. When my intercom rings, I wear a jean jacket over my plaid pyjamas and head downstairs, trying to move within the security camera's blindspots just in case one of my parents are still up. The whole compound is quiet as I sneak my way to the main gate and ask one of the security guards to let me out.

Parked right outside is a dark-grey Range Rover with the halogen headlamps still on. Sadiq dims the lights and comes out of the driver's seat as soon as I come out of the gate; he has already changed into grey slacks and a red T-shirt.

"Thanks for driving all the way back this late," I smile. He has been coming to my rescue quite a lot these past days.

"I don't mind," he shrugs with a smile, "I get to see you again." He hands me the two kits and our hands linger slightly, brushing each other. The smile on his face disappears when he sees the four hundred dollar bills I try to give him.

"What is this? Don't insult this new friendship we have going on," he says with his hands in his pocket, he seems even taller and his chest broader. Without my heels, I only reach his torso, even as I look up at him.

"Oh, that's what we are now – friends?" I ask with a laugh. There is something about standing out in the slight night breeze under the security lights on the deserted street that makes our interaction subtly flirtatious.

"We're anything *you* want us to be, Hafsat." he lowers his voice as he speaks, his eyes never leaving my face.

I open my mouth to respond but I can't; my mouth is dry and for a moment I almost forget all the questions I had about my DNA results.

Zuwaira

1998

I never understood the way people talked about luck. Or maybe I just didn't understand how the thing worked. When something good happened to you, they would say you should thank your luck, that luck must be the reason why you had it. So why was it that when something terrible happened, they blame you? Shouldn't they blame luck for the bad things too?

Or maybe it was the way women talked about the small things, everyday things. Like when my mother's visitors saw my sister Maimuna and me when we returned from school. They would tell my mother: *"kin ci sa'a yaran ki sun biyo ki. Ga gashi, ga hanci;* You're lucky your daughters took after you – their hair and their nose."* Maimuna was just eight at the time, and I was around ten.

Even at that age, we looked exactly like our mother – the straight pointed nose, the thick and dark hair. The only difference was that our hair was not half the length of hers and that we didn't take her complexion; we were more like our father, much darker than she was. She was very light-skinned, the type that bruised easily from all the toiling she did to run a small canteen by the Officer's Mess. This was the job she took when our father lost all his savings to swindlers who showed him a building that he wanted to buy to start a primary school in Bauchi. He had signed the papers, employed teachers, designed syllabi and had set up everything in anticipation for the big opening. One week before they launched, it came to light that the Certificate of ownership documents he kept in a black iron safe in his room were all fake. He found out that all the signatures were forged and the building itself was in an inheritance dispute that had been ongoing for over a year and, as such, could not be bought by anyone or sold by the actual owners.

While my father toiled to pay off the loan he took to pay for the school, he lost our home to the bank. My mother took up a job for the first time in her life to support him and it was a tiring job. She cooked all day and even started making drinks for my sister and me to hawk at the motor park not too far from the Officer's Mess. When my father's relatives learnt of this, they blamed her for the bad luck that had befallen him. *"Ai wasu matan ko ina suka shiga, sai karayan arziki ta biyo, sai dai wani ikon Allah*; Some women, wherever they go, they take poverty along, if not by some special grace of God."

It was my mother's bad luck, they said, that befell me. After my aunties bathed Maimuna's corpse – her body swollen and limp as they wrapped her in the white cloth – they stood over her body and discussed the bad luck in the family. "What kind of bad luck does that Zuwaira have to lose all her family members in one day?"

But maybe it was just my luck that I managed to survived the accident that took their lives. As we laid on the hot coal tar of the express road just a few feet away from the big pothole that the commercial bus driver had swerved to avoid before he collided head-on with a trailer, I held my sister's hand tightly, as she laid next to me, not moving. I was covered in her blood, unable to speak nor cry. I could not even answer the people shaking me and asking if the other two bodies were my parents. When they tried to pry her cold hands from me, I held on for dear life, watching as they covered the bodies with wrappers other survivors gave as we waited for a pick-up from the nearest hospital to carry them.

After that, my life changed. For many weeks after that, I would wake up screaming from dreams of my parents and my sister leaving me on a bus. In the dream, I would keep running after them bare feet, but they would always tell me to wait, to not follow them. Sometimes, I would wake up and see my mother on the bed, all bloodied with her eyes unblinking staring at me. When I lived with my grandmother, the nightmares got so bad that she used to get me *rubutu,* the water washed off a wooden plaque that had Qur'an verses written on it with black ink. I drank the water every night before going to bed as instructed by her older brother. It was meant to ward off the evil they believed I saw at night. Eventually, one day, the dreams stopped. Maybe it was the rubutu, maybe it was luck, who knows.

I could never forget the day *Kawu* Sani talked to me about marriage in the parlour. It was a Friday. After his wife went to work, I hurried up and washed the heap of clothes she left for me, making sure to secure them on the line properly so that the wind wouldn't land them in the gutter. Then I quickly fetched water from the well, filling up the drums in the toilets, the kitchen and even the one on the verandah,and I ran inside to wait for Ibrahim's call. I had so much to tell him. I had written an essay on what I wanted to be in future and why, from the 1995 WAEC question paper that he gave me and was going to read it to him over the phone. I also wanted to tell him about Dan Tala – the meat seller in the market who Ibrahim used to talk to sometimes – he now owned the abattoir where they slaughtered the cows. I was also going to ask him to bring batteries for the walkman when he was coming back in three weeks because I hated going to sleep without listening to our song. It was hard to believe that Ibrahim was six years older than me, I had never in my whole life met someone that I could relate with so much, someone I felt at peace with. It was like I knew him from somewhere else, that was the only way I could describe how I felt about him.

I looked at the clock on the wall impatiently and saw that it was two minutes to nine. I wondered what he was doing at that moment – was he on his way to the phone booth, or was he in line waiting for his turn? He told me that the phone booth was just a few minutes from his hostel, but sometimes when I picked up his call, his voice would sound like he had been running, so I doubted that it was as close as he told me. I had just moved closer to the phone, anticipating the shrill ring, when I heard *sallama,* a greeting at the door. It was *Kawu* Sani on an unexpected visit from Zaria.

Ever since he got the new job and started renovating his house in Zaria, he and Hajiya Tani started fighting very often. He wanted her to move to Zaria, but she said she couldn't live with his first wife, even though he explained that he was adding two bedrooms to accommodate her and the kids.

After I greeted him and gave him water, I start moving towards the kitchen to start cooking but he called me back.

"*Zo*, Zuwaira. Come." Looking at *Kawu* Sani was like looking at my father's face if he had lived another ten years. They had the same dark skin and dark curly hair cut short to the scalp with the same receding hairline. Like my father, his eyes were always tired. Tired, but soft. "You're a very lucky girl, Zuwaira and innocent, too. Yesterday, I came back home to pick up some documents for the textile factory and I saw Suwaiba in a serious quarrel with a woman I had never seen before." His first wife, Aunty Suwaiba, was a troublemaker, even worse than Aunty Tani. But maybe that was his own luck – to be with women who hated the sound of peace and quiet. He continued, "I asked what the noise was about and why there was a stranger in my house. As it turns out, Suwaiba sold her gold to the woman – the same gold she accused you of stealing – and now, the woman wanted to return it," he shook his head. "Can you imagine? She sold it and spent the money." Just at that moment, the phone started ringing, and I froze. *Ibrahim.*

My uncle frowned as he looked at the phone and picked up with a hello. He repeated himself a few times, frowning. "I think these wires are beginning to tangle again. Tani said something about the sound getting faint when I call," he said as he disconnected a wire from the phone, untangling it because he must have thought that was the reason why he could not hear the caller.

My heart was beating wildly in my chest because I did not know what my uncle would do if he found out that a boy was calling me in his house. I imagined that I would be in so much trouble. I must have been shaking as I sat on the floor because my uncle looked at me and said: "Don't be angry, I knew you didn't touch her gold. I never doubted you for a second."

I wondered if Ibrahim would call back. I wished there was a way I could let him know not to call back, that my uncle was around. But at the same time, I really wanted to hear his voice. It had been seven days since we last spoke.

"Allah that separated you peacefully from Suwaiba is going to separate you from Tani soon," he studied my confused face and explained. "Alhaji Ringim has asked for your hand in marriage. His third wife died a few weeks ago at child birth. The man has suffered a great loss."

A woman died giving birth to his child a few weeks ago and he was already looking for another wife. I looked up at my uncle, noticing the bags under his eyes, the dark circles around them for the first time, and the white hair on his head and beard that was not there a few months ago.

"Zuwaira, you know that until I see you married, I cannot rest. The least I can do for my late brother is make sure that his last surviving child is settled in her own house."

Ibrahim. What about Ibrahim? Maybe if I had opened my mouth at that time to tell my uncle that Ibrahim was the one I wanted to marry, he would have listened. After all, he was not a bad man. But I could not. I could not speak.

"Don't cry, Zuwaira. This is all part of God's plan. See how patient you've been, and now, God has blessed you. Alhaji Ringim will take care of you. You're a very lucky girl. You will never lack anything."

What about my education?

My uncle must have translated my crying to be tears of joy because he said. "This is how God works, just keep thanking him. Now, you're going to rest from Tani and all the things she does to you when I'm not around."

When Aunty Tani heard the news, she stood up yodelling and started dancing, calling me *amarya*, bride, and saying things like: "you have gotten someone worthy." When I received three boxes filled with materials, laces, veils, toiletries, shoes, bags and a small kit with jewellery from an entourage of women Alhaji Ringim sent as my *lefe*, Aunty Tani picked out the most expensive ones for herself and her two daughters and from the money Alhaji sent for my sewing, she kept half for Jamil.

In the ten days that followed, she told anyone who cared to listen about how she would miss me because I was like a daughter to her. It surprised me how she could say such lies with a straight face. While she announced the upcoming wedding to everyone in the compound, I hoped Ibrahim's brother or sister-in-law would say something – anything – to my uncle so that he would know that my heart was with Ibrahim. But they said nothing. Or maybe they did not know. Maybe the way I kept him a secret was the way he kept me a secret. Yet, I still hoped. Even when my *lalle,* the patterned henna on my hands and feet, dried, I kept looking at the gate, hoping he would come back earlier than planned because he was worried he couldn't reach me. During the *walima,* I kept looking up, praying, hoping that he would walk in through the gate and get the courage to say what I was too weak to say. But it never happened. He was like a mirage – the more I hoped, the more unrealistic it seemed.

On the day of my *Nikkah,* wedding, Aunty Tani told my cousin to cry as soon as she saw *Kawu* Sani bringing in the dowry to me. She told her to hold me and keep saying she didn't want me to leave. This was a girl that hardly spoke to me, who always waited till I was done washing plates before bringing hers and dumping it in the sink I had already cleaned dry. This was the same girl who would look at her ironed school shirt and storm into her mother's room to complain that it was not washed properly. But on that day, the tears were almost convincing.

"What's this nonsense?" her father asked, annoyed at her drama. She was holding my neck and crying.

"Do you want to follow her? Do you want to go stay with your sister for a few weeks?" Aunty Tani said, her high-pitched voice laced with more saccharine than usual, the way it usually did when she wanted something. "A bride shouldn't be alone, anyway. Maybe you should go with her."

"No," came my uncle's stern voice. "That is not done. Let us hold our honor."

When Aunty Tani led the small group of women that took me to Alhaji Ringim's house at the end of the street after *Maghrib* prayer, it felt like I was in a dream that had gone on for too long, hoping that someone would wake me up. When we arrived at the house, I couldn't believe how big it was on the inside. The fence was plastered white walls with electric barbed wire on top and huge black gates hid the three other gates inside the house.

The first part of the compound was where the cars were parked and the security post. The big mosque was also in this section, just outside Alhaji's section. When the second gate opened, we were ushered towards the section of the *uwargida*, the first wife. She was a chubby woman in her forties, who had pictures of her and Alhaji on the walls – from black-and-white pictures of them looking very young to pictures of them abroad with graduating kids.

When we entered, she was sitting on the big red chair dressed up in a heavy lace material and big gold rings on six of her fingers as though she were taking part in the wedding festivities. The other chairs were occupied by two other well-dressed women. The women who brought me, knelt me down in front of her and Aunty Tani immediately started crying and wiping her eyes with her hijab. "She's an orphan. Her parents are dead. Please accept her as your family."

One of the women – who I recognized from the group that brought my *lefe* looked at me. "This is your *uwargida*. She's called Hajiya Babba; her father is Alhaji's uncle."

Hajiya Babba motions for me to sit on the chair next to her. When I do, she pulls me into a hug and various voices start echoing in the room: *Allah ya hada kan ku*; May God put your heads together. *A yi hakuri da ita, yarinya ce*; Be patient with her, she's just a child.

Finally, when Hajiya Babba moved to speak, the room fell silent. With the practiced gait of someone who had done this whole routine multiple times, she said with a smile: *"Allah ya sa nan gidan zaman ki ne, Allah ya kawo kazantan daki*. I pray that Allah has decreed that this is your future home and may He bring children to mess up your room." It was the usual prayer for newlyweds in our part of the world.

The whole room breaks into a chorus of 'Ameen' and laughter, as if her saying this somehow signified her acceptance of me. The two women sitting by her side look on with no expression on their faces. I wondered if they were the other wives until she said: "Take *amarya* to the other sections so she can meet the others."

The others. I was taken to the session opposite hers and a girl around my age opened the door to let us in.

"Mamie, *sun zo.* They're here," she said as she led us to the living room. This house was decorated differently, with golden frames wrapped around Qur'an verses and Arabic calligraphy lining the walls. Mamie, a woman of average build that seemed to be in her early forties was sitting alone in the living room in a white hijab, as if she was waiting for us.

Like with Hajiya Babba, the women knelt me down in front of her. This time, I found myself praying that Aunty Tani did not display fake tears like she did earlier.

The old woman who was our guide spoke again in Hausa. " This is the new bride. Hajiya Babba said she should be brought here to greet you."

"*Zauna*; sit down," Mamie said to me. " You shouldn't be kneeling down." I was propelled up by the other women and placed on the chair opposite her. "Zuwaira, *ko?*" she asked the women and they said yes. "Masha'Allah."

She said nothing after that and after a few minutes of awkward silence, the old woman, who at this point I believe is the spokesperson, said, "Let's go and see Hajiya Balaraba."

"Okay, thank you," the second wife stood up and even escorted us to the door. When we exited her section, we walked through yet another gate leading to another part of the compound. Like the previous ones, the two sections here were opposite each other but not closely built. I heard them doing *sallama* just as the *athan* for *Isha* rang out from the Mosque in front of the compound.

"Where's Hajiya Balaraba?" the spokesperson asked as we entered the dimly-lit section. Unlike the other ones, the only light reflecting in the living room was from the dining room behind us. A few minutes later, I heard the girl's voice: "*Wai tana Sallah*; she said to tell you she's praying."

And so we waited. But even after the Imam finished the congregation prayer, Hajiya Balaraba remained absent. I assumed she had a few *Ishas* to pray that evening because we were sitting in her living room for about fifteen minutes, when the prayer could be completed in five. We were still waiting when the women started to grumble among themselves: "We also need to go pray"; "It's getting dark. Did you tell her we were waiting?" Then I heard someone whisper behind me: "this is the former *amarya*, right?" and another person whispered back: "Yes, this is her." Someone else joined the conversation: "I thought the *amarya* died?" and her question was answered: "No, that was the third wife; this one is the fourth wife – well, the former fourth wife."

I knew none of these women. They were all strangers to me invited by Hajiya Tani. One of the voice quiped, "It must be hard, thinking your husband will not marry after you and then –" the voice trailed off as someone walked into the room.

"I hope you weren't waiting for long?" she said in English to a group of women who mostly only spoke Hausa. Her voice was so high and sultry that I had to look up. Our eyes met when she switched on the lights. She was a tall, slim woman and if I were to guess, I would say she were in her twenties. She was wearing a long black abaya, with her head uncovered and her hair plaited into multiple tiny braids that fell to the nape of her neck held together by a ribbon,. Even with no trace of makeup, you could tell that she was beautiful. If you looked well enough, you could tell that she had been crying – with her red, puffy eyes and the small bags under them.

"Is this the *amarya*?" she finally asked, never taking her eyes off me.

"Yes, this is your sister, *abokiyan zaman ki,* a friend for you to live with. She came to greet you."

"I never told Alhaji that I needed an *extra* friend to keep me company," her words cut down all the background chatter like a whip. I looked away from her face and at my hands on my lap. "What do you want me to say now? To wish her a happy married life with my husband? I'm not doing that. I'm not a hypocrite like the others."

She went through the hallway into what looked like her kitchen. Some of the women wanted to cajole her but the spokesperson shook her head: "Leave her. We have to make the most important stop before we finally take *amarya* to her room." We left her section awkwardly and walked silently past the section opposite and to my surprise, there was another gate. The security lights were now all on, yellow lights on long poles, and as we walked to the only section that occupied this section of the house, I could see that we had reached the end of the compound.

Hajiya Tani pulled me close. "Of all the women you met today, this is the only one who's support you truly need."

The door was pushed open and we entered a wide living room, rich with the scent of burning incense. There were rows and rows of *Samira*, various colours of covered bowls in different sizes behind a wooden cupboard with glass doors. Her sitting room had big brown leather cushions with Arabic emblems woven on them.

"Hajiya Uwa, *ga amarya*," the spokesperson greeted the elderly woman sitting down on one of the the chairs. She had her arms open like she was waiting for our arrival and frowned as the spokeswoman whispered something in her ear.

"*Maraba*, welcome," she gave me a slight hug as I was made my way to sit at her feet. Her voice was small and as she raised my veil to see my face, her eyes shone bright with the wisdom of her years. "Don't worry about Balaraba; the way she was married into this house is how you're now married into this house. You have the same right over each other, so don't let her words bother you."

She reached for my hand, severing the band Hajiya Tani's fingers made over my wrist. "You are married to my son now. That makes you my daughter. Welcome, Zuwaira." People said that lucky girls were loved by their husbands, but the luckiest girls were loved by their mother in-law. Which was I going to be?

Later that evening, when the women took me to the section opposite Balaraba's, the one that is now mine, they kept repeating the same thing over and over – how lucky I was to marry Alhaji Ringim, to have a place this beautiful and big to myself. There it was again that word –*luck*.

Sadiq

2021

Spending time with Hafast reveals parts of her that I have never been privy to in the past, when all I did was watch her through careless glances when we were in a group of people. Things like how often she talks about her dad and how fiercely she loves her family. The hours she puts in at *H&I* – something I thought was just another vanity project, most graduates from overseas return to Abuja with one. *H&I* was not something she did on the side; it was something she worked hard at with Ilham every day of the week. I also never realized how often she bites down on her lower lip, especially when she's concentrating on something, like when we play scrabble. There are also annoying habits that never change, like the fact that she never picks up her phone the first time you call and how often her phone is always engaged because she's always talking to Ilham. There are endearing things like the little hint of jealousy that changes her whole demeanor, like when she saw me with Halima and just now – as she sees me walking into her Fashion show with Fatima. Fatima and I walk through the crowd to our front row seats and pick up the order cards. Amused, I watch Hafsat's eyebrows shoot up from across the runway from where she stood with Ilham when she sees Fatima lean close to me as the event photographer takes a picture of us just before the show starts. She even ignores my message, even though, I see her bring out her phone to check the notification.

She expertly avoids my gaze for the rest of the evening. After the show, I take Fatima backstage and as soon as Hafsat sees us, those beautiful lips form a thin straight line on her face which is framed by her turban. She crosses her arms over her body, under her chest, a movement that pushes the swell of her breasts upwards, an outline revealing itself over the V-neck of the purple kaftan she wore. It is belted around her waist, accentuating it, making me imagine my hand wrapped around her. The kaftan stopped mid-thigh and she had black skinny trousers underneath that hugged the curves of her hips.

I pull my gaze back to her face, "congratulations Hafsat. It's quite a collection."

"Thank you," she answers without looking at me as she signs a document on a clipboard that a vendor wheeling away some clothes on a rack hands her. She doesn't spare a glance at the person next to me and that makes me smile. The jealousy she's trying to hide, her slow and quiet anger – I want it. I want it all for myself.

"I want you to meet my sister, Fatima." Trying to hide the smile on my face, I watch as the mask of attitude falls off her face when she finally looks up at us.

Fatima speaks immediately, her movements animated with excitement. "I loved every single thing out there. I just placed my order, but the houndstooth patterned kimono is already sold out." Fatima is twenty, just two or three years younger than Hafsat.

"Aww, you're so sweet. What's your size? I'll get the tailor to make one for you and we'll call you to pick it up." She holds my sister's hand as she talks to her.

"Thank you. I wear a small. By the way, I sent you a friend request on Instagram. I've been following *H&I* for months now, I've always loved how modern and edgy your creations are."

"*Haba*? Let me follow you back," Hafsat brings out her phone from a pocket carefully hidden under the pleats on the left side of her kaftan. I see them scrolling through many unaccepted friend requests until she gets to Fatima's profile and follows her back.

"Ya Sadiq told me your sister goes to Edinburgh? I go to Heriot-Watt," Fatima says after she gets her follow-back.

Hafsat looks at me with a glint in her eye, the rich notes of her laughter taking over the conversation. "Actually, *kinsani me?* You know what? Let's get the tailor to take your measurement. *Ya* Sadiq can wait for us in my office."

I shake my head slowly, knowing she's going to keep teasing me with what my sister calls me. I saw it in her eyes when she repeated the name. I walk into her office – a small space with a white desk, two white leather chairs on both ends and a relatively small monitor. The desk was covered with sketches of women's silhouettes, colorful post-it notes on the pages of fashion magazines and a fabric-sample book. My eyes fall on a framed picture on the desk. I pick it up to get a better look; in the picture, she's wearing a graduation gown and hat and next to her is a tall and slim man wearing glasses, from his salt and pepper beard, I deduce that he might have been in his early fifties. He has a proud smile on his face as she plasters a kiss on his cheek. *Her dad.* As I set it down, I hear heels clicking towards my direction, and I turn around. Fatima is holding two big paper bags with the *H&I* logo.

"Thanks for your card. I got some things for Hadiza." Fatima hands my debit card back to me and I return it to my wallet. Fatima and Hadiza are Hajiya Amina's youngest daughters and my favorite siblings. She turns to Hafsat, "thank you for the gifts as well. The silk scarves are beautiful."

"Thanks for dropping by," Hafsat says, "Don't be a stranger." They exchange hugs.

"I love your girlfriend!" she says in a whisper loud enough for Hafsat to hear.

"Oh, he's not my boyfriend," Hafsat laughs.

Not your boyfriend, yet. Soon enough, though, you will be all mine.

The next time Hafsat laughs over a comment someone makes about our relationship is one afternoon after I pick her up from *H&I* and we decide to drive to The Vue for lunch. When we get there, she is surprisingly

96

reluctant to get out of the car.

"You said you were hungry," I'm perplexed at how how comfortable she looks, not budging or attempting to get out of the car.

"Yes, but a lot of people we know come here."

"Okay... and?"

"They'll see us together and they might misunderstand our friendship."

I chuckle to myself. *Since when does Hafsat Gaya care about what people think?* "I don't care about that," I say bluntly.

"Well, I do. They might think there's something more."

It will be interesting to see how she handles the inevitability of our being together but right now, there's no need to rush. If she wants to keep things on the low, we'll do just that. I call the restaurant and they deliver our food to the car. With our seats reclined and her feet tucked under her, we tried to eat from takeaway packs – sharing the salad from one and grilled chicken from the other. We talk about movies, Coachella, embarrassing moments but she laughs the hardest when I say 'well it was nice knowing you' when she admitted that she has never watched a single episode of Friends from beginning to end. By the time we get to dessert, the conversation has slowed down as we enjoyed the chocolate mousse. As she enjoyed the moist chocolate cake, she scrolls through Instagram.

"The influencers you gave tickets to the Fashion show are boosting up our mentions and tags," she shows me the metrics on the analytics tab of her brand's instagram page. Lilybeth and her model friends live-streamed the event and uploaded review videos for the pieces that they bought.

I finish my lunch and type a quick reply to a business email as she continues scrolling. When I look up, she has a crease form in the middle of her forehead as she frowns. "Hey, look at this."

I take her phone and see a post with a lot of comments and likes by that insignificant blogger. Red clouds my vision with every derogatory comment I scroll past, wanting to break something. But seeing how unbothered Hafsat is about it calms me down.

Buygist Blind item

Alexa, play us 'Last Last' by Burna.

Sources have confirmed that Bujtown's resident casanova and playboy has found himself a new paramour.

Rumour has it that he has been spending time at a doe-eyed designer's boutique, who, wait for it, is his friend and business partner's ex!

Is he providing a shoulder for her to cry on or a bed for her to lie in?

We will be the first to update you when this breakfast gets served.

Remember you heard it here first!

"Why do people think we're more than friends?" she laughs as I hand her phone back to her.

As she reaches between us to grab a serviette, her pink and white veil falls off her hair. She seems unaware of it until I slowly lift the ends of the soft fabric from her shoulder and cover her hair partly with it. She looks up at me, her eyes never leaving mine.

Because friends don't look at each other the way you look at me, Hafsat, and friends don't imagine what your lips will taste like pressed against theirs, like I do every waking moment.

"Would you like me to survey random people and summarize the results for you?" I ask.

She rolls her eyes.

* * *

The following month, I'm at Hajiya Amina's house in Asokoro to give her a printed itinerary for her Emirates flight to see her doctor. Her limp has gotten worse over the years and nowadays, something as simple as walking from the living room to her room has become a hassle. Her bedroom had to be moved downstairs last year to reduce the pain she goes through while climbing up the stairs.

Everyone, from her friends to my father's relations believes it's an injury from a car accident she suffered years ago. In fact, Hajiya Amina has repeated the story of the unfortunate accident that happened on her way to Zaria for her sister's wedding so many times this year that I'm beginning to think she's trying to convince herself. Sometimes, when it's just the two of us in her living room, she would rub her left thigh in a circular motion, her face contorting with so much pain that I'm forced to look away. I remember the evening the 'accident' happened, like it was yesterday. It happened in this very house.

"Take all your belongings and leave this house," I heard his voice shouting at her from one of the rooms upstairs during one of their heated arguments. "Leave my house."

"Give me my divorce paper. I'm not going anywhere until you give me my divorce." She shouted back in Hausa.

Even at that age, I couldn't be more than eleven, I remember thinking I would leave with her if she left my father; of course it wouldn't have been possible, but she was the only one who cared whether I lived or died; the other women were too busy keeping themselves in his good graces and shielding their own children from his wrath.

I left the dining room and stood at the bottom of the stairs. The door banged loudly as someone came out from one of the rooms. It was my father. Hajiya Amina was holding his babban riga and from the bruises on her face, I could tell he had already hit her a few times. As I watched, his hands pushed her off him and down the stairs and she fell face first, her body hurtling down the stairs.

"Should I send *kayan bude baki* – food to break your fast – to your place tomorrow?" her motherly voice jolts me back to reality – to the white leather couch I'm sitting on. Today, she's dressed in brighter colors than usual – a bright red lace and sitting in her regular chair, with cushions behind her back.

"For Ashura tomorrow, *ko?*" Muslims fast on the 10th day of Muharram, the first month of the Islamic calendar. "*Kar ki damu*, don't worry about it. I'll have food delivered."

"You're still ordering from that grill house? Don't you get tired of their food?"

"And some other places," I correct. Sometimes, I order from Ranchers. I've been spending most of my evenings there since the change of ownership. Bashir is happy with the split. The recently opened Waffle Drop was no longer co-owned by me; it all belonged to him. The loss I incurred was about 12%, and it was the best possible scenario. I was no longer his business partner, and we were never really friends in the first place.

"Isn't it easier to just get you a cook? You can take one from here, if you want. They're all trained and way more than I need."

"It's not necessary," I say, avoiding the stress of having domestic staff. "I'm fine."

My phone buzzes and I check to see Hafsat calling. I pick up immediately, half-grateful that I didn't have to argue my way out of getting a cook. "Hey, is everything okay?"

"Why do you think something has to be wrong for me to call you?" She laughs as she asks – a sweet, simple sound that makes me want to hear it again. Her voice sounds distant, like I'm on speakerphone. As I listen, I hear the sounds of a turn signal and can tell that she's driving.

"Because I called you twice this morning and you didn't pick," I reply.

"I took daddy to his follow-up appointment and my phone was on silent *ne*" she explained.

"Oh, okay. How is he doing?" she was at the hospital with him a few weeks earlier for eye surgery.

"Alhamdulillah. Much better *gaskiya*. Where are you?" The casual way she asks makes me want to tell her that I was about to call to check on her again. I can't seem to stop looking for excuses to see her. It has to be as a result of spending too much time with her.

"I'm in Asokoro." I say instead, answering her question.

"Are you busy?"

"No, what's up."

"I'm just going to the DHL office to drop a late-order item. Do you wanna come with me?"

"Really? You want us to go together?" The last time I invited her out for a book launch she said it was too early for us to be seen in public together.

"You're kind of slow today, no? *Ko ranan ne?* Is it the sun?" she teased. "Yes, I want us to go together."

"Okay, are we taking my car or yours?"

"I know how much you love driving me around, but I'll drive this time."

"Okay, see you in a bit," I laugh. As I end the call, I look up to see Hajiya Amina smiling at me knowingly.

"I'll come by in the morning to see you off," I stand up. "I have to leave now."

"I could tell from the phone call that you have somewhere to be," she laughs. "So, when am I meeting her?"

"Her?" I ask. "What makes you so sure it's a 'her'?"

"*Haba* Abubakar. I know you like the back of my hand and I've never heard you talking to anyone like that."

I'd love to introduce Hafsat to her.

"Soon, *insha'Allah.*" God willing. I've planned it already. After Hajiya Amina returns from Sweden in two weeks, I'll bring Hafsat to greet her.

"You don't know how happy I am to hear this," the smile on her face widens, "What's her name?"

"Hafsat." Her name rolls off my tongue very easily, like it's a name I've spent years saying.

"*MashaAllah!* I can't wait to meet Hafsat."

As I head outside, my phone buzzes with a message from Hafsat: *Outside*

101

Hafsatu

Exactly seven weeks after my break up, the daughter of a family friend got married. The groom and Sadiq happen to be friends from the University. Umm'Hafsa attended the other events but tonight is the Gatsby-themed cocktail party for only the couple and their friends.

It's just after *Maghrib*. Ilham and I are in front of the mirror in my room making small changes to our perfectly made up faces that the makeup artist spent a lot of time working on when Sadiq calls to say that he's parked out front. We walk out to find him and Usman looking like actors from the movie in a red vintage 1959 Peugeot convertible with its roof off.

"Oh, great Gatsby! Wait a minute. I have to take a picture of this," Ilham says as she pulls up her phone and takes a picture of the car. "Where did you get this beauty?"

"Sadiq is a collector of all things rare and beautiful," Usman says as he does a big show of coming out of his seat and pushing it forward for us to climb into the back.

The interior is refurbished with white leather seats and cigarette holders. "Kinda tiny back here," I say as I scoot over and Ilham joins me. In front of me, Sadiq is in the driver's seat in a light brown peak lapel suit. His inner vest has four buttons as typically favored in that era. As we drive to the venue, I see him occasionally looking at me through the rearview mirror. I play with the layered pearl necklace around my neck and the pearls on my earlobes the entire way as I listen to Ilham and Usman chat about football.

When we arrive at the venue – the Goldenbird Marquee – I reach for his hand and he helps me out of the car, the gold sequins on my black dress catch the light of the cars dropping other guests off.

"No one does costumes better than you," Sadiq says as his eyes linger on the dress I have on.

I put one gloved hand on my slicked-back hair that has a feathered headpiece completing my look. "Take a picture; it will last longer."

I move to help Ilham adjust her beaded headband cap, feeling good about myself as I hear Sadiq's quiet laughter at my quip.

We see mask-wearing entertainers and a fountain of non-alcoholic champagne as we walk into the gold and glitzy decor of the venue, complete with gold and black chandeliers and golden luxe tufted armchairs around tables with white ostrich feather centrepieces. The stage is bedazzled and there's a black-and-gold mirrored backdrop. To the far left corner is a Cuban cigar rolling booth.

I grab a champagne flute and catch up with some acquaintances and clients when I see Bashir walk in dressed in a regular suit like he is attending a business meeting – no regard for the 1920s theme at all. I manage to avoid him until right after refreshments and the silent auction when I feel a tap on my shoulder. "Excuse me," he says to the girls I'm talking to as he pulls me away. "I'll bring her right back."

"What are you doing?" I hold my glass away from me, so it doesn't spill on my dress.

"Bebi, just be honest with me. There's someone else, isn't there?"

"I don't owe you an explanation," I start to walk away. He pulls me back closer to him. I look around the room and find Sadiq talking to two guys in front of the mirrored backdrop, yet his eyes are on me – on Bashir's hands on my arm the whole time.

"Just tell me his name," Bashir insists.

"I don't have time for this." I try pulling my arm away, trying not to cause a scene , but he wouldn't budge.

"Who's he? Is he the reason you blocked me?"

"What?" I asked incredulously, "I blocked you because you're a cheat and a liar." Before I can say more, Ilham comes and pulls me away, leading me to the rotating video-booth platform.

"Dancing time, Bebi," she says as we hop on the platform and the camera starts to revolve around it. It's easy to find our balance in the heels we're wearing as we dance to the music. A few minutes later, while we are watching edits of the slow-motion video, my phone beeps. It's a message from Sadiq: *Let's leave. Just you and me.*

I look up, scanning the room for him – past people posing for pictures, people dancing, others eating and some just trying to be the loudest in the room by trying to sing along to every song playing. In the center of it all – with his elbow on the bar, his eyes on me, swirls of smoke from Usman's Cuban cigar around him – stands Sadiq, giving off some major main character energy.

I rack my brain, thinking of the best way to tell him that the two of us leaving together would not go unnoticed, but his eyes have me transfixed in one spot. The way he looks at me from across the room makes me get tunnel vision, all the sounds around me go mute and all the people disappear into the darkness until he is all I can see.

"Hey, I'll text you. Something came up," I raise my phone at Ilham and she frowns at my vagueness. I promise to explain later as I start walking towards the exit.

Soon, I hear footsteps behind me but I don't look back. I keep walking past the mobile police guarding the entrance, past drivers in parked SUVs waiting for the party-goers. His footsteps behind me are steady and heavy, matching my pace. In the distance, I see the bright red of his convertible and when I reach it, I lean my hips against the door, turning around to watch him walk towards me in the dark. The light from the bulbs brightening the parking lot leaks through the tree branches above us.

As Sadiq closes the distance between us, the cool breeze brushes over my bare shoulders. I remove my gloves, pulling each finger out first, before the whole thing and dropping the pieces of fabric and my phone on the seat behind me. His eyes follow my every movement. When he reaches me, he stands in front of me, his eyes unblinking and his lips pursed. "He touched you," he finally says. "He has no right to touch you. Why didn't you tell him about us?"

"Tell him what about us?" I sigh dramatically. "I think by now he knows we're on talking terms."

He moves closer to me, the heat from his body enveloping mine as he ensures there's no space between our bodies. Our thighs touch and I have nowhere else to look but his face. "Talking?" he asks dryly. "Is that what we're doing?"

I try to think of a sarcastic answer, but my brain doesn't cooperate. His eyes search my face then move to my lips and back in a quick second. I let out an unsteady breath and a whisp of a smile forms in the corner of his mouth.

"Why are you fighting this?" His words are quiet, but his tone is rough. I squirm against him and the wicked curve of his lips increases as he notices my discomfort. *He knows.* He takes a step back and I adjust my headband. He removes his jacket, throws it into the convertible's back seat and holds the door open for me. "Let's go for a ride."

This late? "I have to head back home. My mum doesn't care whose wedding it is; she expects me back before she's in bed."

He nods slowly. "Let me drop you at home then."

I get into the passenger seat and watch him roll up his sleeves as he sits next to me. I push my seat back and cross my legs, my heels tapping the re-upholstered white panel. His hand strokes his beard like he's deep in deep thought as he stares at the hint of skin that peeks through the tasseled fringe of my dress. With one hand on the steering wheel, he drives slowly on the quiet streets. With the stars and moon above us, I understand Chbosky for the first time ever because, in this moment, we are infinite.

* * *

Sadiq parks behind my Mercedes coupe when we get to the house. When I come down from the car, I tremble as the wind blows towards my direction and he drapes his jacket over my shoulders and walks with me to the front door. Besides the security lights around the house, most of the interior lights are off.

"Are your parents asleep?" He asks as he looks around the quiet compound.

I nod. At least daddy is. "See that light there?" I ask and he follows my gaze to the window on the far left of the house. "My mom is still up. I'm sure she's watching us right now," I gesture to the camera that is above the front door.

"Okaay," he takes a step back.

I laugh almost immediately. We stand opposite each other, having nothing to say yet unable to say goodbye. "I'll give you your jacket when I see you again."

"I want you to keep it," he smiles.

He says goodbye and I watch as he gets into the convertible and drive away quietly. When I get to my room, I drop the jacket on the bed, zip down my dress and peel off the Spanx underneath. I open my mini-fridge and pour myself some cranberry juice into a wine glass. I start to light some scented candles when Ilham's message comes in in block letters: *WHERE R U?*

I type and send a reply: *Home already. Sadiq dropped me.*

Leaving now, too. I have a migraine.

Uh oh. Feel better.

In the bathroom, I place the candles and my drink on the wooden bath tray next to my iPad, which is playing soft music, and step into the clawfoot bathtub, leaving my robe on the floor. The dissolving bath bomb infused with rose oil and eucalyptus always feels relaxing.

I'm halfway through my drink and fast asleep in the bathtub when my phone rings. "Hello, Sadiq?" I answer sleepily.

"Hey. You up?"

I look around me, and most of the bubbles from my bath have disappeared, "I fell asleep. Thank God you called – you would have just heard that I've drowned in my own bathtub, or got burnt to death," I say as I blow out the candles.

"This is what you sound like when you're sleepy?" There's a long pause and then: *"Damn."*

My eyes snap open. "What's wrong with my voice?"

I hear him sigh.

"I could listen to you talk *all night*," he says. When I don't respond, he continues: "I just wanted to check in on you. Get out of the tub and get into bed." I'm getting used to the sound of his voice in my ear.

"Don't tell me what to do," I grumble jokingly.

"Goodnight, darling," he chuckles.

I definitely don't mind this – at all. "Goodnight, Sadiq."

When I hang up, I see missed notifications and I pull down the notification tab and see an email from DNA Ancestry: *Your DNA Ancestry results are here.* I click on it immediately and find two links to the results of the samples I got from Shatu and Mohammed. Sara and I told them that she was building a family biological profile for her coursework and it took a minute to get the inside of their cheeks swabbed.

I open both results and look at the careful percentages written alongside the countries in the ancestry results. Around me, I feel the water in the bathtub getting colder and colder. I am freezing, and I start to shiver in the bathtub. I reach for the robe on the floor and wear it as I come out of the tub, splashing water all over the cold gray marble floor. My feet leave wet imprints on my carpet as I walk to my bed, clutching unto my phone. I open my laptop and look at the results again. Side by side. Sara, Shatu, and Mohammed have the same DNA Ancestry result: 60 percent Nigerian, 28 percent Senegal and Gambia, 10 percent Mali, and 2 percent Libya. They have the same ancestors because they have the same parents; *they* are siblings. And me?

I think back to my baby album in Umm'Hafsa's room. There's a picture of me when I was just as a few days old, with a chubby face and a shaved head. In another, I was naked except for diapers. We always laugh at my eyes – at the dark *kwalli,* kohl paste that was applied to them, that gave me raccoon eyes. There were pictures of me in a walker learning how to walk. Even back then, you could see daddy in the background cheering me on as I smiled at him with my two teeth. In another sepia-toned picture, we're in front of the Ka'aba in Saudi; Umm'Hafsa is holding me to her chest, and daddy is next to her. I couldn't have been up to two years old then. Umm'Hafsa also has pictures of Saratu, Shatu, and Mohammed as babies and toddlers. In one album is the collection of family pictures we still take annually. It starts with pictures of Umm'Hafsa and Daddy alone, then pictures of them with me. As the years go by, there are more pictures and additions to the family, as Saratu, Shatu, and Mohammed join one after the other.

So, how – what – I let out a deep sigh, trying to understand. Can Sara's suspicion be right? Am I – But how can it be possible if there are baby pictures of me in all the albums, all over the house? How can my ancestry be different if this is my family? Is this not my family? Am I – Am I really – I can't bring myself to say it.

Hafsatu

My first instinct is to ask my dad if I'm really adopted. I want to show him the mismatched DNA results and listen to the explanation. There must be an explanation.

I lay in my bed, unable to see again. I end up scrolling through the pictures in my gallery, zooming into pictures of my siblings. Sara, Shatu, and Mohammed all wearing their glasses. Is that enough proof that I'm not one of them? By the time I get some sleep, it's a few minutes after 4 am.

"Wakey wakey," Sara's voice wakes me up the following morning. My head is buried underneath the covers, my drapes blocking out any sliver of sunlight from filtering into my room. My terry robe from last night's bath is discarded at the foot of the bed. "Why weren't you at breakfast?"

I open my eyes, pushing the covers down as I sit up. The digital alarm clock on my bedside table says it's 11:20 am. I haven't slept in this much in… well, a long time now. Yet, I'm still exhausted. My closed laptop under the pillow next to me reminds me of the email I spent hours reading and re-reading last night. *What am I supposed to do now?*

I rub my eyes and find Sara wearing palazzo pants and a black tank top. She's at my vanity, spritzing perfume on her wrists. "Sa –" I weakly start.

"Looks like someone had fun last night. I've been seeing pictures on Instagram. You were easily the best dressed person there," she takes the La Mer cream from my moisturizer rack and dabs a bit on her forehead. "You know what?" she asks, looking into the mirror as she applies the moisturizer. I open my mouth to speak, but she continues without waiting for me to answer. "You should have a themed cocktail during your wedding, too. Maybe a Bond theme," her eyes light up, "or Moulin Rouge! Actually, Moulin Rouge will be – hey, why do you look like someone died?" She's looking at me now.

I sigh as I reach for my phone that's still showing the results from DNA Ancestry, and I hand it to her. She walks towards my bed and sits down as she reads Shatu's results, then adjusts her glasses as she scrolls down to Mohammed's. She doesn't look as surprised as I expect her to; in fact, as I watch her, it almost seems like she expected their results to match hers. *Did she already know?*

"You're right," I start scratching at the shellac red nail polish on my nails. "One of us is adopted."

"There has to be an explanation for this," she looks up at me. I keep scratching at my nail, lifting the tip and peeling off the color. "Stop that," she holds my wrist, stopping me from wrecking my manicure, and looks into my eyes assuringly. "There's gotta be an explanation for this. And no matter what the explanation is, they are your parents. You are our sister – our big sister," she pulls me into a hug.

"What other explanation could there be? That I was switched at birth in the hospital?" A part of me is hopeful that I am indeed one of those 'switched-at-the-hospital' cases we hear about sometimes. Maybe daddy and Umm'Hafsa aren't even aware. It beats the alternative that I'm adopted, that someone somewhere did not want me, so they gave me up to the strangers whom I have grown to love. My parents. I stand up from the bed, catching my reflection in the mirror as I walk to the bathroom in my black silk shorts and its matching pyjama shirt.

I'm brushing my teeth when I hear Sara's footsteps. She stops by the open bathroom door quietly. The only sound between us is the hum of my electric toothbrush and the sound of running water from the silver faucet.

She sighs a couple of times as though unsure about what she wants to say. "I – I've been looking at the detailed analysis. The thing is, we *are* related, but – I dunno – maybe not how we think."

I try to remember what I read in the analysis, but it was mostly migration history. I pat my mouth with a white facecloth and leave it on the sink. "What do you mean?" I turn to face her.

She hesitates before answering. "I don't think you're adopted or mistakenly switched at birth."

"Okay…?"

"Maybe I'm wrong, but I've been comparing my analysis to yours. There are some similarities, but I don't – I don't know if it's patrilineal or matrilineal. " she falters as she stumbles over her words.

"I don't understand."

She points at my phone screen. "You see how we both have Nigeria, Libya and Mali – that's an indication." The last part of her sentence is a whisper.

"An indication of what?"

"*Um*, the reports don't say who, but I'm pretty sure that we share a parent."

* * *

We share a parent. The words sit with me, and I mull over the prospects in my head over and over. If daddy is the parent we share, does that mean Umm'Hafsa is not my real mom? Did he have another wife before they got married? Nothing about the stories they have told us about them indicates that daddy had a family before Umm'Hafsa. He always told us about how she brought meaning to his life, how she is his first and only love. Was there another woman before her – one he has kept hidden from us all this while? Is she dead? Is she alive? Does she want to see me?

If Umm'Hafsa is the parent we share – but that's highly improbable. From the pictures of their wedding, my parents got married when Umm'Hafsa was very young – younger than I currently am. Every time the subject of marriage comes up, she's always quick to remind me that, at my age, she was married with two kids.

111

So that brings me back to daddy being the parent that I share with my siblings. That's why he does things for me he wouldn't do for the other kids – like when he surprised me at *TedxEdinburgh* in my final year at university, where I was to give a lecture on 'Rebranding Africa.' Twenty - five minutes before I went on stage, I was practicing my opening lines when one of the organizers brought a guest backstage -it was daddy; he came to the venue straight from the airport after buying a last-minute ticket from Abuja because the previous evening, I told him over the phone that I wasn't sure I could get over my stage fright. Or the time he matched my savings to help me kickstart my failed jewelry business while I was still in school and even that time when he decided to gift me ten store units at ATUM plaza, three of which *H&I* is currently spread across. He hasn't done as much for the others. It makes sense that I'm *his* child, that I'm his baby – not Saratu, not Shatu, not even the baby of the house. I'm his Bebi. So, the only reasonable explanation is that he had me with another woman. But was this before Umm'Hafsa, or during? Were they in a polygamous marriage, or did he cheat? Could he? No, I shake my head. Children born out of wedlock are unheard of in Hausa families. Islamically, a child born out of wedlock doesn't even get an inheritance. I cannot even imagine the kind of disrepute that would bring to a family today, talk less of years ago. So, polygamy, then. If Umm'Hafsa is not my biological mum, then she's a saint in hindsight. Even though she has always been a disciplinarian, she has never given me a reason to doubt her as my mother. And she must really love him – to take care of his child without bringing it up and making it obvious that I'm not her child.

"Bebi?" I'm jolted back to reality – to the sound of laughter across the dinner table. My dad is looking at me expectantly, waiting for an answer. Shatu is laughing, and Sara is looking at me worriedly while she's playing with the spaghetti and meatballs on her plate.

"Sorry, daddy. I was distracted," I reply honestly.

"Mohammed wants a second Nintendo Switch," he laughs as he repeats himself. Next to him, Umm'Hafsa is whispering into Ladidi's ear, no doubt giving her instructions for tomorrow's breakfast.

"What happened to the one he got for his birthday?" I push my barely touched plate away and use a ladle to put some fruit salad in the white bone china bowl in front of me.

"It's broken," Mohammed says with a shrug.

"*Da kyau.* Very good." I scoff to myself.

"I told him he needs to start doing chores, and I'll pay him. When he saves enough, he can replace it himself. What do you think?" My dad pushes his glasses into his face.

I nod in agreement as Shatu adds, "Last summer, I drafted all the correspondences daddy sent out to his staff." We all look towards Mohammed, who has this look of incredulous disbelief on his face.

"That's right. We've all had to work for daddy at some point in our lives. When I was in uni, I used to sort all the mails in his office during the holidays." I smile at Mohammed, who looks as uninterested in the conversation as he possibly can.

"What time did you get back home *jiya*?" Umm'Hafsa asks me pointedly.

Oh boy, here we go again. I look at her: "We got there around 8 and I was there for an hour and half or so. I didn't stay until the end."

"And who brought you back?"

I knew it! She was looking through the camera. "Sadiq," I answer, then I realize she has no idea who that is. "My friend."

She doesn't say anything to me after that, she looks over at Sara, "*Lafiya?* Why are you not eating?" So, does that mean Sara is *her* first child? I wonder quietly to myself as I watch their interactions.

"I'm not feeling too good *ne*," Sara drops her cutlery as she looks at me. I look away as I take another spoonful of my fruit salad even though I had no appetite.

"Daddy, I was born in Jos, *ko*?" I try to poke holes into what they have told us through the years, but Sara discreetly shakes her head at me. I ignore her.

"Yes, at the University Teaching Hospital," he takes a gulp of water from his glass. I push my fruit bowl away and put my hands on my cheek, keeping a smile plastered on my face the way I always do when I want my dad to keep talking about something. It always works.

"There was such a heavy rainfall that day," he continues. *We all know this story. I've heard it numerous times, as most of my birthdays aren't complete without daddy narrating the story of the day he became a father – the heavy rainfall, the flooded road to the hospital, and how my mom's water broke in the car.* "When we finally made it to the hospital, there was no light, right? My love?" He looks at his wife, and she nods distractedly. *So she gave birth to me? Is that what he is saying?* "The doctors were even surprised that she was in labour because it wasn't her due date yet."

Not on the due date? That bit of information is new. "Really?" I glance back at Umm'Hafsa, who's opposite me. Am I imagining it, or does she look slightly uncomfortable? She wipes the corners of her mouth with a napkin, drops it on her plate, and starts toying with the ring on her finger. "I was born earlier than expected?"

Daddy nods, but before he can answer, Umm'Hafsa interrupts him: "Would you like some tea, my love?"

An interruption. Interesting.

"Ah yes. Some tea will be nice," he pushes his glasses into his face, his attention now entirely on her.

She presses a button on the intercom. "Ladidi, bring some water for tea," she says in Hausa. When the blinking green lights go off, she reaches for his hand and switches to English: "Is chamomile okay?"

He thinks about it for a second. "Can you make me that special one?" His voice lowers, the way it does when he talks to her.

"*Wanne kenan?* Which one, my love?"

"*Wannan mai* cinnamon *din,*" he tries to remember the tea with cinnamon, "Karak chai."

Her karak tea is special, with a mix of cardamom, cinnamon, fennel, and cloves boiled in milk and sieved into teacups.

When she lets go of his hand and presses the intercom again to give the kitchen more instructions on what to bring on the tea tray, so that she can make him the special blend. I ask, "how early, daddy?"

"What?" He looks at me, rubbing his beard downwards. He has already

114

forgotten what we were talking about; her interruption worked.

"You said I was born early, so I'm asking how early," I try to sound casual.

"Ah, yes!" he looks at his wife. "Two or three weeks, *ko?*"

She ignores the question, pretending not to hear as she concentrates on the news recap on the television like it's the most interesting thing at that moment.

"I like to think that you couldn't wait to meet your daddy, Hafsatu-Bebi – just like I couldn't wait to hold you."

I smile at how earnestly he says that – so full of pride – and it breaks my heart. Someone has been lying to us both.

* * *

After dinner, I find myself searching for paternity testing labs on my laptop. I'm on the website of a privately owned lab that promises confidentiality and fast results. 99.9% Accuracy promised, their slogan reads.

As much as I want to do this and know the truth of the matter, I couldn't risk doing it in Abuja. The owners might know my dad or someone who knows him might see me dropping off a sample. I can't risk it, so I change my search to labs in Lagos. It's past midnight, and I'm still reading through pages of Google reviews. I close and open multiple tabs as I look for the best lab to solve my current problem. Or rather, my family problem.

I eventually find one. It's an accredited DNA testing center with an easy-to-navigate website and all the pertinent information I need to know on the homepage. It says that they carry out different types of tests: Non-invasive prenatal DNA testing, paternity tests, maternity tests, and even sibling test.

I decide to sleep on it. In the morning, I call the phone number listed on their website. After three long rings, someone picks up.

"Hello, Nike speaking. How can I help you?" A female voice speaks over other ringing phones in the background.

"Hi, Nike. I just have some questions about doing a DNA test."

I hear a shuffle of paper in the background. "Which of the tests are you interested in?"

"Um –" I look at the website to confirm, "Paternal and maternal."

I hear her typing on a keyboard as I speak. When I finish, she stops. "Are these tests going to be used for a court claim, adoption or immigration purposes?" It sounds like she's reading out the words from a screen.

"Err no, none of that. I just want to know."

"Okay, so if it's not a legal test, we're not required to come and collect the sample ourselves; you have to send it to us. But first, you have to make the payment for both tests to our business account and provide your contact details."

"Okay," I say. "What kind of samples do you need?"

"Where will you be sending the sample from?"

"From Abuja."

"Okay, you can send hair samples – just a few strands – in different sealed envelopes. Our website has a labeling kit you can download or I can email it to you. So the primary sample – that's your own sample – should be labeled as explained in the online document; then the samples from the man and woman should also be labeled accordingly."

Am I really going to do this? "Okay," I scroll through the website as she speaks. "I see the labeling kit; I'll download it now. So, that's it – I just mail the envelopes to you?"

"Yes. You can send it to our lab address using DHL or Fedex. Once your payment is received, we'll do the DNA sequencing to check for a genetic match and we'll contact you with the results."

"Okay. How long does it take?"

"We'll send you the results about three days after we get your samples."

"Alright. Can you send me the total cost and account details for the transfer?" I give her my email address, and a few minutes later, I receive a confirmation that my payment has been received. I connect my laptop to the small, wireless *hp* printer in my room that I usually use to print out my sketches that need to go into our collection pad on the days I work from home and, print out the labeling kit, then staple the appropriate sections to three different white envelopes from my stationary stand.

I finally leave my room around noon in my jeans and oversized varsity hoodie – the mellow hum of the central conditioning unit is the only sound in the quiet house. Daddy is already at work, and from the looks of it, Mohammed is with him. I don't think Sara is home either; she knocked on my door some hours ago, but it was locked because I just needed some time to myself this morning.

I head to the smaller living room and see Umm'Hafsa with Joy. Joy owns a mobile spa and comes to our house weekly for Umm'Hafsa's manicures and pedicures. Her feet are soaked in a blue foot basin now, as Joy files the nails on her fingers. They are both distracted by the television that's playing a popular Nigerian series, Riona.

I quietly tiptoe away and go into my parents' private chambers; the scent of Arabian *bakhoor* fills the air; it's coming from a simple black incense burner on gold trays next to a vase of flowers she waters daily and luxury stick diffusers, all arranged on a glossy white table in the open seating area. Around the table is a grey sofa and two green velvet accent chairs. As I walk further through the seating area to get to their bedroom, my footsteps are swallowed by the soft Persian carpet. The multiple light bulbs from the branched pendant light cast a golden glow around me. Their king-sized bed – with the grey upholstered wall-to-wall headboard – is perfectly made, without a crease in sight. The king-sized pillows and numerous square and cylindrical decorative pillows add some height and flair over the cream duvet with brown borders that match the ceiling-to-floor drapes all around the room. At the sides of the bed are two high-mirrored side tables with table lamps with grey hoods. At the end of the bed, there's a padded white tufted bench that had more throw pillows and a fur blanket thrown across.

I walk through the gigantic walk-in closet – almost the size of my room – to get to the bathroom. It has double sinks on opposite ends, white cabinets, and mirrored cubicles. I open a cabinet where my dad keeps his clipper, and I tap it into the envelope labeled 'Parent one' until some hair falls out. I carefully return it to where it was and walk over to the other side. I open the mirrored cabinet, but all I see are serums and creams.

I start opening the drawers; there are dozens of unopened perfume boxes. The next drawer has jars of her Maiduguri and Chadian *humra* as well as tubs of Moroccan black soap. I start getting frustrated until I open the third drawer and find hair creams, oils, and combs. I lift her brown hairbrush, pull out long strands of her hair and put them in the second envelope labeled 'Parent two,' and hide the envelopes in the pocket of my oversized hoodie. I make sure that everything is back in its place and start to make my way out of their bathroom when I hear the door to the room open.

Umm'Hafsa walks into the room laughing, laughing on the phone. By the sounds of it, she's talking to daddy. She is wearing a long, fitted red Swiss lace boubou, with silver earrings and a matching necklace. "Toh, *sai ka dawo*. See you soon," she says into the phone. There's a slight pause and then: "Love you, too." She looks up and finds me coming out of their closet.

"I thought daddy was back. *Ashe ba motan shi na ji ba*; I guess it wasn't his car I heard," I say as I put my hands in my pockets, holding the envelopes in place.

She looks at me quietly for a moment. "*Jiya ko kwalli babu a idon ki*; you didn't even wear eyeliner yesterday. And today your eyes look puffy today. Are you okay?"

"I'm just tired and I have a slight headache." That is true.

She points to the mirrored console beneath a framed picture of both of them, "I have some Paracetamol over there, take two," she says as she walks into her bathroom.

On the console, there are secondary school graduation pictures of all my siblings and me and some holiday pictures of our whole family. I unscrew the cap of the red bottle, take two tablets of Paracetamol, and put them in my mouth as I leave the room.

Later in the evening, I drive to the FedEx office alone.

* * *

A few days later, I wake up to an incessant ringing on my intercom. I pick up not because I want to hear what anyone has to say but because I want the ringing to stop.

"Hello, ma'am. Your friend Ilham just drove in." It is Joe's voice.

I muttered thanks, but it doesn't quite sound like it. The lunch Mariya brought earlier is untouched except for the apple I ate earlier. I move towards the curtains and open them, surprised that the day is already so far gone. My door opens, and Ilham walks into the room in a green asymmetrical tunic over dark blue jeans and big aviator glasses.

"Bebi, what the heck?" She pushes the glasses to the top of her scarf. I have to admit, I have been a bad friend and business partner. I have been MIA for days; I switched off my phone because I didn't want to have to lie about being okay when I wasn't. Regardless of my feelings, I shouldn't have left all the hassle of *H&I* to her. I open my mouth to speak, but her phone starts ringing before I can get a word out. She picks up: "Hold on. She's here," she passes me the phone. I look at the name on the screen: Sadiq.

I clear my throat before I answer. "Hello."

"Hafsat?" His voice is deep and thinly veiled with concern.

"Yeah." Opposite me, I see Ilham throw her bag on the accent chair by the window.

"Are you okay?" He asks cautiously. I haven't spoken to him in two days because my phone has been switched off.

"Yeah," I clear my throat, "just feeling a bit under the weather." Ilham squints as she looks at me closely.

"I thought maybe you were avoiding me."

"Wait, no. It's not you at all." I wish I can tell him about all the drama that's bubbling underneath the foundation of our house. "I'm fine."

"Okay, that's good. Listen, you can't let this get to you. We'll find out who's behind the account and get to the bottom of it. I've got someone on it."

Wait, what is he talking about? I hear a *beep* sound and see that the call has ended. I hand Ilham the phone.

She opens my fridge. "I know that post was brutal, but anyone who knows *H&I* knows that it's not true. But hiding in your bedroom doesn't solve the problem."

"What are you guys talking about?"

"The blind item – everyone thinks it's about *H&I*. The number of calls I've been getting is outrageous! We need to have whoever's behind that account arrested because this is slander."

"Show me," I say as I get my phone and throw it on the white charging pad on my bedside table.

Ilham frowns as she looks at me, "*tsaya*; wait. You haven't seen it?" I shake my head slowly. "Then what's got you in this mess? It's 5 o'clock and you're still in your pyjamas."

"Show me the post."

She scrolls through her phone and gives it to me, then starts pouring some juice into a glass cup for herself.

Blind item

Why call yourself a designer if what you do is ship in clothes from SHEIN and attach your brand's premade labels to the clothes?
A 'designer' who had a big fashion show complete with a showstopper and plus-sized models (all in the name of faux wokeness) is actually just a retailer. YES! My source tells me that all her 'designs' are just ordered off a website on sale and sold to Abuja residents for 5 times the sale price.

Kimono queen indeed! Remember you heard it first

Shein my foot! I scoff as I reread the post.

"This feels personal, doesn't it? I mean, usually the blind items aren't malicious, they feel detached when you read them, but this sounds bitter;

there's definitely some anger behind this post. Am I wrong?"

"I just know that whoever is behind this is gonna have to retract and issue an apology." Ilham returns the bottle of juice to the fridge.

I scroll to the comment section and it is wild. They are bashing the quality of the clothes, calling them overpriced, and a comment about bad customer service has over 200 likes.

"Maybe this should be a crisis management opportunity. Yes, the post is false, but if people are raising other issues they have with the brand, we need to look into fixing them," I say.

"What do you mean?"

"Well, like this person," I look down at the Instagram handle, 'bujpromotions101'. They complained about customer service. Let's reach out to them, get the details of their experience and offer them a discount as an apology." I click on the profile and see that they have no profile picture, no followers, and the only post on the profile was posted 24 hours prior. "Wait a minute," I open the profiles of the accounts with the harshest comments and see that they are all accounts created within the last 48 hours.

"This is a smear campaign Bebi. That's why we're going to shut the whole page down." She stands in front of the double mirrors to my closet, sucks in her belly, turns to the side then exhales.

I ignore everything *Bujgist* says about me and my relationships, but coming after *H&I* like this? I'm not going to just sit and watch. My phone beeps multiple times, and I pass Ilham hers and walk to my bedside table.

"Sadiq kept calling me this morning. He was really worried about you. He cares, you know," she says, now inspecting the elasticity of the skin around her neck.

I check my notifications and see his messages on my phone. They are just regular messages of him checking in on me, but after midnight, when the post was released, I can see that his messages were more frequent and full of concern.

I scroll through messages from friends and extended family members sending screenshots of the Blind Item, and I see an email notification with the subject line: 'DNA Test Results.' *Finally!*

I click on the email and open the PDF attachment. As I read, I feel numb, like everything about my whole life has been a lie. My DNA sample matched only one parent: 'parent two.' Umm'Hafsa. I watch as my hands begin to shake, and I have to tighten my fingers around the phone I'm holding so it doesn't to the ground. I feel lightheaded and nauseated at the same time. How can daddy not be my father? My daddy? How am I not even related to him? My head begins to throb with a migraine, and my legs feel weak. I slowly sit on the bed and read the results again and again in disbelief.

What exactly does this mean? Am I holding proof that my mother cheated on her husband? Made him believe that I am his child when I am not?

Ilham must have noticed my silence as I look up and find her standing over me. She has worry lines all over her face as she sits next to me on the bed; I instinctively turn my phone around and place it back on the charging pad. Her mouth is moving, but her voice fades into the background, overshadowed by the throbbing in my head. I stare at her, making out the words "it's going to be okay" and "it'll all be fine" as she pulls me closer to her; I assume she thinks I'm having a late reaction to the news about *H&I*. I nod, a tear rolling down my face as she pulls me into a long, comforting hug.

Zuwaira

1998

There's a sound that I don't know the English word for, the sound you hear when someone clears their throat like they have something stuck in it or before they say something. That was the first sound I heard every day in my new home as soon as I opened my eyes in the morning. It was a deep guttural sound made by the throat and didn't even escape the lips, but it was audible – and loud. The sound was amplified by the two loudspeakers in the compound, one facing the women's sections and the other facing outwards, towards the street.

That was the sound the *muezzin*, the person who calls for prayer, makes before he utters the first line of the *athan*. Depending on how he cleared his throat, I could tell who the muezzin of the day was. Most times, the sound was repeated twice in quick succession, a sound I came to associate with Abdulwahab. Abdulwahab was Alhaji's first son, who was studying Law at a University abroad. Other times, when the sound was quieter and drawn out, I came to associate that sound with Sufyanu, Hajiya Uwa's youngest son and Alhaji's brother.

Sufyanu was in his late twenties and worked closely with Alhaji. Of all his siblings, it seemed to me that Alhaji trusted Sufyanu the most, even though they only shared one parent, as Hajiya Uwa remarried after Alhaji's father died.

When I was first brought to this house, I used to jolt awake in panic at the unfamiliar surroundings before I remembered where I was. Gradually, my body forgot the feel of the cold hard floor under the raffia mat I used to put in Aunty Tani's living room to sleep. The bed I now called mine was covered by a floral-patterned bedsheet and a red velvety blanket. It was a beautifully furnished room with a bed big enough for three people, and the carved brown wood above the two pillows matched the design of the two-door wardrobe and the carvings above the mirror.

"Before you use up all your money *saboda a mata kayan daki* to furnish her room – don't forget you promised to change my car this year. I'm tired of always calling a mechanic to kickstart the battery every morning after a rainfall," I remember Aunty Tani telling my uncle the day he told her I was to marry Alhaji. I listened as I ironed the clothes I'd washed.

Kawu Sani's reply was calm, asking her not to worry. "Ai, Alhaji Ringim said we shouldn't worry about that, he said he has a furnished place for her." Even though in our culture, the bride furnishes her home, Alhaji Ringim's gesture in taking that responsibility off the shoulders of my Uncle earned him their undying appreciation. It was evident in the revered way they spoke about him.

Her tone changed immediately. "*A'a iyye.* That's good to hear! *Ai kuwa, takun manya daban take*; it's true – the walk of a man is different from a boy. *Ehen*, now we're talking. Why would we even consider a young man like Tanko, who would expect us to furnish her room and bring foodstuff? Do you know that the landlord's son stopped greeting me since he heard about her marriage?" Her voice began to fade as I stopped paying attention and started wondering if Ibrahim would call again.

On the day I was brought here – as I looked around, finding it hard to believe that everything in the section was all mine – the comfortable bed and matching set, connecting bathroom with running water, a kitchen, and a living room all to myself – Aunty Tani came to my side. "You are now a queen – a queen in her palace," she said to me, looking around the house covetously.

As I got off from the bed now and moved to perform my ablution, I thought about how I hadn't seen her in weeks, and I liked it that way. I prayed, took a bath, and got dressed. I had never owned these many expensive things – the *ankara*, laces, and abayas that filled the wardrobes and the dressing table drawers full of creams and nice little perfumes in bottles. In one of the drawers were empty perfume bottles I could not throw in the garbage; they looked too special to be thrown out.

On the days I was alone – when Alhaji was with his other wives – I would go to the kitchen after breakfast to start prepping lunch. Those days were long and lonely without the sound of my cousins doing their homework or Jamil asking me to help him with his further maths questions. On those days, I often found myself wondering a lot, I wondered if this life would be mine if my parents were still alive. My parents wanted Maimuna and me to go to university. I wondered if that would be the case if I had not ended up in my uncle's house. Would I have met Ibrahim if I had gone to university? Would we have had a chance? *Astagfirullah*, I would say to myself as I washed the tomatoes and pepper for lunch, reminding myself that no self-respecting married woman should have those kinds of thoughts.

Peering out of the window as I blended the pepper mix in the white blender, I would see the other wives – mostly Hajiya Babba and Mamie – visiting each other. They also had friends who came to visit them, and from the guests' looks and dressing, I could guess which flat they would be going into. The older ones, the women with things to sell, and the rich-looking ones always came to see Hajiya Babba. They were the ones who had drivers waiting for them outside the gate, the ones whose expensive perfume I could smell all the way from my flat. Hajiya Mamie's guests were always in hijabs like her and never stayed too long when they visited and always left before *Maghrib*. Her family members also spoke a language I did not understand.

Balaraba never had people visit her, but she went out a lot. Every morning, I would see her lock the door to her section and put the key in her handbag. She was always dressed in colorful atamfas or laces, her headtie in various intricate styles – sometimes tilted forward, other times pushed backward around her hair just above her matching veils draped over her shoulder, not over her head like married women were supposed to do. She always had big dark sunglasses and shoes that made sounds as she walked out of the gate.

"*Yar boko*," my mother-in-law muttered with disdain one day. It was during one of her visits and from her section, we could see Balaraba leaving hers. "These educated girls. Always leaving the house to work – what's the point of that? What's the point of working if your husband can provide everything you need?" Her mouth twisted as a hiss filled the room, almost as if the thought of her son's wife working signified a lack that stained her own reputation. "She has to stop this job. The wife of a man of his stature can't be seen outside doing a petty government job." That was when I knew that Balaraba had a job.

On some mornings, I had bread and tea, and other times, I made *sinasir* - flat pancakes made with fermented rice batter and yogurt. I would always put some in a food warmer and take to Hajiya Uwa's section. In some ways, she became like a mother to me those first few months, as her door was always open. But I would come to find out that it was not only because she needed to keep an eye on what was happening in the compound, but because she was also the judge and jury for most of the cases, fights, and disagreements between her daughters-in-law.

* * *

I only saw Alhaji for a few days every few weeks, so I had a lot of free time, and there were only so many Hausa film cassettes I could watch in a day. Eventually, when my head started to ache from the glare of the screen and the isolation in the big section, I found myself visiting my mother-in-law every few days, but I could not go empty-handed, so I always brought some food.

One day, just as I dropped a white-and-brown *samira* bowl on her dining table, Hajiya Uwa came out of her room and into the living room. Her face broke into a smile when she saw me.

"Zuwaira, did you make sinasir today? I can't tell you how much I like your sinasir. Even yesterday, I said to myself: '*kai,* it's been a few days since I had Zuwaira's sinasir.'"

I smiled at Hajiya Uwa's soft voice and kind demeanor. She was a woman I had grown to not only respect, but also love dearly. She always corrected me on things I didn't even know I was doing wrong.

"Good morning, Hajiya. How is your back." She always complained about back pain.

"The pain is still there. Indo just brought me some medicine that I mixed with yogurt to drink; it helped a little." Indo was her younger sister and the woman who acted as a spokesperson on the day they brought me from Kawu Sani's house.

"*Allah ya kara sauki*; may Allah make it better."

"Ameen," she said as she opened the *samira*, a satisfactory smile brightening her features as she tasted one of the sinasir. "When next is your husband returning to your section?" A line appeared between her brows.

"This evening," I answered without looking at her. The rotation was back to me again. This was the first time he was coming over after the one week he spent when we first got married.

"Don't forget everything I told you," she reminded me about not watching Hausa films when he was around; he preferred the news channel.

Later that evening, I made tuwo and beans soup for Alhaji for dinner. He didn't say anything as he watched the news. He never said anything; he was a very quiet man. Tall and broad, with a head full of hair. When he walked into the flat, I knew to keep my hijab on because his brother would sometimes come with him and give him updates on some business-related issues as they ate dinner.

Alhaji was sitting on the carpet with one leg stretched out and the other tucked inwards. He had removed his blue *babban riga* and cap and placed them on the three-seater he was leaning against. I brought the food warmers from the kitchen and arranged them on the mat on the carpet to stop food from staining the white and red carpet and put out an extra plate for Sufyanu, who was crouched by Alhaji's side, showing him some numbers on printed sheets of paper. I took his briefcase and cap into the bedroom before heading back into the kitchen to clean up. I did not come out until I heard Sufyanu leave the section, leaving the plate I had kept for him unused. Only then did I remove my hijab.

As I walked back to the living room, I caught my reflection in the mirrored panels between the white wood of the room divider, and it still took me by surprise. I still could not get used to dressing up like this, applying makeup, and using perfume so late in the evening, but that was the advice that everyone gave me, that's what good married women were supposed to do. As I sat down on the carpet, I added another wrap of tuwo to his plate as he had finished the first two and added more soup. As I filled his cup with water, he asked me to increase the sound on the television.

Most of his evenings in my section were the same. After dinner, he would head out to the mosque to pray Isha, and before he came back, I had cleaned up and used the incense Hajiya Babba sent to me. I was astonished that I got presents from her the second day I was brought into the house –two atamfas, two veils, perfume, and some *turaren wuta*, perfumed incense.

When I got into bed, after changing into one of the night dresses that came in my *lefe*, Alhaji would be going through business papers or the newspaper. He never really talked to me; he talked *at* me. "Pass me my pen," he would say in Hausa when he reviewed his papers and got to a page that needed his signature. "Where's your hijab?" he would ask before answering the sallama when someone who was not his son or daughter waited outside my verandah to see him. "Turn off the lights," he would say when it was time to sleep.

There would still be no words when his hands reached for me in the darkness and as he got on top of me. Only his grunts and the bed squeaks would fill the silent night air, and when he rolled off, his snores would immediately fill the room.

If there was something he did not like, he would never say it to me. Hajiya

Uwa would usually send for me the following morning after he left for work.

"Zuwaira, *su zabin da kajin da aka kawo sun kare, ne?*" I looked up as my mother-in-law asked me if the chickens and guinea fowls that were sent to my kitchen had finished already.

"No, I still have some in the freezer." I even used some to make dinner the previous evening.

"So, why would you just put only three chicken thighs for Alhaji?"

I remained silent. Did I put too much meat? Should I have just put two? My uncle, *Kawu* Sani usually had the two biggest pieces of chicken in his soup. I remained silent because I didn't know what to say.

"He likes to eat meat," she continued. "You should be grilling whole chickens and fowls every evening he comes to you. Two or three, if he's eating with visitors."

A whole chicken in one night? I wanted to ask. That normally lasts a whole week everywhere else I have lived.

"Do you understand?" her kind voice asked.

I nodded.

"*Kuma ya na da shan miya,* he loves a lot of soup. So, make sure you increase the amount of soup that you serve him, okay?"

I nodded.

"If there's anything that has finished in your kitchen, tell Hashim. He knows where to get everything."

I nodded again.

Hashim was the errand boy who was always carrying heavy bags of groceries to various sections. We never gave him money to buy anything; we just told him what we wanted. You want the new *Ali Nuhu, Abida,* and *Fati Mohammed* film? In less than an hour, he would return with a brand-new cassette. Feel like drinking cold coke after lunch and the crate in your kitchen is empty? Hashim would return with a chilled bottle for you and an extra crate to put in your store. He could not be more than two years younger than me, and apparently, he had been the errand boy in the house for over five years. A day after grilling two whole chickens for Alhaji, I sent for him.

"Assalamu alaikum, *amarya*. I was told that you wanted to see me?" his Hausa sounded like the one I grew up with in Bauchi, even though he was from Gombe, a neighboring state, so there were some similarities in how we spoke.

"*Na ce ba,* where can I find fish this evening? You know that one they call catfish?" I wanted to make some catfish pepper soup since that was Alhaji's last evening in my section before he went to spend the next three days with Hajiya Babba. I won't see him for another nine days.

His dark forehead furrowed as his bushy brows drew together. "Alhaji does not eat catfish from the market," he looked at the floor as he spoke to me from outside the door.

I widened my eyes in surprise. I am thankful for my mother-in-law and Hashim; I was constantly learning about Alhaji from them. It would have been hell if I had cooked something he could not eat, as Alhaji had a temper. A very bad temper, from what everyone said. "Oh okay," I said as I adjusted my blue hijab, "so which fish does he eat?"

"I can bring some from the farm. You can choose the ones you want and we'll kill it so you can cook it."

I had never seen live catfish before until that day when he returned with a bucket with four big catfish swimming around, gliding off each other's slippery skins. I pointed at the ones I wanted, and a few minutes later, Hashim returned with them washed and clean.

That evening, as Alhaji finished his food, he spoke the longest sentence he had ever uttered to me: "Tomorrow, the driver will take you to bid your aunty and uncle goodbye. We're going to Mecca for pilgrimage."

Sadiq

I'm boxing alone without my trainer in the spare room that I converted to a home gym when my phone rings. It's my cousin Imran Dankabo. He is in town for a wedding, and we've been trying to meet up, but life keeps getting in the way. I remove my red boxing gloves and answer through my AirPods, walking to the water dispenser to refill my bottle.

"Hello, Imran."

"Sadiq," his voice comes through, "you're a hard man to reach. I was just at Aunty Amina's place. *Na je in mata sallama*; I went to say goodbye."

"Heading back to Toronto already?"

"Tomorrow morning, *insha Allah*. God willing."

"Why the hurry? You've only been here a week." I unhook the punching bag, drag it to the corner of the room and drag back an angled heavy bag to replace it with.

"You know how it is; this was supposed to be a quick trip in and out. Wifey is alone with the kid. So when can I see you *ne*? We haven't even finished our talk from the other day." We met briefly after the nikkah of a family member a few days prior.

"How about *Ranchers* tonight? I'm usually there in the evening, hanging out with the guys."

"Oh, okay. I heard that it belongs to you now, *ko*?" his voice disappears

131

for a few seconds and returns, "Nice one. Okay, I'll see you there after *Maghrib*, Insha Allah."

As I end the call, a message comes in. I'm disappointed that it's only Lilybeth asking if I'm at the gym. I unwrap the grey workout bands around my palms as I take a swig of water and type a reply to her: *Nah. Throwing punches at home today.*

Later that evening, Imran shows up at Ranchers. There's live music inside, but we eat dinner in the outdoor lounge under the thatched raffia and bamboo gazebo, flanked by palm trees and the newly-constructed fish pond. Our conversation is punctuated by the commentary following football highlights on the 70-inch screens.

"I'm a little surprised that you put the Hyde Park flat on the market," Imran says after a while. He cleans his hands using the napkins with our R logo stitched on a corner. He's about ten years older than me, but he has always treated me like an equal. During his vacations in the UK, he always dropped by my boarding school, Stonar in Wiltshire to see me, a practice he continued even when I got into UCL in London.

"Yes, I'll be closing the sale soon. I have a buyer that offered more than the asking price."

He nods as he ignores a call on his phone. "Mohammed doesn't think you should sell that property because it was your father's second home, after the Asokoro house. Surely it holds some sentimental value to you."

Not in the slightest bit. That's actually the reason why I am selling the place – because it has so much of him in it. I remain quiet as Imran continues: "Now, I understand that you might have no plans to live in the UK anymore, but Mohammed is interested in buying it from you. He's hoping you can both reach an agreement on a payment plan."

Before I tell him what I think about my stepbrother Mohammed's interest in my inheritance, we hear the guys approach us. Usman comes with another mutual friend Umar Isa and surprisingly, Bashir, who hasn't come to Ranchers since we ended our business contracts months ago. They all shake hands with Imran and settle into the bar stools around the circular pavilion. Umar's attention is on the screen now showing the opening of a

UFA fight with Kamaru Usman.

"How have you been? Where's Bebi?" Imran asks Bashir, who is sitting next to him.

I take another swig of my drink as the waiter comes to take their orders. Bashir rubs the back of his head. "*Ai* baba, we're going through a slight misunderstanding."

Slight misunderstanding is probably the understatement of the century.

"*Ka kwapsa kenan*, Bash; you messed this one up too? I thought a girl like Hafsatu would be enough for you to hang your boots," Imran laughs as the chatter turns into good-natured banter. "What did you do this time?"

Bashir drops his phones on the table in front of him as he answers. "The whole thing is just –" his voice trails off, "she won't even pick up my calls. I've gone to her house, spoken to her sisters, talked to Ilham... she won't budge."

"Don't drag Ilham into your mess," Usman says as he lights a cigarette. He leans back into his chair next to mine as he exhales away from us, nodding at the waiter that drops a bottle of water in front to him.

Imran puts his hand on Bashir's shoulder, his face dropping the affable gestures; he is serious now. "You know what? Let me give you some solid advice. If you really want her back, show up with an engagement ring and say '*za a turo' kawai*; tell her that your family wants to meet hers."

I look at Bashir and see his brows drawn together. He rubs his chin, like he's actually considering it.

"Seriously Imran, what will that fix?" I ask.

"No, I'm serious, man. Let me tell you guys something nobody knows. Six months before Nasreen and I got married, she broke up with me. Like, it was final; she deleted me everywhere and said she was completely done with me. Nothing, *kai*, no one could make her budge." Nasreen, Imran's wife, is a family friend and Usman's cousin from his mother's side. Their wedding was one of the best Abuja has ever seen, one that is still being talked about, even though it was three years ago. "I showed up to her birthday party, dropped on one knee with an engagement ring, and... well, as they say, the rest is history."

"She didn't turn you down?" Bashir asks.

"Turn down a *Harry Winston* diamond ring?" he scoffs. "Let's be honest. All of them – every single one of them – want a beautiful wedding that will trend for weeks. And if Bebi is the one you want to trend with, just put it on lock."

Bashir nods slowly, a smile already forming on his face. The thought that Bashir thinks he has another chance with Hafsat makes me want to laugh and break something. I am no expert on relationships, but even *I* know that what he feels for her is not love; it is an ego-driven need to possess her, masquerading as love.

"And the reason she broke up with you?" Usman seems intrigued as he stubs the rest of his cigarette on the ashtray.

"All forgiven and forgotten, my guy. *Wallahi*. There are some mess-ups that only a proposal can fix," Imran looks down at his wristwatch, "I have to bounce. Bash, let me know how it goes."

I scoff at the absurdity of it. It makes no sense to me at all. Why would a woman who knows her worth want a man who doesn't respect her enough to change his ways? After I walk Imran to his car and wish him a safe flight back to Canada, my phone beeps, and it's a text message from her: *Hey, U busy?*

Even though her radio silence this past week was crushing, not bombarding her with calls or messages has finally paid off. I call her and she picks on the third ring, her voice distant: "Hello?"

"Hafsat?"

"Hmm..Sadiq?" She's not her usual upbeat self. Is this still about *H&I*? The post was deleted, and the blogger hasn't posted anything about her and Ilham since then.

"You good?"

"Yeah," she replies, yet I can sense the hesitation as she adds, "*um*, are you busy?"

"Nah, what's up?" I look back to the brightly lit gazebos of Ranchers. Even from the parking lot, I can see that more people have arrived. To the far right, Bashir and Usman are talking to some girls who are just making their way in.

"I was hoping I could talk to you."

"Of course. Are you at the plaza?" I glance at my wristwatch; it was almost 8 pm.

"No, I'm home."

"Okay, I can come see you now."

"Alright. Call me when you are outside. I'll come out."

* * *

I'm parked outside the heavy black steel gates of Hafsat's parents' house, skipping songs on the music player as I look for something with Fireboy while I wait in my car. As I watch, the smaller gate opens and she walks out in dark jeans and a dark shirt with a white open abaya on top. The security lights bathe her curves in its glow, framing her silhouette as she walks towards my car. I watch as she adjusts her falling scarf over her head and as she comes closer, I notice that her shoulders are sagging a bit. I have spent months watching her from the sidelines – carefully hidden by my feigned indifference towards her – among friends and acquaintances, to know the pride in her raised shoulders, the ego in her strides, and the aloofness in the arch of her brow. None of these is here now.

I come out of the driver's seat and meet her just in front of the car. She glances up at me as she says "*yadai*" and looks behind us at the gate. It only takes a second for me to notice the redness around her eyes and that her usually painted or glossy lips are bare. Her face is devoid of makeup, and I notice a tiny beauty mark on her chin. I assume the only reason I am noticing it for the first time is because it is usually covered.

"You've been crying." It isn't a question. "Is this still about the gossip page? The post was taken down." I made sure of it, but she doesn't need to know that part.

"Oh, no. This isn't about *H&I*," she looks down at her feet as she wraps her abaya around her.

"Is this about Bashir?"

She scowls as she looks up at me, shaking her head slowly with a questioning look on her face like she's wondering why I would mention that.

"What? No. Why would you even think that?"

I think back to Bashir's words: 'we're going through a slight misunderstanding,' and start getting angry again. I shake off the thought, without taking my eyes off hers: "Tell me what's wrong and I'll fix it right now."

She chuckles sadly. "Can we go into your car? I don't like standing out here." Her eyes shimmer slightly and I wonder if it's tears or reflections from the dimmed headlamps of my car.

"Of course." We enter the car. "What's going on?" I watch as she picks at her nails and notice that they have no color on them. She always has color on her nails.

"I just – I just needed some air. I didn't wanna be in the house." The crease in her forehead deepens as her mask begins to slip, and I can see the tiniest hint of uncertainty in her features for the first time.

If this isn't about H&I or her ex, then maybe it was something at home.

"Is everything okay with your mum- your dad-?" Perhaps there was a fight.

Tears cascade down her cheeks and a deep knot forms in my chest. It takes me to the day I saw her leaving Bellanova in a rush, her hands trembling at her discovery of a cheating boyfriend. Like that time, my protective instincts for her come roaring to life. "Hey, what's wrong?" I whisper as I reach for her, cupping her chin in my hands and wiping the tears off her face.

She sniffles and uses the ends of her black scarf to wipe the tears I miss. A few seconds later, she regains her composure and leans into the reclined seat, pulling her legs up to her chest as she faces me. "You're just the only person I feel like I can talk to right now."

My chest constricts at her sincerity. I want to be the person she trusts enough to vent to, the person she comes to when anything bothers her. I sit in her silence as I watch her quietly, waiting for her to let me in.

"Are you close to your mum?" she finally asks.

That's easily the most personal question she has ever asked me – perhaps the only one. As she waits for my reply, my mind travels to the sepia-toned pictures in my safe, of a woman in her twenties. There were pictures of her and me in front of a birthday cake with one candle for my first birthday. In another picture, we were surrounded by my father's other children holding brightly colored balloons. But the memories of her are almost nonexistent.

"I lost my mother when I was really young," I reply. I have never told any girl this.

"Oh my God, I didn't know that. I'm so sorry," she starts crying again. "*Allah ya jikan ta*; May her soul rest in peace."

"Ameen." I resist the urge to reach over and wipe her tears again.

"I've always wondered why you called your mum 'Aunty Amina,'" she uses her scarf to dab her cheeks.

"That's my step mum. She practically raised me. That is why I am in Asokoro a lot." I say.

"What about your dad – were you two close?"

I flex my fingers, feeling the familiar throb in my temple. Unbidden images of the phone falling from my hand to the ground when I heard my uncle's voice that evening at Stonar flood my brain. I still remember the brief initial shock followed by undeniable relief that flooded me after that call.

"No, we weren't close at all," I answer honestly. I hated the man. "I was sent off to boarding school when I was 11 and when I was 16, my uncle – his brother – called to say that my father died in a plane crash." I have never talked about my father to anyone outside my family. "What about you? Your family seems pretty close-knit," I glance at the wallpaper on her phone as it lights up with a notification; it's a picture-perfect family portrait with all four siblings surrounding their sitting parents as they laugh. It's the kind of laugh you know to be real, one they didn't have to fake.

She bites her lower lip and suddenly looks unsure. Then a sad smile settles on her face as she looks through the windscreen. "So, hypothetical question," she starts rather enthusiastically.

I fight to hide back a smile at how she tries to make it look like this just came to her head. But I can tell that this hypothetical question may be the reason for her unusual behavior, the reason she's here with me. "Give it to me," I match her enthusiasm.

"Okay. What if, one day," she hesitates, "what if, one day, you find out – okay, maybe not find out – you get proof that you're not who you thought you were. What would you do?"

"*Hmm*, I'm gonna need you to be more specific," I turn towards her giving her my full attention. The car's engine is still running, and even though the music had been playing quietly this whole time, I can't tell you what songs have been on.

"So, let's *assume*," she stresses the word while looking at me, "let's assume that you get proof that you're not –" she pauses for a second, "that you're not your father's child. What would you do? Would you confront your mom about it?" she says the last bit with a practiced nonchalance that I'm very familiar with, the type of show you put on to pretend something doesn't matter to you when it does, in fact, matter a great deal. This was the show I put on around her for months, while she was with Bashir.

I raise my eyebrows, then I exhale loudly and lean back into my seat. Not what I was expecting at all. "Interesting hypothetical question." I watch as she raises her phone and gives it her attention, scrolling through her Instagram feed. But I see it for what it is; I know that she's scared. "I think I would weigh the effects that a confrontation with my mom will have," I say slowly.

"What do you mean?" she drops her phone as she looks at me.

"If I confront my mom with this proof I have, what am I hoping to achieve? Do I want to know my real father? What good will that do to me under Islamic guidelines?" I pause as I watch her take it in, the gears in her head going in overdrive as she bites down on her lip hard and her eyes scan my dashboard. "How will this confrontation change my relationship with my mother moving forward and the man I have thought of as my father my whole life?"

"I don't – the person doesn't care about her relationship with the mum. The woman is a cheat and a liar."

"Is she a hundred percent sure? *Zato zunubi*; suspicion is a sin," I watch as she ponders silently. Suddenly, her phone lights up with a call from 'Umm'Hafsa.' She rejects the call. "Is that your mum calling?" I ask.

"Yup. She's probably looking through the camera again. I should go in," she reaches for the door, and I do the same.

I walk her to the front of the gate that automatically swings open. "Hafsat," I call out to her before she walks in through the gate. She turns around and looks at me. "Are you gonna be alright?" I ask quietly. "With the hypothetical question?"

Her mouth twitches as she rolls her eyes at me – not with sarcasm this time, but something more: fondness. "It's for a story I am writing."

"*Ah*! A designer, an artist *and* a writer? Is there anything you can not do?"

"Don't forget slayer of costumed parties."

"That, too," I chuckle, glad that she's returning to her usual witty self, yet sad because I know it's all an act. "I can't wait to read this book!"

"I might send you an autographed copy," she smiles as she mouths good night, disappearing into the darkness.

Hafsatu

The golden frame on the huge family portrait hanging above the living room's television is trimmed with dust. I wonder how Mariya or Ladidi missed that top spot since they clean every morning. It's a black-and-white picture of the six of us in a 20 x 30 frame. When we took the picture two years ago, Umm'Hafsa was redecorating all three living rooms, and she insisted that we take new family portraits for each one. Sara and I came up with the black and white concept for this living room; I thought it would be a good idea if we all wore white as the background was grey and black. Even in the portrait, Umm'Hafsa's husband can't take his eyes off her as she laughs into the camera with her right hand resting on his chest. The only piece of jewelry on her hand is a colossal ring he gifted her on their 15th wedding anniversary. We stood on their sides, with Mohammed and me smiling wide next to daddy and Shatu and Sara laughing next to her.

Looking at the picture from here, it's clear to see that I am the one with most of her features –her arching eyebrows, the thin bridge of her nose, and her full lips. Sara has her full lips too. But Shatu and Mohammed – their lanky frame, the thin lips, their lighter skin, the v-shaped peak at the center of their hairline – that's all from 'daddy,' *their* father.

But who is my own father? And where is he?

A part of me just wants to show the man I've wrongly called my father since the day I was born the result that came from Lagos. I wonder what that conversation will go like. I can be like, "Soooo, funny story, daddy. My friends and I were playing around with DNA kits and it turns out I am

140

not your daughter." Or maybe, I can walk up to them in the dining room one day and leave a printout of the test results on the table next to daddy's food.

Daddy? Do I still get to call him that?

I believe he deserves to know the truth about the woman he adores so much, but I can not bring myself to break his heart like that. Just thinking of the pain that it'll cause him brings tears to my eyes. It is *her* I want to hurt; *her* I want to feel the pain that I'm currently feeling.

Another part of me wants her to know that I know what she's been hiding all these years. That's the worst thing about this whole ordeal – my obsession with hinting that I know. My brain is in constant overdrive, analyzing all my interactions with her, watching every exchange between her and her husband, and observing every single touch, laughter, and hug between them while trying to find an allusion to her falsehood.

I enter the living room upstairs that evening after I return from *H&I* to meet them, sharing a pie as they watch a documentary on the conflict in Palestine. Sara and Shatu have returned to the university, and Mohammed is already in bed, as he has to be up early for school the following morning.

When daddy sees me, he shows me the *Kobo* tablet he got for Umm'Hafsa and asks me to upload some books to her e-book collection: *Kitabut Tauheed* and *Dar al-Taqwa: The souls journey after Death* from his *Darrusalam* account. I sit opposite them with a glass of water in front of me as I sync his black tablet to her new grey one, watching the percentage bar showing the download progress increase in length.

"Now in this small device, you can carry hundreds of books at once. Bebi can create different libraries for you – Islamic books separate, biographies separate and those other ones you read –"

"Is it my Hausa novels you're calling 'those other ones'?" She widened her eyes as he laughs at her addiction to books written by *Arewa* authors, authors from Northern Nigeria, on online platforms.

Before, I would have found this banter 'cute' but looking at them now, I recoil in irritation. Listening to her and watching her act like a saint when she has a 23-year-old skeleton in her cupboard almost has me rolling my eyes.

"Do you miss your friends in Jos?" I can't stop myself from wanting to know more about her life from years ago.

Her attention slowly turns to me and she stops mid-movement, dropping the dessert fork in the pie she's sharing with her husband. *"Me ya kawo maganan Jos kuma*; why are we talking about Jos all of a sudden?"

"Since we left Jos, we've never gone back." If I remember correctly, we left Jos before my first birthday and moved to Abuja.

"No, we have had no reason to go back," she picks up the cutlery again as she looks at daddy, who is still digging into the pie.

"What was Jos like when you lived there?" I ask.

The documentary they are watching ends and I can tell that daddy is paying attention to our conversation. His eyes are on her as she answers, "Jos was lonely. It was so lonely. We didn't like it there."

"Haba? Really?" Daddy adds something inaudible to her that makes her laugh and turn the pie around, eating from his side.

"Why was it lonely? Weren't you together?" I asked innocently, looking up at him.

She sighs. "He was working long hours those days; he left home very early and came back late. I barely saw him. Thank God those days ended after you were born."

Maybe my real father lives in Jos, then? Was he a family friend? A neighbor? Someone who saw how lonely she was, maybe? Someone she turned to for companionship?

I have spent the past few days pouring over old family albums, trying to see if I would see the face of a male 'family friend' who appears often or who shares some of my features. I saw no one like that. All I saw were pictures of my dad's colleagues but the pictures are all grainy, and it was hard to tell.

"It wasn't all bad," daddy interjects now, "do you remember the first time we went to Assop waterfall? It was after we left Shere hills, *ko?*"

"How can I forget, my love? It was beautiful *amma* it was so cold that evening," she looks at me. "Your daddy gave me his jacket to wear over mine. It was a heavy jacket *fa,* but *wallahi* I couldn't stop shivering."

"Wow." My flat-tone reply is laced with cynicism, one they don't seem to notice as they reminisce.

The laughter around the dining room is punctuated by her cough. *"Ki sha ruwa;* drink some water," daddy says, pushing a glass of water towards her. She drinks.

"Thank you love," she reaches for his hands and intertwines her fingers with his.

He worships the ground she walks on. How could she? If she has lied about something like this, what else has she lied about?

* * *

Somehow, I find that I'm spending less and less time at home. I'm usually in the back office at *H&I* most days. In the evenings, I go to Ilham's house with her; today, we're in her room on the cream carpet matching fabric samples to sketches that I made earlier as I chat with Sadiq.

"It's crazy. Since Bujgist redacted that post, they haven't posted anything again – and it has been weeks!" She shows me her phone screen; it's on the Bujgist profile. I look at it properly and see that comments have been turned off.

"Did we find out who was behind the page?" I lean back, the small of my back resting on her white four-poster bed frame.

"Sadiq told me not to worry about it. Last I heard, he found the IP address of the website that was linked to the Instagram account and they've gone MIA since."

"Good riddance to bad rubbish." My phone beeps, and I reply to Sadiq's message about seeing *Spiderman No way home* together: *Maybe...*

I pick up her TV remote and browse through her Netflix home page. As I scroll past her Korean shows, I feel her eyes on me.

"Bebi, are you okay? These days you seem, I don't know... a bit off," she looks at me with squinted eyes as she tilts her head gently to the side.

I fake a smile, "how?"

"Your whole aura seems off," her index finger swirls as she draws a circle in the air around my face. "If there's something wrong, you'll tell me, won't you?"

"Of course, I will," I answer immediately. Although, that's not true. Ilham's mom, Aunty Salame, and Umm'Hafsa have the same circle of friends. There is no way I can tell her about the discovery I made about my parents. I know she'll tell her mother, who might tell her other friends and our family will be at the helm of a huge scandal people will pass around in hushed tones. That will be the end of daddy and Umm'Hafsa's marriage.

But maybe that's what Umm'Hafsa deserves.

* * *

When Sadiq brings me home, we remain in his car giving answers to hypothetical scenarios; they have sort of become our thing now. I do a tiny clap with my hands as I think of another hypothetical question. "Would you rather have everyone you know be able to read your thoughts or have everyone you know see your internet search history?"

"None of the above," he starts laughing, shaking his head.

"You know that's not how we play this game. You have to pick one."

"Okay, they can have access to my internet history. But whatever they see there – that's on them."

"*Hmm hmm*, what are you hiding?" I ask.

He looks at me, and his gaze falls to my lips. "You don't want to know."

I look away and hear him reply: "Okay, I've got a good one. Would your rather lose your sight or your memories?"

"My job depends on my sight."

"Okay, so you would lose your memories?" His finger reaches for a knob on the dashboard, and the song changes to Buju and Wizkid's *Mood*.

"No, I have a lot of amazing memories with my family," I think back to the days when I didn't know what I know now. Memories of our first trip to Disneyland as a family, game nights with my siblings, and helping daddy pick out gifts for Umm'Hafsa. "I'd like to hold onto those."

"Babe, give me an answer, not all this *shalaye* you're doing."

I laugh. "Okay. Memories can go. No, no, wait. Sight. Sight is my final answer."

"That's a horrible choice. You'll be hopeless as a blind person – have you seen the length of your heels? You would be tripping everywhere," he teases.

"I don't judge your answers, but now I'll start," I warn him as I glance at the time on my phone. "I have to go in." We've been in his car for an hour, and it's almost *Maghrib*.

"C'mon, what's the rush? You're already home. Okay, one more round. It's your turn."

I like that Sadiq spends all his free time with me. To be honest, I look forward to our evenings together. "Okay, one last one," I say. "Would you rather go back in time and meet your great-grandparents, or go into the future and meet your great-grandchildren?"

"*Hmm*," he rubs his hands together as he leans back into his seat. "Would I rather meet my great-grandparents or our future great grandchildren?" he thinks out loud.

"Wait. Did you just say *our* great grandchildren?"

He nods slowly, "Yes. Yes, I did."

This guy thinks he's sleek, I think but can't stop the smile that's beginning to tug the corners of my lips. "What makes you think we'll share great-grand kids?"

"Well, our kids will have kids and their kids will have kids. That's how life works you know." He thinks about the question for a few more seconds and then: "Easy answer. I'll go to the future."

"Are you flirting with me?" I say in an Anne-Hathaway impersonation. A really good one, too, if I can say so myself.

He lowers his voice, his eyes fixed on mine. "That depends. Is it working?" The exact answer Steve Carrel gave her in the movie *Get Smart*.

He got my reference! The way we understand each other reminds me of Umm'Hafsa and daddy. As they cross my mind, the smile leaves my face; *Not my daddy*. I sigh, then put my phone in my bag and reach for the door,

"I – I'm gonna go now."

"Hey, what just happened?" He reaches for my arm, stopping me.

A part of me wants to tell him, but honestly, I'm scared. I already feel like I overshared when I asked him the hypothetical question about paternity. "Nothing, It's just –" my voice trails off, and I just shrug. There's no way to explain what crossed my mind and dampened the otherwise amazing moment we just had.

As we walk slowly closer to the gate, it begins to roll open, and I look behind us to see the white BMW X7 with tinted glasses approaching us. The driver drives past, and the gates close behind the car. "That's my mum," I tell him, hoping she doesn't give me another lecture about standing outside the gate with visitors.

"Oh cool. Hey, what are you doing on Friday? Hajiya Amina is back from her trip and I want you to meet her."

"Oooh, I'm meeting your family now?" I start laughing.

"Yeah," he puts his hands in his pocket. "You keep calling me while I'm at her place, so she's curious to know who this pest is."

I gasp, "shut up. I'll stop calling you."

He starts laughing and before I get a comeback, Ashiru, one of the security guards under Joe, opens the small gate.

"*Um, Hajiya na magana*; Madam would like a word."

Oh boy. "Call me when you get home," I say as I start going inside.

"*Da shi wai*; with him," Ashiru says, pointing at Sadiq.

Sadiq

I walk Hafsat to their gate when her mother's car drives past us. A few minutes later, someone opens the gate and says that her mother wants to talk to me.

"What?" the color pales from Hafsat's face as she turns to me. "Hey, you don't have to. I'll tell her you left before Ashiru got here." She starts walking into the house.

"What do you mean? Your mom sent for me; best believe I'm going to see her."

A look of surprise passes her face. "But you shouldn't, if you don't want to."

"I *want* to." I wait for her to walk through the gate, then walk behind her and we walk in silence to the front door. When we get to it, a lady in a brown hijab opens the main door and Hafsat walks past her without an acknowledgment. I assume she's the help. I answer her greeting. The heels of Hafsat's red bottoms tap the white marbled floor as she walks down a hallway, pushes open a heavy white door and removes her heels before stepping on the black and gold woven carpet. I follow her, doing the same, leaving my slip-ons next to her stilettos. I sit down on the grey sofa lined with black decorative cushions.

"Let me tell her you're here," Hafsat says as she walks through an inner door. I track the discomfort in her eyes and the way she fidgets with the rings on her index fingers as she walks away. I look around the air-conditioned living room – from the grey and gold wallpaper on opposite ends of the room, the large green plants, the gold center table in front of me to the massive portraits on the white wall. Some were pictures of just Hafsat and her siblings, and others were just her parents, mostly posing in front of black backdrops. Her father – tall and thin seems open, personable and looks completely in awe of his gorgeous wife in all the pictures. There is something about the way he looks at their mum – not romantic, not platonic... I wish I had the words for it.

As I hear footsteps coming towards us, my pulse jumps with something that can be described as anticipation. I look up to her mother's unsmiling face as her brown eyes meet mine, a perfectly arched brow raised at me like a loaded gun. Hafsat looks so much like her; the resemblance is so uncanny.

She is wearing a long, black dress made of some lace material with stones that catch the light from the yellow gleam of the hanging crystal chandelier above us. The bracelets on her hand chime softly as she adjusts the neckline of her dress.

"Assalamu alaikum," her voice is almost inaudible, almost as if I'm not supposed to hear it. Behind her, Hafsat fiddles with a remote control as the wide television on a white and gold built-in media center comes on, displaying a news channel on mute.

"Good evening, Hajiya." I greet her in Hausa.

As she settles into the sofa opposite me, she answers softly then looks at Hafsat. "Get Mariya to bring something for him to drink." Hafsat's eyes dart towards me, I give her a short smile and she bites down on her lower lip like she's trying to hide her worry.

"What's your name?" Her mum asks the moment Hafsat closes the door behind her. Observing me closely as she gives me a once over, from my blue kaftan to its matching trousers. Her eyes finally settle back firmly on my face.

"My name is Sadiq. Abubakar Sadiq."

"Abubakar Sadiq," she repeats slowly as she observes my mannerisms. "Where are you from?"

"Jigawa state."

She tilts her head slightly, and her eyes light up as she says, "oh! We're neighbors, then." From Hafsat's last name, it's easy to deduce that she's from a town called Gaya in Kano state. Kano and Jigawa share a border. In fact, Jigawa was part of Kano until IBB carved out upper towns from the latter when he was head of state. "So, I see that you've been coming here a lot?" She wasted no time in diving into the inquisition.

I clear my throat before answering. "Yes, I have." I keep my voice as level as possible.

The door opens and Hafsat walks back in, followed by the lady in the brown hijab. She's holding a little bowl with some nuts in it and without glancing my way, she gracefully sinks into an armchair next to me, giving all her attention to the soundless television.

The maid sets a tray with three small bowls filled with almonds, pistachios, and cashew nuts on the side table next to me. She fills a glass with mango juice and even though I would have just preferred water, I say thank you before she walks away.

"Do you have younger female siblings, Sadiq?" Hafsat's mum switches to English, her voice soft yet commanding. There's a slight rustle of fabric as she leans back into the black throw cushions behind her.

"Yes, I have two younger sisters." I think I have an idea where this conversation is going.

"Very good. It means you can understand where I am coming from. Hafsatu's father doesn't like her standing outside the gate or sitting in someone's car outside. *Bai kamata ba*; there's no honor in that. You are both grown and if you are serious about her, you should come into the house like someone with nothing to hide." Next to me, I hear Hafsat snap a pistachio nut open, and her hands slowly reach for her mouth, her gaze still on the television.

Her mother is very direct, I like that. It reminds me of Hajiya Amina. I open my mouth to say something, but she continues. "Secondly, you have been bringing her home very late. As a man with younger sisters, surely you know that's not a good look for a girl from a respectable home, and she knows how I feel about her coming back home late."

"*A mun afuwa*, Hajiya; I apologize." I say honestly, "I'll make sure she's back home on time moving forward."

Her face softens as her mouth curves into a content smile. "I'll take your word for it," she pauses. "*Ya mutanen gida?* How's your family?"

"They are all fine, Alhamdulillah."

"That's good. You didn't take your drink," she gestures to the tray in front of me as she stands up, and I thank her for her hospitality.

When the door closes, Hafsat pulls her gaze away from the television and looks at me, her face covered with her hands: "I am mortified." she murmurs softly.

I laugh quietly, "Personally, I think that could have gone a lot worse."

* * *

Moving back to Nigeria after grad school was one of the easiest decisions I have ever made. I've always known that Abuja is where I wanted to start my businesses and call home. In Abuja, getting things done is easy – there's always someone who knows a family member who can facilitate formalities, paperwork and bypass the red tape of management and government systems. Sure, you have to spend a few hundred thousand, but it's always better than waiting for months following due process.

I returned to Abuja with most of my belongings. A few things took longer than expected to get into Abuja due to a change in the chain of command in Customs because of some cabinet reshuffling by the Nigerian government. Because of this, it takes a while for my Quad bikes – a red Outlander Max and a blue Yamaha Raptor – to arrive. When they finally do, I take a quick picture after signing the delivery forms and send it to Hafsat with a caption: *Do you need me to teach you how to ride one?*

As I wait for her reply, I chuckle to myself. Nowadays, when something interesting happens to me, she is always the first person I want to share it with. My phone lights up with her reply: *Teach me? I bet I can floor you in a quad race.*

I raise my brows as I type back: *Oh word?*

Hafsat is full of surprises. I check her next message and see that she attached a picture of her on a black Yamaha Grizzly, an older model. In the dusty picture, her hands are balanced on the steering bar, her boots on the footrest of the four-wheeled all-terrain vehicle. Behind her is her sister Sara, who I met two days after the Fashion show when Fatima and I ran into them at *Johnny Rockets.*

I smile: *I'll believe it when you do it. Pick you up after Zuhr?*

I see bubbles indicating she is typing, and then: *Asr...*

I have the Quads delivered to Almat Farms, a large piece of terrain sitting on over 100 hectares in the outer parts of Abuja. When I pick Hafsat up a few hours later after *Asr,* the late afternoon prayer, from Ilham's house, she approaches my car in what looks like an unlikely ensemble. She's wearing a peach-colored long-sleeved top with a floral lace bodice hugging her torso. As she hugs Ilham before saying bye, I look through the windows, and my attention is drawn to her perfectly rounded ass in the white jeans she's wearing. I glance back at the dashboard, skipping songs until she comes in and winds down the glass for Ilham to lean in.

"Fam, make sure she wears a helmet," Ilham warns.

I chuckle to myself. The bond between the unlikely pair is fascinating. Ilham is all sharp edges with no filter and on a constant commentary, while Hafsat is zen, adding to Ilham's commentary with only her expressions. Yet, they are as tight as Ted and Coach Beard.

"You know I can't make her do anything," I say. Hafsat is stubborn; her best friend knows that better than anyone.

She looks at Hafsat, "weird flex," and they share a knowing glance, "I'm going to check on Usman; he had his tonsillectomy today."

"Oh, it was today?" Hafsat says. "Say hi to him for me."

We watch as she walks into the waiting Land Cruiser and her driver pulls away. As I get the car back on the road, I turn the volume of the music down.

"Your white is going to get all muddy because it rained last night."

She looks at her jeans. "I don't want to have to go home and change *ne.* Besides, it's just clothes."

Maybe I'm reading too much into it, but she spends more time at Ilham's place these days than at hers. I wonder if this has anything at all to do with the hypothetical question she asked the other day – the one about the story she's writing. She hasn't referred to it again since that evening. "So you Quad? I was surprised," I say.

Her scent – something sweet and fruity – lingers in the air between us. "We used to go to Fifth Chukker a lot. When we were kids, daddy would take us to Kaduna to visit our Uncle. Every Saturday, we'll spend the day at there and he would teach us how to ride."

"Your dad sounds super cool."

"Yes," she says slowly. "He is."

"Fifth Chukker has the best bush trails for Quads. *Ko mu je Kd ne?* Should we drive to Kaduna?"

"*Ba da ni ba wallahi*; I swear I'm not going on that road."

"*Matsoraciya!*" I tease her about her being scared. "When did you become a scaredy cat?"

"Guy, I'm not stopping you. Just drop me off at home but make sure you call me when you get there."

I laugh at her wisecracks. Since the 2-hour road between Kaduna and Abuja got plagued by armed bandits, no one travels on it. But Kaduna has a great Polo Club and Outdoor recreation center called Fifth Chukker. My family went there frequently when I was a kid.

"So you guys all used to go together, including your mom?" As I push down the accelerator, I deftly change lanes, passing the cars on my right.

"Yeah, we used to go together. But she usually stayed back in the Villa to read her novels or watch something. Never really understood why she insisted on coming along, if she didn't want to participate."

"I can't imagine your mom doing any outdoor activity."

"Yeah, but even with the other activities like Tennis or Polo Tournaments – she hardly came out to watch."

I nod as I listen. "I like your mom. She seems nice and straightforward." Ever since I started going into Hafsat's house, I always make it a point to greet her before I leave, something Hafsat isn't ever pleased about. "I just don't understand the way you act towards her."

She sits back, crossing her arms underneath her breasts, a movement that is distracting as hell, because of the low neckline of her top. Unlike other girls who do it to get my attention, she only seems to be doing it to close herself off, to be less vulnerable.

"Yeah, she's not who she seems to be." I see irritation slipping over her features.

The rest of the car ride is filled with songs from the stereo until we get to Kuje. For a girl that is hardly ever impressed, the gigantic grin on her face as she sees the Quads when we get to Almat Farms makes my chest swell with pride. "I'm gonna choose first," she says as we walk towards them, where they are parked on the grassy plains.

"Go for it," I watch as her hands go over the shiny headlights and throttle of the gleaming red four-wheeler, and in a swift, poised movement, she climbs the black leather seat, balancing her wedges on the footrest as she leans forward.

"This one," I haven't seen her smile this much in weeks. I can watch her forever like this.

"Okay, so this is a bit different from the ones they have at Fifth Chukker," I explain as she ties her veil around her head like a bandana; the long ends fall behind her back. "This here is the front break, the clutch is on this side and the gear shifter is down here." I touch the black knob by her knees.

I don't think she was listening because the minute I take a step back, she zooms off like a pro, shouting over her shoulders: "Try and catch up!"

Zuwaira

1998

Alhaji and I never made it to Mecca that year.

On my way to visit Aunty Tani, as Alhaji had suggested, I just could not get over the kind of respect my new status accorded me – from the way the driver, who was much older than me, greeted me and asked for permission before turning on the radio, to the way Aunty Tani welcomed me into the unusually unkempt house. As I entered, I noticed her scrambling to pack up the plates her children ate lunch with from the messy carpet and into the kitchen. She didn't mean for me to see that, but I did.

As she thanked me for the fruits and juice that I brought for my cousins, she shouted at her youngest daughter to go into the kitchen to get me something to drink; this same girl never stepped into the kitchen when I lived here. From being offered drinks to spoken to with respect – no, admiration – it was easy to see that Aunty Tani no longer saw me as the help, I was now like an old friend.

She told me about what I'd missed on the compound. A date had been set for the landlord's son's wedding; the well fell in and had to be rebuilt; and Mallam Isa, Ibrahim's older brother, was building a house, and they would be moving out of their rented flat in a few months. I nodded quietly as I listened to her. When I was leaving, we stopped at Ibrahim's sister-in-law's

154

flat, whose eyes lit up when she saw me.

"Marriage looks great on you!" she said as they both escorted me to the car where the driver was waiting outside the gate.

When we get home, the driver parked right by the inner gate leading to the women's section. As I walked into my section, feeling the cool evening breeze on my skin and watching how it made the trees in the compound sway gently, I watched as Alhaji's younger children played with a football around the house.

I was beginning to know which kid belonged to which wife. The first wife had three boys and two daughters; the girls were all married, and the boys were in university, except for one who was still in secondary school with the second wife's children. The second wife had three kids – all daughters in secondary school. They were usually the last to get into the blue Peugeot station wagon that took all the children to school, and they constantly forgot their homework, sports uniform, or money for recess snacks. I always saw them through my kitchen window, rushing back into their mother's section as I made breakfast while the driver kept honking at the insistence of the other impatient kids. Alhaji's late wife had died giving birth to a son, who was also proclaimed dead upon his birth; she left behind a four-year-old who stayed with Hajiya Uwa and attended school with the other children. Balaraba had a baby who was barely a year old and was always carried on a nanny's back while his mother was at work.

When I walked back to my section, I wondered what to eat for dinner since Alhaji was away for the next few days. I contemplated between yam porridge and indomie with some leftover grilled chicken. Eventually, I decided to wait till I pray *Maghrib*, eat, then watch *Sumbuka*, the Hausa film I'd started that morning. As I got closer to my door and put the key in its lock, I saw it.

A small black bird – like a dove or maybe a pigeon. It lay dead in front of my door with both legs tied together. Upon closer inspection, I saw a threaded charm on its limp feet. *What is this? How did it get here?* All my earlier thoughts about food vanished from my mind. I removed my keys from the doorknob with shaky hands and walked towards Hajiya Uwa's section. I met her on the verandah, and she was on a brown armchair smoking a cigarette. I had learned much earlier that Hajiya Uwa was a chronic tobacco addict; she smoked a pack of cigarettes in two days.

"*Har kin dawo?* You're back so soon?" she took one final drag before dropping the short cigarette stub into a cup of water.

"Yes, I'm back. Aunty Tani sends her regards," I sat on the blue raffia mat on the floor next to the leather cushion that she had her legs on as she fanned herself.

"*Lafiya na gan ki haka?* Is everything okay? Why do you look worried?"

I looked up at her, failing to mask the trepidation on my face. "*Hajiya, bakar laya na tarar a kofar daki na*; I came back to a black charm at the entrance of my door." Images of the dead bird and the menacing way its legs were tied could not leave my mind.

"Black charm?" she raised her voice and she started looking around her chair for something; she picked her long blue veil from the edge of the armchair and wrapped it over her head as she stood up. "Come and show me."

I led the way, and she followed me past the inner gate all the way to my section. The whole compound was now quiet; all the children who were playing outside a few minutes ago were all gone. I got to my verandah and pointed to the dead bird on the floor.

"*Ai kuwa*; indeed. It's exactly what you said." She leaned closer and inspected the charm around its leg without touching it. "I hope you didn't touch it or cross over it."

What would have happened if I had crossed over it? I shook my head no. I'd noticed it just before I stepped over it.

She stood up, adjusted her veil and raised her voice so that the wives in other sections could hear her. "*Nan fa gidan musulmai ne, ba gidan maguzawa ba*; We are Muslims in this house, not pagans. But you people have resorted to charms and black magic? May Allah forgive you all. The way you have stayed in this house and given birth to children is how she will also stay and give birth to children. *Ai baku isa ba!* None of you – I repeat, none of you – is strong enough, except my name is not Uwa yar

Gabasawa." She turned her head in the other direction. "Where's Hashim? Hashim!" She called out.

From the gate leading towards Alhaji's section, Hashim came sprinting out wearing a black jallabiya. Hajiya Uwa didn't even wait for him to reach us.

"*Kai, kira mun Buzu;* Call the nomad for me."

Buzu was one of the guards at the entrance of the house; he was originally from Agadez in Niger.

All I knew about charms were from the little I'd heard when I was in school; there were bad charms, and there were good charms. Even with my basic knowledge of the topic, I knew that anything that involved a dead bird or animal was a terrible omen.

"You have to stand up for yourself. You can't let yourself be turned into something pitiful. Read your Qur'an, intensify your prayers, so that Allah will deliver you from their evil plots," she said to me. "You hear me?"

As I nodded, a tall, dark man with plaits on the sides of his head came towards us. "Hajiya, you sent for me?"

"Yes, I did. Come and take a look at this," her Hausa accent changed to match his deeply accented dialect. The voice inflections and intonations would make it hard for someone to follow the exact conversation, but it was a dialect I'd heard my mother speak with some of her customers in Bauchi, so it was easy for me to decipher.

Without looking at me, he walked straight to my verandah and sat by the dead bird; he whispered some words, dusted both hands and reached to touch the bird.

"Don't touch it!" I said, concerned. But it was too late; he had already carried the bird and was closely inspecting the writings around the threaded charm.

"Don't worry. This one is a protected man," Hajiya Uwa told me quietly.

I looked back at him and saw the multiple dark scars on his hand and several annulets around his neck, including one with a brown gourd on a black string that stopped at his waist. *Oh,* I thought, *that kind of protection.*

As he stood up, he started coughing alarmingly. He dusted his hands again as he looked up at us. "She has to seek protection. A lot of work went into this. Whoever did this – whoever is responsible for this – wants her to run mad."

"It's their mothers that will run mad," Hajiya Uwa countered, taking her hand round her head and snapping her fingers as if to say 'God forbid.'

"The fact that she's still standing is by the grace of God because they want to get rid of her for good," he paused, "I'll take this and after the necessary precautions, I'll open it and get rid of the other items they used to bind it. But she *has* to seek protection," he said in Niger-Hausa.

I could not pay attention to what else he was saying. *They want to get rid of me? Who wants to do that? The other wives? What have I done? I hardly ever see them, and whenever I saw them, we were cordial to each other, and I never say anything bad about them. Even when their children drop by my section to see their father, I always give them refreshments. Some even borrow film cassettes from me to watch. What have I done to them that they want to hurt me?*

* * *

Maybe my prayers weren't enough, or maybe it was just my bad luck, but things got considerably worse as time passed. First, Hashim told me one day when he came to change my gas cylinder that one of Alhaji's biggest factories caught fire in the middle of the night.

"Caught fire?" I asked behind the curtain separating the hallway from the kitchen.

"Yes," his voice was muffled by the distance as he worked to connect the cylinder to my three-plate burner. "Completely burnt to the ground."

"*Innalillahi wa inna ilayhi raji'un.*" No wonder Alhaji had been in a foul mood recently. We all heard him arguing with Balaraba in her section two nights earlier, and the following evening, he didn't go back to her section. That was how Alhaji showed his displeasure with his wives – by ignoring them during their allocated time with him. He stayed in his section until the rest of her days were done. Balaraba, on the other hand, had not come out of her section since that day, not even to go to work. I wondered if he

158

had stopped her from working, but I knew better than to ask.

A week later, Alhaji had just taken a bath in my toilet and was getting ready for work when we heard *sallama* at the door. It was Sufyan's voice. I thought it was odd because Alhaji's brother never dropped by so early in the morning as he had his own family a few houses away. Whatever this was, it must be urgent, I thought.

As I listened to their conversation from the kitchen, I overheard that one of Alhaji's trailers containing harvested food from his farms had gotten into another accident. This was the third time accident that month; the first two happened within three days on different highways to different parts of the country.

Alhaji's mood got worse. He remained in his section of the house for days at a time, ignoring his other wives. Yet from the moment he set foot into my section, things that seemed to go well in the past started falling apart. The rice I made sure to taste before serving him was suddenly too pepperish for him, and soup recipes I had perfected to his taste suddenly tasted too salty. One day, he sat down for dinner in the worst mood ever. He had just received news that one of the multi-complexes he was building in Ungwan Sarki was in an area rezoned by the government for the building of a hospital, this meant that the shops he had spent millions of naira building were going to be demolished, that was the day that Alhaji hit me for the first time ever.

He had just started eating when he bit into a stone in the rice he was eating. We didn't even buy local rice; all the rice that filled our stores was imported, and there were no stones in them. Even if there were stones, I would have washed them out, as I washed the rice multiple times before cooking.

Yet, there it was – the sound of an unmistakable crunch. He spat the rice mixed with saliva back on his plate and just as I started apologizing, I felt my head slam the back of the chair. I hadn't even seen his hand in the air, not even when it descended across my cheeks. All I felt was the sting and the pain.

I was dazed. I could not process what had just happened. I was filled with a kind of surprise that caught me unaware that I continued apologizing while crying profusely.

* * *

One day, my mother-in-law brought rubutu from her mallam for protection, as she did weekly since we found the dead bird at my door. When I did not answer her *sallama*, she knocked on my door and because Alhaji left it unlocked after he left, she pushed it open. She found me on in the living room with a deep gash on my forehead, bleeding profusely. Yet, all I was worried about was cleaning the red stain on the white portion of the carpet. The water in the bucket next to me was tinged with pink, as was the towel I cleaned it with. But the blood stain was still evident on the carpet.

Even though I was bleeding and continuously staining the carpet, I could not stop cleaning. *What if he comes back and sees that I've ruined his carpet with my blood? That will make him angry, and he'll beat me again.* The beating had become frequent by this time; it happened every time he stepped into this section.

"Innalillahi wa inna ilayhi raji'un," she said. I looked up as my mother-in-law dropped the rubutu on the table, a swan water bottle wrapped in a black plastic bag. "What did you do this time?" There was sympathy in her voice and her expression, but she had already assigned the blame to me.

"There was a piece of shell in his eggs at breakfast," I reply. Next to me, the eggs fried in peppers and sardines were all over the floor. There was also oil trailing the wall from where the plate struck it after he had flung it away, scalding his hand and my thighs with hot tea.

"Zuwaira, I always tell you to leave the television off when you're cooking *amma ina*, but you won't listen."

I was going to tell her that I took her advice and that I never cook with the television on anymore, but I couldn't talk because the stain on the carpet was not coming off, and I was panicking and getting lightheaded.

"Go into your room, get your hijab and come, let's go," I looked up at her and nodded as the tears streamed down my face.

Hajiya Uwa was finally able to stop the bleeding; she cleaned the wound and put a plaster on it. Some minutes later, we were in the jeep's back seat, driven by one of the drivers who asked no questions about my forehead, puffy eyes or slight limp.

"Dutsen-Abba," she said in a way that suggested he knew exactly where to go, despite the broad instruction, and he nodded in a way that confirmed it.

When we got to the mud-thatched homes on the outskirts of town, a place so far removed from the city that the car had multiple issues navigating the dusty dirt roads, Hajiya remained unperturbed, just pulling her white *tasbeeh*, her rosary, as the tires went in and out of multiple potholes. When the driver announced that we had arrived, she reached into her bag and gave him three ten naira bills.

"Go and get yourself lunch in that food shop. We'll be out in an hour." She pointed to a house in front of us. "Let's go in, Zuwaira," she said, and I followed her, wondering where we were.

Are we visiting an old relative of hers? Somebody that can intercede on my behalf to Alhaji so that he can stop beating me?

We went into the only house with a corrugated zinc roof on the street , we passed the unpainted mud walls and walked into the quiet compound until we reached a smaller mud hut at the end. Hajiya Uwa bent as she pushed aside the sheepskin used as a curtain to keep the sun out. I followed her in. It looked much bigger from the inside. It was cool inside too, unlike the scorching heat outside. There was no furniture except a wooden bench on another sheepskin on the ground. Hajiya sat on the sheepskin and I did the same. Against the wall was a covered clay pot with a stainless steel cup over it. Next to the pot were different-sized *Allos,* wooden plaques with Arabic verses written on them, and many small clay pots with different powders inside.

"*Ah ah*, today I have a big visitor. Uwa, is this your face I'm seeing?" A thin old man, taller than anyone I had ever seen, came into the room. He was wrapped in a grey blanket, and his white beard reached his chest. As he smiled, I saw that the remaining teeth in his mouth were stained brown, a stain associated with kola nuts and tobacco.

"It is. And that should let you know that this matter is not a small one since I came all the way here by myself." She did not stop pulling her tasbeeh.

I huddled closer to her as the man sat opposite us, separated by the small bench with the most enormous tasbeeh I had ever seen laying on it.

"Does Indo deliver my message?"

"Yes, she does," she turned to me. "In fact, this is the one we've been getting the *rubutu* for."

"Okay, this is the youngest one?" he looked at me for the first time. "I hope you've been drinking what I send to you? That's what is protecting you from those co-wives of yours, especially the oldest one."

Hajiya Babba? Really? The woman who smiled at me when I was brought in? I could not find my voice, so all I did was nod.

"There's something else. That his terrifying anger is back. This time around, he has been unleashing it on this poor girl." From how she spoke, I realized that the incidents in my section had not been as unknown to Hajiya Uwa as I'd thought.

He frowned then laughed out all of a sudden. "One of them must have countered what you and I did to calm him down. They're very resourceful – those daughters-in-law of yours."

"*Munafukai ba;* those Hypocrites? They keep acting innocent, but I can see how they've been punishing him for adding another wife. All his businesses are suffering – even that contract I told you about. Up to today, as I sit in front of you and speak, the government has not paid him his money."

He looked at me and then at my mother-in-law. "Oh, that's not on them. That's on this one right here."

I widened my eyes as I looked at him and my mother-in-law, shaking my head. "Wallahi, I didn't do anythin –" I started crying as Hajiya Uwa squinted her eyes as she looked at me.

He picked up a powder from a small pot, put it on his tongue, and closed his eyes. A few seconds later, he opened his eyes and said: "Of course she's the cause of everything." He closed his eyes again for a bit and murmured. "Yes, it's all her."

"What exactly are you telling me?" Hajiya Uwa asked gravely. All the color from her face is gone now.

"I have not done anyt-" Before I could complete my sentence, he cut me short without even looking at me as he spoke to Hajiya directly.

"Think about the events that have followed since she married your son," he said again.

Hajiya Uwa had a frown on her face as she shook her head vehemently, "no, don't tell me that. This Zuwaira?" she asked.

"Can't you tell? *Ai farin kafa gare ta*; she brought bad luck," he looked at me as he spoke, and I looked at my crossed legs, hiding my feet beneath the hijab. "She's the reason all his wealth is disappearing. It happened to her father when he married her mother."

I mulled over his words: *Mai farin kafa*, a girl who brings bad luck into a house. If she's married, her husband will never progress, or his wealth will eventually dwindle into nothing.

Luck. There it was, that word again.

Hafsatu

2021

My cousin Salma is in Abuja for her visa biometrics. Whenever she's in Abuja, which happens a few times a year, she stays at our house in one of the spare rooms.

"Adda Salma, when is your trip?" I ask as we eat breakfast by the pool, taking in some early morning sun. Behind us, the gardener is trimming the green hedges and watering Umm'Hafsa's hibiscus and sunflowers.

"Wallahi, their father wants us to visit him before the new year, so as soon as I get my visa." she says, referring to the three-year-old twins she left with the maid in Kaduna. Her husband works at the Nigerian High Commission in India, and they visit him every few months. She takes a sip of her green tea and drops her teacup. "How about you? How have you been? Where's Bashir?"

"He's around, *o*," I say, not interested in dwelling on it. I want to tell her about Sadiq, but I decide to wait until he's back from the wedding he's attending in Kano so she can meet him. "How's Uncle? *Wallahi* I miss coming to Kaduna. We haven't been in so long."

"We all miss you too," she says. "*Nace ba*, how about you and I go for dinner tonight? You can tell Ilham to come, too. It'll be my treat."

"Of course," I pick up my phone to text Ilham. At the same time, Adda Salma turns her phone around to show me a restaurant's Instagram page.

"What do you think of this place?"

"Ah, *The Six*? I've always wanted to go to their new location, *amma*, they are always sold out. But it's a nice place. We can try to go at, like, 5 pm?"

She doesn't reply; she types on her phone, her phone beeps, and then she answers, "*Um.*. let's do seven."

"Okay," I say, then text Ilham: *7 pm – you, me, and* Adda *S?*

Her reply comes in seconds later: Adda S *is in town? Yes, of course!*

"Ilham's in," I drop my phone back on the table as I add more pancakes to my plate.

"That's fantastic. I haven't seen her in over a year. I should drop by *H&I* to pick up some things," she has a smile on her face as she reads a message on her phone.

"Of course! Anytime you want."

Later that evening, as I'm dabbing concealer under my eyes to hide the black circles I have been battling with as a result of lack of proper sleep in the past few weeks, Adda S comes in wearing a lovely black kaftan from my latest collection. It leaves a massive grin on my face.

"*Haba* Hafsatu. I'm all dressed up and you're still in the jeans and T-shirt you're been wearing all day?" she pouts to show her disappointment.

"I'm gonna dress it up with heels and these earrings," I turn so she can see the emerald green teardrop earrings I'm wearing.

"C'mon. It's a girls' evening out, you should dress up. Wear something... elegant."

"Understated is more like a girl's night out."

"But still, we haven't done this in so long," she walks into my closet and I follow her. "Look at this place! You have a whole boutique in here. Bebi, I deserve something better than what you're wearing right now."

I roll my eyes; Adda S can be dramatic when she wants to be. "Fine, I'll change."

Two outfit changes later – I notice she's very particular about how she wants me to look – we finally settle on a beige draped top that falls off one shoulder and has slit sleeves. I have a long burgundy bodycon skirt, and on my feet are clear heels with embellished brooches in front. I'm wrapping my scarf around my head when Sadiq's call comes in.

"Hey you," I say, smiling into the phone.

"Heyyy, whats up?" I can hear the smile in his voice.

"Nothing much. I'm heading out to dinner with my cousin and Ilham," I say. "Maybe we can all go out together, when you come back?"

"Cool cool. You're going to *The Six* huh?" he asks. I hear something in his voice I can't quite place.

"Yeah. How did you know?"

He clears his throat. "Nah, it's okay. Tell me how it goes, okay? And say hi to your cousin."

"Okay, I will. Bye," I end the call and look up to see Adda S looking at me questioningly.

"And who is this one that's got talking in such a coy manner?"

I bat my eyelashes playfully at her. "You'll meet him tomorrow, *insha Allah*. His name is Sadiq."

"Sadiq *kuma*? Who's Sadiq again? No, me, I'm team Bashir forever. He's soooo nice. He calls me often just to greet me."

"Bashir still calls you?" I frown. I introduced them during one of Adda S's stops in Abuja on her way to New Delhi, but I didn't think he still kept in touch with her after our break up.

"Listen, I know every relationship has it's ups and downs. Why don't you tell me all about what made you block him at dinner? We shouldn't be late," she glances at her wristwatch. It's already a few minutes to seven.

When we get to *The Six by Lovitoz*, an upscale restaurant that boasts of a fully customizable menu, I am surprised to see that I can find parking easily. It is quiet, which I assume is because they only host exclusively based on a limited number of reservations. The waiter leads us into the Classic room that has a grill and a beautiful skylit ceiling. Before I can fully take in the well-decorated interior, my phone starts to ring. It's Ilham.

"Where are you? We are gonna start eating without you *o*," I say into the phone as soon as I pick up.

"Babeeee, listen, Usman just told me –" static comes through, and I can't hear her anymore.

I look at my phone; I have full bars. I return it to my ear. *"Ina kike ne haka? Where are you?"* I am almost annoyed.

"We're – one min – Usman – Bashir –" the call drops.

Bashir? Did she say Bashir? I'm just about to say that it's nice to have the whole place to ourselves when I see some four people walking in. Three are faces I've seen while hanging out with Bashir; I think he introduced them as his cousins. What is going on?

Then Bashir walks in, wearing a blue checkered shirt, black trousers, and tan brogues. *Bashir in brogues? Uh oh, this can't be good.* A quartet of Accapella musicians come out at the same time that rose petals drop all over the floor. Before I can gather my thoughts together, Bashir goes down on one knee with a ring in his hand. The music starts.

"Hafsatu Bebi – love of my life – would you make me the happiest man in the world?"

I look at Adda S and she has the biggest smile on her face as she records the spectacle on her phone.

The door opens as Ilham and Usman arrive. The look on her face as she sees Bashir on one knee, is precisely how I feel: *What the actual eff?*

* * *

I ignore the voices chanting, "say yes, say yes, say yes," and the music reverberating through the room as I force a smile on my face.

"One minute," I say apologetically to the faces in the room as I grab Bashir's hand and pull him up. As he stands, he has the biggest grin on his face that I begin to wonder if I'm being pranked. I drag him out of the doors and see another door on the left, and I open that one and walk into a room with brown walls, potted plants, and succulents.

"What are you doing?" I feel dizzy. "What is the meaning of this? Is

167

marriage a joke to you?" I say as I ignore my ringing phone. He looks at me, puzzled, like he doesn't know what I was talking about. "You cheated. You were constantly cheating with different girls," I look at him and he looks back, as though he was trying to remember, then he shakes his head as if to say that's not true, but I'm not about to let myself be gaslit. "I caught you having sex with another girl in your apartment."

He closes the door and tries to hold my hand. I pull away from him, rejecting the call without looking at it. "I told you I was going to make it up to you, Bebi. I'm sorry." The look on his face is like that of someone who gives a child something they really want for their birthday, and the child is about to drown them in hugs. Expectant. Except this is not what I want. If this was three months ago, I would be calling my parents, elated, telling them about the news. I would even be taking pictures of my finger sporting the ring to send to my sisters. Now, as I look at him, a question was popping in my head: *would Bashir still want to marry me if he learns the truth about my paternity?* And the sad truth is, I really, really don't know.

"So *this* is you making it up to me?" I try not to laugh.

"Yes," he answers incredulously. He did not see the irony in his proposal. A woman catches you cheating, so you buy her back by asking her to spend the rest of her life with you? *Why does he think that's a deal I'll gladly jump into?*

My phone starts ringing again. I'm about to reject it again when I see that it is Aunty Zainab, Bashir's mum. I widen my eyes questioningly at him, as I gesture towards the phone.

"Just pick up," he says, "or she'll call my phone and ask to talk to you."

Oh my God, what has this guy done? This guy actually involved his mom in this farce of an engagement.

"Hello, Aunty *ina yini*; Good evening," I say into the phone, my voice losing all the attitude from a minute ago.

"Congratulations, Hafsatu! You won't believe how happy I was when Bashir told me he was going to propose. *Haba*, it's about time *ai*," I can hear the smile in her voice. I can't even say thank you, I just glare at him with so much anger at the mess he managed to put both of us in. "I hope you love the ring?" she continues. "The accent stones on it are actually from the wedding ring his father's family presented to me in 1985."

I listen as his mum went on to narrate how her Arab Morrocan grandfather was so impressed with all the presents the family from Kano had brought – so much so that he knew that no one else was worthy of marrying his daughter. I'm brought back to reality, to her asking me a question that needs my reply, or at least so I think from this pause in her monologue.

"*Na'am*? Yes?" I asked uncertainly.

"I said, you should expect a call from that Lagos designer, *Veekee James*. I booked you a consultation. You know, she did Amirah's gown – that champagne pink one everyone was talking about." Amirah is Bashir's sister-in-law, and I remember the dress very well as Bashir and I attended the wedding together about six months ago.

"Oh, okay…" How do I tell her that even though I think that Veekee's gowns are a work of art, I can't possibly go for any consultation because I won't be marrying her son?

"Anyways, I'll let you and Bashir figure out your flight to Lagos and we can start preparing properly when you get back. *Allah ya sa a yi a sa'a*," she prayed for us, still with the same energy and excitement she had when I picked up the phone.

"Thank you, Aunty," I plaster a smile on my face trying to sound as cheerful as I possibly can. As soon as the call ends, I push the ring he's still holding towards his chest. "Fix. This."

"What is it? You're not happy with the ring? Listen, we can get you a bigger one," he opens the box and looks at the ring. "Okay, how about you send me a link to the ring you want and I'll get that for you, instead?"

"It's not about the ring!" I'm shouting now. He looks at me like he still does not understand what I'm talking about. "Bashir, we can not get married. You and I – it's over. We are not getting back together."

"What are you saying?"

Trying to force me into saying yes through a very public proposal like this just further emphasizes my thoughts that he doesn't do these things for me. For my dream proposal, I want something intimate and quiet – just the two of us – after a private dinner on a rooftop somewhere quiet. The ring will be a simple band, something that has our names engraved on the inside where no one can see, like an inside joke, something like *Hafsatu ∞ Sadiq*. Sadiq. I wonder if he has heard about this drama and what he thinks of it. I hope he doesn't think that I'll say yes to Bashir.

"I *can't* marry you," I say again, enunciating this time. "You need to find a way to tell all these people you invited, and your mum, too."

"What, what?" He holds me back as I try to open the door. "Are you being serious? You're actually saying *no*?" From the look on his face, it's clear that he never even considered that it was in the realm of possibility that I might not want to be his wife.

"Yeah. If I knew you were doing this, I would have told you no, without it going public." I glance at the table through the glass panes and see Ilham in deep conversation with Adda S, who looks like she's just beginning to understand the major mess up Bashir made her a part of. Usman just stands by the door, looking at the decorations and the tables. In the middle of the restaurant, the musicians and Bashir's cousins are looking at their phones while waiting for us to come out.

I tap my phone and text Ilham: *Please bring Adda S home. I owe you one* as I quietly leave *The Six* through the side door.

* * *

I just finished a video call with my sisters, who could not believe Bashir's audacity when Adda S returns with Ilham.

"I blindly went with his plans out of excitement. When he heard I was coming to Abuja, all he said was, 'I want to propose to your sister' and made me promise to keep it a secret." She removes her turban and drops it on my bed. "He said it was going to be a surprise because you blocked him

170

due to a misunderstanding and sent me all the details. All I had to do was bring you to the restaurant."

I know how persuasive Bashir can be. He almost gets away with what he wants most of the time. "If I tell you what I caught Bashir doing – *Allah dai ya sawake*; may God forbid. We broke up almost three months now."

"Ilham just told me everything," she hisses. "*Kai* Bashir *ko?* I can't imagine how embarrassing that must have been for you."

I look at my phone. I've been trying to reach Sadiq since I left the restaurant, but it doesn't go through. I purse my lips and add, "I'm seeing someone now."

She glances at Ilham, who just kicks her heels off and opens my fridge. "*Haba?* Who is he? How did you guys meet? Tell me everything."

"That's the weird part; we met through Bashir."

"*Ashe yariyan nan baki da mutunci*; you're not nice at all *oh*," she jokes and bursts out laughing. "What's he like, though? I hope it's not just a relationship? I want to hear wedding bells."

I sigh. "I'm so confused. We're like going out, but not really."

She tilts her head questioningly as she looks from me to Ilham. "I don't understand."

Ilham shrugs and drinks water from the bottle, a hint of a smile on her lips.

"He acts like my boyfriend. Like, he's possessive, but not in a bad way, and we spend all our free time together, but we haven't really had the *talk*," I try to explain. "We don't have a label."

She shakes her head slowly. "That's a red flag for me – situationships, where you're more than friends but there's no concrete label. That's how you get hurt. Breakups from that are even worse than from relationships, because you guys never defined it. Worst-case scenario, the guy can say *ai* he was just being friendly," she pauses, "I hope he's not trying to get all touchy touchy with you?"

"No no. Not at all. He's not like that. Besides, I would never let him."

"That's my girl! *Kunsan maza*; you know how these guys are. Once they get that, they just move onto the next. You'll be left with all the shame."

Ilham stands up, walks to my closet and wears one of my Aldo slippers. "I'm borrowing this." She carried her heels off the carpet. "So – just to be sure – I'm not organizing any bridal shower yet?"

"Sorry to disappoint you," I giggle.

She sighs dramatically. "*Matsalan kenan* – that's the problem with having just one best friend. Adda S, she has just deprived me of my opportunity to throw the best bridal party ever. *Toh,* have a goodnight. Usman is waiting for me downstairs," she smiles and leaves without waiting for a reply.

When we hear her footsteps down the stairs, Adda S whispers, "*har yanzu* her and Usman are still 'just friends'?" The first day Adda S met Usman, she swore that he was Ilham's future husband.

"Yup, for over ten years now," I lean back into my pillows as I redial Sadiq's number. The call doesn't even go through.

"Is it that she doesn't see it, or he doesn't see it?"

"I think they just don't wanna ruin it with a label," I answer honestly.

"Why is your generation obsessed with no-label relationships, *ne?*"

I think about it for a minute. "Technically *fa*, we belong to the same generation, Adda S," I say, laughing as I dodge the pillow she throws at me.

Hafsatu

I gradually pull to a stop at the entrance of *Ranchers* and park my car. Then I look at the screen of my phone again. Still no call, no text message, nothing. None of the calls I made to his phone this morning went through. Unlike most of us, Sadiq doesn't carry multiple phones around; he says he doesn't see the point. I look at the time on my phone 2:01 pm.

I can't shake off this foreboding sense of *deja vu* – the unreachable number, the un-replied texts. It feels familiar. *Is this Bashir all over again?*

Coming here like this is such a bad idea. What if he's in Asokoro? I think as I rotate the gear shift dial back to Drive. There's no reason for me to be here. But as I gently start pulling my foot off the brake, I admit to myself that this is unusual. It's unusual for him to go a whole day without texting or calling me. What if something horrible happened to him, and here I am, contemplating if he's ghosted me? *Let me just go in there, find one of his staff and ask to hear that he's alive. Once I know that he's okay, I'll head back home,* I think to myself as I take the gear shift back to Park.

I open the door and step out of the car, the satin material of the brown belted A-line dress I have on flowing in the uncharacteristically windy afternoon; it's gonna rain, I think, and I don't have an umbrella in my car. I walk on the gravel pathway overlooking a fish pond with multiple fast-swimming goldfish and pass the empty seats in the thatched huts. I go inside the lounge where Simi's *Joromi* is coming from, there's a guy cleaning glass cups just behind the payment counter as the song's video plays behind him on multiple large-screen televisions. He sways to the

173

familiar tune as he mouths the lyrics. The lounge is empty except for a few staff cleaning. Even though it is my first time here, I've seen enough videos on Snapchat and Insta-stories to know that this place only gets busy at night.

"Hi," I walk to the counter.

The man, whose name tag reads 'Promise,' drops the glass cup he's holding on the placemat in front of him. "Welcome ma," he says, as he grabs a paper towel and cleans his hand.

"I'm – I'm looking for the owner. Sadiq," I say, looking around.

"He's in the office. Let me take you," he offers, coming out from behind the counter and leading the way to an inner hallway with the walls lined with big posters of different Afrobeat musicians: Fela Kuti, Burna Boy, Davido, Wizkid, Fireboy, Adekunle Gold, Mr. Eazi. I follow him until he stops just after a black-and-white large print of Joeboy covered in a cloud of smoke. He points at a brown door with intricate paneling that looks like a beehive and gestures for me to go through.

"Thanks," I mutter quietly.

Is it right for me to just show up like this unannounced? The last time I did something like this – well, that was the end of that relationship. Before I can discourage myself, I slowly push the door open and find myself in an office that doesn't exactly look like one. I see more posters on a wall and there's a pool table with multicolored balls scattered all over its green surface.

And there he is, Sadiq. Even with his back to me, I recognize his frame in the navy blue T-shirt and blue jeans, leaning over the table as he concentrates on hitting a ball with the black pool stick.

"Just cancel your flight and we can go together next week." It was Lilybeth, or Halima, or whatever she calls herself these days. She's wearing a tight white top over beige wide-legged pants, chewing gum loudly as she plays with her pool stick.

"I've told you over and over again that you have to choose your battles very carefully. This whole thing won't be easy," he makes the shot and looks up at her. She gestures behind him and he turns around. There's surprise written all over his face when he sees me.

"Sorry, I should have known that you were busy," I turn around and close the door behind me. But before I can take a step down the hallway, I hear him following me.

"Hafsat," he calls. I ignore him and keep walking. "Hafsat," he repeats again as I feel his hand on my elbow. "Where are you going?"

I pull my hand away. " It's okay. You don't h – you don't have to explain anything. It's not like you owe me anything." This was what Adda S meant about not knowing where exactly you stand in someone's life.

"Hey," he stops me with his hands on my shoulder.

I gently shrug him off as I turn around to look at him. "All day, I've been worried sick wondering if something happened to you but you're fine. You're just here with –" I realize that I'm raising my voice and take a second to collect myself. I exhale. "You guys are all the same," I say, walking away from him.

He follows me. "Can we talk about this inside?"

"Nothing to talk about. Go and play your snooker."

"Listen." There's something about the finality of his tone that stops me in my tracks. "Please."

"And your ' gym partner'?" I make air quotes in the air with my fingers, and his eyes narrow as his brows knit closer to each other.

"Who? Lily?" he sighs. "Just come inside, Hafsat."

I adjust my veil to cover my neck as we walk slowly back to the office and he does a double take at my hands like he's looking for something, and his eyes return to mine. We walk back to his office, he opens the door for me, and I walk in.

The pool table is now abandoned. "Please sit down," he says, pointing further into the office to a part well hidden from the door that it's easy to miss. Just behind the wall to the side of the pool table is a wide desk with two chairs in front of it. On the left are two black leather sofas – one empty and the other, a lean guy in a white polo shirt and jeans is watching a golf tournament on the wall-mounted curved television. He's around Sadiq's age, and they have similar features – the waves in their dark hair and dark brown skin. Lilybeth is laying down with her head on his thighs as she scrolls through her phone.

"Oh you are back Sadiq. I was just about to call and tell you we're leaving, then I remembered that you don't have a phone anymore," she sits up and starts to wear her shoes. "*Habibi*, love, let's give them some privacy."

Oh.

"Hafsat – Halima, Assad. Guys, meet Hafsat," Sadiq introduces us, squeezing a black stress relief ball I didn't notice him holding earlier.

They are already standing up to leave when I say hey. Halima starts to clear the plates and Pepsi cans that crowd the table in front of the sofa.

"Lily, don't worry about that. Someone will come pick them up."

"It's okay, I've got it," she says as she takes the last can and puts it on the tray. "*Yadai*, Hafsat?" How's Ilham?" she smiles at me.

"She's fine. She's on her way to Dubai," my voice sounds a bit higher than usual. As Halima and I exchange pleasantries, I hear Sadiq promising to call Assad when he gets his phone. They talk about canceling a flight and calling someone's brother. After a short exchange of polite goodbyes, they leave.

When we are alone again, Sadiq looks at me. "*Kin ki zama*; you've refused to sit," he squeezes the ball again. I look behind me and sink into one of the black sofas. He slowly examines my hands and his gaze travels back to my face with a smile tugging the corners of his lips. "So, I guess you disappointed Bashir last night?"

Oh, that's why he keeps looking at my hands – to see if I'm wearing a ring on my finger. "You knew about that?" I knew that there was something off about how he sounded when he called me as I was getting ready to go to *The Six*. "How?"

"Someone he told thought that I should know," he shrugs as he sits down on the other sofa, away from mine. "Abuja is a small place."

"Why didn't you warn me when you called?"

"Why would I do that?" The smile leaves his face as he leans back into the sofa. "I needed to watch it play out, to know whether or not I'm just a rebound, or someone holding space until your man came to his senses."

"He's definitely not my man, and you are *not* a rebound."

He looks from my lips back to my eyes and the mood in the room changes. "I know that now." His heavy gaze burns into mine and I feel my heartbeat start to pick up.

I look away and glance at the television. "What happened to your phone?"

"Managed to get stolen somewhere between the wedding reception and the airport, but I ordered one this morning. It should be arriving soon," he glances at his wristwatch.

"You could have used someone's phone to tell me."

"Honestly, I couldn't; I didn't know if you were engaged or not."

I roll my eyes. As if I would ever get engaged to Bashir. "I thought you weren't picking my calls, I – I kinda freaked out," I'm looking up at him as I speak. He raises his eyebrow like my admission surprised him, then he nods slowly like he understands my concern. I exhale, "and when I saw *her* here. I thought –" I swallow, "it just felt so familiar –" my voice trails off.

The room stays silent for a few seconds as his gaze holds mine. Finally, he squeezes the ball again and says, "I am not your ex, Hafsat."

I look up at him and there's this look in his eyes; it's the way I've always wished to be looked at. It's a quiet reassurance that there's no one else, that I am not alone in this. He stands up from his sofa and sits next to me, his thighs brushing mine as he reaches for my fingers.

"You should be able to give me the benefit of doubt and not jump to the worst possible conclusion at times like this. When you walked out of here, I wondered what would have happened if her boyfriend wasn't here with us. How would I have gotten you to believe that she is just a friend."

I didn't even know I was dealing with unhealed trauma from walking in on Bashir and that girl at Bellanova until I was walking down the hallway to Sadiq's office and wondering what to expect.

"I probably wouldn't have believed anything you told me." Not after what Bashir did.

"I understand. It's a perfectly logical reaction. But can you see how it can cause problems for us when there aren't any?" His fingers graze mine lightly, "Assad's family are the only family I have on my mother's side.

They don't want him with Lily because she's a model, even though they've been dating for years now," he explains. I nod quietly, feeling a little silly about how I stormed out of his office earlier and how long it took him to convince me to come back inside. He continues, "I'm never going to give you a reason to doubt how I feel about you," he promises.

Listening to him speak makes me realize that I need to unlearn what I'm used to and Adda S's idea of labels. Relationships are more than labels – how a person treats you is what should matter the most. I don't want to define this. This – whatever we have here – is perfect just the way it is.

There's a knock on the door, and Promise walks in with a box. "You have a delivery."

"Finally!" He turns to me, "have you ever had Kwame's grilled fish?"

"Who is Kwame?" I ask as he unboxes a phone.

"The finest spice specialist in town. Have you been living under a rock?" he teases, then looks up at Promise again, "bring our menu; she needs to testify to Kwame's skills."

* * *

The following Saturday, when Sadiq comes to pick me up, he goes into the living room to greet Umm'Hafsa. Daddy is out playing golf with an old friend who's visiting from Belgium. Alone in my room, I can't decide what to wear; I finally settle on a straight dress made from a light pink lace with peach and grey woven designs. I wrap its matching scarf around my head after I wear my jewelry and throw on a grey veil over my shoulders. On days like this, I wish my sisters were around; Shatu would have helped me decide between the crossbody and the satchel bag and Sara might have gotten me to wear an Abaya instead.

I leave the room before I decide to change the whole outfit. I take one last look at the mirror before I leave my room and walk down the stairs, glad that the uncertainty I feel isn't showing on my features. I am anxious. Sure, I've met Bashir's mum at events in the past, but this is going to be the first time I'm going to a guy's house for the sole purpose of meeting his mother – well, stepmother in this case. What if she doesn't like me?

When Sadiq asked Umm'Hafsa for permission yesterday if he could take me, I was surprised that she agreed immediately. I even overheard her telling daddy about it this morning at breakfast, just as I tiptoed quietly downstairs to eat alone.

"As-sallamu Alaikum," I say as I enter the living room downstairs.

"Wa alaikumus salam," they answer. Sadiq smiles appreciatively as he sees me walk in; he's wearing a black kaftan and trousers. Umm'Hafsa glances up to see what I'm wearing and looks back at the television, her face expressionless.

"We won't be long. I'll bring her back home before *Maghrib, Insha Allah,*" Sadiq says as I open the fridge behind the sitting area to get a bottle of water for the road.

"I have no doubt. You have been a man of your word so far. *A gai da mai jiki*; greet her for me," she says. Sadiq must have told her about Hajiya Amina's frequent trips to see doctors when I was upstairs.

I bid my mother goodbye in the cold way I am now used to. Since I got the results from the test, my interactions with her have been restrictive and cold. I avoid going into the dining room when I know she's there and when I get home, I'm usually in my room or the Game room catching up on shows, and that's where Sadiq usually meets me most evenings when he visits.

As we walk out of the house and get into his Range Rover, I wait until he starts driving off before I speak, "you know you could have just waited for me in the car right?"

"I wanted to let your mom know that I would bring you back on time," he raises his hands at the security guards as we drive past them. "I can't wait for when I no longer have to drop you back home."

I chuckle to myself, "what do you mean?"

"When we get married," he says like it's something he has thought about.

179

"I can't wait for your text to read *come home*, instead of *come over*.

I remain silent on the entire ride, listening to the songs that play: *Bloody Samaritan*, Gyakie's *Forever*, and Wande Coal's *Again*. Noting that all the songs I've mentioned I like somehow gain repeat status on his playlist. What makes Sadiq so alluring isn't the fact that he is good-looking or that he dresses well; it's that underneath what I thought was a cold exterior, he's actually the sweetest and most respectful guy I've ever come across.

A few minutes later, he presses the horn and I look up to see the high white iron gate slide open, revealing a long driveway lined with tall palm trees. On the left is a well-maintained green hedge that continues as we drive in. We pass multiple peahens and peacocks with their colorful plumage in full display, and still, there was no sign of the house in my line of sight. The vast greenery continues in both directions until, after what feels like a whole minute of driving, I see the white mansion finally appear in the distance. As we drive closer to it, its sheer size seemed to dwarf all the trees on its sides. A white-stoned water fountain with three big flat stones and lights illuminate the space where the cars were parked.

This is my first time inside, the one time I came here to pick Sadiq up, I waited outside the gate in my car. I know that this particular part of Asokoro had the most magnificent mansions in Abuja, but this is pure opulence and grandeur carefully hidden behind the high walls. This is old money – quiet and unimposing.

Sadiq comes to my side and we walk into the main house together, "She's very excited to meet you."

"I feel like I should have worn something else," my breath is shaky as I exhale.

"This is my favorite color on you. You look beautiful," he says as he opens the door. We walk into what looks like little Arabia – as we walk through mirrored hallways into a large circular gold room, I'm a little taken aback by how much the interior reminds me of the hotels my family and I stay in when we go to Dubai or Doha. The furniture – about three sets of them – are gold and light brown, complimenting the flamboyant designs on the wallpaper. The massive chandelier hanging from the white ceilings with gold-trimmed panels and yellow LED lights is rose gold. The brown marbled floors are so well-polished I can almost see my reflection in them. I have always believed that too much gold in interior decor was out of style because there's the risk of it looking tacky if not done properly, but this room is timeless, and every part of it is exquisite.

We sit in silence as I take slow, deep breaths trying to be less anxious. Every now and then, Sadiq will look up across the room at the Persian-styled archway above the double doors. When the doors finally open, I perceive her scent even before I see her walk in. She is wearing a light green boubou with 3D flower embroidery around the neck, and she looks to be in her late forties. Her face breaks into a wide smile as soon as she sees us and begins to walk towards us, dragging her left leg slowly in an unrushed manner masking the pain Sadiq told me about.

"Hafsatuuu," she calls out to me in a sing-song manner that makes me feel immediately welcome. The smile never leaves her face, revealing a golden tooth, as she slowly sinks into one of the chairs with a red pillow behind it.

"Good evening," I greet her in Hausa, getting up from the chair and crouching as I do so.

"No, no, no. Please sit down," she says, and I obey. "*Sannu*, Hafsatu, my grandmother's namesake," she answers with a twinkle in her eye. "How are you?"

"Alhamdulillah. *Ya jiki?* How are you feeling? I hope you're not angry that I haven't come to greet you since you returned."

"*Wallahi*, I'm not angry. I understand how these things are," she laughs. "I'm just happy to finally meet Sadiq's Hafsat," she says, smiling at him and I hear the sounds of cutlery like someone was setting the table in room adjacent, the dining room maybe.

Sadiq looks up from his phone, "I hear a date has been fixed for Madina's wedding." As if he doesn't want me to feel left out of the conversation, he adds quietly to me, "Madina is my stepsister. She lives in Kaduna."

She looks at him, "yes, her mother called me this morning to tell me the good news. In fact your uncle called me just after I finished praying *Asr* to inform me," she laughs, returning her gaze to me. "I told him that he should expect you soon because you're planning to go and see him regarding the visit to Hafsat's parents."

"Yes, Imran told me he's traveling to Egypt after Madina's wedding. When he gets back I'll meet with him and we can decide on a date to go see them."

"That's great. May Allah spare our lives until then," her hands rub her thighs gently as she prays. Finally, she says, "*ni kam, a ina na san fuskan nan?* Where do I know this face from?" she wonders almost to herself, then, "Hafsatu, haven't we met somewhere before?"

I glance at Sadiq, who just smiles at me. "It's possible," I say politely, even though I know I've never met her anywhere. I wouldn't have forgotten. Her face isn't one that one would forget easily – she has striking features and a complexion so light that I wonder what her DNA Ancestry profile will look like.

"Maybe on a flight or at a wedding," Sadiq offers.

"Possibly," she agrees, although, from the way her forehead creases as she peers at me, it's apparent she's trying to recall exactly where she has seen me before. "There's food for you. Sadiq, the dining room is set. You both have to eat before leaving."

I bite my lip, and sensing my discomfort, Sadiq declines politely, "actually, I have to drop Hafsat back home."

"Why are you leaving so soon?" she asks surprisedly.

I only smile in response as I look downwards, but Sadiq answers, "I'll be back to eat dinner after I drop her. Her mom is expecting her back on time *ne*, that's why."

"*Toh shikenan*, okay then. Thanks for bringing her," she reaches for a big white paper bag I didn't even notice was tucked beside the arm of her chair, and she pushes it towards me. "Here's a little something for you, dear."

"*Haba*, you shouldn't have bothered yourself."

"No way! It's not done. My daughter-in-law can't leave here empty-handed. This is your first visit *fa*."

"Thank you," I say, collecting the heavy paper bag.

As we get up to leave, she adds, "please extend my regards to your parents. Sadiq, drive carefully, *ka ji ko*? You know these Abuja drivers."

"*Sai anjima*," I say, getting up.

"Goodbye, Hafsatu."

Hafsatu

Sometimes, while spending time with Sadiq, I find myself getting carried away by how perfect everything is. It almost feels like he's a missing piece in a puzzle I thought was complete. My relationship with him so far, has been the best in my life. Even though I've had a few boyfriends since secondary school, with him, everything seems so un-chaotic – the way we fuse our lives together is the easiest thing I've ever done. I find myself on his phone with his family members often because every time he talks to them when he's with me, at some point, he'll say, "No, I'm not home, I'm with Hafast," then give me the phone to say hello. I would then find myself with one of his stepsisters, a friend, Imran, Assad, and sometimes Hajiya Amina.

Same with my FaceTime video calls with my sisters, which are now punctuated with Sadiq and Shatu going on a tangent about the latest Marvel shows: *Loki* or *WandaVision*, nothing I had particular interest in. During Sara's study break, when she calls me, she's often with her new bestie, Sadiq's sister, Fatima. The four of us usually spend hours making plans for their graduation and where we'll stay when we visit them.

He has also become a regular face not just at our house, where we spend most evenings watching *Squid Games* in the Game room with Mohammed, but at the back office in *H&I*, and I spend most of my free time during the day at *Ranchers* as he teaches me how to play pool whenever I need a break from work.

"You should come to the gym with me someday," he says to me one evening as we eat dinner at *Cilantro*. Tuesday evenings have somehow become date night, even though we never really talked about it; it just happened seamlessly, effortlessly.

I mock frown as I add salt to my food, "are you calling me fat?"

He shakes his head, "even if I did, you love yourself too much to be bothered by it." Well, he's got that part right. "But, no. You're perfect, and you know it," he cuts into a piece of his chicken breast, picks it up with his fork, and brings it towards my mouth.

I lean forward and open my mouth. I love that he *always* shares his food with me. We always order different things, and a few minutes into our meals, he'll unfailingly give me a piece of his to taste. I chew the meat gently and raise my brow at him, "and what part of me is the most perfect?" Sometimes one is just in the mood to hear unending compliments; today is one of those days.

His thumb reaches for my mouth as he slowly wipes a bit of sauce from my lower lip. "I'd rather show you," he lowers his voice as his eyes slowly leave my lips and meet mine.

It takes everything in me to hide the smile forming on my face. "Show me?"

He pushes his plate away and leans back into his chair. "Yup. As soon as your father gives my uncles a date. I heard that in your family, your uncles are fond of prolonging the investigations. I hope it's not true." There was just the slightest hint of impatience in his voice.

I don't know if it's possible to fall deeper for this guy, but the best part of our relationship is the most surprising one – his restraint. In my other relationships, kisses were regular, pecks here and French kisses there. But with Sadiq, it has been surprisingly more *halal* than the rest. Surprising because you can cut the sexual tension between us with a knife. Just sitting opposite him in this sparse restaurant, and he has already undressed me twice with his eyes – once when I walked in and a second time as I looked at the menu. Yet, he always keeps his hands to himself.

"You're investigating my family's methods now?" I take a sip of my virgin mojito.

"I just want this to go smoothly without any hiccups. I heard about the stress your cousins husbands went through before their weddings."

"That's my dad's older brother, he's pretty old-school. But you have nothing to worry about; daddy's cool."

"Insha Allah," he watches as I reply to a text message on my phone. "So, is that a yes to the gym?"

"I'm not coming to the gym with you." I love him, but public gyms are where I draw the line. "Maybe when you're back from South Africa," I add when I see him narrow his eyes.

A week later, with Sadiq in Johannesburg, I am at *Figaro's* to pick up Pizza for dinner. The rice and beans they made at home didn't appeal to me, and even the pasta the cook made when I asked for something else did nothing to pique my appetite. So, I went looking for takeout. I just paid for my order when an unsaved number calls me. If the past few weeks have taught me anything, it's that Bashir has no shortage of unknown numbers to call me with. I stare at my phone until it stops ringing and continue scrolling through social media until my pizza is ready. When I finally make my way outdoors with a pizza box in hand, I see Bashir coming out of a black Corvette parked a few cars from mine.

"Hafsatu Bebi," he sneers as he walks towards me with his hands in his pocket. "I saw your car as I was driving past and stopped to see if it's really you, *saboda yanzu ganin ki sai da visa*, because nowadays, one has to apply for a visa to see you."

"*Toh*, Bashir. Congrats on getting your visa approved." I keep my sunglasses on and don't look up at him as I open my door. I get into my car and place the pizza on the passenger seat. As I stretch my hand out to close my door, he holds it.

"So where's Sadiq?" His voice is laced with something between anger, jealousy, and disbelief.

"*Lafiyan shi kalau*; he's very fine," I answer curtly.

He starts laughing as he opens the door even wider. "So, it's true? I introduce you to my friend and you go behind my back to date him. Did this start while we were still together?"

I push my sunglasses to the top of my head, "first of all, I do not owe *you* an explanation but just so you know, Sadiq and I never spoke until you and I broke up, so don't come at me with all this bullshit."

"I can't believe you turned me down for Sadiq." His body is still braced between the door and the body of my car. "You know he's just using you to get back at me, *ko*?"

I roll my eyes as I reach for the door, "Bashir, please. I don't have time for this."

"You don't believe me? Ask him about Kalie. Maybe you'll know the truth then."

As he closes my door, I see a glint of wickedness or something just as sinister pass his face. It disappears almost as quickly as it got there, but I didn't think too much of it, not until the following week when I see a post by *Bujgist* on my feed, the first one in weeks.

Exclusive Blind Item

They tried to bury us, they did not know that we are seeds! We will grow and keep growing until we uproot the worst kept secrets that Buj residents hide underneath their holy garments.
Speaking of garments, this one claims to put them on people but all this while she is secretly taking hers off for the camera. Yes! This is a bujgist exclusive. You heard it here first! Her name starts with 'Had I known' and ends with 'Two for trouble.'
We are talking about really shameless pictures and if she tries to shut us down this time, we will publish them! Or better yet, 100,000 Likes, and I promise to publish the first one. Hint: RED LACE!

I read the post over. And over. *They tried to bury us? Garments? Starts with Had I known?*

The more I reread the post, the more I am certain that it is about me. The poorly done and not-so-subtle references to my name and business, and the worst part? Red lace.

In one of the pictures I sent to Bashir while we were dating, I was wearing a red lace push-up babydoll. I even remember the day I bought it – at *Victoria's Secret* on one of our shopping sprees last summer with Ilham. After we picked out regular underwear, sleepwear, and loungewear, we started goofing around with the mannequins that displayed sexy, naughty lingerie, and I decided to buy a few just for fun. In those days, things were going great with Bashir, and he always wanted pictures of me because of how much he missed me. "Not regular pictures like the ones on your Instagram," he said. "Something no one else has seen."

One evening, a few days before our return to Abuja, my whole family visited *Universal Studios Hollywood*, and I stayed back at the apartment, blaming a headache. Bashir was already halfway back to London after spending my birthday with me and my sisters, and I surprised him with a few pictures in some of the lingerie I got. I thought they would be enough, but only a few days later, he continued asking for more, with less on.

I glance back at my screen now. People are already tagging people and encouraging others to like and tag more people so that they can get to 100,000 Likes. If those pictures end up on the internet, I'll never be able to show my face again.

I scroll through my contacts and find Bashir's number, unblock him, and within seconds, his messages start flooding my inbox. I ignore all of them and call him instead. It keeps ringing, and he doesn't pick up. *Oh my God.* With shaky fingers, I start typing a text to him: *What did you do with my pictures?*

I read the message, and then I start to backspace until I delete it. Sending a text is a bad idea; if he showed someone my pictures, who knows what he'll do with this message? Imagine a message like this with my name on it, ending up on *Bujgist* with the pictures – it'll solidify the so-called 'evidence.'

I call him back and start pacing my office as the ringing continues for what seems like forever. When he finally picks up, the background is noisy; I can hear voices belonging to guys and girls laughing.

Are they laughing at me? "Bashir?"

"Madam, so you still have my number?" he laughs, "So, tell me, to what do I owe this pleasure?"

I cover my eyes with my palm, trying to keep calm, but I honestly can't. *What if I'm on speaker right now? What if other people are listening? Is Bujgist one of the people he hangs out with? What if they are with him right now? All*

188

these nerve-wracking thoughts cross my mind one after the other, but I'm in such a state of panic at the pictures leaking, at my parents seeing them, my siblings, Sadiq, or his family. *Oh my God.*

"Bashir, I need to see you." I can't be direct in my conversation with him because who knows if he's recording this call?

I hear a shuffle in the background and then, "you can come and meet me. We're at *Zuma Grill.*"

There is no way on earth I'm driving to meet him at the grill at *Hilton.* I'm a little stunned at this unusual cockiness in his voice that he didn't have in the past when talking to me. It's crisp and rude, and it's all I need to drop whatever subtlety I'm hinting at. It tells me that he knows exactly why I'm calling. I take a deep breath and ask, "what did you do with my pictures?"

The background chatter stops, maybe he moved away, or maybe, they kept quiet to listen. Whatever it is, there's too much adrenaline pumping in me that I don't care.

"What pictures?" he asks. From the way he talks, I can tell that his mouth is full, like he is eating something.

"The Cali pictures. You never deleted them like I asked you to, did you?"

"Oh, those pictures? Why, what happened?" He's trying to play dumb. He's always on his phone, and he's always on Instagram. If I have seen the latest blind item, I'm sure he has too.

"I hope you're not trying to get back at me by leaking those pictures?" I ask. He's so quiet from the other end that I think the connection is off. "Hello? Hello?"

"I'm here." The smug way he answers does nothing to hide the arrogance in his voice as he says, "Well, now my mother will know why *I* broke off our engagement."

My heart drops.

"What? Bashir, are you –" I start, but he hangs up before I finish.

Now my mother will know why I broke off our engagement, the words repeat in my head. I'm in deep trouble.

I leave my office, walking down the hallway into Ilham's office. She hardly stays in there, but it's the end of the month, so I know she is working on payroll and balancing vendor accounts and also trying to do the work she missed while in Dubai. She's on a call when I come in, and from the voice on speaker, I can tell that it's a recent client whose wedding is coming up in a few weeks. She looks up from her laptop when I walk in – looking at me worriedly as I close the door and pace up and down the room as I wait.

"The design that was created for you has tulle underneath, but if you want that part removed that's no problem, the stylists will have it sorted out when you come for your second fitting," Ilham says.

"No, *baki gane ba*, you don't understand. I love the dress, I just want to make sure that no one else will be wearing something similar. You know there's a line-up of weddings this month and next."

"Imitation is the highest form of flattery. If other brides start to copy your style, take it as a compliment, Jamila," she rolls her eyes. A few seconds later, she ends the call after reassuring the bride she has nothing to worry about and continues typing on her keyboard, shaking her head as she looks at the computer screen. "Please promise me you won't be one of these brides that need constant reassurance every five minutes, because I will personally strangle you." She looks up at me pacing about her office, "and what's got your panties in a bunch?"

"Ha – have you seen the *Bujgist* post?"

"*Bujgist?* They're back?" she picks up her phone, types, and starts scrolling immediately. I watch her face as she finds the post and her eyes squint as she reads, then her eyebrows shoot up. She stands up and drags her gaze from the screen of her phone to my face, "wait, this is you?" she rereads the clues. "They are obviously hinting at the *H&I* post from months ago – garments. So unoriginal! *Ha* and *Tu* – they are making it look like they have dirt on you." She looks at my face again, and a shocked expression takes over her features, "wait, this is an empty threat, *right?*" she asks, as though afraid of the answer. I slowly shake my head no. I can feel the tears forming in my eyes. When she speaks again, her voice is a whisper and a scream simultaneously: "How?"

"I sent some to Bash –"

"Yeah, but you cropped your face out, didn't you?"

I shake my head again.

"You didn't crop your face out?" she asks as if there's a universal memo that teaches you to crop your face out of risqué pictures. If there's such a memo, it definitely skipped me.

"I didn't know. I didn't – I didn't expe –" My words fail me. I didn't expect that someone I thought I loved, someone who said he loved me, would ever do this to me. *"Bashir ya gama da ni,* Ilham; Bashir has finished me. What am I gonna do?" I ask; the shakiness in my voice is hard to miss.

She comes to my side and nudges me towards a chair. "We have to make sure those pictures don't see the light of day. Plans are being made for his family to meet yours…." She's back to doing the whisper-scream thing with her voice. She doesn't have to say it, but in our part of the world, marriages can be canceled for much less. This will cause an uproar. I can't bear to imagine how disappointed my family will be. My sisters both follow *Bujgist.* Have they seen this? Have they clued in? I'm the worst possible role model to both of them.

I am sitting down helplessly, all the anger I had in me a few minutes ago has transferred to Ilham, who is now pacing about her office. My hands hover above the *Contact Us* button on the *Bujgist* profile. Should I reach out to them and negotiate? What if it backfires? A part of me knows that it is useless because when the *H&I* Blind item came out, I tried contacting them to retract their post, but to no avail.

"I hate the lawlessness of this country," she reads the post again as she hisses. "If we were elsewhere, this is a police matter. Bashir will end up on a sex offender registry for harassing you this way!" She sits next to me now, exhales, and takes my hand in hers, "Bebi, I know this is the last thing you *wanna* do, but you *have* to get Sadiq involved."

My stomach drops. "Sadiq? No way!" I widen my eyes, "I have to fix this before he finds out. I have to find out how to contact them and get them to hand over my pictures to me. I'll pay."

"How?" she's whispering now. "You don't even know how to reach them.

Nobody knows who they are. The last time they came for us, it was Sadiq who silenced them for months. So if anyone has the power to do that, it's him, babe. You have to tell him."

Exasperated, I stand up and sit back down on the chair, "I can't. *Da wana ido zan kalle shi?* How can I face him and admit that there's a possibility my nudes are floating around somewhere?" I bury my head in my hands. My relationship with him is at a good place. We are happy. And now this bombshell!

"If these assholes do what they are threatening to do, he'll see it in a few hours online. Which is worse – hearing it from you or seeing it while he's hanging with his guys?" she implores quietly, her face mirroring the worry on mine.

"I can't," I shake my head, tears falling from my eyes uncontrollably.

"Call him."

Sadiq

A contract Usman and I submitted a bid for finally got the green light after months. I'm going over the procurement letter from the Ministry of Works and Housing when Hafsat's call comes in. I pick up after a few rings. "Hey, B?" I clear my throat as my voice is hoarse from hours of not talking.

"Sadiq?" her voice has taken the tone of a vet about to tell a six-year-old that their puppy had died. Then came a sniff. *She's crying.*

"What's wrong?" I ask. When I saw her this morning, she was in high spirits; she had gotten us tickets to a movie about tackling corruption in Nigerian politics that she wanted us to go to this evening. A friend of hers from secondary school produced and directed it and she wanted us to go and support the debut movie-maker.

"Um... I... havetotalktoyou," her words are incoherent and rushed. I can barely make sense of what she is saying.

"Breathe, B. What are you saying?"

"Have you seen the *Bujgist* post?" her voice increased by a slight octave, and I hear more sniffing.

Oh, they are back online? "No," I answer; I haven't been on Instagram all afternoon. I put the phone on speaker as I open the purple violet app icon on my phone. "What's going on?" I go to the search tab, type *bujgist* and click on the first account that comes up.

As I read the post, Hafsat is talking, "Bashir is trying to get back at me. I sent him these pictures while we were dating... I was so stup –" I stop hearing what she's saying. The post is an apparent dig at her, talking about pictures of her. Judging by the number of likes the post already has, they are going to leak in a matter of minutes. I sit up in my chair and scroll through the comments. There are a few wrong guesses, but there's a pinned comment on top, which has even more replies and over two thousand likes: *I bet it's Hafsatu Gaya.*

Fuck! I scroll down a few other comments, and each one is worse than the last: *'How the mighty have fallen, KimK wanna be'; 'Bujgist, abeg send your account details, we'll pay to see it'; 'Hausa Mia Khalifa.'*

My temple starts to throb and I refrain from picking up their Instagram handles, reverse searching their email addresses and finding their identities and addresses and...

"Sadiq, are you there?" her voice is a scared whisper.

"Hafsat, what is this?" my voice sounds harsher than I intend.

"It's Bashir, he said – he said – I sent –" she is incoherent again. Either that or my brain is filled with so much rage that I can't make sense of the sentences that she is saying. All I hear is Bashir.

Bashir.

Of course. The pictures he showed me months ago – pictures of her, half naked in lingerie. I never expected Bashir to go this low. I know he's a low life, but this? This is vile, depraved even. His ego took a beating at the embarrassing way his botched proposal went. Unfortunately, he was armed with just the right ammunition to get her executed on the internet's firing squad. Her pictures. Nothing that can't be found in music videos or college movies, but the fact that it is a racy picture of someone who is usually covered up in public has gathered it a lot of interest. The deepest cut to a girl like Hafsat – to any girl really – is to leave her exposed in this manner. No one cares who she sent the pictures to or if he sent her a hundred dick pics back. All that matters is that she has been caught in a compromising situation and will be left hanging to dry. In a society as judgmental as ours, social standing is not only a form of currency, it also goes hand-in-hand with family name and honor. Her pictures leaking will be social suicide for her.

"Sadiq, please say something."

I take the phone off speaker and return it to my ear, "*Ina kike?* Where are you?"

"I –I'm in the car at *H&I*. I couldn't stay in the store, it got busy all of a sudden like they came to –" her voice trails off.

"Wait there," I stand up, pick up my keys and wallet. "I'll come get you."

"No, I'll come to you," she says.

"Okay," I disconnect the call and call Jide.

* * *

Twenty minutes later, when Hafsat's white Mercedes pulls up to *Ranchers*, the slight drizzle escalates to a torrential downpour as the darkened sky makes it look later than 5 pm. I walk out without an umbrella to where she parked right beside my car.

Her door opens, and she steps out, crying, "I messed up, I messed up," she avoids my eye as she speaks, readjusting her white scarf to cover her hair. Her eyes are smudged in black, the mascara streaks her tears and it is smeared around her reddened eyes. She is wearing the same outfit from this morning – a long white dress shirt wrapped around her curves. "I messed up," she repeats again as she finally looks up at me, wiping the rain and tears off her face with the back of her hand.

I remove my lightweight blazer and cover her head with it, but it is of no use in the heavy rain, as she's already drenched, and now, so am I. I lead her to the empty thatched hut.

"What exactly is going on?" I try to keep my voice leveled as I speak to her.

She covers her mouth with her hands, her eyes downcast, breathing heavily as rivulets of rain fall off the side of her face. "My pic... my pictures. Bashir had some pictures of me and he said he would – he said – *Bujgist* has them," she chokes on her words. The sound of the rain splattering around us drowns her sniffles.

"So he knows about us?" It's the only explanation.

The lightning lit her features, her high cheekbones, and full quivering lips, as she nods briefly. The thunder that follows is loud.

"Is… is your face visible in any of them?"

She covers her face with her hands and starts crying uncontrollably, her sobs wracking through her in gut-wrenching sobs.

Shit.

I pull her closer to my chest, and her tears soak my already damp shirt. It hurts to see her like this. Her tears go on for a while, starting afresh every few seconds.

"Let's go inside," I say when she quietens down, my hand on her back as I lead her into my office. She is quiet the entire walk down, her phone beeps twice, and over the disheartened slump of her shoulders, I see her reject Ilham's calls.

I push the door open and wait for her to walk in. Jide is already sitting in front of my desk when we go in. He turns around and looks at us as I close the door.

"Jide, this is Hafsat. Hafsat, Jide. He's on my legal team." I pull out a seat for her and push a bottle of water and a box of tissue to her side of the desk before walking around and sitting on the swivel chair opposite them.

I see her eyes travel to the tablet in front of him on the table, which is on the *bujgist* post, with 98,000 likes now and a much higher number in comments.

"Revenge porn is becoming more common now, unfortunately," Jide says, stating facts. I watch as Hafsat cringes at the word he uses to describe the situation. She looks down at her hands, and it's clear that she's ashamed, an emotion threatening to eat her alive.

Jide leans back into the leather chair, "section 170 of the Criminal Code here in Nigeria –"

I exhale, "English, my guy." It's getting hard to hide my impatience and anger. The clock is ticking.

"Well, if the pictures are eventually posted, the person responsible for the leak is liable to one year in prison or a fine."

I scoff. Nigerian laws fail to acknowledge the law of exclusion that status grants a select set of its citizens. Maybe the blogger, but Bashir is not going to prison for one year over what everyone will call Hafsat a willing party. More importantly, I'm trying to stop the pictures from being posted, not punish the offenders.

"Unfortunately, because it is an anonymous blog, ascertaining ownership in cases like this can take years, but there are many loopholes around it.

I pinch the bridge of my nose as I look at the time, "I can't have the picture on the internet. The internet never forgets and even if it's deleted afterwards, it's never really gone." I look at Hafsat. She's picking the colors off her nails nervously.

"That's very true," he nods. "We can do a *Cease and Desist* like last time. It'll buy us some time and maybe she can talk to the person and make them see reason –"

Hafsat raises her head and her eyes are bloodshot. I shake my head; I will not have my woman at Bashir's mercy, begging him to save her honor. I will never give him that satisfaction. "That's out of the question."

"Okay, I can start the paperwork for the *Cease and Desist*."

"You do that. My IT guy was able to trace the IP address registrant so I have a name and address. Your guy from MTN verified it for me last month." I scroll through my messages until I get to a forwarded message and I pass my phone to Jide.

"Hadi Bilal. There's even a phone number and address, so that makes it easier. I can call as her legal representative and press charges based on harassment and defamation."

Hafsat takes a few tissues from the box and dabs her eyes with them as I nod towards Jide. He brings out his phone, dials the number, and leaves it on speakerphone.

After a few rings, a male voice picks up. "Hello?"

"Hello, good afternoon. Am I speaking with Hadi Bilal of House number 3, Phase A layout Kuje?"

"Who is this?"

"Is your mother Malama Jummai, that works at Samara Stores?"

"How do you know my mother? Who are you?" The voice asks again.

"I'll take that as an affirmative answer. Please bear in mind that this call is being recorded and can be used in future court proceedings. My name is Barrister Jide Moshood of JNP solicitors. I'm calling to serve you with a *Cease and Desist* on behalf of my client on a recent post made by your Instagram account, *Bujgist.*"

Hadi remains silent, so Jide continues. "There are also charges of defamation and harassment faced by my client by the comments made on your recent post. I will like to bring your attention to the Criminal Code Act and Cybercrimes prohibition and prevention act of 2015, for which you are liable to a 7 million naira fine or a 3-year jail term."

"Excuse me, sir, I don't have any picture. The contact paid for the post and promised to send the pictures to me to post once I get the 100,000 likes."

I gesture to Jide to mute the call, and he hurriedly does. "Ask him who the contact is." I know it's Bashir; I just need to hear it on a recording.

"Mr Bilal, who is this contact?"

"I don't know him, sir; he calls with unknown numbers."

"How does your contact intend to give you the pictures?"

"He said he'll send it through DM."

I take a pen and scribble on a notepad: *Get him to negotiate with his contact for exclusivity. Offer any amount necessary*, and I pass it to Jide.

Jide reads the note and says, "Hadi, you seem like a regular guy, a hustler. There might be a way to get you out of this mess."

* * *

Two and half hours later, I look outside my window to see that the rain has stopped and it's pitch black outside. Jide spent a better half of the past hour giving careful instructions to Hadi, who is now working with us to retrieve the pictures. He is maintaining his cover by saying he wants all available copies of the pictures as he wants his blog to be the only outlet with the exposé. Once he gets the flash drive, he'll hand over the pictures to Jide, who is on his way to Kuje, to meet with him. Hafsat was unusually quiet during the whole exchange.

I look at my wristwatch, "Let's go, I'll drop you home. I promised your mom you would stop going back late." She carries her half-empty bottle of water, and I pick up the contract and lock it in my safe, turning the knob to the security combination. My driver meets me by the main entrance and I turn to Hafsat, "he'll drive your car." She nods as she hands him the keys, and as we walk past her car and approach mine, the gravel path illuminated by the headlamps of my Audi A8 come on.

I wait for her to put her seatbelt on before I start driving. The music is off and the ride back to her parent's house is unusually quiet. I feel the dull throb of a stress-related migraine coming on, and I wonder how she must feel after the ordeal she has been through.

When we pull up past the gates, I park behind her father's car and wait for the driver to bring her keys after parking her car.

"*Gobe ka je Asokoro kawai,*" I tell him. I won't need his services the following day, so he can go to Asokoro where there might be errands for him to run for my stepmother. I need to monitor this situation closely and will stay home throughout instead of getting distracted at *Ranchers.*

I give Hafsat her keys and rest the back of my head on the headrest. It's only when I close my eyes that I realize it's been hours since I actually said a word to her, apart from when we left my office. I wait for her to open the door and leave, but she doesn't.

"Sadiq, please say something."

I open my eyes and can see that the lights in most sections of the house are on, which means she's back home early enough. I glance at her and my attention goes to how her hands go from pulling at her nails to straightening the invisible wrinkles on her dress to pulling her scarf over her damp hair. She looks so vulnerable and nervous, and I feel it too. I know what it would mean for us if those pictures come to light. First off, my uncle would not, under that circumstance, rally other family members to formally ask for her hand in marriage. Even if he doesn't see the pictures himself, someone will bring it to his attention as soon as it is known that she's the person I intend to marry. The thought of my family rejecting her makes my neck stiffen, and my heart skips a beat as if to remind me that she's the only one I have ever wanted.

"S-Sadiq," she says again, quietly as her voice breaks.

I sigh as I look into her eyes, "how are you feeling?"

She shakes her head, "horrible. I –I'm so sorry." I wonder why she is apologizing to me; a great injustice was done to *her*, then she adds, "look at all the trouble I made you go through."

I look outside my window, then at my phone. I click on the post again. So far, no update from *Bujgist*. The comments on the post are eager and waiting, reminding the account handler that they had fulfilled their part of the deal by making sure the post trended all day, with well over 102,000 likes.

"I guess I should tell you that I've seen the pictures," I say and her eyes widen at my statement. "He showed me just before we split *The Drop* and *Ranchers*."

A look of absolute devastation settles on her face, "he showed you? Did he show anyone else? Oh my God."

My phone beeps as a text message from Jide confirms that he successfully got the pictures, and I give him the address to meet us.

"Jide is bringing the flash here. Bashir fell for the exclusive deal, Hadi will go dark for a few weeks, and I'll have my IT guys monitor other bloggers for any chatter, but I doubt anything is going to come up. The worst is over."

"Thank you," she says quietly. She doesn't have to thank me. How would I have been able to sleep knowing that such pictures of the person I want to marry were threatening to land on the internet? "If you break up with me right now, I'll be hurt but I'll completely understand." There's a hint of sadness in her voice.

I don't think she realizes how much she owns me. "I need to ask: is there anything else I should know?"

She shakes her head as she looks at me earnestly, "no – wallahi, he's - he's the only person I ever sent pictures to."

I don't doubt her at all, not even for a second.

* * *

The domino effect starts as I drive home. It is clear; there's no denying it. I am angry – angry that someone can have such leverage over her. My blood boils as my thoughts plummet down the rabbit hole dug by the crude online comments in the deep burrows of my brain.

After I pray Isha and am in the small den by my home office, a small 9 by 5 room that the interior designer transformed into a prayer room, I pour myself a glass of water and walk into my bedroom to find my ibuprofen tablets for my migraine. I find the container just as my phone starts ringing through the empty apartment, and I walk back to my office to pick up the call. It's my cousin, Imran.

"Hello?" I tilt the small white medicine container until two tablets fall into my palm.

"Sadiq?" his voice comes through.

"Imran," I look at the white wall clocks showing multiple time zones on the back wall of my office and see that it's about 7 am in Toronto.

"Baba, *yane?* How you dey?"

"Alhamdulillah, just got back home. How's Nasreen and Khalil?"

"They are fine. Listen, I heard some disturbing rumor."

Shit. I add another tablet to the ones already in my hand and throw them back with the whole glass of water. He continues, "when you told me how far you wanted to take things between you and Bebi, you know I gave my full support – 100 percent, regardless of how Bashir might be affected.

But now, I'm hearing that there might be some... well, you know, some pictures of her floating around."

I close my eyes as I rub my forehead, my migraine is unbearable, but I know I have to sound as normal as I could. "What pictures, Imran?" I ask. The speed of light has nothing on how fast bad news travels in these parts.

"Nudes, I heard," he sounds certain. My glass cup clinks as I set it down on the table and sink into the chair. "Sadiq, you're my brother, so I'm going to be direct with you. In a man's life, *kana ji?* Can you hear me? There are girls we love, and there are girls we marry. Sometimes, they are not the same person," he lets out a sigh.

Has he always given such bad advice, or am I just noticing it more recently?

"If what I've heard is true," he continues, "and these pictures leak, there's no way you can marry her. Yes, you guys can continue with whatever you're doing, but you know that when it comes to marriage, it's just not possible. *Haba,* think about your sons in the future coming across a picture of their mother from the internet's deep archive, *ai wannan abun kunya ne, za a zage su da shi*; this is a thing of shame, and they'll be ridiculed with it."

"But the pictures won't leak."

"You can't be sure. *Da ma a ce*, she's already your wife, if she already was, this won't be a problem because no one would dare to even think of messing with our family like this."

Of course, the infamous Ringim/Dankabo immunity. My father's brothers are a bit notorious for taking justice into their hands. Back in the 1970s, during the *Maitatsine* riots in Kano, it was well-known that the rioters could not venture onto any street where our family members lived. They dared not, for the fear of the Ringim/Dankabo repercussion. This image continued through the years and evolved even as the presidency changed from military to democracy due to the part my father and uncles played in different regimes and during elections all over the North-Central and parts of the North-West.

He doesn't stop talking, "It's such a pity, *wallahi.* I've met Bebi a few times, really nice girl. This shouldn't be happening to her. The pictures are from your phone that got stolen *ko? Shegu, yan computer village dinnan;*

bastards, those guys at computer village! How did they even manage to jailbreak it to access her pictures in your gallery?"

My cousin thought that the pictures leaked from my phone. From my phone that had gotten missing a few weeks prior. That's why he still thinks she's a nice girl like he just said. If he knew that she sent them to her ex, he would have called her unsavory names because – by the flawed logic of our culture – we, as men, have to be first of everything, as far as intimacy was concerned, in the mother of our children's lives. Even though it's usual for the man to have many great loves before the woman he eventually settles for because of her chaste image. This convenient duplicity and sexist mindset are so typical in our society that I don't correct his assumptions that the pictures were from my phone.

"The pictures will not leak, Imran," I say again, my tone indicating a firm finality in the matter. The flash drive containing all copies of the pictures is now safe with her.

"You're still going to go ahead *da tambayan*, to ask for her hand?" He doesn't bother to mask the disbelief in his voice.

"You know that I already spoke to Uncle about it. After Madina's wedding, he's going with *Kawu* Sani and *Kawu* Liman to see Hafsat's father. In January insha Allah."

He is quiet for a few seconds, then, "*toh*, I hope – I really hope – the matter dies down. You know Baba – the people around him whisper in his ears a lot; there's nothing that escapes him when it comes to finding out about the reputation of the girls we want to marry. *Asali, Addini da Tarbiyya* – these are the three things he looks for in prospective in-laws. I mean yes, Dr. Gaya is well-respected and they are practicing Muslims, but you see that third point now –" his voice fades away as I stop listening.

Asali, Addini da Tarbiyya. Asali, her lineage – who her parents are, if the roots of her family can be traced, where they come from, and what they are known for. A good name is better than money, my uncle, Imran's father often says. Second, *addini,* religion – does she know the tenets of Islam, the rights of a husband over his wife and the role of a wife in our *ummah,* our community? Will she raise our children according to the teachings of our religion, or at least facilitate it? And thirdly, *tarbiyya*, upbringing – A girl is good until she gets caught in a situation that says otherwise; that's why our women have perfected the pretense and lies in various subtle manners just to be looked at as good Muslims or good northern girls.

There's nothing lacking in Hafsat's upbringing. She knows her boundaries, she knows how to carry herself, and she guards her privacy fiercely. She is a girl who made a mistake. If a guy had done the same thing she did, it would be quickly forgotten and written off as immaturity, but for the girl, it's a testament to her upbringing and flawed character.

"Will Nasreen and Khalil be around for Madina's wedding?" My attempt to change the topic is a weakly executed one, but I need this conversation to end.

* * *

I realized very early in my University days that boxing helps curb my rage. So when something bothers me, I always turn to the gym. It's the following morning and I'm in my home gym right after *Fajr*. The sting I feel as my fists collide with the punching bag overrides every thought that threatens to stray towards Hafsat's laughter, her scent, and how she looks at me even when we're around people.

I am doused in sweat and even as I feel the muscles in my biceps twinge with dull stabs of fatigue, I don't slow down. Every undistracted moment makes me think about the pictures, the looming threat, and the gossip blogger. Hadi Bilal signed an undertaking to not only disappear, but to deactivate the *Bujgist* account. Yet, the now-deleted comments made about the post still taunt me, silently urging me to punch harder and harder as my fists hit the bag repeatedly in successive strikes that increase the ache building up to my shoulder. I get interrupted by *Siri's* voice through my AirPods, pausing my music: "Incoming call from B. Answer?"

I stop punching, breathing laboriously as I hold onto the hanging punching bag. In the wall-sized mirror opposite me, I watch as sweat drips down my face to my bare chest as I took a swig of water from my bottle, waiting for the call to end.

When it stops, my phone beeps an incoming message. I open it and it's from her: *Hey... I need to see you.*

It wasn't even eight in the morning, I have no intentions of going to *Ranchers* today, but I also don't want to go to her house with the way I'm feeling right now. Maybe I need a few more hours to cool off, to see where my head is at. I type my reply: *I have to monitor the online chatter at home.*

Her reply comes in a few seconds later: *I can come by your place.*

I'm not in Asokoro, I reply.

Okay, on my way

She has never come to my place in Wuse in all the time we've been dating. I never expected her to; I'm content with seeing her in *H&I* and at her house, under watchful eyes. Or at *Ranchers*, during the day. I frown as I reply: *Sure.*

I call the security post of the apartment building to let them know I'm expecting a guest, then head to the bathroom to shower.

When the doorbell rings, I'm already in a white jallabiya. I open the door and there she stands – in a long, brown abaya, her face scrubbed clean and devoid of any makeup, yet she manages to knock the winds out of my lungs. I try not to think back to when we were caught under the rain the previous day – the way her white dress got transparent when it was drenched in the rain, and the way the soft outline of her breasts pressed against the thin material, leaving the faintest impression of her nipples implanted in my brain. I pull my gaze away from her, as she adjusts her veil around her head, holding her phone as she looks up at me.

"Hi," is all she says, and I start to feel my anger wash away. How does she manage to capture my attention with nothing but her mere presence?

I move to the side, "come on in." She walks in and stands by the wall, and I close the door and lead the way into the living area. "Can I get you anything – water, juice?" Well, that's all I can offer her. I hardly receive visitors here, and I eat out most of the time.

"No, I'm good, thank you," she looks around, and her eyes settle on the bookends on the white bookshelves to her right; customized gifts from my stepmother, they were carved out of black oak with flat surfaces veneered with pictures from different highlights of my life. "Is that Imran's dad?" she points at a picture of me, Imran, and Uncle Dankabo that was taken at my university graduation. Next to it is one with me, Fatima, Hadiza, and Hajiya Amina.

"Yes, that's my uncle."

She nods like she already knew, "oh, you've been riding for a while." She reaches for a picture of me riding a black standardbred Friesian horse. I must have been twelve or so in the picture.

"Yes, I joined the equestrian club at boarding school in my second year." I know she didn't come all the way to talk about my life events or my hobbies. I sit down on the white leather couch, turn down the air conditioning, and look up at her. She catches my drift and sits opposite me, and I watched as she searches my eyes, probably to gauge my mood before she speaks. "What's up?" I ease us into the conversation.

Her phone rings and she looks down and she rejects the call with a look I'm now familiar with. "Sorry, it's Umm'Hafsa; we had an argument this morning," she says dismissively.

"You know what, Hafsat? I might as well bring this up now – the way you treat your mother really bothers me."

"She's not who she claims to be."

"You've said that multiple times but whatever that means, she is still your mother."

She sighs, "yesterday, when you asked if there was anything else you needed to know, I said no. But that wasn't entirely true..."

My eyes meet hers as I wait for the other shoe to drop.

When she continues, her voice is crisp and her words are clear like she has thought about exactly what to say multiple times. "A few months ago, I found out that daddy isn't my father."

SubhanAllah.

This is what the 'hypothetical' question was about. "Are you sure about this?" I ask, thinking back to the pictures of the older couple I saw in their living room – the way they look at each other, the love in their eyes.

She starts picking at her nails, "yeah. At first, I thought I was adopted, but I got a DNA test done and –" she inhales sharply "– and I'm her child but not his, so she must have... she must have stepped out on him, or something."

"Damn," is all I can say.

"Yup, I'm Umm'Hafsa's best-kept secret," she looks up at me with a forlorn smile on her face. "Anyway, I can't keep a secret like this from you, not after yesterday. You deserve to know the whole truth about me, so..."

Asali, Addini. Tarbiya. Well, there goes *Asali.* That's a second strike, if I go by how my uncle does his things. Her real father could be anybody. *Anybody.*

But does this change who she is – the person the man she thought was her father brought her up to be? Isn't there a case of nurture against nature here? Paternity is more than sperm cells; it's the values, the principles a man instills in his offspring.

"I *hate* her. But I can't bring myself up to tell anyone because this coming out will hurt dad– Dr. Gaya the most, and I can't bear that."

It must be hard for her to open up and share something like this with me. "B, you have every right to feel the way you do, but you being rude to her," I slowly shake my head, "to what end? It's possible *kina nan kina ta kwasan zunubai,* you're here accumulating sins for something she has begged Allah's forgiveness for, something Allah has already forgiven her for."

"You know, sometimes, I catch myself wondering, like, what if I'm just like her? What if I marry a man who loves me so much, but I end up cheating on him too? I mean, maybe I *am* like her; when I was dating Bashir, I started having a crush on you... so maybe I'm no different."

Strangely, I know exactly what her fear feels like, but I'm not going to watch her wallow in some self-prescribed guilt over a man who did not deserve her loyalty. However, her revelation surprises me. Hafsat admitting to a crush on me back then?

"But you never cheated on him." When she looks at me with moist eyes, I feel this protectiveness over her. "We're not our parents." Something about Hafsat makes me want to reassure her that we are not our parents. "There's something I've never told anyone, too," I steady my breath and ignore all the warnings in my head trying to stop me from opening up to her. "My father was a... was a very abusive man." I see the surprise on her face as her jaw slowly drops but I continue before I can stop myself from being completely honest with her, from hiding this part of me the way that I'm used to. "He lashed out at anyone – his staff, his kids, even his wives." The way her eyes widen at the last part of my sentence should stop me, but it doesn't. "When I was eight, he gave me this scar," I roll up my sleeves to show her two keloid incisions on my arm. "And a broken arm. I still have a metal plate and screws from the fracture." I watch as her hands immediately cover her mouth.

It makes sense for someone who grew up around that kind of violence like I did to say that they will never hurt someone they love. That's why I told myself I would never commit to someone until I knew that I would never hurt them. And I'll never hurt Hafsat. "Therapy taught me that being my father's son doesn't mean that I automatically inherit his vices or weaknesses," I finally say. "Like I said, we are not our parents."

The room remains silent for a little while. When she finally speaks, she says, "I'm so sorry you went through all that." Her voice is like a balm that soothes the pain I've kept hidden for so long.

"Find it in your heart to forgive your mother. Your sisters are returning from the university next month; this whole thing is bound to get messy if they pick up on your behavior towards her, like I did."

She sniffs and nods and we sit in silence, comfortable in the shared knowledge that we have opened the doors to complete honesty in our relationship moving forward.

"Should we go get lunch? I'm starving." I notice the relief in her sigh as she looks up at me. "Pick a place for us to go?"

Her eyes light up as she thinks about it, "umm... Kwame's special."

I laugh out loud for the first time since yesterday, and it's genuine. "*Toh,* let's go to *Ranchers* then," I say as I stand up from the couch, and she does the same.

Zuwaira

1998

Pain came in phases. For me, it was every nine to ten days. What we thought we found a remedy for only got worse; the more Alhaji's business ventures declined, the more temperamental he got. Yet, it was only Balaraba and me who bore the brunt. As bad as my situation was with the constant beatings, it was worse for Balaraba because, unlike me, she spoke up and fought back, but the result was never pretty. Most of my bruises were covered by my expensive clothes and veils, but most of hers were on her face, expertly covered by makeup so that it was hardly noticeable except if you went really close to her.

A life I knew nothing about had become mine, *shige-shige*. I was going helter-skelter looking for people who could help remove the bad luck they said I brought into the family and undo the many charms the different people saw.

One day, I found myself in Zangon Kataf, sitting in a smokey room with Hajiya Indo, my mother-in-law's younger sister whom Hajiya Uwa had handed me over to in the quest for *neman taimako*, seeking help, ever since she fell ill. We explained my situation, as I'd done with several other helpers. "It doesn't matter what I do, nothing is ever right. When I cook, it ends up too salty, or pepperish or –" I started.

"*Ashha!*" the pot-bellied man interrupted as he laughed at me. "Young girl, you don't know the ways of the world." The black beads around his neck jiggled as he laughed and swatted a fly away from him, then pointed at me, "listen, even if you cook the best meal he has ever seen, as soon as he enters that your section, everything will taste bad to him, *saboda a iska yake, ya shaka* – because the charm is in the air, and he has inhaled it."

Hajiya Indo leaned forward with a questioning look, "inhaled it? What do you mean?"

The man gestured to the thick cloud of smoke around us, "the incense that your *uwargida* gave you. It has been working silently and it has finally taken hold of him. Yes, great work has to be done to undo it." He looked at me and I blanched, my head full of questions. The incense that Hajiya Babba gave me when I was a new bride six months prior? It was charmed? "Everything she has given you to put on your body or to use around the house has been working to separate you from your husband."

Hajiya Indo started laughing, "this isn't her first time. She's always frustrating the other wives. We have always known this. If not you, Zuwaira, how will a co-wife give you something, and you'll use it? Are you not wise?"

Nobody told me. I didn't know. She seemed so kind in all her interactions with me. The week after I was brought into the house, I cooked nothing for Alhaji or me. All the food we ate was sent to my section from hers.

"Not just her," Hajiya Indo continues, "even that quiet one that wears a hijab that covers her head to her feet. I've seen her multiple times in the crooks and crannies of these lanes, going to see medicine men."

The second wife too? Is this what my life is supposed to become? I thought to myself. Continuously going in and out looking for help from suspicious people who claimed that what we were doing was normal, but they worked with dubious things – a feather from a one-legged ostrich, a snake's tongue, the milk of a breastfeeding woman? I had even sold the set of red *mirzani* beads that came in my lefe to be able to afford their fees. We paid exorbitant amounts of money for the black portions they gave me to rub over my body before Alhaji came into my section or to add to his food to gain his favor and put above my door to eliminate all the other charms.

211

None of that worked.

The nine days circled back again really quickly and the treatment meted out to me was worse than the previous ones. I tried to hide it by not telling my mother-in-law how bad it had gotten whenever she asked. I would say that it was getting better. I did not want to bother her because her health was deteriorating, and she still refused to quit smoking the cigarettes, even with Dr. Ishaya's insistence. She not only hid the brown packs from her sons, but now from her daughters-in-law too. I made it a point to always go and check on her most evenings because she didn't smoke when I was with her.

On one particular day, I saw one of Alhaji's children, Abu, playing outside her verandah. His beautiful brown skin glimmered under the white shirt he had on, which was stained with orange juice. I wondered if he would look this unkempt if his mother was still alive. Hajiya Uwa ensured he was well taken care of, but with her failing health these days, it was hard for her to keep track of his meals or how clean he was. I knew she didn't want the other wives taking care of him because she was sure they would maltreat him. I watched as he played with a yellow toy car and a few pieces of stones. He would try to push the stones away from the toy car's path, a process he repeated over and over. "Abu, *ina Hajiya*? Wheres's Hajiya?" I asked as I removed my shoes outside her section. The five-year-old looked up at me and pointed his yellow car towards the door.

"*Ka dinga magana,* use your words. Don't let your father beat you again." I heard Hajiya Uwa's voice coming from her living room. Her words were immediately swallowed by a nasty bout of cough, which was so bad her eyes watered at the intensity. I reached for the water on a tray next to her three-sitter and passed it to her.

"*Sannu,* Hajiya. Sorry," I said as she drank the water. The cough subsided a bit. She tried to hide the bloodied handkerchief under her wrapper. "Hajiya, are you still coughing blood?" I asked, dismayed because I thought the blood had stopped; that was what she told the doctor on our last visit to the hospital. "*Kina shan magungunan?* Are you taking the medication?" I asked.

212

"*Ai* this is not a case for the hospital. *Wannan jipa ne*; this is a spell. They want to get rid of me," she laughed to herself as she gestured outwards, towards the other sections.

My mouth hung open. Would they really do that? Would they hurt their husband's mother? Was there an end to this wickedness?

I watched her as she brought out a powder wrapped in a piece of paper; she poured it into a cup and drank. "*Ya jiki jiki?*" she smiled, touching my stomach as she asked about my pregnancy. I was still in my first trimester, according to Dr. Ishaya. I didn't look or feel different; I was just very happy that in a few months, I would have someone that would be mine, a part of me. Maybe I would not feel so alone in this world when my child is born. The child would be born into privilege that I never grew up in, and that is something. I would try to endure my marriage with Alhaji, if not for anything, for the birthright my child would be advantaged with.

"Alhamdulillah, Hajiya." My voice dropped with shyness as I looked down at my hands. When people asked about my pregnancy, it was hard to look them in the eye.

Abu walked into the sitting room and stood next to his grandmother, staring at her but not saying anything.

"What do you want?" She asked him.

His bright eyes just kept staring at her, while his fingers played with the tires of his yellow car.

"What is it, Abu? Talk!" She raised her voice at him in a manner that is more concern, than anger. "You have to speak. A five-year-old boy and up till now, you don't want to talk," she reprimanded him but he remained silent. You could see from his face that he wanted to say something, but he didn't know how.

"Abu-Abu," his head turned in my direction when he heard the nickname I sometimes called him. "*Za ka ci abinci?* Are you hungry?" I smiled and he nodded. "Okay, come and eat rice and beans." I said and he gave me a smile.

"Don't indulge him. He needs to use his words. Everyday his father speaks to him and he doesn't answer back, *bulala yake sha*, he gets beaten.

213

I don't know why he doesn't want to talk. His father even took him to Sudan sometime back, and all the doctors say he's fine but he has refused to speak." Another bout of cough shook her and when it subsided, she rested her head on the pillow behind her.

"Sannu, Hajiya,"

Abu came next to me and tugged at my wrapper. I looked at him and he gave me his yellow car to look at.

"What is this?" I asked him. "Is it a car? Say it is a car."

He remained quiet, just peering at me with his hooded eyes.

"Hajiya, let me take Abu. He can stay with me during the day if you permit, he can come back here and sleep."

"*Allah ya miki albarka*, Zuwaira; May God bless you. You see, your heart is the purest out of these women. Are you sure it won't be too much for you with your pregnancy?"

"*Haba*, Hajiya, allow me do this." I watched her as she slowly drifted off to sleep, exhaustion written all over her features and the plate of sinasir I made for her earlier in the day untouched on the table.

"Abu-Abu, let's go eat." I stood up and adjusted my veil around my body and he held my hand as we walked out of Hajiya Uwa's section.

* * *

Abu never spoke a word to me, not once. But he saved my life one day. When Alhaji was not in my section, Abu would come to my living room as soon as he woke up. I usually had his bread and tea waiting for him and would get him ready for school, before he joined his older siblings in the new Jeep that had now replaced the station wagon as the designated children's vehicle. When the driver brought them back home from school, he would come straight to my section with drawings of the sun and trees from his activities at school and give them to me.

"Are these pictures for me?" I would kneel in front of him as I asked. "What did you draw today? Tell me."

He would smile shyly and walk to the dining room, where he would eat

214

lunch. He was a tidy kid with a healthy appetite. When he was done, he would take his plate and cup to the kitchen and put them in the sink. He didn't say thank you, but he would wave at me wildly as the Jeep took him and the other kids to *Islammiya* for Qur'an lessons. Islammiya was hard for him, and he always got beaten by his teachers because he never recited the Qur'an verses along with the other kids.

When he came back in the evening, he would hide behind the curtains, and I would pause my Hausa film or stop knitting the sweater that I was making for my baby to call out to him. Eventually, he would come out, his cheeks streaked in dry tears, as he showed me the lines from the cane on his tiny palms.

"Abu-Abu, please talk. Do you want them to keep beating you?" I would ask him and he would shake his head. "Then please talk. Or else they will keep beating you."

After he ate dinner, he would go to the mosque to pray in congregation with his father, uncles, and older male siblings. He would always bring me a toy or rock from the outer gate when he returned before going back to his grandmother's section to sleep.

Abu never came into my section on the days Alhaji was with me. He avoided his father like he was *Firaun*, the wicked pharaoh of Egypt. On that fateful Sunday morning – on the day he saved my life – Abu peeped into the house after his father had completed his three days with me and saw me laying unconscious on the floor. He panicked and ran into the opposite section to find help.

I woke up in a daze to see Balaraba, the third wife, in my section in a black abaya, with her hair open. She'd sprinkled water on me and the coolness of the water had awakened me from my faint. I tried to pull myself up, but she stopped me with a hand on my shoulder, "wait, I think you dislocated something." Her face pulled into a worrying frown, the red bruise on her lip was already healing but it would definitely leave a scar. Over her shoulder, Abu stood behind her, with tears in his eyes as he watched me with a fearful look.

I looked down to find my arm sticking out at a weird angle. The moment

I looked at it, a tremendous amount of pain flooded my brain, registering the hurt I'd received. "I slipped – I fell –" my voice was a whisper as I grabbled with words.

She looked around the living room at the broken plates on the floor and the brown belt on the carpet by the television. "These new tiles are slippery; you have to walk carefully. Your shoulder is dislocated." She carefully pulled me up into the chair, as I stretched my leg out, a worried look settled on her face, and before I could ask her what was wrong, I began to feel faint. She turned to Abu, "tell the driver to bring the car. Hurry!"

I looked down, and the room started to spin just as I noticed the red stain spreading all over the front of my dress.

* * *

Having a dislocated shoulder was painful, but I was used to the pain at that point. The ride to the hospital was long and antagonizing. Balaraba was by my side, a very unlikely alliance in my time of need, as Hajiya Uwa had traveled to Katsina for a wedding. Even with her ill health, my mother-in-law had insisted on going with the driver for the one-week wedding.

I didn't have tears left to cry – not when the doctor popped my shoulder back, not when he told me that I had lost the pregnancy. They gave me a tablet to flush the tissue out and my face was blank the whole time.

Tissue. It was my child that they were calling 'tissue.' *What kind of father kills his own child? What kind of man is so filled with anger and rage that the pleas of his pregnant wife fall on deaf ears?* We remained in the hospital for a whole day. When the drivers brought lunch from home, I did not eat. Balaraba did not eat, too. We didn't talk much, either.

Later that afternoon, as I sat on the hospital bed, my hand connected to a drip, with my legs dangling off the floor, the door to the gloomy private ward opened. We looked up to see the doctor –not Dr. Ishaya, but another one I had never seen – walking into the room. His tone took a somber tone as he spoke to me, "Hajiya, your body has refused to expel the remaining tissue. We'll have to do a D&C."

I looked up at Balaraba, who had just finished praying Asr, as she folded her praying mat, set it aside and walked to my bed. "What's a D&C?" I asked her in Hausa.

She held my hand, "dilation and curettage. They are going to suction out the –" her eyes filled with sadness as she left her sentence incomplete. There was a certain empathy in them that made me realize – without doubt – that it was a pain she shared, a secret. She had also lost a baby.

"Is it painful?" I asked her, as I forced back the tears.

"We're women," she replied as she helped me up. "Women are warriors, you'll be fine."

I was no warrior. I was not as strong as the first two wives, or as educated as Balaraba. I was only eighteen and ill-prepared for this life I had been thrust into – a life where my co-wife stood outside the door of a surgical room where a doctor was relieving my body of the 13-week-old dead baby that a maternal part of me had refused to give up. In a dingy hospital one hour away from our house, a hospital where nobody knew who we were because our husband's good reputation had to be protected even when his crimes left marks on us that lived with us forever.

There had to be more to life than this. That was the only thought on my mind as Sufyan, Alhaji's brother, and the driver took us back home that night.

Hafsatu

2021

It's December and this month has been the happiest for me because Sara and Shatu are back home from university for Christmas break. There's just something about having my sisters back home that makes up for all the annoying things they do. Like taking things from my closet without permission and borrowing my car without asking, even if I have places I need to be. We spend hours catching up in my room, talking about the highlights of their semester and what they have missed in the Abuja gossip sphere, and spend most evenings in the game room shouting and arguing over words we make up as we play Scrabble since we all refuse to use a dictionary. I even see Umm'Hafsa and her husband more now that I have started joining family dinners in the dining room upstairs.

Today, Shatu and Mohammed are trying to convince the rest of the table to side with their recommendations for the family trip. Daddy lives for this kind of family debates. When we were much younger, whenever he had some free time to play around with, he would give us assignments on Fridays: *pick a family activity you think we should do this weekend, and why.* My sisters and I would spend the whole evening brainstorming ideas and writing a list of pros and cons to present to him the following day in the living room of our former house in CBN quarters in Garki. I was probably twelve or thirteen years old then. "...and with these few points of mine, I hope I have been able to convince you, and not confuse, you that we should go to the family fair today. They even have face painting *fa*." I would add, trying to get my parents to vote for my choice.

"Face painting messes up the toilet when we perform ablution, and Shatu doesn't even wash her face properly," ten-year-old Sara would counter. Our parents would laugh at our antics as they sat on the sofa with the television off, making us feel important with their undivided attention. "Let's just go to the amusement park instead."

I remember pushing Sara, "but we went to the amusement park last month."

"No, Bebi. You know the rules, no pushing," daddy reprimanded me as he pushed his glasses into his face.

Shatu's tiny voice would eventually be heard when there were a few seconds of silence as I apologized to Sara, which I only did because Umm'Hafsa was glaring at me. "Daddy, teach me how to ride a bike."

"Learn how to ride a bike by yourself," Sara would snap at her. We used to gang up against poor Shatu in those days. Right now, history seems to be repeating itself.

Sara drinks orange juice from her glass cup as she listens to Shatu plead, "you guys should side with me on this. The Safari in Kenya is beautiful this time of the year and we have never been to East Africa. Bebi, back me up on this."

I shrug as I rest my spoon in my bowl of oxtail pepper soup. "I don't know. Mohammed's choice is very tempting."

"Yes, *comic-con!*" He imitates gunshots at Shatu with his fingers. He wants us to go to Los Angeles for the comic superheroes convention because he wants to meet Ironman and Spiderman.

Umm'Hafsa's voice breaks into our chatter, "Mohammed, I can stop you right there, that's not happening. International travel with these changing COVID regulations and layovers is going to be too much."

"Yesss!" Shatu pumps her fist in the air.

"No, even Kenya is a stretch. Think local. There are many parts of Nigeria we haven't explored." Daddy immediately said.

219

Shatu nods like she agrees with him, but the sheer shock on Mohammed's face makes me chortle into my soup. My phone beeps, and it's a message from Sadiq, replying to a meme I sent him on the movie Tenet: *That movie was inception on steroids!*

I chuckle at his reply as I type: *I still have no idea what the whole movie is about, not even after the second time we watched it.*

His reply comes in immediately: *I could explain it to you, but you keep distracting me...*

I smile to myself. I would be lying if I said that I didn't think my relationship with Sadiq would be changed by the previous month's events, but it didn't. In a way, it brought us closer because we started opening up to each other more and discussing our expectations of each other. We agreed to be honest and not keep secrets away from one another.

I have to be honest. I am still a bit paranoid. Some part of me feels that Bashir might still have a vendetta against me, so I obsessively check *Bujgist* and other blogs just to see if my pictures will be mentioned. When I wake up, the first thing I check is social media, and the tightness in my chest stops constricting only when I see that people have truly moved on. As negotiated that day in Sadiq's office, *Bujgist* has gone completely dark, and the people on the internet have moved onto the current trending gist, something about Rahama Sadau's outfit at some award show.

My phone beeps again: *What are you doing tomorrow?*

I smile as I reply: *Going to the saloon, then I'm taking Sara to register at your gym. She says she wants to start working out.*

He replies: *#TeamSara. Tell her I'll make sure she gets the best trainer.*

"Sadiq says he will make sure you get the best trainer," I read the message out to Saratu.

"Haha, tell him it's me and Fatima registering tomorrow, so his trainer should be ready for our complaints."

"Tell him yourself, I'm not your *'yar aike.*" My tone is stern as I remind her I'm not her messenger, but inside, I'm smiling. It gives me joy to see my family members interact with Sadiq; they are fond of him. Well, those that he has met so far – all of them except daddy.

The following morning, after getting my hair done at the saloon, I walk past the living room upstairs and hear the television on. I peep in and find daddy snacking on Almonds as he reads the paper. "Daddy?" It feels like it has been a long time since I called him that out loud. "I didn't think you were still home. Is everything okay?" I ask as I walk toward him.

He looks up at me with a smile, "Dr. Ogundare is around, so I decided to take the day off." Dr. Ogundare is my dad's friend and specialist who consults at daddy's hospital every few months. He peers at me as I sit down next to him, folding the newspaper as he puts it away.

"If I didn't know better, I would say you've been avoiding me. Every day I come back home and I ask after you, I'm told that you're at work and when you come back, you don't bother to look for me." He slides his glasses down the bridge of his nose as he talks.

I have been avoiding him. That is the honest truth. Of course, I check on him every now and then, but I don't prolong my visits as I used to in the past. "We've been busy *ne*. We had some bridal clients and you know how weddings are." At least that part is true.

"That's good. A busy business is good business." I see a hint of a smile start to tug at his lips as he speaks. "So, it has nothing to do with a certain young man who has been visiting quite often?"

I reach between us, take some of his almonds, and lean back into the cushions. "No, he's not even here that often."

"He's here almost every evening," his eyes widen with a twinkle as he teases me. "And from what I hear, it's very serious."

I have missed this, talking to daddy the way I usually do. I feel a certain kind of calmness I haven't felt in a while just by this conversation that has not even lasted three minutes. My voice lowers as it always does when I confide in him. "His name is Sadiq. I think you'll like him. Actually, I *know* you will."

He pushes his glasses back into his face, "are you trying to butter me up?"

"No, daddy, of course not."

He laughs at my vehement denial. "So, why Sadiq?"

Because, in a way, he reminds me of you, I think but I can't quite say that, so

I try to articulate the specifics into words. "He's... different, trustworthy, dependable... and he respects me."

"And you – are you all these things to him?" he slowly rubs his beard downwards as he speaks, "Marriage is a two-way street, you know. These things you like about him have to be reciprocated." I nod yes, and he continues, "your mom and I raised you and your siblings with the hope that when the time comes for you all to choose life partners, we'll trust your choices. Nobody is going to live with him but you," he pauses, letting out a soft sigh. "No one is perfect but with marriage, you have to learn to overlook each other's weaknesses. So, be honest with yourself: are his weaknesses things you can live with? I'll ask him the same thing when I meet him." He chuckles as if he just remembered something. "Let me share a funny story with you about your Adda Bilki." Adda Bilki is Adda Salma's sister. "We were sitting in her father's sitting room in Kaduna, after *ya ma sunan shi –*" daddy's memory fails to recall her husband's name. *"Baban su Amal* – Amal's father –"

"Uncle Samad," I say.

"Yes, Abdulsamad," his index finger is pointing in the air as he continues his story. "When she told us she wanted to marry Abdulsamad, I asked her the same question I just asked you: "Why Abdulsamad?" Do you know what she said?" I shake my head no. "She said because she had been dating him for a year, and in that whole time, they had not had one single fight. I was surprised. Not even an argument? She said no, never." A text message comes into daddy's phone and he pauses for a few seconds to see the sender, then he continues. "I told her that she needs to see what kind of man he becomes during an argument before she marries him." I chuckle and he continues. "So, I will ask you the same thing, how do you and Sadiq resolve conflict? I'm not saying go pick a fight with him but you should pay attention, watch how his issues with other people go. Does he lash out? Does he blame? Does he take responsibility? Does he invite other people into your fight? Does he give you the silent treatment? Does he jokingly threaten to hurt you? These are some things you need to know about a man before you sign up for a lifetime with him because in a marriage, conflicts are bound to happen; it's how you handle them that truly matters, especially when the honeymoon phase is over."

I raise my eyebrow as I gently tug my earlobes, looking at the television that's displaying the news channel quietly. My mind goes back to the whole picture fiasco and everything that followed when I called Sadiq.

"There was a… situation," I swallow, "it wasn't exactly a fight but it was something we were both upset over. Um… I think what stood out for me was he didn't make me feel *less*, if that makes sense? Even though I was to blame, he still handled everything with dignity and treated me with respect."

He remains quiet for a few seconds as he ponders my answer. "That's very important, maintaining the balance of respect even during conflicts and it is not an easy thing to do. You have to remember that."

* * *

A few days later, Sadiq comes to pick me up an hour just after Asr. He has a family friend whose husband is into luxury real estate in Abuja, and he tells me that he wants to buy a duplex in one of their developments in Maitama, but before he does, he wants us to look at the floor plans together. As we drive to Cosgrove Estates to meet the sales representative, he turns down the volume to Asake and Olamide's *Omo Ope* playing through the *Bose* speakers.

"Do you know why I decided on Maitama?"

I bite my lower lip as I shake my head, "no, why?"

"There was a day we were at Bellanova, you and Ilham were talking and you said you can't imagine living anywhere but Maitama."

"When was that?" My thumb strokes his as our intertwined hands lay on the white leather handrest between our seats.

"It was at the beginning of this year," he says as he steers the wheel with his left hand. There is something unexplainably hot about Sadiq driving with one hand.

"Ilham and I say the most outrageous things when we talk about the future," I say, but the real zinger is that he overheard that conversation before we started talking and somehow still remembers.

"I didn't think it was outrageous. I love how you know exactly what you want."

I smile to myself, "you never even used to look at me back then. I can't believe you were paying attention to my conversations."

He is silent for a few seconds as the song changes to Ckay's *Love Nwantiti* Remix. "Believe me, I tried everything in my power to stay away." As he makes a right into the estate, he looks at me.

"Well, I'm glad you didn't," I say softly and his hand squeezes mine gently.

As we reach the automated estate, a camera scans our plate number and the gates roll open. He follows the GPS directions to a white boxed duplex where a man in a blue suit was waiting for us by the green carpet grass opposite the paved driveway. We exchange pleasantries and he goes on a spiel on the smart home features, the solar panels and full automation as I walk in through the foyer then the living room. I make my way into the kitchen, with its vast island and the cubic-styled backsplash.

Sadiq looks into the backyard, "so what do you think? Can you see us living here?"

I feel goosebumps on my skin just from the exhilaration at the mental image in my head of the two of us within these walls, calling this place home and doing anything we want. "I dunno yet," I say, failing horribly to hide my excitement, "let's see the bedrooms."

I see a look pass Sadiq's face at my comment. He's about to say something but the sales rep interrupts him by insisting that we use the elevators to the top floor where the master bedroom is.

"That's very unnecessary in a family home," Sadiq remarks.

"I agree," I say, imagining a child getting stuck in the elevator."

We hold hands as we take the winding stairs instead and open the doors to the bedrooms. The motion sensor lights come on immediately, and for the next few minutes, we go through all the rooms and eventually get to the master bedroom, and I'm very aware of Sadiq watching my every expression. I walk into the his-and-hers closet and the bathroom as I listen to the features of the smart mirror. I open a door that leads into the balcony and find myself looking at the other units in the estate. Impeccably pruned and spaced with luxury cars parked in front of their driveways. It's quiet and serene. Just perfect.

I hear Sadiq's footsteps as he joins me on the balcony. He stands next to me, and his hands adjust my veil over my shoulder. "So, what's the verdict?"

My face breaks into a smile, "love it!"

"And there are schools nearby for our kids." He has a roguish smile on his face as he talks to me about kids in the master bedroom of our future house.

I shake my head as I roll my eyes playfully, "I see you've done your research. I love everything."

"Wonderful! Let me tell Fa'iza the good news," he says as he brings out his phone.

"Is that your family friend?"

"Yes, that's her. They moved back to Abuja this year," he says as he puts his phone to his ear and I hear the distant ringing. "Hi, future neighbor," he says when the ringing stops. I hear her light squeal through his phone and look at him as he winks at me, "yes… no, you were right. She loves it." He pauses a bit and then says, "it's great. *Kuna gida?* Are you guys home?" A shorter pause, then, "okay, we'll drop by for a bit." As he ends the call, he holds my hand. "B, they live next door. Let's go and say hello to them."

* * *

After the sales representative gives us different brochures and paperwork, we cross the road to the three-storied duplex in front of us. We ring the bell and a few minutes later, a lady in a white apron opens the door and leads us into the living room.

Okay, this Fai'za has to hook me up with her interior decorator, I think to myself as I take in the foyer's light pastels and bronze metalwork. I see a console desk with plaques that read Award of Recognition for social service and Philanthropy. As we walk into the living room, a perfect blend of the flowery notes of jasmine, white musk, and bakhoor make me inhale longer than I normally do. Almost at the same time, I hear a deep baritone behind us: "Abubakar, *kwana biyu*. Long time." I turn around to see this tall, beautiful man walking down the stairs. Really, I mean beautiful. That is the only word I can use to describe him and his perfect bone structure. I look away and admire the wrought iron art pieces around the living room just so I don't stare at him too much.

"Ahmad." There is a brotherly vibe between him and Sadiq as they shake hands.

He turns to me. "And you must be Hafsat. Welcome, please sit down." He motions for us to sit down, and they immediately start talking about business.

"Sadiq, our *ango,* groom-to-be." A lady in her late twenties, slim and just a little shorter than me, walks in with an easy gait. She's wearing a light pink straight dress I recognize from the *Bottega* collection with a pashmina wrapped around her head. She is a delight to look at. Her eyes meet mine and she stretches her arms towards me, joining me on the couch as she gives me a hug: "Hi, neighbor. I'm so excited you guys will be moving in next to us, *insha'Allah*." She speaks in a North American accent. "Hafsat, how's it going?"

"Good, *Alhamdulillah*." I look around and my eyes settle on a beautiful black-and-white portrait of her and her husband on the wall. They look like models. "You have a beautiful home."

"Thank you, you're so sweet. That's a beautiful bag."

"I love how she completely ignored you once she saw Hafsat," Ahmad says to Sadiq just as the lady who opened the door brings in drinks.

"No surprise there," Sadiq answers. "Are you in touch with Imran, Fa'iza?"

"Yes, they came over a few times in Toronto over the summer, but we didn't meet when he came to Abuja some months ago. I had COVID." The whole time she talks, her husband just keeps looking at her with this look on his face, like he can't get enough of her.

"Oh yeah, you said so," Sadiq looks at his wristwatch; he doesn't joke with Umm'Hafsa's expectations about him bringing me home on time. He raises both eyebrows at me in a swift move that I doubt people around notice, but it has somehow become a signal we use to communicate to each other when it's time to leave. "We'll come back soon insha Allah. *Ina mutumi na* – where's my lil man – Shahid?"

"He's with his Qur'an tutor in the garden," Ahmad answers.

We stand up to leave and just as we get to the foyer, we see a woman who looks Spanish or Filipino and in her forties with a girl of about three years old. She closes the door as they come in through the main door. The little girl, in her pink tutu, runs straight into her father's waiting arms. She has features from both her parents: light brown skin, an aquiline nose and thin lips.

"How was your walk, Sheryl?" Fa'iza asks.

"Perfect. Nadia was great today. We practiced our colours and we counted to twenty." *Not just interior decorators, I'm going to ask Fa'iza for details about tutors and Au pairs for kids too.* "Hello," Sheryl acknowledges us with a quick greeting as she makes her way into a different part of the house.

"When did baby get so big?" Sadiq asks as she buries her face in her father's neck.

"Nadia is a big girl now. Lots of nos and tantrums," Faiza rolls her eyes in my direction like she's giving me a heads up of what to expect. For some reason, I love that she does that. I can imagine my future already. We would be sitting on our balconies, complaining about terrible twos and daddys' girls.

"Sadiq tells me *H&I* belongs to you, *ko*? My sister-in-law shops there all the time. I have to visit one of these days."

"Oh, *haba*? Really?" I make a mental note to ask Ilham later if she knows who her sister-in-law is. "*Toh*, I'll be expecting you. Let me give you my number, so you can call me when you're coming." If we're going to see a lot of each other in the future, I might as well get her number already. Besides, I honestly need her decorator's number. We exchange phone numbers and bid them goodbye as we get into the car and drive off. It looks like I fit perfectly into Sadiq's circle of family and friends, too.

* * *

We went nowhere for the new year – not Obudu Ranch, not even Lagos, which was a shame because Sadiq got me, my sisters and his sisters VIP tickets to the *Mavins Experience* concert. Right around the Christmas break, Umm'Hafsa got ill and her husband put everything, including our holiday plans, on a standstill. By the time she got better, it was already January and my sisters were preparing to return to school. The rest of the family was busy with a different kind of preparation – receiving Sadiq's family for *gaisuwa*. From the bits and pieces I've been able to put together, Sadiq's uncles and one of his late father's friends will be coming to see daddy, who has already informed Uncle Isa as the oldest member of his family.

Ilham visits all the time. As the self-appointed maid of honor, she is not only helping to narrow down lists of wedding planners, but she's also taking the planning of my bachelorette party very seriously. She is currently in the process of ordering custom-made 'W*ould you be my bridesmaid?*' hampers with an assortment of chocolates, non-alcoholic pink champagne, *Pandora* friendship bracelets, scented candles and a few other items that my bridesmaids will receive after a date for my wedding is fixed.

"We should invite them to a chic and exclusive dinner and then you'll pop the question to them," she suggests. She has been spending way too much time on Pinterest looking at unique ideas.

"Pop the question to my friends? No way! I'm thinking of making a WhatsApp group and sending one message with a lot of emojis."

"You must be joking. This idea will make really nice and emotional footage for your wedding video. You know how BigH is fond of nice background music and slo-mo scenes. I promise to act surprised and burst into tears." She leans back into my pillows with a dreamy look on her face.

"You're so dramatic, I love it." I don't know what I would do without Ilham; she's the best friend anyone could ever ask for.

The door opens and Sara stands by the door in black workout tights and a purple T-shirt. From the slight sheen of sweat on her skin, I figure she's just coming back from the gym. "Ilham," she says as she sees my best friend lying on my bed.

"*Shigo mana*; come in. What are you standing out there for?" I ask as she scrunches up her face.

"I need to take a bath first."

"How was the gym?" Ilham asks. "Will you come for Zumba tomorrow evening?"

"Oh yes, for sure," she starts to close the door. "I have gist for you guys when I come back."

The door closes and Ilham whirls her head to me, "I think Sara has a *boarfrenn*."

"Can you please stop pronouncing boyfriend like that?"

"What? You don't like *boarfrenn*?" she flutters her eyelash innocently. "Don't you have *boarfrenn*?" her exaggerated accent gets worse with every syllable that I can't hold my laughter in, especially with how she leaves her mouth agape after saying the word. She stands up, "tell Sara to call me, I need to hear this gist."

"You're leaving already?" I grumble, even though she has been with me all afternoon, and it's now almost Maghrib.

"Yes, Usman got *habbatus sauda* for Umma. I wanna see him before he leaves the house. *Kinsan*, since they got that contract from the Ministry, he's been so occupied."

I nod. Habbatus Sauda, black seed oil, is used to relieve arthritis, something Ilham's mother has been dealing with recently. "Yeah, the beginning of these projects are always like that but Sadiq says by next week, they won't be so busy."

As she puts her bag on her shoulder, she catches the massive grin on my face. "What is it?"

"Nothing," I say in a singsong manner.

"You better say it *koma mene ne*, whatever it is."

"It's just you and *your* Usman, and your little dance of oh-there's-nothing-here but you guys can't go two days without looking for an excuse to see each other."

"*Pfft*, not everyone has caught the love bug. You know two of my aunts are married to some extended family of his. He's like family," she argues. I start fake coughing and clearing my throat. She hisses, "*Ki kware*. Choke." But I see the smile threatening to break free on her lips as she walks out of the room.

After I pray Maghrib, I head out to the dining room to join the rest of my family for dinner. Umm'Hafsa is in the best of moods when all of us are around and spending time together like this.

After Mariya and Ladidi clear the plates, the news plays on low volume on the television in front of us. Shatu and Umm'Hafsa are discussing a book they are both reading – *Atomic Habits* – when she turns to me.

"Hafsa, have you finished the book I gave you?" From the corner of my eye, I see Sara looking in my direction. Since she returned, she has been paying a lot of attention to my interactions with Umm'Hafsa.

"Oh, *um*, I've started." That is a lie, "I'm like halfway now." Since Umm'Hafsa gave me an Islamic book titled *The Secrets of Divine Love* about three weeks ago, I haven't even opened a single page. I just don't think she's in a position to give me recommendations about divine love.

"That's good. Did you see the quotes I highlighted?" I nod convincingly, and she continues, "*gaskiya*, it's an excellent book. When you're done, I have another one for you –*Secrets of a Muslim Bride*."

Fat chance that I would read that too, but I have to be as cordial as possible with her until I leave her house.

"Bebi," daddy says as the segment on the news that he is watching ends, "since you're reading all these books, maybe when Sadiq's family comes for introduction, I'll just ask them for your *sadaqi*, dowry, and if they have it, then we'll just get you two married right there and then. No need for any delay."

"Daddy, no! Please," I shout from across the table as everyone laughs. "Are you trying to get rid of me so quickly?"

Sara widens her eyes, "oh my God. On Twitter today, I read about this guy who went to ask for his girlfriend's hands and her father got them married right there. It was so *Masha Allah.*"

Daddy nods, "Oh yes, it is Islamically permissible. *Ya ma fi lada*, it's even more blessed. Weddings with less noise are better."

"*Tsk tsk*, not my wedding. I want mine very loud." I bring out my phone and type a message to Sadiq: *Daddy just said when you come for gaisuwa, he might get us married there and then. Lol*

I see the bubbles start to form immediately, then they stop. Five seconds later, a message comes in: *YES! ALHAMDULILLAH. ALHAMDULILLAH.*

I chuckle as I shake my head, even though I absolutely love his reaction: *Excuse you? I'm not just going to move into your house like that.*

B, haven't you tortured me enough? I imagine him smiling as he types.

Barely! I want a themed reception and a bachelorette party, I confess.

He sends another message: *You can have as many events as you want, you'd just be attending them from our house.*

Not a chance, I reply before turning my attention back to the dinner table, which is empty except for the platter of fruit we're all picking at.

"Your daughter has a list of performers she wants for her reception *wai,*" Umm'Hafsa tells daddy with a laugh as she bites into a slice of watermelon.

"*Ah toh shikenan*, okay. Bebi gets whatever she wants," he says proudly.

Sara's attention has been on the television for a few seconds when she suddenly says, "look. Isn't that his uncle on the news?"

I look up and see Sadiq's uncle on the screen. It's a replay of a panel interview from earlier in the day about the aviation worker's protest and the subsequent domestic flight shutdown.

Daddy looks up at the television. "Oh okay? The head of airline operations there?"

"No," I say, "the man next to him."

With a slight turn of her head towards the television, Umm'Hafsa takes sight of the grey-haired man talking just as the red ribbon on the screen that has his position flips from Minister of Aviation to his name Senator Sufyan Dankabo.

Daddy picks up his glasses from the table and wears them. "Oh, *shi*

Dankabo? Isn't Dankabo from Kano? I thought Sadiq was from Jigawa. That was my understanding –" I didn't hear the rest of his sentence because his attention swiftly moves to Umm'Hafsa, who is patting her chest as she chokes on the watermelon in her mouth. Daddy moves her glass of water closer to her. She can't drink the water because her cough is only worsening. "Sannu," Daddy says as she raises her reddened eyes. "Did you swallow a seed?" he asks.

She shakes her head and wipes her mouth with the end of her veil. Her expression hardens, and I see a vein pop on her forehead.

"Sorry, mum," Sara says, and as the room becomes quiet again, she adds, "this is his dad's younger brother." She knew about their family as much as I did because of her friendship with his sister.

"Oh, okay. He's Abubakar Sadiq Dankabo *kenan*?" Daddy removes his glasses as he looks back in my direction.

"No, Abubakar Sadiq Ringim." Even his full name sounds so powerful, my husband-to-be.

Umm'Hafsa stands up from the table, her cough still not subsiding.

"Sannu," I call after her as she walks out of the dining room.

* * *

I just got off the phone with Sadiq the next afternoon and I start getting ready to head out to *H&I* when my door slowly opens. I look up to see Umm'Hafsa walking into my room. She doesn't look like she got enough sleep last night – her eyes are red-rimmed, and she has no makeup on, which is very unlike her at this time of the day. It is also odd that she's still wearing her purple robes over her black nightgown. I have never seen her in her robes outside her and daddy's room ever, not since that night years ago when Mohammed had really high fever and she was in his room when I walked in.

"Hafsatu, *muna da magana*; we need to talk." It's Friday. Usually, at this time, she's decked up in an expensive lace or *atamfa*, with her face all made up and her headtie wrapped in her signature turban style, tucking away any sign or tendril of her soft hair underneath. But right now, her hair looks a mess, like she literally got up from her pillow and walked into my room. Maybe she knows I know her secret?

I drop the fan makeup brush I just used to apply highlighter to my cheekbones, a bit of the golden dust shimmer still on its soft white bristles. As I look away from the mirror, I swirl my tufted chair in her direction. I notice that she doesn't sit down on the blue accent chair by her side; she just supports herself on it with her right arm.

"Okay," I say. Normally I would add 'mum' but I have been using that word sparingly in the past few months.

She makes eye contact with me and I see a determined resolve in her eyes, even from the way her brows are pulled upwards. It reminds me of my expression when I make a decision I intend to stand by.

"*Um*, about this Sadiq. *Sadiq dai ba mijin auren ki bane*; he is not the man you will marry. I won't give him permission to marry you."

This has to be a joke. She hasn't exactly been the parent with the sense of humor, but maybe it has finally rubbed off on her. "Mum, it's a few months too early for April fool's jokes."

But she isn't smiling. "I can't allow this marriage happen," she says, shaking her head continuously.

"The same Sadiq you invited into this house? The one you told daddy is a better choice than Bashir?"

"Hafsatu, why must you always argue? *Ki ba shi hakuri*, tell him sorry. Some things have come to light, and –"

"What things?" I stand up from the chair. "His uncles are coming soon to talk about our wedding, and –"

"Then you better save them the embarrassment of coming because they will not be allowed into this house. We're no longer in support of you and him getti–"

"No one is going to stop me from marrying him."

Her face pales as she moves closer to me with her hand on her chest, "What did you say? You are raising your voice at me?"

I raise my voice even higher. "You're not stopping me from marrying Sadiq because I can't wait to leave this house."

"*Kin sha kwaya ne? Are you on drugs?*" She takes another step towards me, her eyes narrow as the lines between her brows furrow even deeper. "*Ni kike wa magana haka?* You're still raising your voice at me, your mother?"

"What is so bad about Sadiq that I can't marry him?" I ask her. I can't think of any reason why she would do a complete 180 on how she feels about us being together except that she was eavesdropping while I confided in daddy. "Is this because his father was abusive? Well, he is not his father. We are not our parents."

She looks at me with tears in her eyes as she chuckles bitterly, shaking her head. "You don't know anything."

"I know enough to know that we are not our parents. He is not his dad, a-and I am not like *you*." I spat out. She can't just make a proclamation, a decision about my future and think that I will accept it without a fight.

Her gaze holds mine and I see her lips shaking.

I continue, "Standing here like a saint and judging other people's parents. Who is going to judge you? I know your secret. I know that I am not your husband's child."

"Hafsatu!" Daddy's thunderous voice echoes through the walls of my room. I whirl my head in his direction and see him in a white Jallabiya. The look on his face is one I have never seen before. Without his glasses, his eyes look like they will pop out of their sockets, and his chest is heaving heavily. He looks shocked. He must have heard what I said to Umm'Hafsa. I never meant for him to find out about her infidelity this way.

"Dad –"

He raises his hand as he stops me. "You need to apologize to your mother right now. I will not tolerate you talking to her like this."

I glance at Umm'Hafsa, and I see her close her eyes as tears fall down her eyes, dampening her cheeks. *Apologize? To her? I should be the one receiving an apology. Or him. Anybody in this room, but her.*

"Daddy, you don't understand. She has been keeping secrets away from you," I say, angry at Umm'Hafsa and angry at myself for crying uncontrollably as I walk toward him. Daddy has never raised his voice at me and I have never been at the receiving end of his rare bouts of anger but here we are today – all because of this woman. "Daddy, ask her yourself," I say as I point an accusing finger at her. "Ask her who my real father is."

Zuwaira

1999

Another day, another discovery, another recommended sacrifice, another dark drink in a swan water bottle, another white powder to add to my bath water. I was tired. I had no interest anymore. It almost felt like my desire to remain married was flushed out of my system along with the dead baby. My nights were filled with dreams, dreams of my child. I would see myself holding her in my arms, and she would suddenly stop cooing, and I would look down only to see my dead sister Maimuna's bloody face. It was frightening and I would wake up screaming.

The hours I spent awake were mostly spent driving to remote villages and communities, from *Tudun Wada* to *Birnin Gwari*. With my ailing mother-in-law's health on the decline, it was still her sister, Hajiya Indo, who was taking me around on the quest for *neman taimako*. I cannot remember the exact point our movements got redirected from *malams*, men who recommended verses from the Qur'an and special prayers, to strange-looking men who called out to djinns and the unseen, but it did. The one thing they all had in common was that there was no shortage of enemies they could see plotting against me – from my husband's wives to my uncle, Kawu Sani, to my uncle's wives. One even said that my mother-in-law secretly hated me. At that point, it didn't matter because I had stopped believing them.

Unknown to Alhaji, his mother and aunt had taken me to mountains and streams to wash off the *farin kafa* they were told I entered the marriage with. I didn't know if all the things that they scrubbed my legs with helped Alhaji's businesses because I had stopped paying attention. I had even removed the charm they gave me to put above my door; it's not like it stopped his rage from coming on every few weeks when I least expected it.

"There's something that has been buried under three trees in that compound and until they have been unearthed, you'll never have peace in your husband's house," one of the shamans said. His name is Djalo, a tall, dark-skinned man with milky eyes. It took me a while to realize that he was blind, yet he peered into a silver bowl with water – or a liquid I assumed was water – that showed him things we couldn't see with our naked eyes. This particular shaman was a very popular man who came all the way from Guinea Bissau with a Hausa translator, Aissatou. According to what I'd heard, he'd spent weeks in Nigeria, traveling from Borno to Sokoto to solve the problems of housewives, and his methods never failed. He had come to Abuja to do the same, residing in a guesthouse in Lifecamp.

"There are tens of trees in that compound. How are we to know which ones they are buried under?" Aissatou translated what I asked and he replied in a language I did not understand in low tones. There was a sour taste in my mouth and I was sweating even in the air-conditioned room. Next to me, Hajiya Indo nodded in agreement, as though she were wondering too.

Aissatou translated what he said again. "We have to make you something to bury in the middle of the night that will cancel out the others. But it's a powerful charm and it has a hefty price."

"If it's about money, go ahead and do it. That's not a problem," Hajiya Indo said, and the woman whispered to him again.

"Djalo says it is not just hefty in price, but in the sacrifice."

"And what kind of sacrifice is that?" I stopped wiping the sweat off my forehead. We had already sacrificed chickens and goats at the other places we have been.

"It's a blood sacrifice. Human blood."

My jaw dropped. "What did you say? Like, a human being? A person? You expect me to take part in killing a person? God forbid!" Definitely not a price to pay to remain in a monster's house. If this was the only way I could remain in his house or the only way to stop him from beating me, it only meant I would die in his hands one day because this was not a sacrifice I could partake in.

"Oh, come on. What are you saying? We're not heathens or barbarians. We're not slaughtering anybody. After you bring the money, all we do is put a charm like this," she reaches into a clay pot and brings out a small gourd with inscriptions around it, tied with a red cloth, "and we put it on a busy road, like an expressway. That is all."

I widened my eyes, "and how does it work?"

"We leave it there and if there is an accident on that road, it means we get our blood sacrifice."

The chill started from my feet and climbed up my legs to my stomach until it reached my fingers, and they started to tingle. My vision blurred as I saw my father, mother, and Maimuna laying bloodied and mangled on the expressway under the commercial bus. *Were they someone's sacrifice?* The tears started to sting my eyes and I could feel the bile climbing up my throat. The disgust at who I had become was so revolting that my breakfast could not stay down. I stood up and hurriedly ran to the open door that led to a bathroom and crouched over the toilet and threw up.

"*Ba da ni ba*; I shall not be a part in this," I kept saying over and over, loud enough for them to hear as the vomit kept coming.

When I came out of the toilet, I went straight to the chair, picked up my handbag, and looked at Hajiya Indo. "Hajiya, *ni na tafi*; I am leaving."

"Listen to us, *Yar Saratu*, daughter of Saratu." Aissatou's voice stopped me just as I reached the door, and I turned around to see Djalo whispering into her ears. I wondered how they knew my mother's name. Even Hajiya Indo did not know these details about me. "If you won't do it for yourself, at least do it for your children. The water just told Djalo what happened to your last pregnancy. It was a girl, a beautiful girl just like you."

My baby. It was a baby girl. I knew it. I felt it.

238

I covered my eyes with the end of my veil as I sobbed until I reached the car where the driver was waiting. Hajiya Indo joined me a few minutes later and we drove back home in silence. That night, I promised myself that none of my children would be snatched away from me before I got to hold them again. I would die before I allowed that to happen. I would find a way to protect them, one that did not involve human sacrifice.

* * *

Over the next few months, Balaraba and I had a few more moments of something akin to friendship. We were not best of friends, but I saw humanity in her and we understood each other's pain. At this point, my eyes were open to the fact that the two other wives did not go through what we dealt with. It was like the vault to his anger was only turned on on the days that he spent in our sections.

"Why don't you go out anymore?" I asked her one afternoon. We were attending an event for the ribbon-cutting ceremony of one of the antenatal clinics our husband had just commissioned on behalf of the governor. We sat on one side while the other two wives sat on his other side. We were all wearing attires made from the same fabric and posed for pictures together after he finished his speech.

She adjusted her dark sunshades on her face and answered, "his witch of a mother made him stop me from working."

I knew that the relationship between Balaraba and our mother-in-law wasn't as smooth as mine. Hajiya Uwa always complained that Balaraba was too stubborn. "*Idon ta ya waye da yawa*; she is too exposed," she often said, like it was a flaw in Balaraba's character. Over time, I had come to find out that Balaraba used to be Alhaji's secretary. We were at another event a week later, a fundraiser for women with VVF, which was so prevalent in Northern Nigeria.

"What does a secretary do?" I asked her as we clapped softly after Alhaji announced his huge donation to the crowd of journalists pushing their microphones and news cameras closer to the platform where he stood.

"I used to book his flight tickets, schedule his appointments and screen his guests. We used to work until late most evenings and he grew really fond of me. He even paid for me to get a university degree because I only had my Higher National Diploma, when I started working for him. After I graduated, they retained me at the Civil Secretariat, where I did my NYSC. He even used to come and see me there," she replied. *Oh, so they had a love story before they got married.* I tried to imagine a softer side or romantic side to Alhaji, but nothing came to my mind. "When he said that he wanted to marry me, I made him promise that I would continue working after marriage, but here I am." She kept quiet as the servers came to drop soft drinks in front of us. "The painful part is that my father warned me; he told me not to marry Alhaji, and I didn't listen. I went ahead, converted and married him."

"Oh, your family is not Muslim?" I was surprised.

"I'm a Kalabari girl *oh*," she said proudly. "My name is Eremina. I'm from Rivers, *kawai girman Kano*; I just grew up in Kano."

I was astonished because I would never have guessed if she hadn't told me; she carried our culture and religion so well. She never joked with prayers, and during Ramadan, all that could be heard coming from her section was the recitation of the Qur'an on the radio. "Because your name is Balaraba, I just assumed –"

"It's Alhaji's sisters and his other wives that started calling me Balaraba. At first it was Balarabiya, then they said I was born on Wednesday or something."

Balarabiya – an Arab. I could see why they would call her that. Her skin was very light, so she could almost pass for an Arab. "When I converted, the name that I chose was that of the mother of Prophet Muhammed."

"*Sallalahu Alayhi Wa Salam*," I invoked blessings on our prophet the way we always do when his name is mentioned. She picked the perfect name for her personality – Amina, the straightforward and honest one. She was too straightforward in fact. She didn't shy away from conversations that women were not supposed to talk about with other people, like bedroom matters. There was a day she peeped into my section as I was getting

Abu-Abu ready for the inter-house sports competition at his school. She stayed by door as she watched me tie the laces to his shoes, gave him his lunchbox, rubbed his head, and told him to hurry up before the driver started honking.

"*Allah sarki*, seeing you like that almost reminded me of how his mother was with him," she said as he ran past her and towards the car. "This section used to be hers, maybe that's why Abubakar is so comfortable here."

I stood up and went to the window to watch him enter the car. "Were you and her close?"

"*Allah ya jikan ta*, May her soul rest in peace," and then she answered my question. "Not really, she was a very quiet woman."

Balaraba never came into my section unless it was urgent, and she certainly never stayed long enough to engage in conversations, so I wondered what this was about. I must have been staring at her pointedly because she said, "I overheard your fight with Alhaji two nights ago. From the way he left here in anger around midnight, I suspected the reason."

As she spoke, I looked away, embarrassed. It was the first time something like that had happened. I had stopped using the incense Hajiya Babba gave me and it was long gone in the garbage. I had also stopped using all the powders the shamans gave me to rub over my body to gain his favor because I was tired of trying. And still, the evening had gone better than usual. He ate his food, watched the news, went to the mosque to pray, and read his newspapers when he returned. Later that night, as his hands groped my body in the dark and he climbed on top of me, I didn't feel the usual pressure between my naked legs. I heard him grunt in frustration, then it became anger. When he got off, pulled up his trousers and left my section to return to his, a part of me relieved.

"It's what his wives do, they've entered phase two," Balaraba said. "Instead of frustrating you, now they are frustrating him."

"What do you mean?"

She lowered her voice and pointed to her pelvis, "his *thing* won't work when he's with you anymore, and you won't be as lucky next time. That's how I got this one. He'll eventually take out his frustration on you," she pointed to a small scar across her forehead, very tiny but still a scar from a healed wound. I sighed. *Does this ever end?* She passed me a small white and blue box. I looked down at my hands and saw the words 'Viagra' written on it with black letters.

"What is this?"

"Medicine. No, not *that* kind of medicine," she said hurriedly as I started to shake my head. "This is from a pharmacy."

"What does it do?"

"It'll help him get it up," her voice took on a conspiratorial tone. "I usually crush one tablet and put it in his food." I must have looked confused because she continued trying to convince me. "I get it from a pharmacy across town. It's safe," she said, pushing it into my hands, "It'll save you from a broken head."

I opened up my hands, loosening the grip of the medicine she'd thrust into them. Of course, I could crush one of these small white tablets and put it in his food, but if it worked like she said it would, then he would have his way with me at night. I was not looking forward to that. If anything, the night Alhaji stormed out of my section was the best night I had had in months. All by myself in bed, all I had to worry about was sending his breakfast to his section the following morning.

I returned the small box to her. "Can you get me sleeping pills, instead?"

She looked confused for a minute before she broke into a laugh, "why didn't I ever think of that?"

Ibrahim

1999

With my housemanship in Lere coming to an end, I was looking forward to two things. One, finally getting a whole day's worth of sleep; and two, I was looking forward to going to Kaduna for my niece Salma's 6th birthday party. I was definitely not going to miss being on call 24 hours a day.

In Lere, I shared a room with two classmates of mine, Dapo, the most practical man I knew, and Suleiman, a happy-go-lucky fellow. On Friday evenings, which happened to be our least busy days, Suleiman would carefully hang the kaftan he wore to the mosque carefully on a nail that stuck out of the back of the door to avoid it getting rumpled or creased. After Maghrib, they both headed out to the girl's hostel of Lere Polytechnic for *tadi*, night chats, where they talked beneath the canopy of trees and were surrounded by a multitude of snacks, soft drinks, and suya vendors strategically positioned by the gates.

"*Ibro, ba za ka zo mu je tadi ba?*" Suleiman would ask if I would go out with them. He would brush his beard with a stiff bristle brush, then bring out a can of masculine-scented spray and douse himself all over, like he was using air freshener.

I would look back to the book I was reading on the mattress on the floor, *Fiqh us-Sunnah* by Shaik Syed Sabiq. "No, Sule. I'll stay indoors today."

One day, he sat next to me as he opened a small circular can filled with shoe polish. "You always say that. *Haba*, mallam. You should come out and see what the world is saying. *Wallahi* Khadija's friend always asks after you. She made me promise to bring you one of these days," he said as he carefully dabbed the brush in the black paste and brought his shoe close to his chest, moving in quick strokes as the worn leather started to shine.

"So this perfume you're trying to block my nose with is all for Khadija?" Khadija was a second-year nursing student Suleiman hoped to marry.

"*Baza ka gane ba*; you won't understand. The love I have for that girl *ko*..." he left his sentence incomplete and started to whistle a love song from a popular Hausa film.

I was sure I could not understand why a man would spend so much time polishing a shoe that she wouldn't even be able to see in the darkness. I had followed them there once in our first month in Lere, and I didn't care for waiting for 20-to-30 minutes by the trunk of a tree while the Sule and Dapo peaked in through the gates, hoping to find someone going to the same block as the girl they wanted to see so they could call her for the boy. The exchange went the same way. "*DanAllah, baiwar Allah*, please. Help me carry word to Khadija in C Block, Room 5."

"Who should I say is looking for her?"

"Please, tell her it's Sule."

Depending on whether the girl wanted to see you or not, you could spend another 15-to-45 minutes waiting around chatting couples and laughing friends while the aroma of *suya* from the nearby grill enveloped your Friday kaftan. It was an experience I found oddly interesting, but I ruled it out completely for myself. So, I never called on a girl.

On the days I did not want to be bothered by my roommates' insistence that I come with them to meet their girlfriends' friends, I would make up an excuse. My most frequently used one was that I was going to Lere Low Cost, an area with affordable housing provided by the government for civil servants, to visit my maternal aunt, Baaba Kande.

Baaba Kande was a widow whose late husband used to be a government clerk. She was a very jovial and tall woman in her forties with a toothy smile enhanced by her *wushirya*, the gap between her two front teeth. I never visited her until I knew I had enough money to buy her some fruits from the fruit seller who pushed different kinds of fruits on a wheelbarrow just outside the hostel and even offered some to the buyer to taste before purchase. Baaba Kande especially loved the small, dark, sweet mangoes we called *Binta suga*. On this particular evening, my black nylon bag was filled with them. Whenever I returned to the hostel, she would always measure some rice or beans to give me. She never allowed me to leave empty-handed. One day I even returned to the hostel with a tuber of yam to the delight of my roommates.

"*Likita Likita*," she sat on the living room chair facing the door as I said my sallama and removed my shoes. She wore a dark-colored hijab and cooled herself with a brown raffia handheld fan.

"Baaba, I got those mangoes you love," I said as I set the nylon bag next to the foot of her chair and I sat on the mat.

"Are they already in season?" she feigned surprise. "*Kai*, you're a blessed person. I've been craving them since last Friday. *Bari a zubo maka pate*; let me get you some porridge," she started to stand up.

"Don't worry yourself, I already ate." Street food was very cheap in the boy's hostel. We never lacked variety – from tea and bread from the *mai shayi* by the mosque to the *mai masa* by the traffic light to *kosai*, fried yam, and sweet potatoes from the old woman who we all called 'mama.' As long as we had our lab coats on, mama would give us food without asking for money because she knew that we would always settle our outstanding bills as soon as we got our allowance.

"Ibrahim, there's a girl I want you to meet. She's our neighbors daughter," Baaba said as her fan pushed the hot air around. I imagined it did nothing to cool her off from how she was sweating.

" Baaba, I don't have the time to be seeing anybody. We're very busy at the hospital."

"You didn't even allow me to finish. This girl is well-behaved, she's educated in western and Islamic teachings and I know looks are not everything but I must tell you that out of all the girls on this our street, she is the prettiest. *Wallahi kun dace*; you two are a match. Please go and see her, I've already spoken to her mother about you."

"I can't always come into town to meet with this girl, because I don't have a car, and getting a bike back after Isha is hard."

That was the first of many excuses that I gave my aunt regarding this girl she wanted me to meet. But one evening two months later, when I went to greet her, she heralded me at the door after my sallama.

"*Likita na*, my doctor. Welcome." She was in a dark blue hijab that fell all the way to her feet, with thick black socks underneath.

I wondered why she sounded in an even better mood than usual as I took off my shoes at the door and sat on the mat next to her like I usually do, pushing the yellow and black nylon bag with a watermelon and oranges to the foot of her chair.

"Good evening Baaba."

"*Oyoyo*, welcome. I'm so happy you're here on time today," she leaned back into her chair with a satisfied smile. "This is my neighbor's daughter, Laila." I look up to see a young girl come out from behind the curtain. Baaba Kande was not exaggerating; the girl was pretty. Not even her high forehead could take away from her comely features.

"*Ina wuni*, good evening." She had a shy smile on her face and I noticed her dimples. It reminded me of a girl I knew some time ago, a near-distant memory beginning to feel like a dream from another lifetime.

"Evening, Laila," I looked away. "How are you?"

"I'm fine."

My aunt stood up and headed into her room; Laila remained by the door, "Go and sit down, Laila. Let me get the dress sample for your mother. I hope I can find it where I kept it." She disappeared into the room to find this supposed dress that had somehow managed to get legs and run away. At least, that was the only thing I could assume since she was in her room for a while, leaving me to pay attention to a spider on the corner of the ceiling as it weaved a web. Its multiple legs were hanging on unseen thin threads one at a time. I kept my gaze away from Laila and her dimple so I wouldn't think too much of Zuwaira, but I could not stop myself. I couldn't help but wonder how she was, and I was sure she had no spiders in her house.

"Can I get you water?" Laila asked.

I looked back at her, "ah no, thank you. I'm fasting." I usually did on Mondays and Thursdays.

She glanced outside at the almost setting sun, "oh it'll soon be time for you to break your fast."

I nod in agreement and my attention returned to the ceiling. A wall gecko was moving dangerously close to the spider. By all indications, this spider would end up as the gecko's dinner. Zuwaira was scared of geckos, almost as much as she was scared of snakes. *Astagfirullah. Astagfirullah.* I chanted my mantra in my head, as I always did whenever I found my thoughts returning to her.

Minutes later, when my aunty came back with a fabric in a bag and gave it to Laila, she said to me, "*Likita*, it's getting late. Please, escort Laila home. Their house is just at the end of the street."

I got up and Laila led the way. We walked out of the small white gate and unto the street. When we got to their house, I stopped at the gate to bid her goodbye. "*Toh* bye, Laila."

"Bye, *a sha ruwa lafiya*," she said about my fast, wishing me a good *iftar*.

"*Na gode*," I thanked her and headed straight to the mosque a few houses away. After praying, I returned to my aunt's place and she had tuwo out for me.

"So, how did it go? What did you two talk about? Did she tell you that she's in Teaching school? She wants to become a teacher." Her eyes twinkled with delight as she told me more details about the girl like she was reading from a bio-data page.

"Oh, that's good. Teaching is a good profession," I said as I ate some dates and opened a pure water sachet with my teeth.

"She told you, *ko*?"

"No, we didn't talk."

"What do you mean you didn't talk?"

"I escorted her home like you asked me to and then I went to the mosque."

"Ibrahim, you didn't say anything to her? Why are you like this?" She looked visibly annoyed. I knew that my aunt would not stop trying to find girls for me to get married to, so I reduced my visits to her house.

* * *

The Federal Medical Centre in Lere was one of the approved medical centers for internship training in Nigeria. While most of my classmates opted for University Teaching Hospitals and those with the means completed theirs in Private hospitals, I ended up in Lere not only because I was running out of time for my posting, but also because it was close enough to Kaduna for me to visit Ya Isa and Ya Aisha regularly.

Unfortunately, I hardly visited them because we were busy, especially during my Paediatric rotation. Those days and nights were hectic due to the fact that the medical center was situated right in the middle of about seven communities and five villages with poor drainage systems, making cases of water-borne diseases frequent among children. On the final week of our internal Medicine rotation, we worked closely with the senior doctor, Dr. Aji, attending ward rounds, making treatment notes, and clerking new patients with Matron Oza, a robust motherly figure with a short temper.

During unplanned breaks, when things had quietened down and we had a few minutes of silence while we carried out treatment instruction, she would tell me about her son, who was in his first year in medical school at ABU. You could see the pride on her face even as she complained about the expensive textbooks that she had to buy for him.

We had a staff room where we ate lunch. Eating lunch as a house officer meant one or two bites of your fried yam before you hurried away for emergency call duty. One day, after an emergency call, I hurried down the hall with Dapo, trying to finish the sachet of pure water I was drinking while putting on my lab coat, we stopped at the sink just behind the nurses' station by the patient wards to wash our hands. As I waited for him to soap his hands, I heard the two nurses on duty talking among themselves.

"*Na wa oh*, I told you they'll be back." She was wearing white trousers under her white dress as she wrote notes in an unnamed patient file.

"Last time, she came with one woman that looked like her sister. Doctor wanted to admit her but this same man insisted that they had to leave and they left here around midnight," the other nurse in a straight white dress added as she chewed her gum silently.

After Dapo rinsed his hands, I lathered and rinsed mine, drying them hurriedly on the clean cloth provided.

Dr. Aji's voice filled the small ward we entered. "The patient is a car accident victim with a simple clavicle, collarbone fracture due to possible impact." We quickly huddled around him as he pointed to the tent-like bump of the fracture site under the patient's neck. As she turned her head away from her sagging shoulder, I tried to gauge her age by looking at her face, and my jaw dropped as my mouth formed a silent O.

Zuwaira.

As Dr. Aji confirmed that no nerves or blood vessels were damaged when the fracture occurred, he gave her a slight nod, and she readjusted the neckline of her abaya. Her eyes were downcast, but I could tell she was in obvious pain from the grimace on her face due to the broken bone. She was wearing a black abaya and her hair was covered with a matching veil in a hijab style, and on her feet were silver shoes, most accident victims don't have both their shoes when they are brought to the hospital, and they were usually dusty and disheveled. There was not even a speck of dirt on Zuwaira.

"Ogundare, lead the patient for an X-ray," Dr. Aji said to Dapo. My attention returned to the senior doctor as I hurriedly looked away from her. He lowered his voice as he spoke to her in Hausa, "don't worry, we'll just do a quick X-ray." He motioned for her to follow the nurse and Dapo into the imaging lab. One that Dr. Aji funded by himself when he returned from the United States after spending years there as chief medical director of a hospital in California.

"Gaya, immobilization using a sling should be enough to send the patient home." He left me with directions, and while I waited for them to return from the X-ray lab, I looked into her chart and was surprised to see that this was not her first time here. How did I miss seeing her the last time she was brought here?

By the time she came back, she had a grumpy man in his late twenties or early thirties in a bright white kaftan and trousers with her. It was not Alhaji Ringim, her husband, but he had to be somewhat related because he was arguing with the nurses about how long the whole process was taking. This man did not look like he had been near an accident scene that day.

My attention went back to Zuwaira, who was being assisted by a nurse as she held onto her right hand. She sat down on the bed right by where I had everything needed to put her hand in a sling on a stainless steel sterile tray.

"Put your palm on your shoulder," the nurse instructed and she did as she was told even though her eyes were fixed on the floor. She made no eye contact with anyone in the room – not even me.

I gently passed the triangular bandage under her arm, then around her back, and tied it in a reef knot. I moved closer to her to secure the knot and the ends of her scarf shifted, revealing a side of her neck. As she moved swiftly to cover her body, I saw red bruises on her neck – discoloration against her skin made by what I could undoubtedly conclude were finger marks. Someone had their hands around her neck in an attempt to strangle her. Very recently, from the lesions I could see. I cleared my throat.

"Where was the accident?" I asked. It was a standard doctor-patient question.

I watched as the long lashes of her eyes slowly flickered upwards and her eyes widened as she looked up at me for the first time. The look of surprised recognition was quickly replaced by fear as her eyes darted behind me to the man who was watching us closely.

"Um, um..." she frowned as she tried to think of an answer.

The man behind me answered just as I had expected, "on the way to Zaria." He moved closer to inspect what I was doing.

I looked away from him and noticed that Zuwaira was blinking rapidly to stop her eyes from filling up with tears. "The roads there are so bad," I said, mainly to him as I tucked in the extra bandage around her arm. He murmured something unintelligible and I continued, "but isn't Zaria on the other side of town? Must have been a long drive here. About three hours, I suspect. Why didn't you go to the General Hospital?" I asked, fighting the urge to add 'or the countless other clinics between the road from Zaria to Lere.' Why did they come to this medical center on the outskirts of town? I looked up at him, but he didn't answer. Behind him, the nurse shook her head toward me like she was prompting me to keep quiet.

As soon as we were done, Zuwaira reached for her handbag with her other hand, almost like she was an actress acting out a well-rehearsed script. She stood up and walked out of the ward and the man followed behind her, keeping a respectable distance between them. I went to the desk on the pretense of looking for some paperwork and watched him pay with wads of crisp cash. He even kept an extra envelope on the desk. "For your staff," I heard him say before picking up her pain relief prescriptions. She waited just by the exit of the medical center as a black Pathfinder jeep that was parked by the trees outside pulled up towards her. The driver came down and opened the door to the back seat for her, while the man who came with her laughed and exchanged pleasantries with Matron Oza and some nurses outside before he got into the front seat. The car disappeared back on the untarred road, leaving behind a massive gust of red dust. There was not a single scratch or dent on that car.

Zuwaira

The few things I knew about marriage were things I heard during the first few years of Islammiya until my parents could no longer afford for us to go because Maimuna and I helped our mother hawk drinks in the evenings. Other things I knew about marriage I heard in bits and pieces from my aunty's gossip, Hausa films, and the rushed advice multiple women gave me the day I was brought into Alhaji's house. On that day, all the women emphasized in their advice were the things I needed to do to please him. His rights. I didn't even know that I had rights as a wife.

I knew that there were three strings that held every marriage and that these strings can be snapped one after the other and the marriage will still hold, but when the third string breaks, then the marriage is over. Apart from that, I knew nothing else about divorce; I did not even know that a Muslim woman had rights over her husband or that maltreatment was grounds for her to initiate separation.

The first time Alhaji pronounced a divorce to me was around the period when the first of his three food trucks had an accident, before the beatings started. Before Hajiya Uwa even started taking me out. I was crouched on the floor when he said, "I divorce you." It was because of undercooked meat in his food. My whole body went still as I heard those words, those dreaded words. After he left, I picked up my veil, wrapped it in a hurried frenzy around my body and walked to my mother-in-law's section as fast as my legs could carry me without running.

"Hajiya, he just divorced me," I sobbed into the ends of my veil as I slumped to the floor with my back against her wall. What would I do now? I hadn't even been married for three months. Does this mean I would go back to my uncle, Kawu Sani's house? This was a thing of shame – that I had only been married for three months and he had divorced me already.

"What happened?" My mother inlaw crushed the cigarette she was holding on a yellow and red ashtray. "*Kai*, Alhaji *bai da hakuri*; he has no patience."

I kept crying, wondering how I messed my marriage up so badly so early. The marriage everybody kept telling me how lucky I was to be in.

"Listen, stand up. You don't have to cry." Hajiya Uwa said to me, " this has happened to all of us. I remember the first time his father gave me a divorce. I stood up, packed my box and left his house, *na yi yaji*." *Yaji* was when a woman angrily left her husband's house and returned to her father's house, but Hajiya Uwa came from a long line of privilege and a big family, from what she had told me. My case was different; I didn't have a father or a mother. My uncle would not take kindly to me returning to his house. Worst of all, Tani would mock me. "I stayed in my father's house until his relatives came to talk to my father. They reconciled us, that's when I went back." She tapped the chair next to her for me to sit on. "That's why I'm here. I'm the elder here, so I'll tell you to go to your section and observe your *Iddah*."

"*Iddah*?" I asked with tears still streaming down my face.

"Yes, your waiting period. He'll come back to his senses. Just wait and see. This has happened to most of your co wives."

I wiped my tears, "How long am I going to wait for?"

"*Iddah* is three-months long and if in that period he doesn't come into your section or touch you, then at the end of the three months, that is when you're divorced. But don't worry, I'm here. It won't come to that." She instructed me to return to my section and not to leave for any reason – not even to go to the salon to get my hair washed, or to visit family. I waited, and I waited while life continued. In the mornings, I heard the other wives laughing as they went about their daily activities. In the evenings, I could hear the children playing around the compound. At night time, I saw him going in and out of the other wives' sections as scheduled.

Eighteen days. That was how long I waited without seeing him. During that period, Hashim regularly brought foodstuff for me; my store, my fridge, and freezer were always full. I never lacked anything, but I woke up alone, I ate alone, and I slept alone. One night, after I had taken a bath and was about to change into my nightdress, I heard Alhaji by my front door. I knew it was him because I heard him talking to Sufyan, giving him instructions about the truckload of Sallah rams that he needed to deliver to some politicians' houses. He always did this as a form of goodwill.

I froze as I heard him close the door behind him, and without even switching on the light in the living room, he came straight into the bedroom, not even sparing me a glance as I stood rooted to the floor in my white towel. *Did he come to ask me to leave his house for good?*

He dropped his newspapers on the bedside table, and as he removed his wristwatch, he said: "when you're done, switch off the light."

Later that night, we had sex, and he stayed in my section for the next three days after coming back from work. And that was it; we were no longer divorced. But now, our marriage was held by two strings. I knew I had to work to maintain it at two strings. That was then – before all the beatings and hospital visits. Now, I had no interest in maintaining those marital strings.

As I watched Alhaji doze off in the living room as the television played the news loudly, surrounded by the empty plates he ate his food, I wondered why he had not uttered more divorces to me. Was the first strike done just to scare me into submission? It worked, because after that first divorce, I was on my best behavior to avoid him getting angry. I treated him like a master, but he got angry anyway yet he never uttered another divorce. Why not the second and the third, instead of hitting me every time he was displeased? From what I had gathered, Mamie and even Balaraba also had one strike against them. The only woman he had never uttered a divorce to was his first wife, Hajiya Babba.

His head rolled off his palm in his deep slumber, and he was jerked awake, looking around the living room in a surprised manner like he could not believe he had fallen asleep as soon as he finished his food. His eyes kept searching around the living room until he saw me sitting at the dining table, far away from him. I had a blank expression on my face.

"What are you waiting for? Clear the plates," he snapped angrily as he stood up and staggered to the room. Through the curtain from where I sat, I could see that he did not even remove his kaftan and trousers; he just went straight to bed and his snores began as soon as his head hit the pillow.

That had been the routine for the past few days, and I relished it. The day Balaraba dropped the sleeping pills with me, a part of me was scared that one tablet would not work, so I crushed two tablets and sprinkled them in his soups. The nights that followed were nights of peace of mind. I could sleep soundly next to him, knowing that he would not even lift a hand to touch me, not out of anger and definitely not to force himself inside me.

My peace of mind came to an end on a Friday when the greatest calamity befell us. Hajiya Uwa died. The doctors said she died of lung disease due to her smoking habit. After they brought her body back from the hospital in Egypt and buried her, all the wives sat in her section in our hijabs. When guests and dignitaries visited Alhaji to pay their condolences, the women would come into the inner section of the compound to do their *ta'aziya* to us. Members of their large extended family dropped in first, and they all went to sit next to Hajiya Babba, excluding the rest of us. She was not only their relative, but she had been married to him the longest, so their allegiance was only to her, a point they proved well in those three mourning days.

Hajiya Mamie cried the loudest, "our mother is gone. Hajiya, please don't leave us." I knew they were not close; she barely even checked on Hajiya Uwa when she was sick for months.

Balaraba did no such theatrics; she was quiet the whole time as people trooped in and out of the section. She sat next to me and read the English translation of the Arabic text in a green Holy Qur'an she always brought with her. We listened as Qur'anic recitation filled the air from the mallams outside who were completing a full recitation of the whole Qur'an.

I felt so alone in a kind of grief that I could not explain to myself. I had only known her for less than a year, yet her death weakened me completely, the last of my strength leaving my body with every breath I drew after Hajiya's demise. That night, I held Abu-Abu close to me as he slept in my bedroom for the first time, breathing evenly as his fingers gripped his yellow toy car. I wondered how many more of the people who genuinely cared for him he would lose because I truly felt like I would be next.

* * *

A few weeks after Hajiya Uwa died. Alhaji collapsed over what I wrongly assumed was grief. On the morning it happened, the call for morning prayer was done by his second son, Mohammed. I was already awake and had even done my ablution and was patiently waiting on my praying mat for the prayer to start so that I could follow the congregation from my room. When Alhaji woke up, he went to the toilet to perform ablution, changed into a jallabiya and left my section, barely acknowledging my greeting.

He was only gone for about 10 seconds when I heard screams of '*Subhan Allah*' ringing across the compound. I ran to the window in the living room and saw that Alhaji fainted by the gate leading into his section. His sons, who were heading out to the mosque from their respective sections, were running towards him. I saw the lights come on in Balaraba's section, then the other two sections, and then doors flung open. I heard them sending Hashim to run to Sufyan's house down the road to call him. At the same time, his oldest sons, Abdul and Mohammed, lifted him, his hands spreading over their shoulders as they carried his limp body into a waiting car. Abdul jumped into the driver's seat while Mohammed sat in the back seat with his father, his head slumped over the son's shoulder.

His third son, Zakari, led the prayer for the first time that morning in an unrushed manner as soon as the car left the compound. I doubt the neighbors who came from various houses on the street to pray in the mosque even knew what happened inside the inner gates of the compound that morning.

As I stood on my praying mat, I skipped lines in my verses, and I miscounted my prostrations. I was shaking. *Is death knocking again? Is this my fault? First his mother and now, him. Is this the farin kafa that they warned her about?*

There were different cars waiting to take us to the hospital after prayer. Balaraba and I went in the same car and when we got to the quiet ward on the second floor of the private hospital he was admitted in, we met the other two wives there already. Mamie was sitting on a praying mat in one corner, and Hajiya Babba was in a chair right by his bed. As soon as she saw us, she raised her head and started admonishing us.

"*Kada ku kashe mana shi*; don't kill him for us," she said as one of her sons put his hands on her shoulder to console her. "I've slaved with this man since we were young, since we had nothing and until now that God has blessed him. Please allow him to enjoy his wealth and see his grandchildren. You girls should not kill him."

Balaraba had already opened her mouth to retort when the doctor came in to adjust the IV lines going into Alhaji's hands. It felt so odd seeing him surrounded by multiple beeping machines; he looked so frail, laying down on the white sheets with his eyes closed. A nurse came in and they took blood samples from him to run tests to see what was wrong with him.

It had been a few hours by the time the results came back, Alhaji was having breakfast, Balaraba was sitting on the couch, and I was in a chair by the window. Alhaji's sons were in the waiting room; they left the room after their father regained consciousness. When Sufyan came into the ward, I saw him head to Hajiya Babba and whisper into her ear just as the doctor came in with multiple sheets of paper.

"Alhaji, I have the results here." From where I sat, I saw 'toxicology report' written on one of the papers.

"Was it food poisoning?" Hajiya Babba asked, and Balaraba sent her a death glare.

"No, but something worse," the doctor shifted closer. "There was a mix of multiple reactive drugs in his system."

"Doctor, you know I don't take anything apart from the blood pressure medicine you prescribed for my hypertension," Alhaji said like he didn't believe the doctor's report.

Blood pressure? Alhaji has hypertension? I was not that educated, but I had watched enough movies to know that there were some medicines you shouldn't mix. Balaraba was giving him Viagra, I was giving him sleeping pills, and all that while he was taking hypertension medicine! No wonder Hajiya Babba said we were trying to kill him.

The doctor continued, "there was a deadly amount of sleeping medicine in your system, as well as erectile dysfunction med –"

"Oh, *Innalillahi wa inna ilayhi rajiun*," Mamie screamed from her praying mat. "Do you two have the fear of God?" She was looking at Balaraba and me.

Balaraba spoke almost immediately, her voice was calm, confident and her speech was eloquent. "I would like you to prove that we had something to do with this. Respect yourself and stop pointing fingers this way. You're not innocent *ke kan ki*. We all know this."

How is she so composed? I was shaking where I sat, so much so that I had to hold my hands together because my fingers wouldn't stop trembling. I looked up to see Sufyan looking at me. I swallowed. My long pink hijab was beginning to suffocate me. I watched him walk toward Alhaji and the doctor, giving him a familiar-looking medicine bottle. The sleeping pills. He must have found them where I hid them in a cabinet filled with spices and condiments.

"I found this hidden in amarya's kitchen," his accusatory tone was hard to miss.

The doctor brought out a pill from the container and inspected it. "Yes, this would do it. A few more days of ingesting this in such doses and you would have had a heart attack, or even gone into coma."

Mamie raised her hands dramatically to her head, calling all the names of Allah that she could fit in one breath.

"You searched our house?" Balaraba shouted at Sufyan. "Who gave you the right to enter our sections?"

He remained quiet; he didn't do as much as look at her. He still accorded her the respect she deserved as his older brother's wife.

"I gave him permission," Hajiya Babba said. "And even though we didn't find anything in yours today, I know you also have poisons you've using on Alhaji. Your bucket is almost full and you'll be caught soon."

All this drama was happening around me, but I could not even move. At one point, I stopped hearing what they were saying. All I knew was that a few minutes later, Sufyan and the doctor rushed to their middle to separate them as Balaraba slapped Hajiya Babba across the cheek.

When everywhere eventually went quiet, I looked up to see Alhaji looking at me. "Zuwaira, listen carefully, for this thing you have done – *na sake ki*. I divorce you."

* * *

I asked Alhaji for permission to go to my uncle's house to observe my *iddah*. He said he would not be responsible for my upkeep if I left his house. When I got back to my section, I was in a rush to leave before he changed his mind. I hurriedly packed a small box with my praying mat, hijabs, and a few clothes. I was dragging it out of my section when Balaraba came to me.

"Zuwaira," she looked down at the box. "Wallahi, I didn't – I'm sorry, you have to believe me. This was not my intention. Wallahi."

She did me a favor without even knowing, and I was not holding it against her. "Amina, please I need you to promise me something," I called her by her Islamic name for the first time ever.

"Anything." Her eyes looked tired.

"Abubakar. That boy has nobody else left. Please, I'm entrusting him in your care. *Amana dan girman Allah*, for the sake of Allah. Please do this for me." It pained me that I would not get to say goodbye to him because he was in school.

"This is only your second strike. You're coming back after your iddah," she said as though she was trying to convince herself. "I'll watch him until you return."

I shook my head no. "Promise me you'll hold him as your own child, even if it takes longer than three months."

"Zuwaira, you're not coming back?"

No, I had no intention of coming back. The only reason I was going to do my iddah outside this house – away from this compound, away from Alhaji – is because I would cry from devastation or even kill myself if Alhaji decided to take me back during my waiting period, like he did last time. But I did not say this. I just gave her a weak smile and left.

When I got to Tani's house that afternoon, one look at me and my box and her face contorted into the meanest frown – a look I had not seen in a while. She barely answered my greeting. After Maghrib prayer, she got on the phone and called my Uncle in Zaria. Her voice was inaudible, but I heard the part where she said, "*ga ta nan dai, an sako ta*; well, here she is, divorced." When she called me from the kitchen, where I was sitting on a stool, and said, "your uncle wants to talk to you." She didn't even look at me as she passed me the phone.

"Good evening, Uncle," I held the receiver to my ear as I greeted him in Hausa.

"Zuwaira, I just got back from work. What is this I'm hearing?" I could hear children playing in the background.

"He divorced me this morning," I said quietly into the phone, aware that Tani was paying attention to every single word I said.

"How many divorces did he give you?"

I hesitated, "this is the second one."

Behind me, I heard Tani clap her hands three times in disgust and shock as she exclaimed, *Tabdi jam!* Wonderful. It has not even been a year."

"Ikon Allah," he was quiet for a little bit, then, "but Zuwaira, according to the Qur'an, you're supposed to do your Iddah in your matrimonial home. Allah knows that sometimes things are said in anger and your waiting period is a favor by Him, an opportunity for husband or wife to realize their mistake and reconcile." His voice was calm as he spoke, like someone giving a counsel. *Please don't make me go back. Please don't make me go back,*

260

I thought as I remained quiet on the phone, clutching the telephone coil as my breathing got heavier. He continued, "except, of course, you fear for your safety – that's the only time it's allowed for a woman to do *Iddah* in her parents' or guardians' house."

I remained quiet.

"Is that the case?" he asked.

"Y –Yes, *kawu.*"

"*Subhan Allahi,*" he said, then remained quiet for even longer. "*Toh shikenan,* okay then. Stay there. I'll see you when I come in one week. Give Tani the phone."

I passed the phone to her, and as I returned to the kitchen, I heard her hissing over the phone as she talked to my uncle in an angry tone.

* * *

In my hurry to leave Alhaji's house, I did not pack all my essentials. Two days later, I was looking at the calendar and realized I would need sanitary pads. I swallowed my pride and asked Tani for some because I had no money, not even a few naira, to buy something as small as pad. Coming back to Tani's house was the most trying thing I had ever gone through in my life. She had no shortage of snide comments to throw my way from my first morning there. I had no problem doing the chores; I had never had a problem with chores. In fact, I was looking forward to them because they would take my mind off my predicament, but Tani enjoyed saying things like, 'don't think because you married a big man, you won't lift a finger here,' or 'make us food. I can't be the one to house you and cook for you.' or the one I heard multiple times a day, 'if marriage was easy, you should have stayed in your husband's house.'

One day she asked me to go to *gidan markade* and grind tomatoes and peppers for stew. I told her that according to the rules of *Iddah*, I was not supposed to leave the house I was observing my *iddah* in.

"Then go back there to his house and complete your *iddah*. Only God knows the black character that you showed them that made them pursue you out of their house, they could not even allow you do *iddah* there. God forbid!" She made sure to shout so that the other tenants could hear her.

Soon enough, I heard footsteps as someone approached the flat. "Haba Tani, you know she's right. You know that there are rules governing the period of *iddah*." It was Aisha, Ibrahim's sister-in-law. She was at the well fetching water and overheard the conversation.

"So, because she cannot keep a husband we should starve? We should not eat? I just asked her to grind tomatoes. She can cover her face if she's ashamed of people knowing that she is a divorcee."

"How were you doing your *markade* when she was not here? Were your daughters not the ones taking it? So send them now."

"They are in Islammiya." She said.

It was a lie. It was Friday, and there were no classes on Fridays. They were in their mother's room watching a Hausa film.

"*Shikenan toh*, it's okay. I'll send Salma; she'll take it for you." Aisha said, then began shouting her daughter's name until she arrived still in her checkered green uniform. Then she placed the pail on her the small girl's head and instructed her to go and grind. As I sat in my hijab on the stool in the small kitchen, all I could think was: *I have to leave this house as soon as my Iddah is finished. I will go anywhere. Anywhere but here.*

That evening after Isha, I cried my eyes out because I had still not gotten my period. It was a week late. *Ya Allah, please let me not be pregnant; please, I don't want this man to have any reason to insist that I return to his house.* I cried well into the night as I sat on my prayer mat, pulling on a *tasbeeh*. But the next morning – and every morning after that – my underwear remained clean every time I checked. For the first time in my life, I contemplated suicide.

Maybe I should just end it all.

Oh, ni Zuwaira, Why is this my luck?

Ibrahim

1999

I heard that Zuwaira was back in her Uncle Alhaji Sani's house the day I returned to my brother's house after my housemanship in Lere. I finally had the chance to visit Kaduna and my nieces were so much taller and more brilliant than the last time I had seen them; their squeals and screams swallowed my sallama and they were loud enough for Ya Aisha to stick her head from the kitchen just as I entered the living room, wondering what the commotion was about.

"Uncle Ibro, Uncle Ibro," the girls ran towards me.

I carried them both, "look at how big you've both gotten!" I pretended to almost fall backwards and their shrieks got even louder.

"Uncle Ibro, you forgot my birthday," Salma pouted as she brought her face just inches away from mine.

"No, I didn't. I missed it, but I didn't forget it," I gestured to the wrapped gift in a nylon bag, "look, I brought your gift."

The sulk on her face was immediately replaced with excitement as she came down from my half embrace and rushed to open the gift.

"*Oyoyo.* Aha, Salma, what do you say?" Ya Aisha said, stopping her from pulling the white plastic flower off the pink wrapping paper.

"*Um...* mummy, can I open it?" she asked with a hint of uncertainty.

"Before that," Ya Aisha prompted. "Before you ask to open it, what do you say?" There was a strong emphasis on the last word.

Salma turned her head towards Bilkisu and me just as I sank into the three-seater with her sister on my lap. "Thank you very much, Uncle Ibro."

"No problem, Salma." I laughed.

"Next time you get a gift and you forget to say thank you, I'll take the gift away. Do you understand?" Ya Aisha wiped her hand on a piece of cloth.

"The smaller one is for you," I urged the more shy sister. "*Oya* go and open it." I urged the more shy sister as she said thank you quietly.

"Ibrahim? *Sai yau?* How was your posting?" Ya Aisha asked.

"Alhamdulillah. *Ai mun ci kwakwa*; we saw hell," I sighed, then started telling her about early mornings, late nights, Baaba Kande's quest to get me married and the polio vaccine drama between Dr. Aji and *mai unguwa*, the village head where the medical center was situated. Ya Aisha was laughing at my demonstrations when we heard a high pitch voice, like an argument or a fight.

"*Al masifatu*, troublemaker. She has started again," Ya Aisha hissed as we heard insults being hurled. But there were no retorts. It was like she was talking to herself.

"Hajiya Tani?" I asked, laughing at the nickname my brother's wife called her.

"*Wallahi* her. Day and night, it never ends with her."

"Who's she fighting with?"

"Zuwaira," she replied. I opened my mouth, but the words made no sound. Ya Aisha continued, "the poor thing – she got divorced."

"Oh," my voice finally came back, and that was all I could say.

"Tani has been making her life unbearable since she got back. *Kai*, it's terrible," she said, shaking her head.

I watched Salma and Bilkisu play with the cups in the kitchen set as they brought their dolls to the living room and made me join them in eating the pretend food. The whole time I played with them, my mind was filled with various thoughts. *Zuwaira is out of her husband's house? For good? Or just temporarily? How long has she been here?*

Over the following weeks, everything I learnt about Zuwaira, her marriage, and her in-laws was not because I asked but because my sister-in-law vented to me. I didn't sleep in their flat anymore. Ya Isa had just finished building a house in Mando, an area further away from Ungwan Rimi. It was a four-bedroom bungalow with a big backyard; he had installed some light fixtures and window coverings, and due to the vandalization of uncompleted buildings in the area, he moved some furniture into the house and asked me to spend the nights there. I didn't mind; the bed was more comfortable than the couch in his living room, and there was light and running water for my ablution and basic necessities in the morning. In the mornings, I would get some breakfast, buttered bread, and tea from the *mai shayi* on the street and when Salma and Bilkisu returned from school, I would go to Ungwan Rimi and help Ya Aisha with chores.

One day, as we were pulling down the curtains so I could wash, iron and pack them into the empty cartoons that Ya Isa and I have been moving gradually to the new house, Ya Aisha said to me, "it's very surprising to me that Zuwaira said she won't go back to her husband's house." She removed the cord from the curtains on the floor.

I stood on a high step stool as I reached up to the curtain holder to remove the heavy material that served as coverings to the door.

"She said so?" I tried to keep the interest in my voice at a minimum.

"Yes, she refused to go back when his family came last week. Alhaji's aunt insisted that they come and ask for her to return because apparently Alhaji's late mother really liked Zuwaira and that is what she would have wanted but the girl said no."

"His mother died?"

"Yes, she died some months ago in Egypt. Very strong-looking woman! I was shocked to hear about her death."

"*Allah ya jikan ta*; may her soul Rest In Peace," I said as I brought out the last rod from the top of the curtain and came down from the step stool. So that meant that it was not a final divorce. There was still a chance of reconciliation between her husband and her. Was she just prolonging the inevitable as a bargaining chip, like most women would do? Is that what she was doing? *Yaji?* So conditions in her marriage will be renegotiated?

"Ya Aisha, where's the soap?" I asked. She went into her store to cut a piece of bar soap and I went out to the well to start soaking the curtains.

I had already filled the buckets with water when she met me outside a few minutes later to hand me the green bar soap and some detergent. Even as I scrubbed the curtains roughly, it didn't occur to me that I was taking my anger out on the curtains. But why was I angry that there was a chance that Zuwaira would be returning to her husband?

I kept looking towards Hajiya Tani's flat, hoping to maybe catch a glimpse of her. Was she really back here? I still hadn't seen her, not even heard her voice. On some nights when I was leaving for Mando, I would hear movement away from the dark well or sometimes by the water drums on Hajiya Tani's verandah. But I never actually saw her. I chuckled at how ridiculous I was being – hoping to catch a glimpse of a woman in her *iddah*, who wasn't supposed to go about her affairs for 90 days. I sighed. *Perhaps I should talk to my Aunty in Lere and tell her that I would like to see Laila again and start discussing marriage with her. Maybe that would help me get my mind over Zuwaira,* I thought.

The following day, as I ironed the curtains on a mat layered with multiple wrappers in the living room, folded them, and added them to the ever-growing pile, Ya Aisha came to sit on the chair dicing Okra for dinner.

"You missed the shouting match Tani had with herself this morning."

"With herself?"

"*Toh* the person she keeps shouting at doesn't answer her," she shrugged.

It was the same thing before Zuwaira got married. Tani would berate the girl, and she would never even react. At this point, I was used to listening to Ya Aisha talk about the daily ordeal that Zuwaira went through, but I was not used to how angry it made me. I kept ironing the hard edges of the curtain roughly, trying to steam the vein-like creases away.

"She told the girl that if she happens to be pregnant, she had better return to that house and complete her *iddah* there because she can't be saddled with taking care of a pregnant girl for nine months. If I were Zuwaira, honestly, I would just go back because *wannan irin wulakancin har ina?* When does this indignity end?"

I thought back to the bruises around her neck and the broken bone months ago when I saw her at the hospital.

"But you don't know why she doesn't want to go back."

Ya Aisha finished cutting the okra and stood up to go to the kitchen. As she reached for the door, she turned to me.

"Let me tell you something, Ibro, whatever the case may be, there's no place that a woman's respect is highest but in her husband's house."

As much as that sounded right because that was how it was supposed to be if we all followed the teachings of our religion and what our culture dictates, but I knew that it was mostly just on paper. I was proven right a few days later, on a Monday afternoon, when the kids were in school while the workers in the compound were at work. I was fetching water for Ya Aisha, and I planned to leave earlier than usual because I needed to go check on my NYSC posting at the state office in Barnawa. I was filling up the last bucket when I heard it. It sounded like someone was retching. I stopped mid-movement, holding up the pail that was now half filled it water when I heard it again. It was coming from Hajiya Tani's flat. Before I could stop myself, I hurried in that direction.

"Assalamu alaikum," I called out loudly to announce my presence. I heard no reply, but the retching continued. I looked in through the net and found someone on the floor by the kitchen door convulsing – or at least that was what I assumed from the rapid, jerky movement and clenched fists. I pushed the door open and it was Zuwaira on the floor, foaming from the mouth. From a first glance analysis, it looked like ingested poisoning, judging from the redness around her mouth. I crouched next to her and was hit by the smell of kerosene. *Did she drink kerosene?*

I lifted her and put her on my laps, trying to get her in a sitting position. Her skin was cold, clammy and her eyes were wide open, but it didn't seem like she could see me. From her low pulse, I could tell she was losing consciousness. I turned her to the side, held her mouth open with one hand and forced my index and ring finger into her mouth to trigger her gag reflex. She immediately threw up a clear liquid and small white pills. When she regained consciousness and realized I was holding her, she started crying.

"You're fine, you're okay." I was trained to talk to overdose patients calmly and reassuringly, but what I really wanted to do right was to shout. *What can be going so wrong in her life to warrant her doing a thing like this? Is divorce the end of the world?* But I stayed level-headed and told her she would be fine. "What did you take?" I finally asked. I needed to assess if there was anything else in her system that required going to the hospital.

"Just... just that..."

"Are you experiencing abdominal pain or having difficulty focusing right now?" I rechecked her pulse.

She nodded slowly, "my stomach hurts." I watched as her hand reached for her stomach and she cradled it before bursting into tears. I allowed her to cry; she looked like she needed it. "My life is over, it's all over," she said in between sobs.

"*Haba*, has it comes to this?" I asked. When she didn't reply, I continued, "there's a risk of permanent lung damage with what you did," and paused, then added, "and the religious implication."

"I just want to end it. I am tired of being someone else's problem. Everybody will rest when I die," she started crying all over again. "I can't go back to that house. I cannot go back to that house." She was not even looking at me as she spoke; it was like she was talking to someone on the wall, with a trembling lower lip and puffy eyes. "He'll kill me, and he'll kill my child."

"You're pregnant?" It almost felt like my world had stopped spinning on its axis.

She squeezed her eyes shut. "I can't go back. Ibrahim, he'll kill me." She had a half-crazed look on her face. "And he'll kill my baby again. I can't lose my child." She pulled herself away from me and dropped her head to her lap.

It shouldn't have surprised me because I knew about the D&C from her hospital chart the day I checked. However, miscarriages in the first trimester were common. That was what I convinced myself when I saw it; it couldn't possibly be connected to the bruises around her neck. An abusive man.

I stood up and looked towards the door. "You should tell your uncle the full truth. I'm sure he won't make you go back and you can stay until the baby is born." I knew it was not ideal; Tani would make her life a living hell. But it beat the alternative.

She looked up at me, "and then what? Give him *my* child?"

"Zuwaira, Islamically, the child can stay with the mother until they mature..." or until the mother got married to another man. I knew that a man like Ringim would take his child away as soon as she remarried. Hausa men never wanted their children growing up under another man's roof; it was our pride.

"He'll separate me from my child as soon as I give birth, he has the money for a wet nurse. He will never leave his child with me except I am under his roof."

"Maybe that's what has been destined by God."

She started crying all over again. "I know how this world treats a child whose mother is not with them. This world is cruel to orphans, and my child won't live the way I did. My child won't be at the mercy of other people. No way." She shakes her head repeatedly.

Could I blame her? Honestly, no. The world was cruel; the world had been cruel to her since her parents died. First, her uncle's wife who maltreated, beat and accused her of stealing, then her uncle's other wife who maltreated her, stopped her from going to school and emotionally abused her at any given opportunity. As if that wasn't enough, there was the husband who maltreated her and only God knows what else. It seemed that the common theme for orphans was this – mistreatment.

"I'm going to run away," she said with a determined look on her face. She nodded as she thought about it again. "I'll keep this to myself and when the three months is done, I'll quietly leave for good."

"Are you mad? Can you hear yourself?" The words were out of my mouth before I could stop them. The world was cruel not only to orphans but to women without *gata*, women with no one who would stand for them. "Where will you go? What will you do?"

269

"Far away from here. I'll find a job, even if it's as a maidservant." She answered. The face of the girl I knew from a lifetime ago – the one who laughed at my jokes, who solved complicated equations in minutes, who knew the lyrics to a song I shared with her – was gone. That girl was long gone.

I rubbed my eyes with my left fingers. Listening to her was giving me a headache. The horrors that could happen to a girl as vulnerable as she was, there was no shortage of men out there who would take advantage of her helplessness at the drop of a hat. I looked outside the door again. I knew that someone seeing me with her like this would bring on further complications for her. There was no explanation I could possibly give that would exonerate us from their suspicion – I was alone in a house with a woman who was supposed to be in *purdah*, away from the sight of men and strangers.

"Listen to me. You have to promise me that you won't do this again. There has to be another way out." She didn't look at me, so I called out her name, and her head jolted my way. She was lost in her thoughts. "If I *ever* meant anything to you, promise me you won't do this again." She didn't look like she heard me, but eventually, she slowly nodded. "Where are the pills? I have to take them."

Her voice cracked as she answered. "T-Those were the only ones I found at the bottom of the drawer.

Even when I left the flat to return to the well, my attention was with her the whole time. I was relieved when I saw Jamil return from school, and started asking for his food as he removed his shoes. At least now someone was with her.

That evening, after I prayed in the Mosque two streets away from us, I stayed back in the big building going over the events of that afternoon. In Islam, matters regarding paternity were not to be joked with. The Qur'an clearly stated everything so that there would be no ambiguity – a woman hiding a pregnancy from a man is wrong. That was part of the reason *iddah* was dictated for divorced women or widows – so that there would be no uncertainty in the paternity of their child, should they be pregnant. This was done to protect the woman, to ensure that the man did not skip out on his responsibilities to his child and to the mother of his child.

But she wanted nothing to do with the father of her child. She wanted him to have nothing to do with the child. Would that be possible? Could it be possible in a town where everybody claimed to mind their business but they really knew every minute detail about their neighbors' households?

I thought back to the bruises on her neck. There was no way she could leave her child with a man like that. But would a father really hurt his own child? Wasn't the man the protector, the one who ensured that no harm came to the ones under his care? The ones he loved?

I loved her once; I knew I had to protect her. But how could I do that? I could not marry her —not while she was pregnant with another man's child. In our religion, the marriage would be invalid.

Over the next few days, the magnitude of how dire her situation was continued to be a constant ball of pressure on my mind, and the fact that Alhaji Ringim's smiling face on big posters that read 'Vote Honorable Ringim as Councillor' was plastered on every available wall in the area did not help.

Honorable indeed. If we were a sane society, a man's character would be tested by how he treated his wives. After all, the Prophet said, "the best of you are those who are best to their women." As a community, we had deviated from that – choosing instead to name the best of men as those with the deepest pockets while blatantly ignoring their sins.

A week later, on a Friday, I made up my mind and left her a note under the black tank: *We need to talk.*

Just the way we used to communicate before she was married off. I wondered if she would see it: and if she saw it, would she reply?

The following morning, when I checked the well as I fetched water to wash Ya'Isa's car, I saw a piece of paper different from the one I'd left there. I looked around to make sure no one was around, then reached for it. It read: *Tuesday 10 pm.*

* * *

271

After *Isha* prayer on Tuesday, I helped my nieces with their homework. While I ate dinner with my brother, he informed me that a painter would be coming to start work at the new house the following day, and he wanted me to supervise the indoor painting as he was planning to move in with his family even before the outdoor painting was completed.

"I paid for seven big buckets of paint and one bucket of wall primer. Please keep an eye to see that they are using Dulux. That's the premium brand I paid for."

"I will," I reached into my pocket. "The plumber gave me this." I passed him the paper, "the leak from yesterday was caused by the wrong pipes in the toilet in the children's room."

"*Wallahi mutanen nan*, these builders, they can frustrate you. When I saw the pipes he was fitting that day, I asked him if those weren't kitchen pipes. He insisted it was the same thing. And now, look. I will deduct it from his fee. If not because you're here to help me supervise, only Allah knows what else would have gone wrong."

When I left that night and bade Ya Isa goodnight, I heard him lock the door behind me. I walked to the gate and made it look like I was leaving but I just lingered around. I sat down outside the gate and thought about the decision that I was about to make and the consequences of the thing I was about to embark on. How would this affect my future and hers? Would she even agree to it? If she didn't, what did that mean for her, and this child she was carrying? These thoughts went through my mind as I wandered on the street, for hours before I looked at my wristwatch; it was a few minutes to 10 pm. I walked back to Ya Isa's rented flat, carefully using my feet to dislodge the piece of stick I had placed to prevent the bolting mechanism from locking me out and walked silently to wait by the black water tank. I looked around the compound and apart from the dim verandah lights outside flat 3, the whole place was pitch black. I had almost given up hope that she would come out when I noticed movement by the door and a dim flicker of the yellow lights. I saw her walking towards the well in a long black hijab covering her whole body except for her face lighted by the moon. The face I haven't been able to get off my mind even after all this time.

I cleared my throat to alert her of my presence, and she looked surprised to see me standing in the dark.

"I didn't think you would be here," she said, dragging her feet as she approached me, holding large buckets stacked inside one another. She bent and started removing the buckets one after the other. I counted eight in total.

I went closer to her, "Do you do this every night?"

"Yes," she nodded. "It's the water I need for the chores throughout the day. I prefer to not do this when the well is so busy in the morning."

I reached for the pail, opened the cover of the well, and start fetching water to fill her buckets. I had just pulled out the small pail filled with water and poured it into her first bucket like I used to do in what felt like a lifetime ago, when she reached for the second pail and started to bend as she tried to fetch water.

I stopped her, "you shouldn't be doing this…" I lowered my voice, "in your condition."

"When am I not going to have to fetch water?" she asked as she continued pulling the pail upwards.

I took it from her. "It's okay, you sit down. Today, I'll do it." She looked relieved as she leaned against the tank and thanked me. "You still haven't told anyone?"

Maybe just maybe, she had decided to come clean and abandon that terrible plan of hers, of running away. Maybe by some miracle, a maternal part of Hajiya Tani took pity on her situation and understood her plight.

She chuckled sadly as she shook her head, her eyes glistening in the moonlight. "I'm always in my hijab, and I have been asking her for pad every four weeks…" she looked away embarrassed. She appeared out of breath and sat down on the concrete under the tank, sighing deeply as she did.

I looked up at her as I filled the 4th bucket, "do you have any morning sickness?" She looked confused, so I added, "any nausea, or vomiting?"

"No vomiting, thank God. Tani would have thrown me out by now. But

I'm so tired. I wake up tired, I'm tired all day..." her voice trailed away as she gazed into space.

"That's normal for your first trimester." We spoke in hushed tones, constantly looking around us to make sure no one could hear us.

"You might get food aversions or cravings as time passes. Things you used to like might disgust you and things you never cared for, you might start to crave."

She looked up at me and nodded slightly, "I smell things I never used to smell before, and the smell disgusts me, like milk... even eggs."

"Eggs?" I raised my eyebrows. *Do eggs have a smell?*

"Eggs, *fa*." She said in exasperation, like she was also surprised, then burst into laughter. It seemed so out of place that she would laugh despite her predicament, but it was a joy to hear. When I finished filling up the last bucket, I looked up to see that her laughter had turned to tears. She sobbed with such desperation that I couldn't see a way out other than the one that had been churning in my mind.

I leaned against the tank, realizing that there was no way I could comfort her without touching her. She was still a married woman in her *iddah* period, I shouldn't even be alone with her. So, I just stood against the tank and listened to her hushed cries in the dark, the knots in my chest tightening at their intensity.

"I'm leaving to start my NYSC in Jos," I finally said when the sobs seemed to have reduced a bit. "Let's leave together." I had initially planned to gently ease her into this outrageous plan of mine, to see how she would take the idea of another marriage before going into specific details, but somehow it came out rushed.

It was suddenly silent. Not even the sound of water dripping back into the well from the holes on the perforated cover could be heard as she looked up at me, holding her face in her hand with a confused look on her face.

"Leave together? What will people say?"

"No, what I mean is we should get married. When do they think your *iddah* ends? In a few weeks, right?"

"Ibrahim…?"

"Of course, it's not a valid marriage, I know. But they don't have to know that. When we get to Jos, you can attend your antenatal at the hospital I'm going to work at. You'll have access to healthcare," I looked at her, and she looked even more confused than before. "We'll be away from people who know us, people who might suspect the truth. When the child is born, then we can make the lie we are going to tell our families now a truth, we can get married then. The proper way." I watched as she thought about it, blinking rapidly. I sighed, then added: "Sleep on it, think about it properly. I'll be here tomorrow evening to talk to Ya Isa about a leak that's being fixed in the new house. If you leave your reply under the tank, I'll see it."

"Yes," She surprised me with an answer that sounded sure, "Yes, I agree."

* * *

The first person I told about my intention to marry Zuwaira was Ya Aisha. I came by earlier than usual from Mando the day after I spoke to Zuwaira at the well. "Ya Aisha, I think I'm ready to get married."

She looked up at me from the braid she was finishing on Bilki's head. The hairstyle had some swept to the side of her head and the rest braided to the back. "Ah *ka ce za mu sha biki*! We have a big celebration ahead of us! Who's the girl?" she asked as she stopped braiding, looking at me with a smile on her face.

"You know her." I peeled the orange I was holding with my fingers, the sound of my voice tense over the voice of Big Bird from *Sesame Street* playing on the television. The yellow color on the screen appeared faded due to the glitch lines disrupting the transmission every few minutes.

"Is it Laila?" I could not help but notice that big smile on her face got wider as she spoke. "*Ai* Baaba Kande told us how beautiful she is. *Masha Allah!*"

"Laila? No, it's not her."

"Is it any of my cousins? Hauwa?" She seemed more excited.

I had even forgotten about her two cousins who came for Eid earlier in

275

the year. She always mentioned how well-read they were in the Qur'an, but it had never dawned on me that she was trying to get me interested in them, so I treated them like my younger sisters.

"Oh – *um*...no, not her." I watched as the smile disappeared from her face.

"Is it someone from your university?" She didn't seem too pleased at the prospect. "I hope *dai tana kallon gabas*." Literally, she meant she hoped the girl faced east when she prayed. Which translates into wanting to know if she was a Muslim.

"Marrying a Christian is allowed *ai*. Islam is only against Muslim men marrying any woman who doesn't believe in God. Christians believe in God."

She removed her hand from her daughter's hair. "So, she's not a Muslim, Ibro? With all the Muslim girls around, you went for a Christian? *Toh*, what's her name?"

"Jennifer." I took a bite of my orange as I watched her eyes widen. Jennifer was the first name that came to my mind because I had an old course mate by that name from the university.

She shook her head as she started combing Bilki's hair, rather forcefully this time.

"Me, I don't know any Jennifer and I can tell you right now that your brother is not going to be in support."

My niece started squirming as Ya Aisha's hands pulled her hair into neat thin braids, "mummy, *zafi*. It hurts."

Ya Aisha didn't even acknowledge her daughter.

"I don't even know how Baaba Kande is going to take this your news."

Baaba Kande was visiting from Lere. She came to Kaduna every few months because she was part of a women's outreach group that educated lower-class families on family planning. It was no easy feat convincing most uneducated women to use birth control to space their children for their health and that of their children. Those who agreed were threatened with divorce from their husbands. Still, Baaba Kande, being a hijabi who could quote and translate verses of the Qur'an at the drop of a hat, seemed to get a lot of success reaching them.

Just then, Baaba Kande came out from the toilet and joined us in the small living room. "How will I take what?"

Ya Aisha looked at me before answering, "ask him. He'll tell you himself."

"Ibrahim *meye ne*? What is it?"

I moved to the floor as my aunt sat on the three-seater, then gave a piece of orange to my niece, and she quietened down.

"Baaba, I was just telling Ya Aisha that I've found the woman I want to marry."

Her face broke into a bigger smile than the one my sister-in-law had for a few seconds. "This is good news. Tell me, who is this girl that has finally caught you for me?"

From her seat, Ya Aisha glowered at me, half disappointed and half resigned.

"Her name is Zuwaira," I put the last piece of orange in my mouth. "Ya Aisha knows her."

Ya Aisha dropped the comb she was using to part Bilkisu's hair and covered her mouth with her hands. "Ibrahim, really? This is good news. *Kai kai kai*, wait. Are you sure about this?" She asked as an afterthought.

"Who is Zuwaira?" My aunt asked.

"She's our neighbor's niece, a very well-mannered girl. You should see her – a black beauty." Ya Aisha seemed almost relieved that I didn't say Jennifer.

"Ah ah, Masha Allah. Look at my *likita! Ai* with his looks, he can only end up with a beauty that matches him. I've always known this. Which of your neighbours are we talking about? The landlord?"

"No, Tani. You met her the last time you came," Ya Aisha answered as she paused mid-plait to answer the question.

"*Ah barkan mu.* Congratulations to us then! It'll go smoothly since Tani is your friend," she paused then asked, "how come I haven't seen this girl?" Aisha glanced at me and looked away, concentrating on her plait. So, Baaba Kande fixed her attention on me. "I come here often, but I have never seen her. Doesn't she live here?"

"Maybe she was still in her husband's house when you came," I said honestly.

The room fell silent. Ya Aisha's eyes darted from my face to Baaba Kande and back.

"*Bazawara ce*? She's a divorcee?" From the disbelief in her voice, one would assume divorces were not very common in our part of the world, as if it was unheard of.

"Yes, she was in an unfortunate marriage for less than a year, and she came back –"

Baaba Kande did not want to listen to me anymore. She was shaking her head, "*gaskiya*, honestly, I don't support it. There are issues with marrying a divorcee." She spoke as if she was stating facts from well-documented research.

Ya Aisha heaved a long sigh as she started oiling the lines between the braids in her daughter's hair.

"What are the issues Baaba?" I asked, even though nothing could change my mind.

"You're young, so you can't understand. First of all, do you know if it's her bad character that made her husband divorce her?"

"Zuwaira doesn't have a bad character, even Ya Aisha can tell you."

"*Gaskiya*, she's a good girl. She –" She was cut short before she completed her sentence.

"Aisha, *ki ji tsoron Allah*, fear God. If Ibrahim was your younger brother, would you advice him to marry a divorcee? Why didn't your older brother Shehu marry a divorced woman? You should be the one advising Ibrahim against this, but you're in support? That's very disappointing."

"Baaba, please. Ya Aisha just heard about this matter the same time you did. Don't blame her," I pleaded, knowing Ya Aisha would not defend herself in front of someone she considered her mother-in-law.

"And you – a young man like you? You want to start your life with a woman who has tasted marriage before. I'm not saying that you can't marry Zuwaira oh, no that's not what I am saying," she shook her head from side to side with a wide-eyed expression, "but marry an innocent girl first, a maiden. Then after a year or so, you can go and marry your Zuwaira."

"A maiden?" I asked just to be clear.

"Yes, a virgin. There are tens of them around for you to pick from."

I nodded as I listened to her list of girls who would make better wives for me. Better life partners than the one I had never stopped thinking about since the first day I met her at the well a year ago. The only reason any of them would make a better first wife for me, according to Baaba Kande, was because they had their hymens intact.

My brother, Ya Isa, had a different reaction when I told him. We had missed the congregational Isha prayer because we were on the highway driving back from Mando after inspecting the finished painting of the house. As soon as we got back, we performed ablution and prayed in the living room, with him leading us in prayer. When we finished, I told him about Baaba Kande's reaction earlier that afternoon.

He leaned against the chair, "even our prophet Mohammed –"

"Sallalahu alaihi wassalam," I finished.

"His first wife was a divorcee. So Baaba Kande's opinion has no basis in our religion. At no point should we pick what is culturally normal over what is permissible in our religion or what is *sunnah*."

"I was not swayed by what she said. I still want to marry Zuwaira," I said as a matter-of-factly. *"Wallahi* I haven't been this sure about anything since when I was filling my first and second choices on my university form years ago."

Ya Isa chuckled at the memory, "when you put MBBS as your first and second choices, *ko*? Everybody told you to have another option in case you didn't get Medicine, but you refused."

"I knew I would get it because *na yi istihara.* I prayed for Allah's guidance before filling those forms."

"And what about this matter – did you pray *istihara*?" he asked as he turned down the volume of the television, something he did when we had something important to discuss.

"Yes, I've been praying about it for days now." It was true. On the one hand, I was committing a sin, but on the other hand, it felt like it was the *right* thing to do.

"*Toh*, I can talk to Alhaji Sani. Has she finished her *iddah*?"

I pretended to think about it for a while, "I don't think she has."

"Well, in that case, don't raise your hopes high. You have to know if she's pregnant, or not. If she is, then you have to wait until the baby is born before we can start talking about marriage. You know that *ai*?"

I nodded forcefully as I cleared my throat, "yes, yes I know this."

"*Allah ya zabi mana mafi alheri*. May Allah choose the best option for us."

"Ameen."

Hafsatu

2022

As I roughly drive through the gates, making a sharp right to get on the road that leads to the traffic lights, I play the past few hours' events in my head. How did something everyone was excited about lead to a fight? How did it lead to the biggest fight in our household? How did we go from Umm'Hafsa reminding her husband to tell his colleagues in Jos about an upcoming wedding to her telling me that Sadiq's family will not be received by ours, that their answer is already no? How did we get here in the span of days? What changed?

After my siblings left the dining table yesterday to check on Umm'Hafsa's cough and it was just me and daddy on the table, I confided in him. I told him that Sadiq's father was abusive. He was unusually quiet throughout that talk, but I want daddy to understand the level of trust Sadiq and I have. Umm'Hafsa must have overheard that conversation when she returned for her phone, which is why her opinion about Sadiq changed overnight.

Umm'Hafsa has never been one to give us relationship advice. In fact, when we were younger, she pretended not to know that we were dating even though in senior secondary school, my sisters and I came back home with Valentine's gifts every year. The first time she talked to me about relationships was when we were in Kaduna for my cousin's wedding. I remember her saying to Adda S and me, "if a man ever hits you, leave him immediately because he will do it again." That's one of the reasons I never talk to her about relationships; her stance is always too rigid. Daddy, however, would listen and would talk about motives and triggers even though he also never condones violence.

I'm jolted back to reality by the aggressive horns behind me; the light is just turning green. I hiss and press down on the accelerator as my car speeds through the intersection. If there's something Abuja drivers all have in common, it's impatience at traffic lights.

I get to *H&I* and park my car in my usual parking spot under a tree in the shopping complex's parking lot and dial Sadiq's number. I know he'll be busy because they are right in the middle of his sister's wedding festivities.

His voice comes through right after the second ring. "Hey, B?"

"Sadiq?" *We have a problem.*

"Hey, I just got Imran from the airport. His wife and son are here too. I cant wait for you to meet them." He is in such high spirits. I'm supposed to attend the wedding dinner with him tomorrow evening. I spent most of last week carefully curating my look, outfit, and accessories for the event because this will be the first time I will meet most of his stepsisters and stepbrothers.

"Oh, that's nice," I manage to say. In the background, I can hear a lady's voice shushing a whining toddler. *"A gaishe su,* my regards to them."

"Za su ji, I'll let them know." He lowers his voice, "hey, are you okay? You sound kinda off."

I bet I sound considerably different from how I did the last time we spoke. He had called me while I was doing my makeup earlier today, just before Umm'Hafsa came into my room.

"I need to see you." As soon as I said it, I bit my tongue. What if they were already in the car and I was on speaker? I would sound like the extra clingy girlfriend that doesn't want him to spend time with his cousin's family.

"Is everything okay?"

I sigh, "not really."

"Kina gida? Are you home?"

"No, I'm at *H&I.*"

282

"Okay, we're just going to drop su Nasreen at home, then it'll be time for *Jummah* prayer. We can have lunch after I pray."

I'm on a juice cleanse. I'm always on one before a big event I want to look good for. But I didn't even take my kale smoothie before I rushed out of the house in tears. I have no appetite, but I answer nevertheless, "sure."

"Where do you wanna go?"

"Wherever you pick." That doesn't even sound like me; I never miss out on an opportunity to choose restaurants when we go out.

"*Toh fa*, okay. Now I know something's wrong," he paused, "our usual spot then? Since It's close to *H&I*."

When Sadiq comes into Cilantro about an hour later, he finds me sitting in the quiet far-end corner, absentmindedly scrolling through Instagram to take my mind off the events of that morning. His sister Madina is not usually active on social media, but her pre-wedding pictures and pictures from the ongoing wedding events are already gaining traction online.

"Hey B," he leans down to give me a half hug; his cologne fills the air as he settles into the wooden chair opposite me. He was in a well-fitting army-green kaftan and a dark brown cap. "Is everything okay?"

I force a smile, "I just placed an order for us; it should be out soon," I glance over my shoulder to see if any of the waiters are approaching us.

"Thanks, *kaman kin san* I'm starving," he smiles as he pushes the drink menu away from him. "So, what's up?" His eyes search mine as he leans closer to me.

"Eat first, then I'll tell you." I don't wanna ruin his appetite as mine is already gone.

"The food can wait. What's going on?" He isn't smiling anymore.

I chew down on my lower lip as I consider the best way to break the news to him. Which one should I even start with?

"There was a fight at home," I say quietly. He remains silent as the tiniest hint of a frown settles on his face. "A fight between me and Umm'Hafsa."

"Babe, I thought we talked about this?" he looks worried. I assume he thinks I was rude to Umm'Hafsa because of what I know. When I confided in him about my DNA results weeks ago, he advised me to still treat her with as much respect as I could regardless. He said she is still my mom, and whatever she did is between her and Allah, but how I treat her is a mark for or against me on the day of judgment. A piece of advice that made me cut her some slack. "So, what happened?"

"She said that we can't get married," I blurt out.

There is barely any change in his demeanor except for a slight movement of his eyebrows.

"Who said? Umm'Hafsa?" It almost sounds like he doesn't believe me. I nod, and he chuckles, but the amusement doesn't reach his eyes. "Is this a joke, babe? My family is coming to meet yours in ten days." I open my mouth to answer and close it as the waiter approaches us with a tray. He drops a platter of garlic prawns and naan bread in the middle of the table and leaves as swiftly as he came. "Wait, you're serious?" He leans back into his chair, his eyes not leaving mine the whole time.

"I wouldn't joke about this."I say quietly.

"Walk me though it." He completely ignores the food between us.

I inhale deeply. "After you and I spoke this morning, she came into my room and she said I should tell you sorry, but they are no longer in support of our relatio–"

"They?" He cuts me short. "So, it's your dad who's against this."

"No, it's not him. It's her."

He shakes his head, "c'mon, I've met your mom multiple times and not once did I get the slightest hint that she doesn't want me to marry you. She even gave me permission to take you to see my stepmom. Now all of a sudden, they are against it? It's definitely your dad."

"Sadiq, I –?"

"You've told me how close you two are. I know dads like him. They believe no one is ever good enough for their daughter."

"No, daddy is not like that. *Wallahi* it's Umm'Hafsa."

I don't know how to explain it to Sadiq. Multiple times in the past, we would have planned something as a family – a trip or an outing that my siblings and I would be excited about – then at the last minute, Umm'Hafsa would mention her discomfort at the idea, and daddy will cancel the plan.

Every single time.

"Is there something you aren't telling me?" His phone starts ringing and he silences it without looking at the caller ID. I looked down at my hands as the waiter comes back with a bowl of rice and curry. *Maybe I ordered too much food. Who's going to eat all this after this conversation?* "Hafsat?" He is looking at me with a questioning look on his face.

They say honesty is the best policy. They don't say how nerve-racking it sometimes is, especially when you know you've messed up.

I exhale loudly and purse my lips. "I told daddy about your father... and I think she might have heard."

His eyebrows rise up and he slowly nods his head. "Now it's beginning to make sense."

"Babe, I was just confiding in him about how much we trust each other and – and I didn't know she was listening. Daddy was still okay with you after. It's her."

His hands reach for his chin as he rubs his jaw in a downward motion. When his hand leaves his face, his fingers tap on the table as he gazes away from me at the empty table next to us.

"Babe, I'm sorry. I know you told me that in confidence and I wasn't supposed to tell anyone..."

"That's not the issue here Hafsat. The problem now is they think I'm something I'm not. And you know what? I can't even blame them. If our daughter wants to marry someone and she tells me something like this about his father, I'll react the same way."

Our daughter. Sadiq is still thinking about our future together, our family, and our kids. "How do we fix this?" I ask.

He removes his cap and drops it on the table. "My uncle was given the impression that this is already a done deal. He believes your family is aware and in support of the relationship and his visit is just a formality. I can't have him come all the way with an entourage and be met with a refusal," he sighs. "It's a slap on his face. You understand that, don't you?"

I shudder as I remember Umm'Hafsa telling me his family won't even be allowed into the house. *Why is this woman hell-bent on destroying my life?*

My head falls into my palm as I bow my face. "Oh, God," I mutter, mostly to myself.

"Hey," he pushes his chair close to me and pulls my hands away from my face. His finger finds mine and he doesn't let go. "It's okay, *haka fa maganan aure yake*. This happens with most marriages. There are always obstacles that come up from both families," his smile is fading away now. "Before we start this fight, I have to know: are you gonna be in this with me?" I start saying, *of course*, but he stops me, "no, Hafsat. Think about it properly. If one day you're going to wake up and tell me that you'll follow your parents' decision, then we might as well end this relationship here."

"Are you breaking up with me?" My eyebrows shoot up even as my voice lowers.

His grip on my hands gets tighter, "babe, you need to *hear* what I'm saying. If we're going to win this, we'll have to keep a united front and it could take months. Look at my cousin Assad and Lily. Family has been saying no for years, but they haven't given up on each other."

I look at him. Sadiq doesn't give up on us. He didn't give up on us even during the picture fiasco. He always has my back, and he has proven it over and over. I can't remember wanting anything more in my life, more than wanting to marry Sadiq Ringim. "I'm never gonna give up on us, Sadiq."

What comes next from him is a sigh of relief. His thumb strokes mine and his features soften, the furrow between his dark brows disappears, and he kisses me gently on my forehead. We remain silent for a few more minutes, the food on the table cold and untouched in front of us.

"Is there anyone your dad listens to, like an Imam or someone close to him? Maybe a family member he really respects?"

"What for?"

"To talk to him on our behalf."

I don't have to think about it for too long; I know the person he holds in the highest esteem. "I have an Uncle in Kaduna, Uncle Isa. He's his older brother."

He ponders on what I say for a minute. "Okay. I'll go to Kaduna to see him then."

"You're gonna travel to KD?"

"I have to. This needs to be fixed before *ranan tambaya*, and we've got less than two weeks. The earlier the better."

"I'll call Aunty Khaltum so she can tell him." Uncle Isa isn't the kind of man I can just call on the phone and talk to about Sadiq. He is not liberal, like daddy. He is very traditional. With him, things have to be done according to the expectations of our culture.

"Is that your Adda S's mum?"

"No, stepmom. Their mom is his first wife, Aunty Aisha. She died some years ago."

He nods, "*Allah ya jikan ta.*"

"Ameen." If Aunty Aisha was alive, she would be the one to talk sense into Umm'Hafsa, as Umm'Hafsa respected her so much, and they were quite close.

Sadiq continues, "explain the whole situation to her. Tell her I want to come and see him and send me their numbers." He thinks about it for a minute, then adds, "send me Salma's number too. I should probably drop by and see her while I'm in Kaduna." He starts typing a message, and because he's sitting so close to me, I see it's a message to Imran about going to Kaduna.

"Are you sure about this? The roads to Kaduna are so unsafe, babe." I think about reported incidents of armed bandits attacking innocent civilians on the road and the recent attempts to kidnap passengers aboard the Abuja-Kaduna train. "Sadiq, let's think about this properly. If anything happens to you on the way there, I won't be able to forgive myself."

"People go to Kaduna everyday." His voice was calm.

"And some don't make it out alive," I added.

"It's okay, I'm not driving. We chartered a small, 13-seater jet to bring family from Kaduna for Madina's wedding. I'll have them take and return me Insha Allah."

All my life, I never thought I would find myself in a situation where I'm trying to convince my parents to allow me to marry someone. I used to tell myself that no one would ever be worth the trouble and that if my parents ever objected to my relationship with someone, it must be because the person isn't a good match for me. I was clearly naive then because here I am, ready to stand with Sadiq for as long as it takes until we win Umm'Hafsa over.

By the time we leave Cilantro and walk to our cars, it's already time for him to head to the mosque to pray *Asr*. He's on a call with Imran, and when he's done, he looks towards me, "so you're telling me that I can't come to your house to see you anymore?"

I shake my head no. Umm'Hafsa has probably left strict instructions at the gate. "There's something else," I add. He doesn't say anything, so I continue, "I confronted Umm'Hafsa with the truth, and – and unfortunately, daddy heard."

He doesn't blink. His hand with the phone remains mid-air as he fixes his stare on me. I open the door to the car and wedge myself between him and the open door. "What truth?"

"The truth about the DNA test."

"And he heard?" This part is a whisper. I can't ever remember hearing Sadiq whisper. "What the fuck, Hafsat? Why would you do that?"

"It just came out. I didn't plan it, I was just so angry, Sadiq. And it was all happening so fast." I enter the car and sit down.

He looks like he is deep in thought then he asks, "what did he say?" His voice is still a whisper.

"He was shocked." But weirdly very calm. He only seemed shocked when I went to my drawer and got the results from Lagos I printed out months ago and thrust them into his hands. He kept looking at the results without saying a word.

"And your mom?"

I feel a tightness in my chest at the memory of my words from this morning, but I push it away. It is not my guilt or my shame; I did nothing wrong.

"She was just crying."

"This is messed up, Hafsat. I wish you didn't."

Well, it's too late for shouldn't, wouldn't, and didn't. It happened, and that's that. Even though now a part of me is dreading going back home, another part of me is relieved that this secret is now in the open. She can finally stop holding her righteousness above my head, face her marital problems and allow me to live my life. "I'll keep you posted when I get back home."

Zuwaira

1999

One, two, three, four, five…nine, ten.

I found myself counting a lot in those days I spent in Aunty Tani's house.

Seventeen.

That's how far I had to count when I woke up to allow the heavy fog of dizziness to dispel before I could stand up from the mat. Even as I rolled up the mat to return it to the children's room, I could still feel the ground moving around me, but I had to act like I was strong enough; I could not afford to allow anybody know what was going on with me, even though I almost gave myself away a few times.

"*Ya na ga kaman kina kara haske?* Why is your skin getting lighter?" Tani asked me one morning as I fried kosai for breakfast one weekend.

I hadn't noticed when she entered the kitchen because she never did when I was there. I looked up to see her eyeing my face and stomach suspiciously and my heart rate got faster as beads of sweat started to gather on my forehead from the heat of the kitchen. "M–may –maybe it's the soap," I stuttered.

"Oh, so you remembered to bring your bleaching soaps and creams, but you didn't remember to bring all the jewelry they bought for you? *Allah ya sawake*, God forbid."

I didn't even bring the Lux toilet soap and body cream I used at Alhaji's house. I barely brought back anything of value in my hurry to leave that compound. But I couldn't tell Aunty Tani that. I allowed her to think the change in my complexion was due to bleaching and not the pregnancy hormones. For once, I was grateful that she always thought the worst of me. I tried turning around because her stare was fixed on my stomach, but her voice stopped me.

"Are you still getting your period?" she asked me like she did every month unfailingly. As she waited for my answer, she brought a small bowl of *kayan ciki* from the fridge with a heavy coat of condensed oil over the top. As she used her spoon to stir it, the globs of fat floated around the broth as the smell of boiled meat wafted toward my nose. *Please don't vomit. Please don't vomit*, I prayed silently.

"Ye –yes, I am," I nodded as the taste in my mouth started to turn sour. I could feel warm bile climbing up my throat, and sweat was beginning to drip down my face as I took the fried *kosai* out of the hot oil. *I am going to vomit right now, and she will find out I am pregnant. Innalilahi wa inna ilayhi raji'un.*

"Warm up this soup and bring some *kosai* for me," she turned around and left the kitchen. I heaved a sigh of relief as I rushed to the window and leaned against it, counting up to twenty, trying to breathe in some fresh air to forget the smell of the soup as much as possible.

Eleven.

That was how many days I counted between *Kawu* Sani's visits from Zaria. I was always happy to see him. It felt like I was beginning to forget what my father looked like, but every time I saw Kawu Sani, I felt like my father was still with me. Kawu Sani never mentioned remarriage when he came back. But he always asked if I had changed my mind and reminded me that I could still return to my husband's house if I wanted, that time was not yet up.

"Zuwaira, what you did is a very grave offence. What if Alhaji had died from the sleeping pills you were putting in his food? Don't you know that would be murder? You're lucky that he has even forgiven you," he would say.

Still, my answer never changed. I had made up my mind. I was not going to go back.

Eight.

That was how many times Ibrahim and I exchanged tiny notes carefully hidden under the wooden plank that served as a foot to the black GP tank by the well. It was mostly him just checking on me, asking how I was and if I needed anything. One night, when everyone had gone to sleep, I went to the well, and after fetching the first bucket of water, I had to sit down to catch my breath because it felt like I would fall over due to the dizziness. I reached for the wooden plank and saw a note from him. That was the last note I ever got from him under the tank: *Off to Jos for a few days. See you at the end of this, insha'Allah.*

I recognized his neat handwriting, the long lines of his j, f, and y's, and the curves of his e's, a's, and o's. As I read the note over and over again, I felt the same despair from long ago, on a moonless evening like this one, when he told me that the strike had been called off and that he was returning to University in Zaria. That was the end of that chapter, except I didn't even know it then. *Is this another unsaid goodbye?* I couldn't help but wonder.

When Ibrahim said we should leave together, I immediately said yes, but after long days and sleepless nights spent thinking about it, I wondered which man would want a woman who was carrying another man's child. I reread his note, trying to find any hint of hesitation between the lines. Maybe he was having second thoughts? Maybe he found me at an unfortunate moment and wanted to give me a glimmer of hope so that I wouldn't try to hurt myself again. *If he had changed his mind, maybe it was for the best. This way, he will be spared from my farin kafa.* I reread the letter again and then once more under the dim yellow lights before folding it carefully and tucking it into the ends of my wrapper, then I carried the buckets back to Aunty Tani's flat one after the other, filling up the drums on the verandah and the kitchen.

Three.

That was how much longer I had to the end of my *Iddah*, and Ibrahim was still not back from Jos like he said he would. I had already planned my escape from the house. When my Uncle returned to Zaria, I would leave a note saying I had left for my mother's grand-aunt in Gombe, and I would leave for Lagos.

I chose Lagos because, according to what I saw on the television, there were a lot of people there, so it would be hard for anyone to find me. I could even change my name. The first thing I would do when I got to Lagos would be to find a mosque. I planned to tell them that I was a pregnant widow and ask for a househelp or nanny job. With time, I would figure out the rest.

As I washed the plates that night, I wondered how much the bus fare to Lagos would be. I looked at the money my uncle had given me during one of his visits when he heard his wife insulting me for asking for Panadol. Since then, he had been giving me twenty naira on all his visits so that I would stop asking her for little things. I had forty naira now, and if forty naira couldn't get me to Lagos, I would tell them at the motor park to take me as far as it could. Every town had a mosque. What mattered was that I left Kaduna before Alhaji found out that I was pregnant with his child. I didn't even want to think of the consequences then.

Two days later, I was pounding yam for dinner when Aunty Tani came into the kitchen. Without even realizing it, I sucked my stomach inwards, something I found myself doing whenever anyone was in a room with me.

"Is the soup ready?" She peeped into the pot bubbling with okro and dried fish on the stove, then bent down and pushed a finger into the mortar as I removed the pestle to check for lumps. She looked disappointed that she didn't find any lumps in the yam I pounded to complain about.

"Yes, it's ready," I answered as I rolled the pounded yam into moulds and served it on different ceramic plates for her and my uncle. I had already poured garri into hot water in a big bowl on the sink and covered it for my cousins and I to eat eba.

"Leave this. Your uncle wants to talk to you in the palour." She started serving out the soup for her family in smaller bowls. I would eat whatever would be left in the pot when she was done, which was usually barely anything.

I walked out of the kitchen and found my uncle in the living room watching a *tafsir,* commentary on the Qur'an on the television. He had just returned from the mosque after praying *Maghrib.*

"Kawu, you sent for me?" I crouched by the chair, hiding myself behind the wooden side table.

He looked towards me as he heard my voice.

"Zuwaira, come and sit down," he gestured to the chair by his right. I adjusted my hijab to properly cover my body as I slowly sat down, thankful for the dim lights in the parlour. "Yesterday, at the mosque, Mallam Isa came to talk to me about you." The kitchen suddenly got very quiet, and I could tell that Aunty Tani was listening through the door. My Uncle continued, "he has a brother, a younger one. His name is Ibrahim and he's a doctor. Mallam Isa came to ask for your hand on his behalf."

I kept quiet. My heart was beating so fast I thought it would burst. Ibrahim didn't run away? He actually meant what he said to me that night?

"I told him that your *iddah* is finishing today and so tomorrow, *shi* Ibrahim can come and the two of you can talk." He continued. "If you like him, then we can set up a wedding date for you two because it's not suitable for someone who has been married to stay unattached for long. It comes with many risks and tests from the devil," he said. I nodded even though I didn't know what risks and tests he was talking about. "I know that before now, I've been asking – through your aunt – but now, I have to ask you directly because of this development. Is your *iddah* really over now?"

I looked at my Uncle to see him scrutinizing my face seriously as if he would find the answer written on it. I had been able to get away with small lies my whole life, but the past three months spent lying to Aunty Tani had been really hard. Even now, just looking at an older version of my father's face staring at me, waiting for an answer, I almost blurted out the truth.

But then, at the back of my head, I envisioned my child growing up without me in that house, with those women. I had seen how Abu-Abu was treated like a second-class citizen in his own father's house just because his mother was not there with him. I remembered how Alhaji's bouts of rage came unexpectedly on whoever was around him at that unfortunate time, and most times, it was the poor boy. I could not imagine how bad it would be now that Hajiya Uwa, who usually protected him, was gone. This thought – of the fear that my child might end up like that little boy with no love and no protection – somehow gave me the strength to look up to my Uncle.

"Yes, uncle. My *iddah* is over."

He remained silent for what felt like a whole minute. "*Toh*, I'll send word to Alhaji that you're not pregnant and that your *iddah* has ended as decreed for divorcees according to the Qur'an. Your marriage to him is officially over. I hope you understand?"

The following day, after *Asr*, Jamil returned to the mosque to say that Ibrahim wanted to see me. I finished mopping the kitchen floor, hurriedly rinsed my face in the kitchen sink, and went to the living room. My uncle and aunt were nowhere in sight, but Jamil remained in the living room with us, watching a program with some children debating and naming chemical compounds.

"Assalamu alaikum," I said, a little taken aback by how formal he looked. He was wearing a light grey kaftan and trousers.

"Wa alaikumus salam" he looked up as he answered my sallama.

I sat on the chair away from him. "Can I get you some water?" I asked in Hausa.

"No, thank you," he answered. "How are *you*?"

"Fine."

An awkward silence followed, I didn't know what else to say because I had never discussed marriage with anyone before; unlike many girls my age, I had never done *zance* before because men did not call on me. The silence continued for another minute, and even though Jamil's attention was completely on the screen, Ibrahim and I could not be as honest as we had been that day by the well.

"How was your tr –"

"I wanted to ask –"

We spoke at the same time. Ibrahim chuckled, bowing his head a little. "You go first."

"No, please. Go first. You wanted to ask me something."

"I insist, what did you want to say?" he asked.

"I was just asking how your trip was?" From his note, I got the feeling that his trip to Jos was urgent.

"It was fine, *Alhamdulillah*. I went to settle some things regarding accommodation and my shifts at the hospital," he looked up as he talked. "Um... I wanted to ask if your answer is still yes and if you have a preferred day for the *nikkah*."

Next to me, Jamil hissed loudly as a girl on the green team got a question wrong and the buzzer rang.

I nodded, "any day you choose is fine by me." I couldn't tell him 'the earlier, the better' because we had a chaperone with us, yet he nodded as if he knew, as if he knew that I was scared that I would be caught if I stayed under that roof any longer.

"My family is hoping it can be as soon as possible because I have to go back to Jos to resume my posting."

"There's something you should know," I whispered. His eyes darted to Jamil and back at me, and he raised his eyebrow, but I continued. "They said *ina da farin kafa*, I have bad luck." I just thought that it was unfair for me to carry this much bad luck into his life. He deserved to know all the truths about me.

"Who said?" He was more amused than worried. I told him about my mother-in-law, her sister, and the few others who confirmed it. "First of all, all that *shige-shige, haramun ne*; it's forbidden in Islam. And wealth is from Allah alone. He alone can give and he alone can take away. To think that a human being can be the reason for loss of wealth is sinful."

The following morning when I told my uncle that I had accepted Ibrahim's proposal, his wife hissed as loudly as she could.

"You that you're supposed to wait to marry someone richer than your former husband, you're downgrading. What are you even rushing for?"

You, Tani. I'm running away from you; the thought flashed across my mind like a lightning bolt.

Ibrahim and I got married a week later. Right there in my Uncle's living room. Unlike my previous marriage, no boxes were brought for *lefe* because Ibrahim had told me he used his savings to pay rent for our house and get it furnished during his trip to Jos. I did not care for any of that; he had already done more than I could thank him for. I wore an old but beautiful dress made with a light yellow-and-black material that belonged to my mother and draped a yellow veil above my head. My *sadaki* was two thousand naira. I watched Ibrahim through the window as he came in with his brother and another man I didn't know. In his white kaftan, trousers, and black cap, he looked every bit like the groom of my dreams, and as happy as I was, I was filled with a twinge of sadness because I badly wished that our marriage was not a farce.

When I was taken to Mallam Isa's flat later that day, I was received by Ibrahim's sister-in-law, Ya Aisha. His nieces, Salma and Bilkisu, were so excited to see their Uncle Ibro's *amarya* that they dressed up in their *Eid* dresses and showed me their toys as they asked if they could come and spend their holidays with us in Jos.

When Aisha gave me a lace, atamfa, and Qur'an, she sat next to me on the chair. "*Kin yi sa'an miji,* you got a good man, Zuwaira. Ibrahim is a very kind soul. I don't even think of him as a brother-in-law; he is my brother. But I'm not even praising him because he's family. Anyone who has met him will attest to his character. *Allah ya ba ku zaman lafiya.* May your marriage be peaceful."

I knew he was kind. Only a kind man would offer to help me in the way he has. But why was I still scared? *What if he changes? What if my uncle finds out about this big lie?*

I wondered if I was supposed to say 'Ameen' to people's prayers and good wishes for us when I knew that the marriage was not valid, that it was only a means to escape my fate. We left for Jos very late that evening. His brother drove us to the motor park, where we boarded a taxi, and Ibrahim paid for all four seats of the small commercial vehicle so we would be the only passengers in the car. He sat in front with the driver, and I sat at the back, clutching the Qu'ran Ya Aisha gave me. We didn't say a word to each other the entire car ride there. Eventually, the long windy roads lined with tall trees gave way to houses with congregated brown roofs in an area called Pankshin. It was already nighttime when we arrived and the driver helped Ibrahim bring out our luggage from the boot and wished us a happy married life. We were far away from Aunty Tani, Alhaji Ringim, and most importantly, anyone who knew me in Kaduna.

* * *

Our house in Jos was a rented one-bedroom house with its outside walls made of red bricks. The day we arrived in Jos, exhausted, I followed Ibrahim as he dragged both our boxes, his big black one and mine, a small box containing my most prized belongings. He fumbled with the keys on the tiny verandah that had some potted plants. The clay pots were either half broken or cracked, but the plants were thriving. He opened the door and pushed the curtain covering the doorway aside for me to enter. When I did, I found myself in a parlour with a three-seater, an armchair made with brown cloth with flowery patterns, and a wooden center table opposite a small television. The walls were bare and painted light blue, and the window was covered with a brown curtain that fell to the floor.

I watched as Ibrahim dragged the boxes across the small parlour and pushed open a white door. I must have been standing awkwardly by the table because he looked at me with concern on his face. "Ki shigo mana, come inside."

I left my black skoll slippers by the door and followed him through the doors. It was a bedroom with a regular-sized bed, pink checkered sheets, and two pillows. To the left was a black wooden dresser with an oval mirror mounted on it, and to the right was a matching standing wardrobe; its two doors were wide open as he placed the boxes inside. Like the living room, this room also had the faint smell of fresh paint.

"This is the toilet," he walked to the door just to my right and switched on the light. I watched as he turned on the tap on the sink. It sputtered, and light brown water started spitting out into the white ceramic sink. "I'll leave the tap on until the water runs clear."

I nodded as I clutched the Qur'an in my hands.

"*Ga gabas*, that's East." Both his hands pointed to the wall I would face to pray, the one the wardrobe was leaning against. "The kitchen is on the other side of the parlour."

I nodded again. I seemed to have lost my voice. The water coming out of the tap was now clear so I walked into the bathroom to wash my face and perform ablution. When I was done, I looked around; there was a flushable toilet and an elevated bath area lined with small yellow rectangular tiles. There was another tap in the bath area with a white bucket placed carefully underneath. By the time I came out, Ibrahim was no longer in the room. I brought out my praying mat and hijab from my box and prayed, facing the direction he'd shown me. When I was done, I laid on the praying mat to say my *du'a* but I must have fallen asleep because when I heard his voice again, it seemed to have awakened me from a trance.

"Zuwaira, *kin idar*? Have you finished?"

"Y–Yes," I croaked. I had to clear my voice and repeat myself again. "Yes, I have."

"Come and eat before you sleep." I heard his voice by the door before he disappeared back to the living room. When I went to the living room, the TV was on. A popular show, *Samanja*, a mock military drama with the leading actor – well-known for his ungroomed moustache and funny antics in Hausa and English – was on. Ibrahim had changed into a white Jallabiya, and I realized I had never seen him in one before. He was sitting cross-legged on a blue mat with some black polythene bags in front of him. He looked up with a smile as I came out of the room and gestured for me to sit across him so that I could lean on the three-sitter couch.

"*Kina cin koda*? Do you eat kidney?" He asked, and I nodded. He brought out oil-stained newspaper wrappers from the bags and placed them between us; they had grilled meat garnished with onions and tomatoes, grilled kidney and masa. To the side, there was cold yogurt and pure water,

"Where did you get it from?" I hadn't realized how hungry I was until my stomach started to rumble audibly.

"There's a *mai suya* just down the street. I wanted to tell you before I headed out, but you were praying."

I adjusted my long pink hijab around my head as I sat on the mat and tucked my legs to my side. I reached over, took a piece of masa and ate, "have you prayed?" My voice sounded timid.

He nodded, "there's a mosque a few houses from us. Why aren't you eating any meat?" He pushed more pieces of meat and kidney in front of me.

I picked up a slice of the spiced meat, bit into it, then another. The kidney was tasty, too. It had been months since I had suya. I followed his gaze to the TV as we continued eating silently, with our hands dipping into the papers in front of us one after the other.

When we were done eating, I boiled some water with the boiling ring, took a bath, and changed into my nightdress in the toilet, wearing my hijab even before I returned to the empty room. I was so exhausted, but I could not sleep immediately. I kept tossing and turning on the bed. My mind was racing with so many thoughts: what *will living with Ibrahim be like? Who else is living in the compound with us? Is this a good idea?* I didn't know when I drifted off to sleep but when I woke up thirsty, I was alone, but someone had covered me with a blanket. I guessed it was Ibrahim. As I got up to get some water from the kitchen, I looked up at the small white wall clock. It was only 11:30 pm.

When I opened the curtain into the living room, the television was off, and the light was dimmed, but I could see him laying on the three-seater, looking up at the ceiling with his hands on his chest. He slowly sat up as I came out of the bedroom.

"Is everything okay?" There was concern in his voice.

"I just need some water; I get really thirsty at night," I said quietly. He nodded as I walked to the kitchen and filled a cup with water from the tap.

"Goodnight," I heard him call out softly behind me as I headed back to the room.

I glanced at him and saw his eyes already closed. "Goodnight, Ibrahim."

When he came back from work the following day, he brought with him a covered plastic jug, and when I woke up in the night, I found it on the dresser next to a cup. The jug was filled with water.

* * *

There was only one bathroom in the house. Most mornings, he would come through the bedroom on his way to the toilet to take a bath and get ready for work; either I had become a deep sleeper, or he was very quiet because most times, I did not even hear him. I only saw him as he came out fully clothed or was rubbing his hands and feet with the small tub of Vaseline on the dresser.

When it was time to leave for work, he would leave a few naira notes on the table for me; "just in case you need anything," he would say. I never needed anything; the house was stocked with enough food items to take us through the week.

After my first antenatal appointment, I busied myself in his absence by practicing the old WAEC and NECO papers he gave me before I got married. I wanted to pass English the next time I took the exams. I needed to further my education and get a job so that if Ibrahim turned out to be anything like Alhaji, I could escape with my child and be able to provide for us.

But Ibrahim never changed. What stood out to me during this period was how considerate and kind he was. It was not big gestures; it was in the little things he did. Like how he would always spray insecticide in the bedroom every evening when I was in the kitchen. "We don't want you getting sick," he would say as he switched off the light and closed the door for the insecticide to work.

One day, he returned home and found me drying our washed clothes on the line. He didn't say anything but two days later, as he left for work, he told me that a boy in the neighborhood, Panshak, would be coming to do laundry every Wednesday and that by Friday, he would return with the ironed clothes and bedsheets.

301

I kept waiting for the other shoe to drop, waiting for the day I would do something to set his temper off. But the day never came. He remained kind, even on days I did things he didn't like, like the day we had our first fight.

He usually sent *keke napep,* commercial tricycles to get me from the house because he did not want me in crowded buses on the days I had to go to the hospital. He usually scheduled my appointments during his break at work so that he could sit in with me during the assessments and make notes of the changes we needed to make. Every day after I was done, he would walk me to the front of the hospital and wait until the tricycle was out of sight before returning to his job. But on that day, he had the day off, so we returned home together after my appointment, stopping by the pharmacy at Pankshin Market to buy some medicine for my increasing blood pressure.

"Wait for me, I'll be back soon," he stopped me from getting off the tricycle, then turned his attention to the teenager driving in front. "*Bawon Allah,* please get off the main road and park on the side, because these bus drivers drive roughly." Following Ibrahim's instructions, the boy pulled us off the busy road so that an oncoming vehicle won't throw us off the narrow road that had many conductors from different buses shouting their destinations into crowds that scrambled to get in. I followed him with my eyes as he looked both ways multiple times, crossing the road with a few steps at a time as tires screeched to a halt and horns blared at him from both directions.

While we waited, I looked to the side and saw a woman in a long, white dress standing under a tree and looking at me earnestly. Her shoulder-length dreadlocks were covered with a white cap, and she wore no shoes or earrings. Every time I looked away, I would look back again only to find her looking at me like she knew me. *Innalillahi,* what if she knew me from Kaduna? As I used my handbag to cover my now-protruding stomach, I looked past the cars and buses and towards the pharmacy. I could not see Ibrahim.

"Sister," I was startled by the voice, so I looked to my other side and found the woman in the white dress so close to me. "They have sent me to you. It is well with you." She spoke in English.

"*Ba turanci*, no english," the boy in front of the *keke* started saying, but she cut him off, her determined unblinking eyes not leaving mine, not even for a second.

"She can hear me; she understands what I am saying," she held onto the steel separating the driver's section from the passenger's side. "Sister, it is well with you *oh*," she repeated with a knowing smile on her face. I looked to my other side again, as if I could telepathically communicate with Ibrahim to come back with my mind. "Sister, they are still after you."

I whirled my head in her direction and my mouth fell open. She shook her head as she spoke: "Not just after you, but after anybody that's helping you right now. That man, the one you are waiting for, his life is in danger. There is a black smoke all around you," she moved her hands in the air, creating a halo on her hand.

My heart started beating fast. *Is Ibrahim in danger? My Ibrahim? What are they going to do to him? This is all my fault.*

"Until you are anointed, you can never marry again oh. They have done wicked things to make sure of it," she added.

"*Ke!* Marry? *Tana da miji. Um… meye ma ake kiran miji a turanci?*" the boy started in my defense, trying to tell her I had a husband so she would leave me alone. "*Yauwa!*" he remembered. "Husband. She have husband, madam."

"Nooo," the smile on her face widened. "No, that man is not her husband. Am I lying, sister? You know I am not lying, *ehn?*" She knew. She knew the truth. She knew about my past. "We have deliverance on the mountain. Come, let us help you. Light will always defeat the darkness," she looked at my stomach with an unsettling smile on her face. "*Toh,* me I have delivered my message."

By the time Ibrahim returned, the woman was gone; he showed me the *agbaluma* he got for me. On a good day, I would have started eating the fleshy fruit right there because of how much I liked its sour and mild sweet taste, but I didn't. Ibrahim must have wondered why I was so quiet the entire ride home, but he didn't ask me. From the corner of my eye, I saw him glance in my direction a few times as I stared at the road ahead. I refused to look at him because I knew I would cry if I did.

How do they know that I'm with Ibrahim? Do they know that I'm pregnant, too? When we got back home and Ibrahim went to the mosque, I ran to my box and removed everything I'd packed from Kaduna – the unsewn lace and atamfa at the top of my box from Ya Aisha, the envelope containing my *sadaqi*, and walkman that Ibrahim gave me. At the bottom was a small brown gourd with white cowries around it; I had paid a lot of money to Djalo, the man from Guniea-Bissau for it. It was a protection charm, all I had to do was put it above our front door, hidden by the curtain from the inside and everybody in the house would be safe. Ibrahim would be safe, and that was all that mattered to me.

Later that evening, Ibrahim found it when he was changing a light bulb. I was sitting on the bed, with the earphones to the walkman in my ear when he came in. The batteries were dying and I had to hit the walkman multiple times to get the music to continue every time it stopped.

"Zuwaira, what is this?" He asked in Hausa as soon as he came into the room. I looked up to see him holding the gourd and thought my heart would burst out of my chest out of fear. *Is he going to beat me? Push me against the wall and leave me unconscious on the floor?* I subconsciously wrapped my hands around my stomach to protect the baby. "Did *you* put this above the door?" He asked again and even though his voice was quiet, I could hear the anger in his tone.

My throat felt dry and my palms got sweaty. I could not speak, so I nodded.

"Innalillahi was inna ilayhi raji'un." It was a low whisper.

"You don't understand; your life is in danger." I did this for you, I wanted to add, knowing I wouldn't be able to live with myself if anything happened to him because of me.

"What are you talking about?" His voice remained calm as he spoke, even though there were frown lines on his forehead and his movements were restrained. I could tell he was livid. So, I explained what happened with

304

the woman in the white dress. "Did she give you this?" He looked puzzled.

"No, it's from Djalo." By the time I told him all about Djalo and the protection charms and the blood sacrifice I could not take part in, Ibrahim sat on the edge of the bed and held his head in his hands.

"So, you brought this *all* the way from Kaduna?"

I nodded.

"Zuwaira, this is *haram*. It's forbidden. It is wrong on so many levels," he rubbed his eyes.

I moved closer to him, "but she *knew*. Wallahi, she knew about us. She knew that we're not really married." The last part of my sentence was a whisper. "I did this to protect you. I need to protect you. I know what those people are capable of."

"My love, I need you to understand something," This was the first time he ever called me 'my love' yet for some reason, it felt familiar. "This is shirk. Only a person who doesn't believe that Allah is sufficient will believe there are human beings or djinns with powers that can protect them. Do you see how terrible that is?"

"I thought since Djalo was a muslim –"

"People like this Djalo – they prey on the common issues that people have and exploit them. Nothing happens to us – good or bad – except by Allah's will. If you're so worried about our safety, there's no greater thing you can do for us than to wake up at night, do your ablution and pray *taraweeh*. Only Allah can protect you. Seek protection from Him and Him alone." I nodded as I recalled that I usually heard him praying late into the night in the living room a few nights every week, especially on the days he fasted, Mondays and Thursdays.

"Okay." My voice was apprehensive. I knew he was angry, but he was not acting angry towards me. It confused me. Maybe Ibrahim doesn't lash out when he's angry; maybe he was not one of those men with a rage they could not control.

"Do you know how to recite the yastasheer prayer?" he asked. I shook my head. I had never heard of it. "Okay, I'll teach you. Wake up any night you can, offer a *few raka'ats* and then recite it as many times as you can.

It'll serve us better than this coconut thing they gave you. Do you know how to recite *Ayatul Qursiyu?*"

"Y –Yes," I nodded. My mother taught me.

"Read that three times every night before going to bed." He kicked the gourd with his leg and the cowries rattled. "You have to promise me something."

"Anything."

"You can't continue these *shige shige*. I understand that your previous circumstances forced you into it but this is not the kind of life we want for ourselves."

I nodded fervently, "I promise." And I meant it.

He sighed and remained seated on the bed for a few minutes, just looking at the gourd by his feet. "I'm going to throw this away. Is there anything else you brought that I need to take along?" his eyes fell on the walkman and moved towards my closed box on the side of the wardrobe. I shook my head and he left the room.

The following evening, when I came into the room after my bath, I saw brand-new batteries for the walkman on the bed. In the days that followed, I listened to *As long as You love me* by backstreet boys over and over, except this time around, I felt like the lyrics were specifically written for Ibrahim and me.

Ibrahim

1999

Z uwaira was scared.

All through the ride from Mando motor park to Zaria, she had this look of sheer terror on her face as she sat in the back seat of the small Mitsubishi Lancer. The driver, Ado, was a robust man in his forties who gave us a detailed account of the trials that the recently sworn-in Nigerian president Olusegun Obasanjo went through in prison. I almost asked him how he knew about the torture and ill-treatment because he narrated the stories as if he was Obasanjo's cellmate.

"That is why of all his wives, he chose Stella to be his first lady." His voice was gruff and loud. "She was the only one who used to visit him in jail."

"Mallam Ado, are you friends with the jail guards? This one that you even know who his visitors were." I glanced at the back seat through the side mirror. Her eyes were downcast; I almost thought she was asleep until I saw her sigh out loud as she looked out of the mirror on her left. The yellow veil was now resting on her shoulders and her hair was completely covered with the scarf she tied tightly around her head. Even with the worried look on her features, she was still the most beautiful lady I had ever met. Zuwaira was still exactly as I remembered – innocent eyes, calm demeanor and small frame. It was hard to believe that she was even pregnant; she was still not showing. This was a saving grace for us in what we had embarked on.

"*Ango*, ai sometimes these women are known to abandon their man when he's at his lowest point. A woman's loyalty to a man is tested when he has nothing; and a man's loyalty to a woman is tested when he has everything."

"May Allah help us pass our tests."

When I came to Jos earlier in the month to find a house close enough to the FUJ hospital where I was posted for NYSC to rent, most of the places I looked at didn't have running water. I was insistent that I needed a place where we wouldn't have to rely on a well. When one of the matrons at the hospital told me that her sister had an unoccupied quarter at the back of her house she was thinking of renting out, I went to see it.

Maman Nancy was a dark-skinned middle-aged woman with an immobile arm in a cast. She had kind eyes and a stutter that disappeared as we spoke longer. As she showed me around the flat, I noted the little repairs that needed to be made and estimated the amount of money I would need to make the place appear decent.

"Are you married? Baban Nancy doesn't want bachelors living here. Nancy is still at an impressionable age, you know."

I thought about the girl who opened the door when I knocked on the flat in front; she must have been thirteen or fourteen. "Yes, I'm married." The lie came out so quickly that it startled me. "I'm bringing her at the end of the month."

"How wonderful! You said your name is Ibrahim? Are you an ECWA church member?"

"No, I'm a Muslim."

"Oh, okay. My brother's name is Abraham; we all call him Ibrahim. I was wondering if you were an Abraham, too." Northern Nigeria was interesting in that way – in that it was hard to differentiate between Christian and Muslim northerners. They all dressed and spoke the same way, some of them didn't drink or eat pork just like us. Most of them even had Arabic versions of anglicized names.

After I had paid the rent and collected the keys two days later, I brought the handyman – who was a painter, plumber, and electrician, as was typical for most people with vocational trades in Nigeria – he told me that the bathroom heater was damaged beyond repair, but he was able to fix the pipes, so we could have water from the taps.

Later that afternoon, Maman Nancy checked in with pure water sachets to see how we were doing.

"*Ya aiki?* How's the work?" she asked as she inspected the bedroom frame we were putting together and a new mattress that was leaning against the wall.

"Alhamdulillah." I stood up from the floor and dusted my jeans as I walked towards her, careful not to stumble over a box with bedsheets and pillows in the small room.

"I brought you some water." She dropped the tray on the floor. "I hope my brother Jeremiah gave you a good deal?"

I nodded as I drank the water. I hadn't eaten all day because of how busy we were. "He did. Thank you." Maman Nancy had introduced me to her brother, Jeremiah, who owned a furniture store down by Pankshin Market, where I bought everything on her recommendation. I would come to find out that Maman Nancy called everyone in Jos her brother; it was just her disposition. Once she warmed up to Zuwaira and me, she took her like a daughter. Zuwaira on the other hand was not as trusting, choosing instead to stay indoors and as quiet as possible, like she was scared.

Zuwaira was scared of a lot of things. One day, I got back home an hour later than I usually did because I left the hospital late, missed the bus and had to walk home. When I got back, Zuwaira was in her hijab by the three steps leading towards the main door in front of the potted plants she had fixed with some clay. Her eyes were reddened and fixed on the gate, and when she saw me, she stood up immediately.

"Are you crying?" Did something happen while I was gone? I looked at her hands and face, looking for a telltale sign.

"I didn't know if you were okay, and I had no way of knowing."

My heart swelled with pain and contentment at the same time. *Is this what it feels like to have someone waiting for you?* "Sorry, Zuwaira, work was hectic today, then I missed my bus and I had to walk. Let's go inside; there are mosquitoes out here." I had no appetite due to some childbirth losses at the hospital. Still, I ate it for her because no matter how late I was, Zuwaira never ate without me.

She nodded and led the way into the house. There was a medium-sized food warmer and water waiting on the mat where we usually ate dinner in front of the television. That was something I was still not used to – the regular home-cooked meals. Every day I got back home, there was always food waiting for me. From the first day I had to go to work after we moved to Jos, I was already on my way out when I heard her calling my name timidly as if she didn't want anyone to hear her voice. I turned around and saw her holding a small bag. "You forgot your lunch," she said, panting slightly from the short run to the gate.

"You made me lunch?"

"Yes. You said you would be at work until evening." She handed me a cloth bag. I opened it and saw a small food warmer, cutlery, and a bottle of water.

Is this what it feels like to be cared for? "Thank you."

She shook her head with a shy smile. "What should I make for dinner?" she asked as she tugged the top of the cap attached to her hijab to cover her hair, even though it was not slipping.

I looked away, embarrassed that I had been staring. "Anything you want. Is there anything we need in the house?"

She looked into space as she thought, "*um*, maybe some bread for tomorrow's breakfast?"

Getting bread was easy; I usually passed the market on my way back from work and was already getting familiar with the various shopkeepers. On the days we needed anything from the market, like potatoes, kerosene, or tomatoes, I would drop off the bus a few stops away from the one close to home, get the items we needed and then walk home just in time for dinner.

On a few occasions, I would meet her in the kitchen finishing up our food and would join her to help with the dishes, take the garbage out or just keep her company. One day, I entered the kitchen to the smell of burnt food as she frantically cut up peppers and onions to put in the blender. "S-sorry, food will be ready soon," she was shaking, and her voice was breaking, "I – I slept off, and it – it got burnt." As she picked up a big spoon to stir the rice in the pot, I saw a reddened patch on her palm.

I walked towards the overhead cupboard behind her, where we kept indomie and spaghetti and reached for the medical supply kit I had in there, and she flinched. *She flinched at me.*

"I –I'm s–sorry," she already had tears in her eyes and her body had tightened up as she ducked down a little like she was bracing herself for a slap.

"Zuwaira?" My heart sank. "I'm just getting bandages."

From the look on her face, she didn't believe me. She was still shaking as I opened the cupboard slowly and got out the bandages. "Let me see your hand." There was a look of surprise on her face, as if she hadn't even realized that she was hurt. "What happened?" I asked, examining the blistered palm as I held her hand in mine.

"I don't know. I think it was when I took the burnt pot off the stove."

I wrapped the bandage around her hand, gutted at how her hands were still trembling in fear just because she had burnt a meal. *What did he do to her?* I thought, unable to stop thinking of the way she flinched when I raised my hand. I wanted to ask if it hurt or if the bandage was too tight. I wanted to ask when he started hitting her. I wanted to hold her for all eternity and never allow her to get hurt again. I wanted to tell her that I loved her.

She slowly raised her head as she looked up at me with questioning eyes. The tears were gone now, but she still looked shaken.

"Zuwaira, I'm never going to hurt you." *Or hit you, not over burnt food, not over anything else.*

She gently pulled her hand away from me and walked to the sink. That was the first time I had seen her without her hijab on, without even a scarf. She was wearing a black abaya that was snug over her growing bump. I looked away as she started washing the plates in the sink.

"You need to keep your hand out of water. Leave that, I'll finish up."

That night, we ate the overcooked rice with the oversalted stew that I managed to make.

* * *

The following morning as I left the house, I stopped by Maman Nancy's flat; she was just returning from her morning walk.

"Doctor, *ya amarya*? How's your wife?" Maman Nancy did not know that Zuwaira and I had only started living together only three months prior. No one in Jos did.

"She's fine, thank you. *Dama* I was going to ask you. I need someone to help her around the house for a small fee; you know her due date is fast approaching."

The first time we went to the hospital together for the dating scan, a few days after we arrived, her pregnancy was calculated to be 15 weeks old. The doctor congratulated us as he wrote down the due date on her file.

"Nancy can come and help; she just finished her junior waec and is on holiday now." Since then, Nancy started spending most days with Zuwaira when I was away at work. After work, I found myself rushing back home to spend that quiet hour where she waited in the living room for the smell of insecticide to leave the room where she slept. During that hour, I made corrections to the English essays she worked on during the day. She had a quirk; she chewed the bottom of her pen whenever she was thinking of the right answer to mark for the multiple choice questions.

"How was work today?" she asked one evening after I gave her the dates for the National exams I had registered her for. Zuwaira was constantly getting 90 percent and upwards in the most recent exams I'd marked, and I was confident she would do well.

"Alhamdulillah. How are you feeling?"

"Better than yesterday."

When Zuwaira was 25 weeks pregnant, she was diagnosed with preeclampsia. Her first trimester was easy on her, she said, but with the second and third trimesters came headaches, vision changes, and pain under her ribcage. I made sure that she never missed an appointment at the hospital and that her blood pressure was managed at home.

As her due date approached, I thought I had managed all contingencies to ensure we were well prepared when her baby arrived. I had even picked up extra evening shifts at Premier Clinic for the extra expenses, and we had bought everything that the baby would need. Zuwaira spent a lot of time walking around the house to relieve her swollen legs, unfolding and refolding the baby clothes. She read a book by Catholic missionaries that Maman Nancy gave her about caring for newborn babies and what to expect in the first three months. But we were still grossly unprepared.

First of all, the baby came early. About three weeks early, at 37 weeks, when Zuwaira started having contractions, she thought they were Braxton-Hicks or false contractions that I'd told her about. But these were more intense and frequent, so she got Maman Nancy to get her a taxi and they went to FUJ hospital. Her water broke in the car and she was admitted immediately. I was at Premier Clinic during my evening shift when Dr. Gyang, a colleague from FUJ Hospital, dropped by.

"Gaya, they just brought your wife in, oh. The baby is breach and she's losing a lot of blood." It felt like I had been doused in cold water from the cold rain pouring outside and was grateful to Dr. Gyang for offering to drive me back to FUJ in his Volkswagen. Throughout the ride on the near flooded roads, I felt like we were driving too slowly and by the time we got to the hospital, there had been an unsuccessful ECV and the baby's position could not be turned to head toward the cervix.

"How's her heart rate?" I asked as I reached for Zuwaira's hand. "Zuwaira, look at me," her eyes fluttered, but they didn't open, "I'm here. You can do this."

"It's dropping," came the reply from the nurse on duty, Anna.

I felt her nails as they dug into my palm; she was in a lot of pain. I had seen a lot of women in labor; some shouted out, and others had no strength to shout. There was no sound from Zuwaira; she looked depleted, barely conscious, and extremely pale.

I glanced at the screen of the ultrasound; the machine was running on the last emergency power. The readings indicated that the baby's heart rate was dropping rapidly as well, and there was no fetal movement. I moved closer to the screen, and saw that there were hardly any dark patches to indicate the presence of amniotic fluid.

"Did her water break already? So, why are we attempting to turn the baby?" I asked Anna.

Her eyes opened weakly, and her parched lips opened as if to whisper my name, and no sound came out. I could not imagine the amount of pain that she was in. I had seen this particular scene more times than I wanted to recall since I started working at this hospital. I knew how it could end. How would I explain to her uncle and my brother that she died while giving birth after barely five months of marriage? How would I live without her?

"We need to wheel her to the theatre." I made the decision without thinking twice.

"Emergency CS?" The attending doctor didn't ignore my blatant override.

"We're losing her. That's the only way."

"Gaya, there's no light, and we are out of fuel." Dr. Gyang tried to reason with me.

"Get the reachable lamps," I was raising my voice now as we ran through the dimly lit hallways, my hand never leaving hers. I could feel the scar from the burn on her palm scratching my hand.

"Ibra –" she tried to speak.

"I'm here. You'll be fine. We're just going to do a CS. You have nothing to worry about," I said as a screen was placed across her body. I watched as her eyes closed as the anesthesia kicked in.

"I'm scared... don't leave me," she said to me, and I felt like I would die. *Never* – that was what I would have said if I thought she could hear and understand me. It was the longest forty minutes of my life. I was alternating between wiping tears that dripped into her ears to the sweat on her forehead, even though her skin was getting ice cold.

The baby was born at 10:31 pm on the 30th of June 1999 in the dim theatre of the FUJ hospital, flanked by about 10 rechargeable lanterns, two doctors, and one nurse. A healthy baby girl with a head full of hair, measuring 20 inches and weighing 7 pounds. While one doctor sewed Zuwaira up and the nurse checked her vitals, I had Zuwaira's blood all over my shirt as I held the tiny baby in one arm. When Zuwaira woke up, she burst out crying when she saw that our hands were still intertwined; I hadn't let go of her hand since they gave her the anesthesia. As I faced east and recited the *Athan* into the baby's ears, I leaned to carefully place the baby on her chest.

"Thank you," she mouthed to me as she stroked her baby's hair, she looked down at her baby with her eyes full of love.

"What are you going to name her?" I asked as I pulled my chair close to her and reached to cover the baby with a white frayed blanket.

"I never thought of names because I knew I wanted you to do it," she answered. "Can you name her?"

"No, *haba*, Zuwaira –" That was an honor too big for me to take.

She stopped me with her hands on my arm, "please. That's the only thing I want."

I looked down at the baby's perfect face as her eyes glanced at the world around her. It took a whole minute for me to find my voice, "I –let's name her Hafsatu, after my late mom."

Zuwaira smiled for the first time. "I love it. It's a perfect name. Hafsatu." Her hands continued stroking the baby's hair gently, and I was sure I had never felt love like that before. "*Allah ya jikan mama, Allah ya raya ki Hafsatu na.* May Mama's soul rest in peace. May God raise you, my Hafsatu."

Is this what it feels like to be alive?

Sadiq

Kaduna, 2022

My memories of Kaduna are very limited. I was born in this city and I lived here for the earliest part of my formative years, yet I don't feel any connection to it at all. As we drive from the airport, I watch the many billboards from the window displaying MTN and Airtel advertisements, and as we drive further into town, I catch a glimpse of the red spectator seats in the famous Ahmadu Bello Stadium. I remember evenings when Imran would take the keys to one of the cars in the house, and we would drive to the stadium to watch football matches. Back in the day, we used to drive past the green and white domed building called 'Lord Lugard Hall' on our way to school. Now the driver even passed the road to Essence International School, where I had my primary school education. Still, I felt no iota of connection to the metropolis.

We arrive at Ungwan Rimi, and from the road sign, I see that the street we used to live on is now named after *him*. The only thought that crosses my mind is that the roads leading to the house are considerably narrower than I remember. I watch as the big black gates are rolled open by a stranger, a man in his early twenties, and the car slows down after the first gate and just before the inner gates that lead to my late mother's section. My memories of her are fuzzy; they have always been unclear. Sometimes she is a brown-skinned woman with kind eyes I almost recognize from the pictures in my safe. Sometimes she has a different face, a warm smile with a characteristic dimple.

As the car gradually comes to a halt, I look around the compound; it still looks the same, but in an inexplicable way, smaller than I remember. When I used to play between these palm trees decades ago, they looked like they reached the skies and touched the clouds. Even the mosque looked bigger then; now, it was just a regular-sized mosque, big enough for twenty adults at most.

"*Bari a wanke babban motan. Na ji ka ce za mu fita anjima kadan, ko?*" The driver interrupts my thoughts to tell me he's going to wash the white Lincoln Aviator parked in front of us and get it ready for the outing I'd informed him about.

"No, just give me the keys to this car." I reply in Hausa, I know that they usually drive my stepmother, Hajiya Mamie, in the Lincoln Aviator, and I was not close enough to her for me to take such liberties in her absence while she was away in Abuja for her daughter's wedding event. Truth be told, I was not close to my other stepmothers – not even Hajiya Babba, my father's first wife, before her death. I hardly visited her in Kano, where she relocated to after my father eventually separated his wives from living together.

"Welcome, Alhaji Abubakar. Is this really your face I'm seeing?"

As I take the keys to the car from the driver, I turn around to see an old caretaker of the house, Mallam Hashim, coming my way. He has worked here since I was a child. I haven't seen him in over six years, but he hasn't changed much; he is still as lanky as I remember, with close-set eyes and a beard. He extends his calloused hand to me in the cultural handshake that ends with our fingers touching our chests.

Mallam Hashim started as an errand boy in this compound and worked his way up to being in charge of hiring all the domestic staff, from drivers to house helps to security guards for my stepmothers. Now in his forties, he has as many wives as my father did and just as many children, all of whom depend on the goodness and generosity of the Ringim and Dankabo family to cater to their needs. His oldest sons, Hassan and Hussain, were among the most recent recipients of our family's tertiary scholarship awards.

"It's me. How have you been, Mallam Hashim? And your family?"

"We're doing well by Allah's grace and many congratulations to you. I hear a date will soon be set for your wedding." He smiles wider and I notice that two of his front teeth are missing. "May it come and meet us in good health."

"Ameen," I adjust my cap as he mentions the wedding and my mind immediately goes to Hafsat. Throughout the short flight to Kaduna, I kept envisioning how the meeting with her uncle would go this evening. Based on what I have gathered about him, Alhaji Isa, a former lecturer and head of department at Kaduna Polytechnic, is a well-respected, no-nonsense man well known for being straightforward.

My phone starts to ring and I look down to see Hajiya Amina calling. "Give me a minute Mallam Hashim." I answer as I walk toward the mosque, "hello, Hajiya?"

The static comes through before her voice does. "Hello, Abubakar. Did you arrive safely? Very unlike you not to call to say you've landed. I was worried."

I was on the phone with Hafsat the entire ride from the airport, but I can't say that. "Sorry, I just got to Ungwan Rimi, and I was actually just about to call."

"*Toh*, Alhamdulillah. Have you seen Hashim? Tell him to give you the things I told him to find for me. Please don't forget to bring them along, they are for the remembrance album."

A pulse ticked in my jaw.

"You's still going ahead with that?" Hajiya Amina had plans to compile pictures of my father's philanthropy through the years in a twelve-year death remembrance memorial. The other wife and my older brothers said they would not be a part of it as it was not our culture, and our religion does not encourage commemorating a person's death. I'm not in support simply because I didn't think he deserved to have his image whitewashed and his memory upheld after everything he had done. Yet, she refuses and insists on getting old pictures from the house in Kaduna for the magazine.

"*Haba*, Abu. Whatever his shortcomings were, everything we have today – everything we enjoy today – is all thanks to him."

"As much as I respect your wishes, this is something you and I will never agree on." How is it possible that I'm holding unto her pain, but she chooses to forgive him? I still have images in my head of her bruised face, her torn lip, of the day I found her on the floor unconscious in this very house. I shook and shook her trying to get her to wake up, but she never did. Whenever I bring that topic up, she insists that she has no recollection of that incident. She alludes it to a bad dream that I must have had as a kid. It haunts me so much that I brought it up in therapy. Maher Zubin, my therapist in London, says that memory isn't as trustworthy as we like to think, and that the human brain sometimes fills gaps with details, especially as a response to trauma. But I know what I saw. I know she's just trying to protect me by denying it.

Before we end the call with brief goodbyes, she makes me promise to bring back the pictures. I look up to see Mallam Hashim hovering.

"Hajiya says there is a package you have for her, *ko?*"

"Most pictures were damaged from the flood many years ago. The few that were moved into storage from her former section were hard to salvage because we didn't know there was a water leak there, too. Most are partial prints from the Councillor election around Hameed Ali's time." He went on a long explanation that I didn't really care for. All that stood out to me was the name Hameed Ali, who was the military governor of Kaduna until 1998. I went to primary school with his daughter.

"Can you bring the ones you found, so I don't forget?" The call for Zuhr prayer starts, and we walk to the five taps in an elongated cemented area to perform ablution. After we pray, he brings some pictures in a big office envelope to me.

As he updates me on things I'm not interested in, like the recent renovations they completed, I open the envelope and look through the pictures. They are mostly faded due to age and humidity. At first glance, I can make out the faces of my father, a much younger Uncle Dankabo, and some politicians at political campaigns, fundraisers, and ribbon-cutting ceremonies for various philanthropic endeavors. There were pictures of my stepmothers in matching outfits, but before I can inspect the pictures closely, my phone starts to ring.

I look at the caller display to see Hafsat's cousin, Salma, calling me back. I clear my throat as I pick up. "Hello? Assalamu alaikum."

"Wa alaikumus salam. Sadiq?" Her speech is fast-paced and resonant, the kind of voice you hear on the radio, which matches her bubbly personality. I met her the last time she visited Abuja. "Sorry I missed your call. I was on another call."

"That's okay. How are the kids?"

"They are fine, see them here bouncing off the walls. So, Hajiya just called." Since she did not name the 'Hajiya' she was talking about, I could only infer that she meant her stepmother. "She spoke to Baba about you and he said that he's willing to meet you and listen to what you have to say."

Alhamdulillah. "That's great. So can I come this evening?"

"Actually, that's why I'm calling. He's not available this evening. Can you go now?"

"Right now? Yes, of course."

"Okay I'll text you the address."

"It's in Mando, isn't it? I think I have the address here. Hafsat sent it to me."

Ten minutes later, I am back on the road, alone this time. It's easy to forget how different driving in other parts of Nigeria is from driving in Abuja; there were a lot of unanticipated reroutes due to the multiple road constructions and new building infrastructures. Luckily, Hafsat used a landmark to describe the area to me. Once I get to the Nigerian Defence Academy, it's easy to find the street her uncle's house is on, even though the houses are numbered out of sequence.

"I think I'm here," I say when she picks up on the first ring.

Her voice comes through the speakers, "you see a house with a white gate?"

"Yup, white gate, red roof and..." I glance out of the window, "blue overhead water tank?"

"Yes, that's the one." she affirms excitedly. "Oh God, I'm panicking."

I start to reverse as I park the car on the roadside just before the gate. "Why?"

"Who knows what he's going to say?" The nervousness in her voice is hard to miss; by the modulation of her soft voice, I can tell that she's pacing around, and from her whispered tone, I know she is at home.

"How's everything at home?" I ask her.

Her voice lowers even more. "So tense. I haven't seen either of them."

"Up till now?" I was surprised when she told me that she did not see her parents when she got home the previous day.

"I don't think they know that I'm home today. Shatu has been out with my car all day and I haven't gone downstairs. After I prayed, I saw his missed call."

"Your dad?" Or stepfather, rather.

"Yes, I think he wants to talk to me. But he has been in his study all day." She sighs, and her voice takes on a somber tone, "I don't even have the words for how I'm feeling. I feel so sad for him."

There is something unsettling about the way this whole thing is playing out. When she unintentionally blurted out that she is not his daughter, he took it all in stride, calmly even. No man is that forgiving, not with the damning evidence of a DNA result. Is it possible that he was already aware? "And your mom?"

She sighs, "she's still in her room."

I look at the gate that looms in front of me, behind which is the backbone of whether Hafsat and I have a future together. If her parents' refusal continues for months or even years, how far are we willing to go? How far is she willing to go with me?

"I'll call you back when I leave here."

"Okay. Aunty Khaltum has already told him everything, but he wants to hear it from you," she hesitates for a second before adding, "I love you."

"Love you too, babe." *It's you and I against the world.* I press the ignition button and step out of the car. As I lock the doors, I catch my reflection in the tinted windows of the white Toyota Prado, and I adjust the brown and white stitched cap I'm wearing over a white kaftan and trousers before pushing the gate open.

It's a modest house with a vast compound with two cars parked a few meters away from the water tank. The paved interlocking tiles leading the way to the bungalow's entrance are lined with tiny pebbles. As I get closer, I see an open verandah just before the front door. On the mat is a pot-bellied man in a blue kaftan who seems to be in his fifties or sixties, judging from the grey hair on his head. Next to him is a black transistor radio tuned to a Hausa service station vocalizing the news, and in his hands, a newspaper he seems deeply engrossed in.

"Assaalamu alaaikum," I drag the phrase as I announce my presence.

"Ameen, wa alaikumus salam," he looks up at me and folds the newspaper deftly as he sits up. I remove my slippers before stepping on the mat, crouching towards him to shake his extended hand.

"Alhaji, good evening. I hope I meet you well," I greet him in Hausa.

"Fine, alhamdulillah," he motions for me to sit opposite him as he switches off the radio and studies me closely as he speaks. "Remind me again – what's your name?"

"It's Sadiq, sir. Abubakar Sadiq."

"That's right, Abubakar Sadiq. Sit down, sit down," he insists again, watching as I move into a sitting position on the mat.

"What do you do for a living, Sadiq?"

"I'm a private contractor for leasing and automation. I also have some smaller businesses I manage in Abuja."

He nods as I answer, but his eyes keep inspecting mine closely, almost as if he is more interested in my mannerism than my answer. "Ah, alhamdulillah. What about your parents?"

"My parents are late, but my uncle and stepmother are aware of my interest to marry Hafsat. In fact, they don't even know this issue has come up and are still preparing to come for *gaisuwa* as scheduled."

"May their souls rest in peace," he pauses. "You see, that is the part I don't understand. Hafsatu's father called yesterday to tell me that it has been

322

moved to a later date, so I shouldn't bother coming next week. But from your side, I'm hearing something different. Explain to me *dalla dalla.*"

I rub my hands together as I think of the best way to proceed. "Toh, to the best of my understanding, her parents are no longer in support."

"And who told you that?"

"*Ita,* Hafsat."

"Did she tell you the reason?"

"At this point, we can only speculate because she was not given a reason either."

He looks at me quietly, "There must be a reason. You may not know the reason yet, but there must be a reason. I know her father and won't just turn away prospective in-laws without a concrete reason."

* * *

Later that evening, as the driver takes me back to the airport for my flight back to Abuja, I call Hajiya Amina to tell her that I have the pictures with me.

"Apart from the remembrance album, there's also something I need to verify in those pictures," her voice fades away as she talks to someone who is with her. "Go easy with the lipstick. Do you have a nude color?"

I hear a voice I don't recognize say something about her makeup, and then her voice comes back to the phone. "Sorry, Sadiq. We're getting ready for the reception."

I could tell. Our family has a lot of weddings, and I know the hours of preparations the ladies go through for the various events. "I'm surprised you're not done. *Ba kuyi latti ba?* Aren't you late?"

"*Wana latti?* Don't you remember how late she came for my birthday last year? *Ai nima* I'll make sure I show up fashionably late for her daughter's reception."

I wondered which was worse – the way they exchanged coded jabs at each other through songs and proverbs when they lived together or the pretend tolerance heavy with this unforgiving passive aggression they displayed whenever they met, even after his death.

"Hajiya, you're still upset at that?"

"Of course I'm still upset *mana*. When someone offends me, I have to give them a taste of their medicine."

I'm about to say something about letting bygones be bygones but decide it's not going to change anything. "I'll call you when I land," I say instead.

"Is Hafsat coming to the reception?"

"Yes, she is."

"Okay, I'll see you both soon, dear. Have a safe flight."

When I land in Abuja, I'm about to call Hafsat to let her know that I'm going home to freshen up, then will pick her up for the reception when I see her message: *At your place.*

When I get to the apartment, it's already dark outside, and the night air is chilly. I see Hafsat's car parked in one of the visitors' parking spots. The engine is running, the doors are closed, and she's scrolling through her phone casually. I tap on the passenger window, and her whole face lights up as she opens the locks.

I pull the door open and get into the passenger seat. She's wearing dark jeans and a white T-shirt with a polka dot veil that falls from her head as she leans towards me and gives me a hug. I hold onto her for a few seconds longer than I normally do.

"B, why aren't you ready yet? We're already late for the reception." I ask as I pull away from her. I can still perceive the coconut scent of her shampoo from when my nose was buried in her hair and how soft she felt with my arms around her.

"Babe, I'm so happy. Uncle Isa called. He said he's coming to Abuja tomorrow."

Maybe it's the sudden turn towards uncertainty that our relationship has taken, or maybe it's the fear that I might lose her, but there is something in me that doesn't allow me to take my eyes off her. I follow her excited hand movements and how her skin glows from the security lights that partly illuminate the interior of her car.

"Yes, he told me. I told him we can fly back together tomorrow but he

324

said he wouldn't be coming with me, that he would prefer to come by road. I tried to make him change his mind, but he said he was not afraid of death."

"Yeah, everybody is stressed out about his trip now." Her chest rises and falls as she lets out a sigh.

I pull my gaze up to her face instead. Her hair is tied in her usual updo, exposing her neck. She has a thin gold chain around it, and the pendant is nestled snugly between the swell of her perky breasts. *"Wallahi* I had already told the pilot we might spend the night in Kaduna, but your uncle remained adamant."

"That's how he is. Even when daddy paid for my cousins' masters in the UK, he thought it was unnecessary. He said sending people abroad to study was the reason Nigerian universities were deteriorating."

He isn't entirely wrong, though. "He said that the governor has mobile security manning regular intervals of the road. *Allah ya kawo shi lafiya.* May Allah bring him safely." I reach for her hands and hold them in mine.

We were quiet for a few minutes, and then her face breaks into a smile. "I spoke to Aunty Khaltum, *ta na ta yabon ka*, she kept praising you. She said you are so respectful, well spoken and that you love me very much —"

I couldn't stop myself. I reach for her face and gently pull her towards me as my lips crash into hers, tasting her, feeling her breath mix with mine. My pent-up desire for her is beginning to get overwhelming.

When our lips part, she stares at me with her mouth half-open. She is so beautiful even when she's caught unawares.

"I thought we were waiting?" She asks me.

"I shouldn't have done that right?"

She bites her lower lip, smiles, and says, "took you long enough

I chuckle as my gaze holds hers. *Hafsat. My Hafsat.*

"Are you going to get ready?"

"Babe, I can't come. *Ko yanzu*, I'm already cutting it close. I have to go back home now. If she finds out I'm with you right now, it'll turn into another issue... and you know how the situation is at home."

"C'mon, Hafsat. Everyone is expecting to see you. If you don't come, it's going to be obvious that something is up."

"Insha Allah it will be resolved tomorrow, so it doesn't matter what they think anyway."

Zuwaira

Jos, 1999

I finally wrote JAMB, the national exam that universities based their admission cut-off marks on, on a Saturday. Ibrahim took the day off to stay with the baby, so I was not distracted. After my exam, I found them waiting for me on a bench under a tree in the empty compound of the Government Secondary School that was my assigned venue. I could not even mask the joy on my face as I saw how content she was sitting on his lap as he read from his pocket Qur'an to her. He stopped reading to answer my sallama as I carried an unwilling Hafsatu into my arms. She preferred to be carried by him, except when she was hungry. When she was hungry, she happily came to me.

"How was it?"

"Ibrahim, it was haaard." I sat down next to him and adjusted my blouse underneath my hijab to feed her. As she suckled, I opened the tiny zipper by my neck that the tailor put for air circulation. Functional and still modest even while going about my mummy duties in public.

"You just need 250; that was the cut-off for Gwags last year." When we filled out the forms, we put the University of Abuja, Gwagwalada, popularly known as 'Gwags,' as my first choice because the week before my exam, Ibrahim had a job interview in Abuja and he was expecting to hear good news. If all went well, we would be relocating soon.

327

"I went over all my answers multiple times, then I started second-guessing them." As I told him about the exam, he chuckled, opened a bottle of water and passed it to me.

"You've been doing well with your past questions. I'm sure you will get over 300." Sometimes I don't know where Ibrahim got his considerable belief in my abilities, but it felt good to have someone who placed me on a pedestal for once in my life.

Hafsatu started getting fussy, and that was our cue to head back home to Pankshin. That house in Jos was my haven. For the first time in my life, I had a peaceful home that I could call mine, where I did not feel like a stranger, where I didn't feel like a burden, and where my child was safe.

I am sure every mother thinks her child is the cutest, but it didn't feel like maternal pride when I said that Hafsatu was the most beautiful baby I had seen in my life. Everybody from Nancy to the conductors on buses to women in the market said the same thing. She had the chubbiest cheeks and the most inquisitive eyes. She hated being still, so I always had to walk around the house when I was carrying her on my back. She loved bath times, and she would always sleep off right after.

There were nights I would wake up frantically in the middle of the night and rush to her small white bassinet by the dresser. Nightmares had me worried that her father would find us and take her away, but I would always find her sleeping peacefully with her little hands at the sides of her head. Her beautiful brown skin was beginning to darken, just like mine. She was the most perfect blessing.

I'd return to bed, careful not to wake Ibrahim up but as I pulled the cover over me, he would open his eyes.

"You went to check on her again?" he would mumble sleepily as he pulled me closer to him. "*Toh*, now that you know that nobody has kidnapped her from us, are you going to sleep?" I would nod and snuggle into him, but we never slept entirely through the night. Our lips always found each other and he kissed me with a tenderness I had never experienced before. At the beginning of our marriage, I didn't know what to do or how to respond until his tongue, always gentle, slowly swiped my lower lip, coaxing me to open up to him. After then, my body just started obeying his directions without even thinking about it.

We couldn't get enough of each other. I didn't feel like sex was just for him, like in my previous marriage, where it was only a duty to my husband and my responsibility as a wife. Something I endured because I could not say no. With Ibrahim, it was different. He was selfless, playful even. He didn't just touch me at night. Throughout the day, he would find an excuse to give me little kisses on my forehead or cheeks, like after I cooked or folded his clothes. Sometimes, it was just to cheer me up when I was sad. He would give me little pecks before leaving for work or while we watched television in the evenings. When we made love, he would constantly check in to make sure that I was okay, asking if I wanted to try something new. It was like it was important to him that I enjoyed it.

When he worked night shifts and returned home around 4 or 5 am, it would be raining heavily outside. I would be in bed, and I would hear him walk to Hafsat's bassinet to check on her, before he quietly removed his damp clothes and joined me in bed. I would feel his hands as they wrapped and pulled my back closer to him and the soft kisses he planted from my neck to my shoulder. The contrast between his cold skin, wet from the outdoors, and my warmth was electrifying.

My faint sighs became moans as I rolled to my back while he moved lower and lower over my body underneath the covers. He kissed every part of me with equal parts devotion and reverence. His eyes always found mine in the darkened room as he kissed to shut me up. "Don't wake Bebi up, my love." And he would go back to killing me with sinful delights.

Sometimes I found it hard to have an orgasm, and he always knew. He would stop me when I tried to get off the bed to take a bath before the call for prayer. Wedging me between the pillow and his chest. "Are you okay?" He would ask me seriously, and I would nod. "But you didn't cum, though."

"How do you know?" My whisper was barely audible in our room, bathed in the soft light of the lantern by the toilet's entrance, which we used as a source of light since the transformer malfunctioned and our whole street was plunged into darkness. We usually cracked the small window in our room open for the fumes to escape.

"I can tell." His voice would turn husky as an indication of what was to come. I tried not to get distracted by the familiar feel of his lips on my neck as his fingers traced my nipples or the poke of his arousal just below my stomach. "I can *feel* it when you do. It's hard to miss."

Oh.

The first time I ever had an orgasm was with Ibrahim. It was after we got married in a mosque by airport road in Jos, away from our neighbors who already knew us as husband and wife. We started going out once in a while, on short walks on the weekends. He took me to places around the city, teaching me about the rich history of the Nok artifacts in the museum, telling me the feeding habits of wild animals in the zoo, and showing me the unique rock formations Jos was famous for. Even though we slept on the same bed, we didn't have sex because of what felt like the longest bleeding in my life and my unhealed stitches during the 6-week wait that the doctors at the hospital said I needed to heal.

On the rainy night he made love to me for the first time, he went slow, finding a rhythm that picked up as he moved in and out of me, covering me in kisses and soft caresses that made my eyes well up with tears at how gentle he was. Then a strange feeling started deep in me, building up with an intensity I had never experienced before. It felt like I was hanging over a cliff of an overwhelming emotion that made me forget about my past and how miserable life was before him. His name escaped my lips in muffled cries before I could stop myself, and I felt him move faster until he collapsed over me. I expected him to roll away from me and sleep off immediately, but he didn't. He held on tightly to me as we struggled to catch our breath.

"Tell me you're okay." He said as he kissed me on my forehead and then my lips.

Am I okay? I thought. My legs felt like jelly, and it was a struggle to get words past my lips. "What was *that?*" I asked shakily after he rolled over to his side, his head brushing mine on my pillow.

He was watching my face and it took a moment for me to realize that he looked surprised. "What was... what?"

"That. The – the end... when I..." I didn't know how to articulate my combustion or how it felt when my fingers dug into his shoulders, leaving nail imprints.

"When we came?" The look of confusion on my face must have told him something because he suddenly raised his brows. "You've never cum before?"

I shook my head. I must have looked like a mess because my scarf came off at some point, and his fingers were wrapped in my hair. I was sure my eyes were red because I had cried. Still, he looked at me like I was the most beautiful person in the world. His eyes fell to my chest, and that was when I realized we were both completely naked. I started pulling the velvety brown blanket to cover my breasts, and he stopped me. "Don't, I can never get tired of looking at you."

Weeks later, Ibrahim told me he didn't get the Abuja position he had applied for. He was passed over for the son of a well-known businessman who had returned from abroad, and I was filled with a familiar pang of guilt.

"I have to keep working at FUJ until I find a better position," he said.

"But you hate that place." Sometimes, during the night, as we rocked Hafsatu Bebi to sleep, he told me about fatalities caused by sheer negligence by some staff there.

"Allah will provide us with something better, my love." He continued eating the jollof rice and fried fish I made.

My love. He did not blame me for the misfortune, but still, I heard Hajiya Uwa's voice in my head: "Mai farin kafa."

Has the inevitable started? Would our marriage lead to the gradual disappearance of any wealth he was supposed to get in this lifetime until he turns penniless? He already spends all his money caring for Bebi and me. *Should I ask around for someone skilled in these matters, mai taimako, who can help get rid of this issue, the issue I clearly brought into his life?* But I could not forget Ibrahim's voice the day he found Djalo's charm in the living room, the day he made me promise that I would never do things like that again. He said they were all exploits and that they don't work.

Later that night, I could not sleep, so I got off the bed, went to the toilet, did my *ghusl* - purification bath, prayed tahajjud, read the Qur'an and *Dua Yastasheer* just as Ibrahim had taught me. Every time I prostrated my face in sujood, I cried my heart out to Allah, told him my fears, begged for forgiveness, and asked him to take away the problems we could see and the ones we didn't even know of. I didn't relent.

* * *

Ibrahim didn't have to say it, but from his actions since Hafsatu's birth, I knew that he had taken her as his. He was there when her ears were pierced, he was present for all her immunizations, and he never missed any of her hospital check-ups, not even when I told him I could manage just fine. When we went to the market together, he would spend long minutes reading the vitamin and mineral content on different packages before he finally decided which brand of fortified baby cereal he would buy. It didn't matter to him if it was the most expensive option. As long as it was for Bebi, he would spend whatever amount.

One day, as I was buying sanitary pads in a store in the middle of the market, I heard a voice call out my name. "Hajiya Zuwaira. Who is this looking like Hajiya Zuwaira?" I froze. The only people who added the title 'Hajiya' before my name as a mark of respect were the last people I thought I would ever see again. I turned around to see Hashim, the errand boy from Alhaji's house.

What is he doing in Jos? My eyes darted behind him as my eyes frantically searched for Ibrahim. He was with Hafsatu, and they were in a toy shop opposite us.

"Ha –Hashim?"

"Good afternoon Hajiya, I didn't know that you live in Jos now."

"Afternoon, Hashim." I looked around us. *Is Alhaji or Sufyan here too? Did they follow us here?* "Are you alone?"

"No, I'm with my uncle. My younger sister is getting married and we're

332

here to buy some things for her room and kitchen."

Oh. "Okay, that's good." I heard Hafsatu start to cry, and Ibrahim shushed her as he picked up the toy she had dropped. *If they come here and Hashim sees them, he might be able to add two plus two and know she is Alhaji's child. How did I have a six-month-old already when I left his boss's house just a year ago? He would know that she belongs to Alhaji, and I couldn't allow that to happen. Ya Allah, please let him walk away before he sees Hafsatu.* I prayed silently in my heart.

"So, you got remarried in Jos? We didn't know. We thought you were in Kaduna this whole time."

"No, we – I stay in Lagos, I just came to visit… alone. I have a friend here." As I paid for the pads, I collected the black plastic bag from the shopkeeper and said goodbye. He stopped me and asked if I knew somebody had died, one of the drivers in Alhaji's house. I didn't know. "*Allah ya jikan shi.* May his soul rest in peace," I said, even though I could not remember which of the drivers it was. I could not think straight.

I looked up to see that Ibrahim had started walking in my direction. A frown crossed his face when he saw me fidgeting while talking to a stranger in the busy Jos market. I panicked and started walking in the opposite direction, praying to God that Ibrahim would not call out loud for me. Hashim looked puzzled as he shouted goodbye to me and returned to his uncle.

When Ibrahim caught up to me, he reached for my shoulders to stop me. "Umm'Hafsa, what was that ab –?" He stopped when he saw me silently crying and looking behind him, fraught with worry to see if Hashim was looking at us, but he was long gone.

"My love, they know… they know we… they know we're here." My voice came out in broken whispers.

"Who knows we're here?"

"Hashim. He works in Alhaji's house. He's going to tell them that he saw me in Jos."

"And so? Zuwaira, you are my wife. You got remarried; it's not a big deal." My eyes drift to Hafsatu as she puts her fists on his face, sucking on her pink pacifier; his eyes followed mine, and his features softened. "Oh."

As we carried nylon bags filled with diapers, meat, vegetables and fruit that would last us for the week, our walk was very quiet.

The following day when Ibrahim got back from work, he met me making dinner in the kitchen as Hafsatu cried her lungs out in her bassinet in the room. I was exhausted. I hadn't slept the night before because of my encounter in the market with Hashim, and Hafsatu didn't want me to carry her even though she was fussy. On days like this, I felt like I was failing at the only job I ever truly wanted – being a mom.

"Zuwaira, *lafiya*? Is everything okay? I heard Bebi's cries from the gate."

"She's been crying all day…" I mumbled as I turned the plantain I was frying over, turning down the black knob on the side of the stove to reduce the flame. Ibrahim picked her up from her bassinet and started singing *Hafsatu Bebi,* a song he had made up for her. She immediately quietened down as he rubbed her back.

"She's colicky. I'm going to go and buy gripe water. It'll help the gas."

He always knew exactly what was wrong with her, unlike me. I thought she was hungry, so I kept feeding her. Then I thought she was sleepy, so I put her on my back, carried her outside, and sang to her, but she only turned redder as she wailed. I felt like I would pull out my hair from the roots in frustration and exhaustion. Eventually, I just left her to cry it out, but she didn't stop until Ibrahim got back.

As I took the hot oil off the fire and splashed some water to douse out the stove's flame, Ibrahim pulled me close and kissed me on my forehead. "Listen, it's not easy, but you're doing great. On days like this, you don't have to cook. I will understand."

"How can you come back from work and there's no dinner?" I wiped the tear that fell from my eye. I didn't want to be the girl that always cried because she couldn't manage being a mother and a wife.

"That's why I give you money weekly. On days you feel overwhelmed, just send Nancy or Panshak to buy us dinner from Maman Bomboi." Maman Bomboi was the woman who fried yam, sweet potatoes, and *kosai* a few meters away from our gate. "You know me, as long as there's cold Pepsi, I am happy to eat *kosh and dosh* for dinner."

Despite myself, I laughed when he called *kosai da doya*, beancakes and fried yam "kosh and dosh."

"Check my briefcase," Ibrahim said quietly so as not to wake Hafsat up; she had already started sleeping with her head resting on his chest. "There's something I want you to see." I washed my hands and reached for the brown briefcase on the top of the fridge.

I pulled out a white envelope with an emblem that read National Hospital Abuja.

"This?" I asked, and he nodded. As I read it my eyes widened as I read the starting salary and benefits. "A job offer?" He smiled as he nodded again. "Alhamdulillah. Thank you, Ya Allah." I said, almost jumping happily. *I was not bad luck to him. Maybe I was never even bad luck at all.*

Hafsatu stirred, and he pretended to frown at me, shushing her back to sleep with an ease that I almost envied. I was married to the best man on earth, and he deserved all the best things in this life and the next. After Ibrahim put her in her bassinet and went out to the mosque to pray Maghrib, all I could hear in my head were his words: 'A house where the inhabitants wake up at night to pray will always progress.' I have seen the proof.

Since then, I never joked with Tahajjud, confident that seeking help from any other means or person was not only a sin but absolutely useless.

Ibrahim

Jos, 1999

نَّ ُهَلْمَحَ نْعَضَي نْأ نَّ ُهَلَجَأ ِلْامْحَألْا ُتَالْوُأَو

And as for pregnant women, their Iddah term shall end with delivery. (Qur'an 65:4)

After Zuwaira and I got married, we went through a stage filled with uncertainty and self-consciousness because I was used to seeing her covered in front of me, and now that we were *halal* for each other and in such close proximity, we kept stumbling over our words.

One morning, I entered our bedroom to see her struggling to tie a thickened wrapper Maman Nancy gave her around her stomach. When she saw me enter the room, she pulled down her blouse to cover her scar and looked away, even though I cleaned and changed the gauze over the incision wound on her lower abdomen every two days. When she pulled her blouse, I wanted to say what was on my mind: 'You never have to hide any part of yourself from me. To me, you are perfect.' Instead, my eyes caught hers in the mirror, and I asked, "do you — do you need help with that?"

She peered up innocently, beautifully. "I just need... to tie... this knot." She huffed and puffed as her hands twisted to tie the ends of the cloth behind her.

I dropped the cup of tea I was holding on the dresser. "Here, let me help you." I stood behind her, and as I started to tie it, I wondered why there was cultural pressure on women to go through a lot of discomfort to flatten their stomachs after pregnancy. The stomach will contract naturally with an active routine and proper diet. Zuwaira didn't seem to agree with me when I told her that weeks ago, so she kept tying her stomach.

"Can you make it a bit tighter?"

"Are you sure? It seems pretty tight already. Can you even breathe?"

She nodded, and I made it tighter.

As I tucked the knot into the material, my fingers touched the skin on her back, and I heard her sharp inhale as she tensed up. *Good.* It gave me satisfaction to know that my touch affected her as much as her proximity affected me. All those months we spent physically apart while living together felt like torture and a grueling test on my self-control. There were nights when I'd come into the room to ensure the windows were properly closed and see her fast asleep on the bed. As I covered her with the blanket, I'd remind myself that the Maliki *madhhab*, our Islamic Jurisprudence, stressed that when a man had sex with any woman during her *iddah*, she became forbidden to him forever. *Forever.* The thought of that alone was enough for me to stay on the couch in the living room the whole time we were fake-married.

Zuwaira's nineteenth birthday was the month after Hafsatu was born. When I returned from work that day, I told her we should go for a walk.

"Where are we going?" she asked after we dropped Hafsatu off with Maman Nancy, who I had told about my plan earlier in the day.

Zuwaira and I went to a restaurant for a late lunch, and she was surprised to see that I had gotten her a cake. "I have never had a birthday cake!" she said with a huge grin on her face as she blew the candles out and opened her gift, a wristwatch and earrings. She wore her gifts every day after that, making me feel like I'd waited so long for that, without even knowing or realizing how much I wanted it, wanted that. To look into her eyes and see genuine happiness reflected in them and to know that I had a part in why

337

she felt that way. It was a blessing from Allah to have someone to share not just the happy moments but sad and uncertain ones too. Zuwaira was my blessing, my companion in every aspect of life.

A week later, I planned to take her to *Shere Hills* and *Assop Falls*. As I packed Hafsatu's diapers to put in the bag we usually dropped with Maman Nancy, she came out from the bedroom. "Should I wear this?"

I looked up to see her in a grey abaya I had gotten for her a few weeks prior. She had wrapped a scarf around her head and used a pin to keep it in place. She was wearing makeup, darkened eyes, red lips, all smiles, and the wristwatch I got her. She looked very beautiful.

I could barely keep my eyes away from her as we sat together on a picnic mat and ate fruits while watching the waterfall. I did not anticipate how cold it would get, so I gave her my sweater. Even as we walked through the busy night market in Pankshin, we kept stealing glances at each other. I found excuses to hold on to her hand – while crossing the road, when someone walked or drove too close, when we heard a dog bark. After a while, I just stopped letting go of her hand until we got home.

When we picked up a sleeping Hafsatu, the tension between us had increased. There was no light at home, so I used a pen touch to light our path to our flat. Zuwaira opened the door while I dropped the bag containing Bebi's soiled clothes and unfinished milk on the chair. As she lit the kerosene lantern with a matchstick, her face was illuminated by the yellow glow, and she followed me with it as I went into the room to drop Bebi in her bassinet. I heard as she dropped the lantern on the dresser, but I didn't hear her when she walked back to us, so when I turned around, I bumped right into her, and had to catch her to stop her from falling.

"Sor –"

"Sor –"

We spoke at the same time. Our first words since we came back home broke the silence and tension teetering on the consuming connection we had shared since the first time we met at the well in Kaduna. A friendship formed from the days we walked to Ungwan Rimi market together, affection from long afternoons spent talking to each other on the phone when I called her uncle's landline from Zaria. Desire from when I gave her the walkman to listen to *our song*, the song that reminded me of her. Up until the day we left Kaduna for Jos with nothing but complete trust in each other. I had never wanted this with anyone else. I had never had this with anyone else.

I reached for the pin in her scarf and pulled it out, unwrapping the material until it fell to her shoulders. I could not get over her hair. How it looked after she loosened the two braids she usually had it in. Frizzy and long, sometimes covering the sides of her face like curtains that hid her eyes from me. Or how it looked right now, wrapped around a black ribbon with the ends falling to her back.

I kissed her for the first time.

She was every dream I had had about love come true. I never imagined that she would come back into my life or that we would one day have a family of our own.

* * *

No member of our family came to Jos because I didn't inform them about the birth of Hafsatu until four months after she was born. I finally sent word with a commercial bus driver going to Kaduna. The package I addressed to my brother contained some sweets, Hausa kola nut, and a letter informing them of our child's birth and her name.

My brother's congratulatory reply came the following week. It had some money in an envelope, some *Zamzam* - holy water, and a letter that informed us that Hajiya Tani said that she could not come for *wankan Jego*, the hot bath administered to new mothers. The letter said Ya Aisha would be arriving in Jos in a few days to help us with the baby and asked me to be at the motor park to receive her.

When I got back home, Zuwaira had just stepped out of the bathroom. Her long hair was washed and fell in wet curls over one shoulder. I showed her the letter, and as she read my brother's words, her eyes widened, and the corners of her mouth twitched.

"*Innalillahi wa inna ilayhi raji'un*. What are we going to do?" The white towel she tied around her small frame was damp from the water that dripped from her hair, down her neck to her bosom.

I watched as our four-month-old played with a rattle and my stethoscope on the bed as she cooed to herself. There was no way we could pass her off as a newborn baby. According to my letter, she was just a week old.

"I will write back and say that the doctors said you can't do the hot water baths, because of your CS." At least that part was true. She couldn't do *wankan jego*.

She stopped me with her hand on my arm, "but what if she still wants to come and help with the baby? Especially if they know that it is CS, and that I'm not supposed to be carrying heavy things or doing a lot of work."

She was right. If Ya Aisha heard that Zuwaira went through surgery, she would board the next available commercial vehicle to Jos. But when she arrived, she would see that the scar from the surgery had already healed, and the baby was already sitting and blabbering.

So I wrote back to them, including a picture of Hafsatu we took on the morning of her naming ceremony. For extra measure, I added that we moved to a remote village away from Jos as part of my posting and that it was hard to get to. I also assured them we were all doing fine and had the help of neighbors and the villagers in this remote place I had made up.

* * *

Two of us came to Jos, and three of us left for Abuja. Ever since the country's capital changed from Lagos to Abuja, the town has seen exponential growth. When Ya Isa and I sold our inheritance in Kano to a man who was buying all the houses on that road to build a shopping mall, that was when Ya Isa started building his house in Mando. I used my share to buy a piece of land on the outskirts of Abuja. Except now, it was no longer the outskirts.

When we came back from Hajj, which was something I had been saving for since I left Kaduna with Zuwaira, a hectic life began in Abuja. We lived in a two-bedroom apartment in the staff quarters allotted to doctors who worked in the recently commissioned National Hospital in Abuja. After a few months of saving, I bought a second-hand Honda and taught Zuwaira how to drive. When she received her admission letter to study Banking and Finance, we already had a routine. On the days she had lectures, she would leave Hafsatu with a nanny who came from Dawaki every morning and left in the evening.

While I was struck by Zuwaira's kindness and intelligence, people were often struck by her beauty. During one of our physician's wedding, a colleague, Dr. Girei, met Zuwaira for the first time, and he pulled me to the side to talk to me, 'brother-to-brother.'

"Dr.Gaya, *ka dai sake shawara*, have an honest rethink. You have a wife like this, and you're allowing her to go to that University?"

"Is something wrong with the University? Are their courses not fully accredited, *ne?*" I wondered out loud.

"No, I see that she's young *ne*. You know that place is a hunting ground for all these Abuja politicians; they have no shame. *Wallahi*, my neighbor's wife left her marriage of three years to follow one rich man like that. Her university friends introduced her to him, *fa*. Can you imagine?"

I looked back at the table where Zuwaira was talking with the wives of other staff; Bebi was on her lap drinking Capri Sonne. I thanked Dr. Girei for his advice and told him I would consider what he told me.

But I knew my Zuwaira. She had seen money and wealth that even I had never come close to, but she chose to leave it all behind and we had been content in our humble marriage for years now. Zuwaira was not going to heed any politician's interest. I knew my wife. I trusted her just as much as she trusted me.

The longest time I spent away from the house was a two-week training I went for in Lagos. Zuwaira and I spent most of the nights on our newly acquired GSM phones, matching grey Sagems. We took advantage of the free night calls MTN was offering the entire time, and during the day, at my training, I would receive text messages from her. *Yawnin thru out lecture 2day. Luv u*, she would send.

I deleted other text messages from friends and colleagues just to make space for hers. I never deleted hers. When I was alone, I got rid of the loneliness by rereading her text messages and when I finally returned to Abuja on a Thursday afternoon, she was back home from her morning lecture, and the nanny had taken Hafsatu to collect Sallah clothes from the tailor. We had the whole apartment to ourselves. I could not even hide my erection. I didn't even try. I had been hard all day just at the thought of coming back home to her.

She pulled me into her, wrapping her hands around my neck and kissing me so softly that the only sound that could be heard in the room was a loud groan. It took a few seconds for me to realize it was coming from me. Her hands hurriedly pulled the buttons on my shirt apart, and I fumbled with the zipper on the back of her dress.

"Hurry," she moaned into my mouth like she craved the same urgency I felt, like I would die if I didn't get it right there and then.

My heart was pounding in my chest. "I know, baby. It's been so long." I think I wrecked her zipper that afternoon. I was just wound up so tight.

She giggled against my lips as she walked backward into the bedroom, and we fell into the bed.

* * *

Our second daughter was named Saratu, after Zuwaira's mother. By then, we had made a habit of traveling to Kaduna regularly to see family.

After Zuwaira completed her NYSC, the Central Bank of Nigeria had a directive to hire qualified candidates from Northeastern Nigeria. Zuwaira passed all three exams and we became a two-income household. Together, we managed our financial affairs, and she always gave me advice on what kind of investments to make. When I thought it was time to start developing my land, she discouraged me from building us a house. "Build stores there instead, so that the rent will be an additional source of income, and as the value increases, we can use the money to build a house."

For the next few years, most of my salary went into building a shopping complex in Wuse. Eventually, we moved to CBN quarters so that I wouldn't be paying out housing allowance from my salary and I could cover both our daughters' school fees.

Alhaji Ringim had become a staple name in Nigerian politics by that time. After he lost the gubernatorial election, he became a member of the House of Representatives. A few years later, he became a senator. We never mentioned his name in our house. Sometimes we would be watching the news and he would come on in an interview segment. Just the discomfort on Zuwaira's face was enough for me to quietly check other channels to see if they were showing something else.

There were also close encounters like the one Zuwaira had in Jos market before we left. One day, we took the girls to a family fair in Garki, but when we got there, Zuwaira turned pale as she gripped my hand tightly and asked us to leave.

"Why? The girls are excited that we finally brought them here." We had already bought tickets and were just in a line-up for snacks.

"Please, my love. That woman over there is one of Alhaji's wives." She covered Hafsatu's face with a veil as she whispered, like she was scared the world would suddenly see a resemblance between Hafsatu and the other kids. I looked behind us to see two women with about seven kids entering the fair. I didn't know which one was Alhaji's wife, and it didn't matter. We left immediately. That evening, Hafsatu didn't eat her dinner. It was the first of many times she was angry at her mother for cutting a family outing short.

Later that night, as we laid in bed, talking about everything and nothing, Zuwaira sighed as she stared into space.

"*Meye ne?* What is it?" I asked.

"Sometimes, I just get so worried about Hafsat. What if like –" she hesitated. "What if she, I don't know, ends up falling in love with someone related to her?"

I didn't understand exactly what she meant, but the fear in her eyes made me probe. "What do you mean?"

"Her surname is Gaya, but what if a Ringim boy ends up liking her, or she likes him back? I know it sounds stupid, but – "

It didn't sound stupid. I knew exactly what she meant. There was a reason why what we did was a sin. We had created an enormous sinkhole in the delicate matter of paternity and blood relations that our religion did not take lightly. Still, I knew I had to reassure my wife.

"*Haba*, Zuwaira. With all the Muslim boys in this country from Kwara to Katsina, what are the odds of her ending up in a relationship with one of her stepbrothers?"

Hafsatu

2022

I pull in through the gates after Isha, and I'm relieved to see that the garden lights opposite the pool are on, and I can hear my sisters' voices and laughter. The pool used to be empty the first year we moved into this house because Umm'Hafsa didn't think it was safe. She said the possibility of someone drowning gave her nightmares. The pool is only 4 ft deep, and the first time it was filled up was after Mohammed's 10th birthday.

I park in my parking spot and follow the gravel-stoned path flanked by bright white security lights, grateful that I didn't have to walk past my mother and her husband in the living room if I had entered the house through the front door.

At the back of the house, just in front of the green shrubs and the yellow sunflowers and hibiscus, are two outdoor sofas and a brown wicker hanging egg chair on artificial green grass.

"*Meye kuke yi?* What are you guys up to?" I clean off a dried piece of leaf resting on the brown waterproof cushion and sit in front of a platter of peppered gizzards and grilled chicken my sisters are feasting on.

"We swapped games night for outdoor grill night," Aisha looks up as she picks up a piece of meat with a toothpick. She takes in the sight of me in my black jeggings and white Moncler shirt. "Wait a minute, I thought you were at the wedding."

I open my mouth to answer but to her side, I catch Sara giving me a look I can't quite decipher in the moment. Her face is unsmiling and when she sees me looking at her, she quickly looks away. I kick off my brown Hermes slip-ons and tuck my feet underneath me.

"Sara, can you pass me a drink?" I gesture to the canned Coca-Cola on the table and she silently passes it to me. I wonder what she knows about this whole fiasco. She was at the gym yesterday when Umm'Hafsa and I had the loud argument in my room. "*Kin fita yau?* Did you go out?" I ask after taking a small gulp of the drink. I really don't feel like eating or drinking. I just want to sit with them to ease the tension on my mind.

Her head jerks as if she is surprised I'm talking to her. "Um – no, well I went to the gym in the morning, but I've been home since."

Maybe she overheard the parents discussing something earlier today. How much does she know? Should I confide in her and Aisha? Should I wait for them to bring it up?

Aisha leans back into the sofa's backrest in her long pink maxi dress. "You didn't show Bebi what Fati Ringim sent to you." She prompts Sara with a mischievous twinkle in her eye.

"Show me what?" I look between the two of them.

"Hold on. I sent it to my phone from hers," Aisha reaches for her phone tucked between one of the cushions, opens it, swipes it a couple of times, then hands it to me.

I raise the phone and look at a video of a woman I don't recognize working hard over at a set of purple travel luggage. They could have been *Briggs and Riley*, but I can't be sure because of the big red and white ribbons she's knotting in big bows over the handle covering the brand names. There's indistinct chatter in the background of what looks like a private living room.

"What's this?" I hand the phone back to her, uninterested, as my phone beeps with a message. I open it to see a picture from Sadiq, completely dressed for the occasion in a grey babban riga with intricate embroidery and a black cap. *Looking great, babe.* I reply.

"Fati sent it to Sara. Apparently, it's for you."

"For me? Is that supposed to be from my *lefe*?" I direct my question to Sara, who is forced to look at me as she answers.

"Oh, their mom's personal shopper got back into town today. It's not from the *lefe*; it's just what they are bringing for gaisuwa."

"They are not supposed to bring anything for gaisuwa." I remember Adda S and Adda B's gaisuwa. They were relatively short affairs, filled with chatter as members of both families got to know each other and had conversations that unearthed known mutual friends or acquaintances. Something I learnt is that no one is ever really a stranger. There is always a connection somewhere, if you dig deep enough.

"Well apparently, this is how they do it in their family," Sara said. From behind me, Ladidi brings more peppered meat and gizzard from the kitchen. "Thank you, Lads. Has Umm'Hafsa come downstairs?" She switches to Hausa.

"*A'a, tana daki.*" Ladidi answers, saying that she is still in her room.

I take another slow sip of my drink as the conversation gets me uncomfortable.

"She really got a bad cold this time. I hope she feels better soon." Sara says without taking her eyes off me. It makes me think that she knows about the argument.

"I hope so too," I say as I pick up Ilham's call. "Hello?"

"Bebi, is everything okay?" She's screaming so that I can hear her over a rendition of Ed Sheeran's *Thinking out loud*, no doubt playing as the couple has a first dance together. Every couple in Abuja has danced to this song since 2014. I would rather dance over fire than have this song played at my wedding.

"Yeah." Wait. Did something happen? Did she hear something?

"When we spoke earlier, you didn't tell me you weren't coming." Ilham and I were on the phone about a missing order of sequins we had ordered from Aba. We had changed our supplier from Cyprus because of the declining value of the naira and the pain it was fast becoming to pay for supplies in dollars without it inflating the prices of our designs.

"It was a last minute cancel –"

"*Kuna fada ne*? Are you guys having a fight?" Her voice lowers dramatically as she interrupts.

"Who, me and Sadiq *wai*?" I throw my head back and laugh. He was right. Me not being there with him right now will have people jumping to conclusions. "Nah, we're good babe. I was just at his place *ma*."

"If there's anything –" From the background voice, it seems like the DJ is urging the groom to do something to the bride, and the laughter in the background stops me from hearing what Ilham says. "I said, if there's anything, you'll tell me, won't you?"

"Of course, babe." Maybe. Probably.

I go to bed late as I'm on Instagram looking at pictures and short video clips from the event I missed out of respect to Umm'Hafsa telling me to break up with Sadiq. The event was full of dignitaries from different parts of the country. His stepmoms – both impeccably dressed, although Hajiya Amina stole the show from the little I could see of the outfit she wore – were surrounded by their even larger entourage of children, friends, and extended family. Even though I haven't met most of his brothers and sisters from his other two stepmothers, I've spoken to a few of them these past months. From the pictures, it's clear to see that Sadiq stands out the most. He is easily the most handsome of the Ringim brothers.

My night ends after a FaceTime call with Sadiq close to midnight, telling me about the event – and the excuses he had to come up with every time a family member or a friend asked him where I was.

* * *

The following day, I'm on my way out of the house before breakfast when I see Joy upstairs in the small living room.

"Madame Joy," I say, catching my reflection in the mirrored panels of the door as I close it. I'm wearing an oversized white shirt over faux leather trousers. My hair is slicked back into a low bun, and I'm wearing my favorite shade of matte red lipstick. The coolness of the air conditioning makes me wonder if daddy spent some time in here earlier this morning.

"Madame Bebi," she replies, as she has done for years. She has the massage bed in the middle of the living room and the TV was tuned to spa music with the sounds of waterfall and Chinese instrumental music, while the air is filled with lemon scent from an orb-shaped diffuser expelling warm mist in the air.

"What are you doing here today?" Umm'Hafsa's home spa sessions are never on the weekend; she usually does this when her husband is at work. Usually on Mondays. Except on rare occasions when something happens, like she has a trip and needs to reschedule to an earlier day.

"Just a relaxing facial and a foot massage. Doctor sent for me, but it's like she's still down with a cold." Joy looks disappointed that she might have to clear up everything without providing the services she came for. "Or, do you want to hop on?"

"As much as I'd love to, I have somewhere to be." Since Sadiq can't come over to spend time with me at the house anymore, I have to drive all the way to his place so we can hang out for a bit before my Uncle arrives from Kaduna. As if on cue, Aisha walks into the living room. "Oh, look at that! Shatu can volunteer."

"Volunteer as what?" Aisha asks suspiciously as she walks closer.

"As tribute." I roll my eyes. "Umm'Hafsa's session since she can't make it."

"Oh, sure." She claps her hand excitedly. "Can I just have a shoulder massage and a facial – Joy, do you have one of those chemical peels?"

Before Joy can answer, I interrupt, "what do you need a chemical peel for?" She has blemish-free skin. We all do. While most of our friends suffered from acne and skin discoloration due to hormonal changes and imbalances at puberty, my sisters and I remained clear-faced, a blessing from our mother's genes.

"I've always wanted to try it." She perches her bum on the massage bed and plugs her AirPods into her ear as she eases into Joy's waiting hands.

Five minutes later, I'm driving slowly towards the gate when I see some frenzy among the security guards, and the gates open quicker than they usually do. I watch as a gray Peugeot 508 drives in slowly until it stops by the main entrance of our house.

Uncle Isa is here and so early too. I immediately remove my dark sunglasses and drop them on the passenger seat that has the box of Scrabble I'm taking to Sadiq's place. I lift my scarf from my shoulders and cover my hair with it. I leave the engine of the car running as I open my door and walk towards his car. By the time I walk around to his corner, his door is open, and his brown leather slip-ons and the brown *shadda* of his trousers are the first things I see before his full height comes out of the car, dwarfing me instantly.

"*Kawu ina kwana.* Good morning, uncle."

He looks at me slowly with no expression, and I subconsciously pull down my shirt unsuccessfully over the trousers I have on. He has reprimanded me in the past about wearing trousers to leave the house. I was just in university then. Seeing me like this on my way out just lets him know that I didn't listen to him and a small part of me wishes I left the house before he arrived.

"Hafsatu," he nods at me, then looks over his car as his son, Nabil, comes out of the driver's seat. Nabil is his designated driver when he has to take a trip because he doesn't believe in paying someone else to drive him around.

"*Ya hanya?*" My voice sounds meek and tiny as I ask about his trip, even though he didn't answer my first greeting.

"Alhamdulillah." He adjusts the folds of his *babban riga* over his shoulders. He is not a man of many words. He didn't say anything about Sadiq's visit to him the previous day or even indicate whether he supports the parents or us. He just slowly walks towards the front door and I know that by now, the gate has informed daddy that his brother has arrived. Before he even stretches his hands to the knob, Ladidi opens the door and ushers him in. I wonder what Umm'Hafsa thinks about me going behind their back to get Uncle Isa involved. I just hope it shows them how much we are willing to fight for our love.

"Adda Hafsi." Nabil is taller than me even though I'm four whole years older than him. He gets his height not only from his father but from his

Fulani mother, Aunty Kalthum. He is the lightest of all my cousins, with bushy brows and a chipped tooth that gives him a roguish look. Growing up, we used to fight over toys the most, especially when he tried to bully my sisters when we visited my Uncle and aunties in Kaduna, but as we grew older, we grew fonder.

"Ya Al-Hajj," I tease him as I give him a quick side hug. He joined us for Hajj on our last trip to Mecca before the pandemic. "Tell me you out-raced those bandits!"

"*Ai da Yasin muka bar Kaduna*. We didn't leave the house until we had completed Suratul Yasin, and we didn't stop reciting until we got here."

"*Sai da haka*. It's necessary."

"May God bring an end to this banditry." He pulls his beeping iPhone from his pocket. "Ya Hafsi, charger, please. You know how travelling with Baba is. I could not even pack everything I needed to bring; he rushed us out."

"Mine is upstairs, but you can ask Shatu to give it to you." I almost contemplated not leaving so I could hang out with him while the elders had their discussion downstairs, but I already promised to see Sadiq this morning to make up for not coming to the reception with him. "I'll be back soon. I just have to drop something at the store." A little white lie.

Fifteen minutes later, when I knock on the door to Sadiq's apartment with my scarf back on my shoulder and Scrabble box in hand, I'm not expecting to see him without a shirt when he opens the door. All he has on are low, snug, faded blue jeans. His face breaks into a smile as soon as he sees me. "Well, aren't you a sight for sore eyes?"

I walk inside as he moves for me to enter his apartment for the second time since we started dating. He closes the door and leans in for a hug.

"Hi, babe." My hands go around the warm skin on his back, and strong muscles flex under my palms.

"*Hmm*. Love that scent. What is it? Kilian?" He asks. I nod, still basking in his voice. It is dreamy and low, with his hands still around my waist. I feel my heart rate start to quicken.

"Guess who just arrived?" Let's focus this energy elsewhere.

"Who? Your Uncle?"

I nod as I walk into the living room, my bare feet sinking into the plush carpet. I throw two pillows from the sectional onto the ground and sit down on them. I place the Scrabble box on the table and start to bring out the pieces.

"Did you really just walk past this?" There is surprise in his eyes. I look up to see him wearing a light green shirt and buttoning it up as he walks toward me. I follow his gaze to the dining room on the other side of the room, to the rectangular glass table and white and gold trimmed flatware and drinkware. It looks like it has been set up for breakfast for two: cinnamon rolls, croissants, eggs benedict, hash browns, juice, tea, and decadent macaroons.

"I thought we were playing Scrabble?" I ask, standing up to take a picture of the spread for my Snapchat.

"I wasn't sure if you had breakfast before coming, so I had this delivered." He pulls out a chair for me.

"You're so sweet but you know I'm off carbs," I said, wondering if to add "until the wedding." I've already started dieting for all the dress fittings I'll have to make time for in the coming few weeks. I sit down, remove the golden ring from a white napkin and fold it over my lap. As I reach for the teapot to pour myself some hot tea, he puts an egg benedict on his plate, the pale yellow sauce moving slightly as he does.

"So, how did the conversation with your uncle go?"

"Oh, he just arrived. Just as I was leaving." The steam from the flowing sprout curls up gently between us.

"Are you nervous?" He asks me quietly. His gaze holds mine and I see him glance at the low neckline of my shirt and back to my face.

"No, not really." I adjust the bracelet on my wrist and inspect my nails.

"It's okay to say you're nervous, *if* you are." His cutlery moves from his plate to his mouth.

"Why? Are you nervous?" I take a slow sip of my tea, ignoring the scald on my tongue.

I watch as he leans back into his chair, sighing. "Nervous isn't the word

I would use. Maybe anxious," he says with a slow nod after thinking about it for a few seconds.

"Yeah, I'm anxious too. But Uncle Isa being here is a good sign, right?

"Yeah, it's the best possible scenario. Imagine if he said, 'well just take it in good faith.' That would be bad."

"Haha, take it in good faith," I start laughing out loud.

"Yes. He could have said that it's destiny; they are her parents and she has to obey their wishes, yadi-yada. That's what my uncle would say."

Interesting. "So you haven't told anyone about this?"

"I told Imran. Hopefully, he's the only person I would have to tell." He wipes his lips and places the napkin on his plate.

And what will happen if my parents are still against Sadiq even when my uncle speaks to them? A part of me feels that Sara knows more than she lets on. Should I tell her about my fight with Umm'Hafsa?

"What's on your mind?" Sadiq's voice breaks into my thoughts. I look up to see a deep furrow between his brows as he stops eating, still looking at me with a worried look on his face. I shake my head, but he doesn't relent. "Come here, talk to me," he stretches his hand and urges me to stand up and come towards him. I do. I stand up, his hands pull me into his lap, and his hands rest on my thighs.

"I think I messed everything up. Like even if they let us get married, I've brought out a secret that she has kept hidden for years. I don't know what that means for all of us moving forward, especially him. You know what I mean?" It's hard to keep the tears in at this point. I keep pretending like I've got it all under control, but the uncertainty of the future makes me feel like a lost child. My relationship with the man I have called father my whole life has now been altered. Forever.

He wipes the tears from my eyes. "Babe, don't cry."

That only makes me cry more. I keep using my finger between sniffs to stop the tears from falling and ruining my winged eyeliner. My phone starts ringing and I lean across the table to grab it and see that it's Umm'Hafsa calling me. We haven't spoken since our shouting match two days ago. "It's my mum."

"So, what are you waiting for?" Sadiq gives me an encouraging look.

I swipe the tab at the bottom of the screen to accept the call, sniffing as I say, "h-hello?"

Her voice comes on crisp and clear, "Hello Hafsatu? *Kina ina?* Where are you?"

I can't tell her that I'm with the guy she asked me to stop seeing, so I avoid her question, and instead, I reply, "*Ina hanyan dawowa.* I'm on my way back."

"I want to see you when you get back."

"Oh, okay." I wait until she hangs up and stare at her name on my call log, my shoulders are all tensed. "She wants to see me."

"That's good, right? You guys have a long overdue conversation." He rubs my shoulders gently. I sigh out loud. "It's okay, babe. *Khair,* Insha Allah. It's good news."

Ibrahim

Abuja, 2021

The COVID–19 situation in Abuja changed every day. With the emergence of new variants with completely new symptoms and higher latent periods, providing treatment got more complicated, especially when patients refused to acknowledge that they have been infected. Abuja residents insisted on saying that they were down with Malaria and Pneumonia.

I was on the bed flipping through pages of *The Muqaddimah: Classic Islamic History of the World*, looking for a page I had read earlier in the day. Zuwaira was sitting in front of the tri-fold vanity mirror in her black silk robes as she reapplied moisturizer to her palms. Her hair, much shorter, was braided and fell lazily to her back as she meticulously performed her bedtime routine.

"You know Architect Jabir's son tested positive three days ago? I told him to quarantine – just for me to run into him at the golf club this evening. He didn't even have a mask on."

"The one that lives in Italy?" she laughed softly as she turned around on the chair and looked at me, raising her eyebrows in surprise.

"That same one." I flipped to the next page, looking for the quote I wanted to share with her. She stood up and walked towards the bed as she reached for her phone that was charging next to it.

"Isn't that the same one whose wife and son infected a few kids in their estate last year because they didn't quarantine when they returned from their holiday?"

"My love, that's just hearsay. We don't know for sure that those other kids got it from their child, *kinsan* a lot of people are asymptomatic."

"*Ni dadi na da kai ke nan*, this is my thing with you. You always expect the best in people." She picked the perfectly fluffed pillows one after the other, like she does every evening, and hit them gently, and before she even asked, I sat up to allow her do the same to the ones behind my back. After so many years of marriage, the routine flowed seamlessly. Satisfied with how many layers she placed for my neck support, her fingers touched my shoulder slightly, and I returned to my reclining position. She picked up her phone and I saw her squinting at it with a frown on her face.

"You need to stop monitoring them so much," I said. "They are all responsible kids."

"Look at this." She passed the phone to me, and just like I guessed, on the screen was live footage from our CCTV security cameras. When we installed the cameras, she picked the option of logging into the feed with her phone. She said it was the only way her mind would be at rest if she was not at home. "This is the second time he's here today, and look at the time *dan Allah*."

I couldn't see much. All I could see was a black car – a Lexus maybe – driving from the gate. The camera view changed, and I saw a hooded figure I could only imagine to be Hafsatu making her way into the house. "Is that Bashir?" I asked.

She kept zooming into the screen with her beautiful henna-stained fingers. She had a particular dislike for Bashir and his 'overfamiliarity', as she put it. She nodded slowly, "I wish she could see that she can do so much better than him. I dread the day she'll actually tell us that she wants to marry him."

"*Aha!* Here it is," I finally found the quote. I cleared my throat and pushed my glasses into my face as I read it out to her: "Throughout history, many nations have suffered a physical defeat, but that has never marked the end of a nation. But when a nation has become the victim of a psychological defeat, then that marks the end of a nation."

She listened attentively as my voice filled our room, a more luxurious space than where we first started our life together. She sighed as she pondered upon my last sentence. "Are you alluding to Boko Haram, or an individual person?"

"Well, it can be both."

"*Gaskiya*, I agree with the quote, especially the part about psychological defeat. You require more strength to overcome psychological abuse than physical abuse."

"So if that's the case, isn't it a form of warfare then – to constantly expose people to desensitizing news of kidnapping and massacre until the value for human life is nothing in their eyes?"

"Of course. When everyone is trying to stay alive, who is going to be bothered with the bills that the senate is passing–"

We heard gentle knocks on the door, and from the three taps, I could tell who it was. She is the only one who checked up on us this way. If she doesn't hear a reply, she will walk away, unlike Mohammed, who would barge in without waiting to be summoned in.

"Come in," I said as Zuwaira dropped her phone on the table and got comfortable in bed, covering her legs with the Egyptian cotton duvet while Hafsatu entered the room.

"*Assalamu alaikum*," Hafsatu's smile was plastered on her face as her eyes met mine. All these years and sometimes, I am still amazed by how much of a living replica she is of Zuwaira at that age, everything but the dimple.

"*Meye ne*? What is it?" Zuwaira asked her.

"I got this for daddy," she handed me a navy blue-wrapped parcel.

"*Ah ah*, this is for me? Is it father's day already?" I opened the box and I saw a well-crafted leather deep green palm sandals.

"No, I went to a friends store opening, and they had your size." She picked the glass water carafe on my bedside table, walked to the water dispenser, filled it with water, and returned it. Ever since she was a little girl, she always made sure that the water jug by my bed was filled by

357

Maghrib. There are days like today when she forgets, but she always comes as soon as she remembers. That's the thing about Hafsat – she is the most concerned about me and my health. Even though unknown to her, the reason I keep the water next to the bed is because Zuwaira gets thirsty at night.

"Thank you. *Gashi ko* I don't have shoes in this colour." I looked up to see an amused expression on my wife's face. "See the shoes Bebi got me!" I always rub the gifts I get from Hafsatu in the face of whoever is around me.

A few months later, I was having breakfast with Zuwaira. After she resigned from her position as a Director of Reserves Management at the CBN, she spends most of her time overseeing her scholarship trust for less privileged girls.

"Remember the boy I told you about?" she added honey into our teacups. "He asked for permission for Hafsatu to meet his mother."

I looked away from the newspaper as I flipped to the next page. "Bashir?"

She bursted into laughter. "*Wana* Bashir? I haven't seen Bashir in this house in months. *Allah ya karbi addu'a na*, Allah has answered my prayers. No, the one I told you about. Sadiq."

"Oh, yeah. That's right," I recalled that she told me about the polite young man she met a few weeks prior. According to her, he looked very decent, and she could tell he respected Hafsat. I was surprised that she approved of him because Zuwaira was critical of suitors in general. "He's still in your good books *kenan.*"

"*Ka san*, since the day I talked to him, Hafsat doesn't even stay out late anymore. She prays Maghrib at home and he leaves here at a respectable time when he visits. From his countenance *ai ni* I can already tell he was well brought up."

"Do we know where he's from?" I asked casually. When Hafsat was in secondary school, Zuwaira used to interrogate her every time she brought a gift back home on her birthday. "Who gave you this?" "What is his name?" "Where is he from?" "What is his father's name?" I knew what she was afraid of, but I had to bring her attention to the fact that those questions were inappropriate for children that age to be subjected to and explain that our children wouldn't understand them. As a matter of fact, they might misinterpret it as her being only interested in them being friends with people of particular households.

"He's from Jigawa." She looked pleased with herself.

"That's good, then. I trust Bebi's choice. *Allah ya zabi mata mafi alheri*, may Allah give her the best option."

"You keep saying you trust her. She hasn't exactly been a paragon of good behavior." Her face tensed up.

"That was years ago." I reminded her. When Bebi was in her final year in secondary school, a month before she left for her A-levels in the UK, she snuck out of the house to go for a party. Zuwaira's instincts have always been spot-on when it comes to our kids. She woke up that night to pray, and after *tahajjud*, she went downstairs to check the doors because she felt something was amiss. Lo and behold, she ran into Bebi tiptoeing into the house at 3 am with her heels in her hands. I still remember how she kept beating Hafsat, chasing her around the living room.

"*Ba za ki kashe ni ba.* You will not kill me," she repeatedly said as she threw anything she could lay her hands on at Hafsatu — slippers, throw pillows, remote controls. "*Me ya sa ba kya jin magana ne wai?* Why don't you ever listen? *Kina san duniya ta sa ki a baki?* Look at how you are dressed! *Kaman ba musulma ba?* Like you don't come from a Muslim home! *Innalillahi wa inna ilayhi raji'un.*"

I heard the commotion and when I went downstairs, they both were in tears. My wife was in her long white hijab and my daughter in something I had never seen her wearing before.

It took a whole week for Zuwaira to talk to her. She threatened to call the University to defer Hafsatu's admission. "There is no way you're going abroad. I can't trust you to make good choices while you're away."

"Let's not get ahead of ourselves here, my love." I tried to keep the situation from turning volatile again.

When a colleague of mine told me that his older sister lived in London with her husband and children, we reached out to them for guardianship for our sixteen-year-old. It turned out that Hafsat went to primary school with their daughter, Ilham, in Abuja before they relocated. So, they were happy to be Hafsat's guardians.

"Hafsatu, your mom and I won't always be around you to watch your behavior but if it's something you have to hide from us, then you shouldn't be doing it at all."

She started crying, "daddy *wallahi*, it was just a graduation send off party."

"Overnight? *Haba*, Hafsatu? That's unacceptable. What kind of get-together can't take place during the day? You should have known better. How you portray yourself to the world is how the world will treat you."

She was remorseful. With time, it got better, with Hafsat making better choices. There was never an altercation between mother and daughter again until one morning when I heard the words I never expected to hear come out of Hafsatu's mouth.

"I know I'm not your husband's child."

SubhanAllah.

* * *

Abuja, 2022

The previous evening, when Hafsatu pointed out Sadiq's uncle on the TV, I was shocked. Over the years, like his late brother, Senator Dankabo's name has been prominent in Nigerian current affairs but to me, he will always be the man who drove his brother's battered wife to hospitals on the outskirts of the city. The brother who enabled abuse. It is easy to ignore his prominence because we belong to two different industries.

At that moment, I did not expect the worst. There was a possibility that Sadiq's father was one of the Dankabos. It was a very large family, after all.

"Abubakar Sadiq Ringim." Hafsatu said. Like falling dominoes, I watched it all happen in quick succession, one after the other. Zuwaira choked on

360

the discovery at the realization of what was about to happen. She hurriedly stood up and left the table.

Like a cruel twist of fate, Hafsatu took that particular moment to confide in me, something we have always done since she was barely eight years old. We were each other's secret keepers, and whether it was broken plates or sibling fights or poor test scores, we kept it all from Umm'Hafsa.

"I only got 55% on my spelling test. Please don't tell mum," she would say when I picked her up from school. In those days, Zuwaira and I took turns with school drop-offs and pick-ups

"You know that I don't keep secrets from mum," I would say.

"Please, daddy, pleaseeeeee. She will beat me. Okay, I promise to get 100% next time."

I would pretend to think about it as I drove through the heavy Abuja traffic. "Promise?"

"Pinky promise."

But this was not one of those small pinky promises we used to talk about when she was a preteen. This was something more serious, even though it had the same caveat.

"Daddy, the other day I was talking with Sadiq and he told me – daddy, you can't tell mummy this. He told me that his late dad was abusive."

Fate was cruel. It had to confirm my suspicion, leaving no room for doubt or even the hesitation in my mind telling me that maybe – just maybe – he was from an entirely different brother.

"He was not just abusive to his children, but even his wi –" She never finished her sentence because Zuwaira returned for her phone. But she didn't have to finish the sentence. It was something her mother had divulged to me many years prior.

"They used to charm him to be violent," my wife had told me one night in Jos. It was one of those rainy nights as we remained in the darkness due to a lack of electricity. Even then, I found it hard to digest. I sighed out loud. He *was just a weak man, don't blame any charm. A wicked man is a wicked man.* I had said.

* * *

When I enter our bedroom a few minutes later, I meet Zuwaira sitting on the carpet in the middle of our bedroom, frantically googling the name Abubakar Sadiq Ringim. Rapidly scrolling through pages and pages of academic papers from University websites and LinkedIn profiles.

"Asiri zai tonu. The secret will be out. *Innalillahi wa Inna ilayhi raji'un.* It's Abu! It's my Abu-Abu."

I watch her fall apart as she repeatedly whispers the same things to herself over and over in despair.

"Abu?" I manage to ask, but her speech is incoherent. It is like she is talking to other people in the room.

"The boy," she says as she reaches for my hand. "*His* son. I –I told you about him. His mother, his mother died, the little boy. I told you, do you remember?"

I don't remember. How can I? It has been over twenty years since she spoke about her first marriage. I crouched next to her. After all these years of being married to her, I can never get used to the sight of tears in her eyes. The tears flow freely down her face, making the knot in my chest bigger. I take the phone away from her grasp in a futile attempt to stop her from spiraling downwards.

"It's him, *wallahi shi ne. Innalillahi wa Inna ilayhi raji'un.* What have I done?" she asks with devastation written all over her face. Her eyes widen, and her hands tremble. "Ibrahim, I have to put an end to this. *Shikenan asiri zai tonu.* My secret will be exposed."

I can't find my voice. This is our worst nightmare come to life. The one thing she has feared the most, something I reassured her would not happen, is about to unfold right before our eyes. What is the probability of Hafsatu choosing a Ringim boy out of the hundreds of boys in our vicinity? Zuwaira is the one with a Master's in Statistics, but I'm sure the answer to that is negligible. However, the possibility still exists even when something has a low probability. Low odds, but still possible.

She puts her hand on her head, "*na shiga uku, na shiga uku, na shiga uku.* Ibrahim, I'm in trouble! *Asiri zai tonu,* this secret will be out."

The last time she was distraught over something was after her second miscarriage, before the birth of Mohammed. Even then, she was not this vocal.

I had back home one evening from a work trip in Cape Town and I met her lying in the tiny twin bed with three-year-old Aisha. On the other side, on a wooden bunk bed, Hasfat was sleeping soundly at the bottom, and Saratu was on top. Zuwaira looked up as she heard me open the door. I moved forward to block the flood of light from the hallway that could have stirred the girls awake. "My love, why are you here?" Sometimes, after Isha, she read *Stories of the Prophet* to them before they went to bed, but as soon as they slept off, she returned to our bedroom.

She stood up with a long sigh, adjusting the blanket around Aisha's sleeping form, and I saw that her eyes were puffy. I instantly knew what was wrong. "I lost the baby," she closed the door behind us and started walking down the hallway. "*Ka ci abinci?* Have you eaten?" She asked as she picked up a toy from the carpet.

She used duty as a way to deflect from her feelings. It took a while for us to work through that, to get her to allow her emotions out and process them in a healthy manner.

I held onto her arm with a frown on my face at the way she said it, like losing a 12-week pregnancy wasn't something that bothered her a lot. "Come here," I pulled her towards me, holding her close to my chest, with just the sounds of our breathing in our two-bedroom home, buried by the sound of the generator outside CBN quarters.

Later in bed that night, with her head on my chest, she voiced her main concern. "This is the second time since Aisha. What if I can't carry another pregnancy to full term? Is something wrong with me?"

"Miscarriages are common. This has nothing to do with you. *Kaddaran Allah ne,* it's Allah's will. We are already blessed with three healthy children, what else are we looking for?"

She remained silent for a few seconds, and then she said, "But I *have* to give you a son."

"Where's this coming from, Zuwaira?" I leaned to the left and turned on the bedside lamp. The room was immediately flooded with the dim glow. "Have I in any way made you feel like our kids are not enough?" Sitting up, I pulled the pillow behind me to an upright position.

"No, you haven't." She stared into space, avoiding my eyes.

"Then, what is this?"

"Let's not pretend you don't know how our culture looks at these things. You need a son to carry your nam –"

"My daughters will carry my name."

"Ya Isa remarried again after all this time," she said quietly.

"What has that got to do with anything?"

"Ya Aisha feels like if she had a son, he wouldn't have gotten a second wife." Ya Aisha and Zuwaira got closer than I could have imagined over the past few years. She was a big sister in many ways to Zuwaira, a solid pillar for her after she lost her closest living relative, Alhaji Sani. During their phone calls, and our visits, they not only shared recipes and prayer texts, but confided in each other as well.

"Not everyone can be as lucky as Ya Aisha," Zuwaira continued, "*ka ga* her and Khaltum *suna zaman mutunci*, they live peacefully. But what if you marry someone else and she ends up being someone who doesn't want peace, or she's into *shige-shige*? I cant go back to that life."

Zuwaira's previous marriage had scarred her in ways I could not explain. Every once in a while, I am reminded to be more gentle in understanding her worldview, even though it was very different from mine.

When Mohammed was born a year later, the girls were ecstatic, but Zuwaira was the most content. In her mind, she had solidified her position in my life, a position that had been solidified since the day I married her as my wife.

* * *

Zuwaira didn't sleep a wink the night we learned about Sadiq's paternity.

She spent the whole it crying and lamenting. The following morning, tired and exhausted, I step out to the balcony to make an important call. It rings twice before it is picked up. "Baban Hafsatu, *lafiya dai, ko?*" My brother's worried voice comes on the other line after we exchange pleasantries. I normally call him in the evenings, so this is an odd time to be calling him, especially on a Friday. "Is everything okay?" he asks again.

I look into the room, and Zuwaira is sitting on her praying mat with her head against the wall, staring at the ceiling. "Everything is fine. I just want to inform you that we're postponing the *gaisuwa.*" It is better to tell him that it was moved instead of explaining why we were going to cancel it.

"Postponing? Why? Is everything okay?"

"Yes, we need more time to organize everything."

"What needs to be organized?" He doesn't sound convinced. "So, it's no longer next week?"

"No, please don't worry yourself with coming. I'll let you know when a date has been set insha Allah," In a month or so, I will let him know that it was not a good match and it has been canceled altogether. Maybe, just maybe, our secret doesn't have to come to light.

He is quiet for a few seconds, and then he responds, "*Toh, Allah ya sa haka shine mafi alheri.* May Allah decree that this is the best option for us all."

"Ameen." I end the call and return to the room, surprised to see that Zuwaira isn't there. Her crumpled purple hijab remained on her pale pink praying mat. She even left her shoes, even though she always complains about the cold marble floors that lined the hallways. I follow her down the hallway and heard the unmistakable sounds of an argument, with Hafsat raising her voice at her. This has never happened in this house.

Innalillahi wa inna ilayhi raji'un.

I hurriedly push open the door to Hafsatu's room, and I see her in tears. I cannot see my wife's face. Her back is to me. They didn't even hear me enter the room or the heavy door closing behind me. Then I hear Hafsatu: "I know your secret. I know that I am not your husband's child."

How on earth did she find out?

I thought that was the worst of it until the following afternoon when I receive a call and the caller ID named the caller as my brother.

"*Assalamu alaikum*," I say into the receiver.

"*Amin. Wa alaikumus salam*, Ibrahim. *Gobe dai zan kama hanyan Abuja.* I am coming to Abuja tomorrow. I trust I will find you at home?"

I am surprised. "But the trains are not running anymore..."

"No, I will be coming with Nabil by road." I hear him talk to someone in the background, asking if he had filled the tank, followed by something indiscernible.

"Is everything okay?" A trip out of the blue like this.

"Well, that is what I want you to look me in the eye and tell me."

Zuwaira

2022

The most remarkable thing about mathematics and, by extension, statistics is how practical it has always been for me. The answer to any equation is always definite; it doesn't change over time. Equations are always the same on both sides of the equals sign, even if they look different.

More than solving equations, I like correcting wrong ones. It's something I did for my course mates throughout university. The symmetry on both sides pulls me towards solving complex mathematical problems and it always feels like a reward when I pinpoint the exact step where they went wrong. Like in my life story, I can pinpoint the exact choice I made that has brought this hurricane of shame over my family.

Strangers usually look at our family and see perfect symmetry. The kids have both me and Ibrahim's features, especially Saratu and Aisha, but there was always that one comment that hung in the air when people meet Hafsat and me together – about how she is my carbon copy. But then again, Mohammed is an exact replica of his father, from the light skin to the thin bridge of their noses and tall build, so it balances out, or so they think.

The first time Ibrahim and I visited Kaduna with Hafsat, who had just turned a year old, I had just gotten my admission letter to the University of Abuja. Throughout the road trip, as she slept in the back seat of our blue Honda Prelude. I kept glancing at Ibrahim in the driver's seat to see if he was as worried as I was about his family seeing Hafsatu and figuring out the truth, but he wasn't. Instead, he kept pointing out landmarks to me, telling me the names of villages as we drove on the busy road between both cities. Our trip was occasionally punctuated by sellers who thrust fruits into our open windows when we got to the Toll gates. Sometimes, it was boiled or roasted corn, biscuits, or a wrapped beef sausage snack I had never had before but it would become my favorite on those trips. It was called Gala.

"There's a man here that sells baskets of potatoes at a reasonable price," Ibrahim pointed to the right side of the road as the car came to a gradual halt. The road by my window was lined with male and female vendors sitting in front of their wares under thatched roofs in a makeshift open-air market. There were various food items on display – big juicy red tomatoes, bright red chilli peppers, purple bulbs of onions bigger than the ones I used to see at Garki market, tubers of yams, and bunches of ripe plantain.

"Can we get them tomatoes as well?" I tried to mentally calculate how much space we had in the car's boot. "We should probably buy them plantain, too; it's usually so expensive in the market."

"Do you need anything? Water, fru –" he was interrupted by Hafsatu, who had woken up as soon as he switched the car off.

"I have water here." I pointed to the swan water bottle sticking out of the brown handbag I carried from the house that morning. I didn't sleep well the night before. I repeatedly woke up to repack the box we were carrying for the two-day weekend trip with Ibrahim's brother and sister-in-law. Hafsat sometimes slept between us in our bedroom; most nights, when she was fast asleep, we would take her to the crib in the other room, but not that night. That night, as the first light of day broke and peeked in through our light blue curtains, I found myself staring at Ibrahim asleep in a white singlet and shorts. Hafsat had managed to turn herself around during the night and her face was now settled on his chest as she sighed deeply in her dreamy state.

Maybe if she was lighter in complexion, at least she would have something in common with Ibrahim, and I wouldn't be so anxious about this trip. What if they could tell that she was not his when they finally met her? Her hair was too curly, and her eyes were set wide apart, a clear distinction from his.

But all my fear and trepidation disappeared as soon as we finally arrived at Mando, the new house that they had moved into. Ya Isa excitedly stood up from the verandah to open the car door just to carry Hafsatu into his arms. His look of pure love and adoration at the child he believed to be his blood, his brother's firstborn child, was so moving that it was easy for the rest of the family to find a resemblance between Hafsatu and Ibrahim in the littlest things.

"Ah ah! *Likita*, a doctor like her father," Ya Isa said when Hafsatu was playing with a toy stethoscope that Salma and Bilkisu gave her while the adults caught up in the living room.

At dinner time, when she started eating the piece of chicken first before diving into her food, Ya Aisha quipped, "*Ai kuwa*, Ibrahim *ta gada*. She inherited that from her father." And the whole room burst into laughter.

They loved how she stuck to Ibrahim like glue and talked about how she had the same fingers as a distant relation. When she threw a tantrum, they said her temper was exactly like their grandmother's. May her soul rest in peace. All the while, in my head, I knew that those fingers were exactly like mine and that temper was a Ringim trait, but by the end of that evening, I felt more at peace.

As we drove back home to Abuja on Sunday evening, Ibrahim was in the best of moods. Living in Abuja meant we could visit every month and now that they didn't live on the same street as Alhaji Ringim, I was looking forward to spending more time with his family.

"I told you that you had nothing to worry about, didn't I?"

He was right. Our secret was safe. No one doubted the age we said she was, no one figured she was actually sixteen months and nobody measured her height. All they said was that it was brilliant that she was already walking. It excited them that she was surpassing her expected milestones. Not even the birth of Saratu, Aishatu, or Mohammed was met with that amount of love. Hafsatu was Ibrahim's first child who was named after his late mother; that enough made her special. To them, she was the first sum of his lineage and mine.

The day I hear that Alhaji Isa was coming to Abuja on such short notice, I knew it was already the beginning of the end. We are now at the other side of the equation and it is time to reap everything I sown. I spent the whole day and night in bed, unmoving – numbed by the words that Hasatu uttered to me, paralyzed by the realization of who Sadiq actually was.

"How did she know?" Ibrahim asked me in disbelief, the day she stormed out of her bedroom in tears, leaving me with a shocked expression that matched the one on his face. "How did she know to do a DNA test?" He kept looking at the paper she forced into his hands as she flung our well-guarded secret right into our faces.

How did she get our DNA samples and run tests without us knowing? Hafsatu has always been smart and resourceful. She doesn't wait around for things to be handed to her. She knows to exhaust all possible options before asking for help. I taught her that. But clearly, it has made her more of a go-getter than I could have imagined.

"She has had this since last year, fa," Ibrahim said as he showed me the date on the top of the page. He kept going over the percentages of the result even though we both knew exactly what the results showed.

She has known since last year? That would explain how detached she has been getting, not just from me but from her father. I just assumed that she was trying to make the inevitable separation from him after she got married easier on him. *Ashe,* it's because she found out that she is not his daughter.

My daughter, *mai zurfin ciki,* has a deep belly for secrets. You would never know when something is bothering her, a trait that she clearly inherited from me. Aishatu is like Mohammed; they take after their father and wear their hearts on their sleeves. When something bothers them, it's very easy to see. In fact, they will mention it.

Hafsatu and Saratu, however, are two peas in a pod. You can't really tell what's going on with them unless they want you to know. During her second year in university, Hafsatu bashed my car when she returned home for the holidays. It was a birthday gift from Ibrahim, and every one of them knew how much I loved the car; I never gave anyone else the keys. But Hafsat found them in my absence and took Saratu in the car with her. Luckily, nobody got hurt. Between them, they put their pocket money together, took the car to the auto shop, and fixed it without anyone else in the house knowing. We would never have found out if Ibrahim's mechanic hadn't called him while we were in Kaduna to ask if he offended us because he saw my car in a rival auto shop, the only other Mercedes Benz authorized refurbisher in Abuja at the time.

I am shaken out of my reverie by the sound of Ibrahim saying the *sallama* as he looks from his right and his left, a gesture that signifies the end of his three-*rak'ah* Maghrib prayer. He raises his hands as he supplicates quietly and I look back downstairs through our bedroom window. The world is still carrying on even as mine balances uncertainly on its axis. The security guards are doing their evening handover and I see the maid, Mariya taking food to the guards at the security post.

"Ya Isa called me a while ago. He said he's coming tomorrow."

He didn't have to say it. I already know, deep in my heart, that it has something to do with Hafsatu.

"She's going out again," I say instead. From where I sit, hidden behind the heavy drapes, I watch Hafsatu's car drive out of the open garage. I can't take my eyes off her customized number plate, 'BEBI,' as she speeds away and the gates close swiftly behind her. I wonder where she is going. Is she going to see him? I monitored the video feed of the main gate all day, and he did not drop by, which means she has already told him that he is no longer welcome at our house anymore.

"We can't keep delaying this. We have to tell her the truth."

"She hates me. Did you not see the look in her eyes yesterday? She hates me."

"Only because she doesn't know the truth," he pulls the chair opposite me to my side and sits down. In front of us is the oval table we sometimes have breakfast on. On it, my dinner is untouched, just as lunch was before the plates were picked up. The fact that I haven't eaten is probably the reason my head feels like it will split into two halves.

"What exactly am I going to tell her?" I never knew this day would come without warning or with this kind of tribulation. My husband and I took specific steps to ensure that Hafsatu felt secure enough among her siblings to never doubt her paternity. This is a secret I never thought would see the light of day, and definitely not in this manner. "Where do I start from?"

As usual, Ibrahim comforts me with his silence. He just sits next to me and listens to me as I wonder out loud with my head on his shoulder.

* * *

The following morning, when the security post calls to inform us that Alhaji Isa has arrived, I pick up the first veil I see when I open my closet, drape it over my head, and head downstairs. On my way down, I see Aishatu and Nabil in the hallway.

"Umm Hafsa, *ina kwana*. Good morning," he crouches as he greets me.

"Nabil, *lafiya kalau*." The pleasantries are over in about thirty seconds, but not before he gleefully tells me about his current GPA at the university. My challenge to all of them has stayed the same from when his sisters used to come and spend their holidays with us in Abuja during their university days: Remain on the dean's list, and I will have a gift for you at the end of the school year. He is still on the dean's list.

When I get to the main living room, where we usually receive guests or colleagues, I find his father sitting on the leather couch just in front of our large family portrait. The television is on a local news channel and Ladidi is pouring him some tea. Alhaji Isa has a very magisterial air around him, the kind of presence that either makes you feel safe or prompts you to watch what you say in front of him.

I remember the first time I actually heard him talk. It was in Ungwan Rimi when I lived with my uncle's wife. I was cooking in the kitchen one evening when I heard the windows banging due to heavy winds that indicated an incoming storm. My heart dropped because I had washed Tani's new lace that she had worn to a wedding that weekend, so I raced out of the flat to pick them off the drying line before they ended up in the gutter. I met him there, removing his daughter's clothes from the line that his wife had washed earlier in the day. He helped me with a hard-to-reach peg that evening.

"Watch your step," he said as I almost tripped and fell. Those were the only words he ever said to me the entire time I lived there, apart from answering my regular greetings on the few occasions I saw him. Over the years, during our regular visits to Kaduna, he treated me with utmost kindness. He loved his brother so by extension, he accorded me that much.

"*Assalamu alaikum.* Alhaji, *ina kwana*," I say as I walk further into the air-conditioned living room, pulling the lace at the top of my veil over my forehead as I tighten it across my neck.

"Umm Hafsa." He looks up from his phone and answers my greeting with a rare smile he always has for me.

"*Na'am. Ya hanya?* I hope you had a good trip?" Even as I go on to ask about his wife and the rest of the family, I can tell that his answers are just out of courtesy.

"*Alhamdulillah. Alhamdulillah.*" He wastes no time diving into the matter at hand as he asks me almost immediately about Ibrahim, "*ina shi mai-gidan naki?*"

Right on cue, Ibrahim walks into the living room in a crisp white kaftan with black needlework and trousers. His demeanor is jovial and welcoming, although it does nothing to ease the already palpable tension in the room. They exchange greetings as they shake hands, making a quick comment about the roads between Kaduna and Abuja.

"*Bari na leka abincin.* Let me see what's taking them so long to bring out breakfast." I stand up from the sectional to give them privacy, but my brother-in-law stops me.

"No, sit down. Umm'Hafsa *ai* this matter concerns you as well. *Ba abinci ne ya kawo ni ba,* I am not here for food."

Ibrahim gives me a look that would have been reassuring on any other day but right now, does nothing to alleviate my distress. I sit back down and sink further into the cushions behind me, picking up a black velvet pillow trimmed with gold tassels and placing it on my lap, almost like it is an amour to protect me.

"There is no need to beat about the bush. I am here is because yesterday afternoon, I received a guest. A young man, err.. Abubakar Sadiq, came all the way to Kaduna to see me," he starts. A long sigh escapes me before I can stop myself; hearing that adds to my headache. In the armchair opposite me, Ibrahim nods as he listens attentively, his face not giving anything away. "We always have to do everything with the fear of Allah. Marriage is not something that is taken lightly, you know this. You cannot give your permission for people to come and see you and then turn them away without a concrete reason." He looks up at us as he speaks, his words calm, calculated, and mainly directed at his brother. "It is not done. This is not who we are; it is not what we are known for. Tell me honestly, what is really going on?"

My eyes immediately find Ibrahim's and I know the man I am married to. I know that he will tell his brother the truth; he is not a liar. Sometimes, he would omit the truth so as not to hurt someone, but not when asked outrightly.

"Yaya, you didn't have to come all the way. You should have just said you wanted to see me and I would have come to Kaduna by myself," he said.

"Well, since I am here already, *sai a bar wannan maganan*, we can forget about that. Just tell me: do these children have your support or not?" It's clear that Alhaji Isa is in no mood for any long tangent; he did not find Ibrahim's attempt at deflecting amusing. This will be a tough conversation. Maybe I should give them some privacy. He continues, almost as if to give us a grace period until we eventually find our voices. "From my interaction with the young man, he seems to have a good head on his shoulder. He is a Muslim, he has the means to take care of her, and she has chosen him as the person she wants."

Ibrahim clears his throat and speaks up, "*Ai* the truth of the matter is – actually– um, the truth is they cannot get married. Atleast, not to each other."

"*Allahu Akbar,*" he says almost immediately. He drags out the words in the phrase very slowly in a soft manner as a hint of dejection crosses his face, almost as if he is sad for the young man he had only met the day prior. *"Toh meye hujjan?* What is the reason for this?

My eyes find a piece of white thread on the black Persian carpet that the vacuum must have failed to pick up this morning. I am no longer looking at the men in the room. My eyes just keep looking at the little imperfections around the room. The white and gold incense burner has dark coal burns on its square edges. It's apparent now that we could have gone with a lighter color for the carpet in this particular living room. It's interesting how from afar, things look great, but the closer you get, the further away from perfect they seem.

I hear Ibrahim's sigh. "In life, everyone has their test. Allah tests every one of us, and... *um* sometimes, these tests come in the most unexpected of places."

Alhaji Isa neither nods nor makes a sign to show that he is following Ibrahim's words; he just fixes him with a stare as the fingers of his left hand slowly touch his beard. My husband does the exact same thing when he is listening to something he is trying to make sense of. "I don't understand what you are trying to say."

"Hafsatu can't get married to him, *saboda*, he is – the young man is actually – he is her brother."

Alhaji Isa's eyes catch mine as soon as Ibrahim says it. I look away but not before I see them narrow slightly as his brows bunch up together in something that looks like shock.

"Ibrahim, what are you saying?" His voice is as worried as it is shocked as he leans toward his brother. "Are you telling me you have a child outside? You fathered a bastard outside your marriage?"

That is a more logical conclusion; it makes sense that this is the worst possible scenario he can conclude because no one would expect Sadiq to be related to Hafsat in any other way. Especially Alhaji Isa, who has always regarded me with the most respect in all the years I have been married to his brother. He even goes as far as using me as an example for his daughters to emulate in their marital lives. But to accept this fallacy is another crime itself. It is bearing false evidence against a dead woman. Accusing a chaste woman of adultery, whether dead or alive, is a major sin in Islam, and Ibrahim would never have an affair or have a child out of wedlock. He is too honorable a man to do that.

"No, that is not what he meant." My voice breaks the unbearable silence, but Ibrahim takes over.

"When we left Kaduna, Zuwaira was pregnant."

From the look on Alhaji Isa's face, it looks like he would have preferred to hear that his brother fathered two more bastards. "I don't understand.... Preg – pregnant with... with whose child?" He looks from me to Ibrahim like he doesn't recognize us anymore. His body moves away, further into his chair.

The room starts getting too hot for me. I realize my palms are moist and clammy, and my breathing is shallow. Ibrahim's eyes don't meet his brother's as he answers quietly.

"Her ex-husband."

"What is this you are telling me? What about the marriage we conducted between you two before you left?" he looks up at me, but my guilt doesn't allow me to meet his eyes. I almost start praying for the ground to open up and swallow me.

The room is quiet for what feels like a lifetime until Ibrahim speaks. He bridges the distance between them by moving to the edge of his seat. "We found ourselves in a situation that was between life and death. That was the only solution."

"You made me a witness to something that had no legality in our religion?" His voice was low, but he was angry, like what we did was a personal affront to him. "You ignored the words of The Holy Qur'an? You ignored the warnings of our Prophet *sallallahu alaihi wasaalam*? No, I don't believe this. I don't believe my brother would do such a thing. Tell me this is not true. Tell me this is a joke. If someone else had done this, *da na yadda*, but I find this hard to believe that you – Ibrahim – as well versed in the Qur'an as you are, would do this. Why?"

Love. Unconditional love. Unquestioning love. Unreserved love in its purest of forms.

"Did I not ask you to confirm if her *Iddah* was really over?" Alhaji Isa asked, shaking his head. Ibrahim opened his mouth to speak, but his brother did not allow him to. "You know the rulings regarding divorce, remarriage and children. Did you not come back to tell me that her *iddah* was over, that she was not pregnant?"

Ibrahim nods and I feel myself shrink into the cushion even further.

"You lied to me, *kenan.*"

"He had hurt her so much. She could not go back to him," he says. My fingers are now damp from the tears I have been wiping silently as I sit quietly.

I was barely eighteen then, helpless and bruised from unseen wounds, ready to go into a world I knew nothing about to ensure that my child and I would not be subjected to maltreatment and abuse. Ibrahim stepped in without reservations and saved me. He saved us.

"And the child she was carrying? That child was not yours to keep. Did you ever stop to think about what could happen in the future?" he asked Ibrahim. I hold my head in my hand as I listen. "So this young man I met yesterday, he is the politician's son? Ringim?"

"Yes. We just found out."

"*Toh ai kun gan irin ta,* you have seen for yourselves. All the rules in the Qur'an are there to protect us from things like these. What if God had taken both of your lives before today? What if she and this man got married after your death because no one else knew the truth?" He turns to me, "Zuwaira, are you not aware that every time they lay with each other and unknowingly sin against themselves, you would be woken up in your grave to bear witness to what you caused?"

Kai, innalillahi wa inna ilayhi raji'un.

"Do you know what it means if anyone knows this? From what I saw yesterday, that young man will not stop until he rallies all the family members that he can get on his side because he has Hafsatu's full support. They will not relent." He leans back into the chair, the hot tea in the clear cup now completely cold from the air conditioning in the room. "*Kai, amma wannan babban jaraba ne*, this is a big issue. You have deprived her of her inheritance from her biological father, and Islamically she cannot inherit from you."

His words take me back to when Ibrahim gifted Hafsatu ten stores from his forty-store shopping complex in Wuse. She had just turned 18 when he gave her the deeds and the papers naming her the undisputed owner of those specific units.

Even she was confused. "Daddy, why does this document have my name?" She looked at me as if she would find answers, but Ibrahim didn't even tell me that he was planning to do that. I was as surprised as she was.

"The building belongs to you and your siblings; there is nothing wrong in me putting your name on specific units," he said.

She didn't know it then, but he gifted them to her because she has no share in his inheritance. He had already started removing what he wanted to give her from his wealth so that she wouldn't be left empty-handed when his property is shared in accordance to the Sharia between Aishatu, Saratu, and Mohammed after his death. She doesn't know it, but that was the explanation for all the gifts he showered her with.

Alhaji Isa keeps shaking his head, staring at the center table in front of him as he says the shahada, saying no one is worthy of worship except Allah, over and over. Ibrahim looks at me, "call Hafsatu. Tell her we need to talk to her." He pushes his glasses into his face as I reach for my phone.

Hafsatu

2022

I have not even gotten to the first red traffic light after leaving Sadiq's place when the music playing in my car stops abruptly and I glance at the display screen to see his call coming in. I touch the answer button on my steering wheel with my thumb as I speak. "Hi, babe." My car comes to a slow halt behind a blue Isuzu truck in front of me. I look into the rearview mirror, trying to fix my lipstick that Sadiq's reluctant and drawn-out goodbye kiss smudged.

"B," his voice fills my car through the bass speakers. "You forgot your boardgame."

I use my index finger to clean off a red line just below my lip, "oh yeah. I'll get it when I come tomorrow. Wait, is that why you called?" I look back through my windscreen as the lights turn green and I start moving past oncoming traffic.

"Yeah."

"It's okay to say you're missing me already," I laugh, and I hear him chuckle.

"Well, you caught me." After a few seconds, he adds, "am I gonna see you later?"

"I dunno. You kinda made it hard for me to leave a few minutes ago." I hint at how our bodies were pressed against each other in the elevator before the doors opened and he walked me to my car. Even when I got into the car, he still repeated his offer to drive me home.

"I can't promise to keep my hands to myself. Left to me, you would already be my wife by now."

Left to me, I would have spent all day at his place. But I have to hear how my uncle's meeting with Umm'Hafsa went. I wonder if she has changed her mind. I am very optimistic that she has.

"When are you going to Asokoro?" I ask. He told me he has a parcel to drop off for Hajiya Amina.

"I'll leave after Zuhr."

I glance at the digital display on my dashboard; it's only eleven thirty. "Okay, I can meet you at Ranchers before *Maghrib*," I say as I make a left turn, "but I'm bringing Ilham. We can all play Scrabble together."

"Oh, you don't trust yourself to be alone with me, *ne?*" He teases.

"More like I don't trust *you*." I bite my lips to keep myself from smiling.

"Well, you better, 'cos you are stuck with me. For life."

"I love you, babe." With my whole heart.

"Love you, too. I'll tell Lily and Assad to drop by for games night."

"Sounds good."

When I get home, I park by the green hedge as my uncle's car is in my usual spot. I quietly walk upstairs to my room and change into a long black skirt, tossing the black faux leather pants in my laundry basket. For my Uncle to see me twice in trousers when I know how he feels about girls wearing them is just disrespectful.

I close the door to my room behind me, and as I walk down the hallway, I peep into the living room and see my sisters with Nabil, who is stretched out on the couch. A lecture by Mufti Menk plays on TV.

"Did you guys go out?" I ask as I enter the living room and see empty ice cream cups and various flavors of cupcakes in front of them.

Aisha looks up from Nabil's phone, "Yes, we went to Chloe's. We got you your faves, but I know you are off carbs ko?" The mischievous smile on her face is a dare for me to try the cupcakes.

"You just reminded me, let me tell the kitchen to make me salad for lunch." I walk towards the intercom and dial 5. After I specify that I want no onions, eggs, or Heinz salad dressing in the salad, I return the handset to its white cradle.

"Ya Hafsi, did you hear that they lifted the Twitter ban?" Nabil asks as he adjusts the pillow under his head.

"There was a Twitter ban?" I look away from the creamy swirl of white chocolate over the cupcake. *Maybe I should just eat one. I can continue my diet right after.*

"There was."

My mind wanders as I pretend to listen to him tell me what led to the government placing the ban, his sentences punctuated by Aisha's additions. She is active on Twitter, but I no longer go on the app. With all the conversation around me, it is apparent that Sara is awfully quiet again. She's on her phone, with a half-eaten cupcake in her hand, and she hasn't looked up at me since I walked in.

When I get downstairs, I am surprised that the frosted glass double doors leading into the living room downstairs is closed shut; they are usually wide open most days. As I brace the handle to push it open, bits of conversation flow to me. It's my Uncle and daddy speaking in hushed tones, mainly in Hausa.

" – this matter is very serious," my uncle says.

"I understand everything you are saying, but you need to look at the intention behind it," Daddy replies.

"It does not matter. You took matters into your hand and you had no right to do so." That is my Uncle's voice. I have never heard him lecture my dad before. They agree on most things, usually. "Allah creates every single person and provides their sustenance from birth until death."

"I understand, I understand. I am not arguing that. I'm just saying –"

They both look up as I push the door open.

"*Assalamu alaikum,*" I say, surprised to see that it is just two of them in there. Umm'Hafsa is absent.

"Hafsatu, you're back?" Daddy pushes his glasses into his face as he addresses me.

381

I feel a twinge of guilt about the last conversation he heard between my mom and me. Even as I search his face to see if something has changed, all I can see is the usual care and concern in his eyes as he peers up at me from where he sits on his armchair.

"Yes, daddy. *Ina kwana*," I sit on the chair closest to him. "Kawu, *ina kwana*." I greet my Uncle again. If he notices that I changed into a skirt, he doesn't say anything.

"Hafsatu," Uncle Isa says in a tone that makes me feel like I have done something wrong.

"*Na'am, Kawu?*" I sit in my oversized shirt and a long, flowy black skirt, but I still find my hands tugging the material to cover my hips. I hope he won't say the skirt is too tight. Maybe I should have worn an abaya.

"I made this trip *domin in cire hakkin ki a kai na*, to fulfil your right over me as my niece," Uncle Isa says. I look over to daddy, and I see him lean back into his chair, his eyelids drooping as his forehead creases. My Uncle continues talking, "when that young man – *shi* Abubakar Sadiq – came to see me yesterday, I told him that your parents have the final say, but I will come to Abuja myself because it is the right thing to do."

Through the curtains behind him, just next to our family portrait, I see that my sisters have walked out with Nabil, who is talking to them animatedly about something. Watching them stand by the cars, I can almost hear their laughter.

"About your marriage, your parents have something important to tell you." I look at daddy again, and he sighs as he rubs his beard downwards. "What I need you to do is listen to them carefully."

"Okay, Uncle."

"Something I want you to keep in mind is this: everything is preordained. Destiny has been written, and as Muslims, we have to accept *Qadr*. Two people can go through the same test, and one of them will gain blessings from that scenario, and another will only accumulate sins. Do you know why, Hafsatu?" My uncle keeps quiet for me to respond. *Where are all these Islammiya questions leading to?* I shake my head no. He continues, "because the first person understood that it was a test and he or she did not lose faith in Allah's will while the second person doubted or even threw the religion away altogether as a result."

I sigh out loud. This is not looking good. If Uncle Isa cannot convince my parents, who else can I get to talk to them? Is this what Sadiq meant when he said this won't be an easy fight? How many more family members do we have to get on our side for my parents to allow us to be together? Do I have to go a level above Uncle Isa to my grandaunt? Kaka Kande is almost 70 now, so she can't travel, but if she talks to them, even on the phone, I'm sure they will reconsider.

He puts his cap on his head as he stands up, "I am going to head back to Kaduna now. You know it takes more than three hours – sometimes four – to travel that road nowadays."

Daddy stands up, "lunch is ready. Let us eat and pray before you leave."

"Ibrahim, I will be very honest with you. After what I heard today, I cannot eat anything," he looks at me as he shakes his head.

What did he hear?

Even as I told him goodbye, I can't stop thinking about what he said. Maybe daddy told him about what I found out? That would explain Umm'Hafsa's absence. Are they going to get divorced? Is that why Sara isn't talking to me?

I look out through the window and see him and daddy still talking as they walk down the stairs toward the cars. The door opens and I look up to see Nabil. "Ya Hafsi, *sai mun zo biki,* till we come for your wedding."

I force a laugh as I hug my cousin goodbye, "*Insha Allah,*" I say in the most unconvincing tone, surprised at the loss of vigor in my own voice.

* * *

Seven minutes and twenty-one seconds later – I know because I checked my wristwatch multiple times – daddy returns to the living room. He looks fatigued as he shuts the door behind him, like he hasn't had a decent night's sleep in days.

"Daddy, I am really sorry," I blurt out, before he even gets to his chair.

383

He looks up at me, brows bunched up like he is surprised at my statement, as he removes his glasses and places them on the glass side table.

"What are you sorry about?"

"About what I said during my fight with Umm'Hafsa." Really, what I was apologizing for was that he found out that I was not his child in that awful way.

He nods as I speak. Just then, the door opens and Umm'Hafsa comes in. I lock eyes with her for the first time since Friday, and my breath catches. She walks slowly, allowing the veil to fall from her hair down to her shoulders. I'm surprised she sits next to me on the leather couch. I didn't think she would want to be anywhere around me.

"How's your headache?" He asks her in Hausa

"I took some medication." She rubs her forehead as she answers.

"Advil?" As he talks to her, he leans toward her the way he always does. It seems like my statement on Friday changed nothing about their relationship. So they are definitely not getting a divorce.

"Tylenol."

He nods again. "We don't have to do this now if you don't feel up to it, my love. We can just –"

"There is never going to be a good time, and like you said, she needs to know the truth."

They are talking about me like I am not right here in the room with them. I look at my nails and start scratching the white gel color off my nails. I am on the second finger when daddy speaks again.

"Bebi, I want to know. Why did you get a DNA test done?"

"Oh." My voice is soft as the single syllable escapes my lips. I have almost forgotten about Bashir's involvement in this whole paternity saga. If only I had never met Bashir, I would never have discovered this family secret. But then again, I might not have met Sadiq. "It was just a dumb thing my friends and I were playing around with." He looks perplexed, so I explain further. "There's a kit you can get online, send your sample and the results will tell you what part of the world your great-great-grandparents originate from..."

The frown leaves his face. "Oh, one of those DNA tests from the US? Ancestry something, *ko?*" He must have seen the television ads I came across too.

"Yes. So we all tried it, just for jokes."

"*Su wa kenan?* Who and who tried it?"

"Me, Ilham, and Bashir. We were still dating at the time." I see him glance quickly at Umm'Hafsa's face and then back at me. "I gave Sara an extra box I got, and when our results came back –" I find it hard to complete the sentence because this is the first time I am actually narrating how I found out.

"Your results weren't identical." Daddy completes it for me. As I nod, he chuckles sadly, almost as if he was blindsided by something he never saw coming. He shakes his head slowly, "*Allah mai iko*, God is mighty." He rubs his eyes as he stares into the space between his feet and the center table. Next to me, I hear Umm Hafsa sigh.

"Hafsat, there is so much I have to tell you." This is the first time my mom has spoken to me in days. I am stumped that there is barely any anger in her voice after everything I said to her. "Yes, you are right. The test was correct. Daddy is *not* your biological father, but he is your father in every other aspect that matters."

This piece of information is not new to me. There was a week last year I spent every single night reading and rereading the DNA results I got from the lab so often that I started having dreams about it, wondering if there was a mistake somewhere, wondering why my feelings for the man I call daddy didn't seem to change even though I tried to disconnect myself. I still felt like his daughter. I felt no different towards my siblings, either. At this moment, it is hearing it out loud – hearing Umm'Hafsa actually say it out loud – that makes me burst into tears. It makes it even more real.

"We never wished for you to find out like this," Umm'Hafsa cradles my shoulder as she pulls me closer to her,

We. We? He knew? Has he always known this thing that I thought was *her* secret?

I look up to see daddy wiping a lone tear from his eye discreetly. His eye is still fixed on a spot on the ground. He knew. He has always known. No wonder nothing changed between them. No wonder he wasn't mad when he heard me. He was only surprised that I found out.

None of this makes sense to me. Daddy and Umm'Hafsa told us stories about being young sweethearts; Umm Hafsa has literally used the phrase, "he is my first and only love" when raising a toast to him. Multiple times. How was there someone else before him? "So, so… who is my father?" I finally ask.

"I was married off at seventeen. I was married to –"

"I thought you got married at nineteen?"

She nods with a sad smile on her face. "To your daddy, yes. But I was married to your biological father before then, and it was a horrible marriage, Hafsat." Her voice drops, as her voice shakes, "he had this… he had this temper. He would hit me often, and… and there was nothing I could do. When I lost my first pregnancy, I knew I had to leave. I wasn't safe. My children wouldn't be safe with him."

Umm'Hafsa was in an abusive marriage? When she was young? And I was here thinking that she cheated in her marriage? I simply assumed the worst of her without even giving her the benefit of the doubt or thinking of other possible scenarios. Not only that, I was constantly rude to her because of that.

I look at daddy as he listens keenly to her and on his face is an enormous amount of pain written as if he lived through that hurt with her. Maybe he did. As she recounts how she found out she was pregnant with me and the choices she made to keep me safe, she starts crying so much that he stands up from his chair and sits next to her to console her.

I watch as his hands find hers, and their fingers intertwine like they always do. He was with her through all these trials. As I watch them, my mind goes to Sadiq, I wonder what he will say when I tell him of this development. Sadiq. Still, this doesn't explain why she doesn't want Sadiq and I to get married.

"But wallahi, I never knew that choice would have such a painful consequence, that the choice I made would end up hurting you so much,

Hafsatu," she keeps sobbing. "I didn't think it would affect your future like this."

Like this?

Somehow my voice manages to be audible as I speak, "No, mum. I'm sorry. It's me who hurt you with everything I said." I am ashamed that I raised my voice at her after everything she went through to keep me safe.

She holds my face in both her hands. "You don't understand, Hafsatu. You can't marry Sadiq."

"Why?" I understand now why she doesn't want me with someone whose father was abusive. "Sadiq would never hurt me mum."

"H-He is your brother. His father is the man I left. He is your father's son."

My mouth hangs open, my vision starts to darken and I feel like the world starts moving too fast as I hear multiple voices around me.

Sadiq's voice: *"My father was an abusive man"*

Umm'Hafsa's voice: *"he had this... this temper, he hit me so often"*

It's a fast-paced recall to four days ago at the dining table at dinner as I said his full name to both my parents as we watched the news: "Abubakar Sadiq Ringim." The way Umm'Hafsa's cough worsened as soon as she heard. Her voice in my room the following day, "Sadiq is not the man you will marry because I won't give him permission to marry you." It all made sense in a gut-wrenching way.

This nightmare cannot be real.

"Hafsatu, *kina ji na?* Can you hear me?" She looks at me worriedly as she repeats herself, but the shock of her revelation doesn't allow me even to say a word. I want to say something but words fail me, and my voice fails me. As I stare into my mother's swollen and puffy eyes, she swallows and blinks a few times. Her expression is yielding as if all of her facial muscles were tired of holding all her emotions in, and she can no longer manage to contain them. "If his family comes here and we refuse them – as we must – they will figure out why."

All I can do at that moment is lift my left hand slightly as my fingertips touch my lips as if to check if the wrath of God has wiped them off my face. But they are still there.

I can still feel his lips on mine and it's all I can think of. The way he fixed my scarf when we entered the elevator earlier. How his lips brushed mine apart, and how I melted into him. The way he gently bit my lower lip after he kissed me softly. "I love you so damn much, Hafsat,"

That was about twenty minutes ago... That was my brother.

My brother.

* * *

After Aisha was born, Sara and I started fighting less; we actually bonded for the first time ever. We had a new baby sister to be excited about. We were fascinated by how Aisha would lay on her back all the time, how she had no teeth in her mouth, and how she reached for her toes as her eyes followed the rotating toys atop her crib. We were delighted anytime Umm'Hafsa sent us to get her something from the room – diapers, dusting powder, or diaper rash cream. We would sit close to each other, watching wide-eyed at how quickly the baby slept off after drinking milk. As we played on the carpet in our parent's room with our dolls, we copied Umm'Hafsa as she put baby Aisha's head on the piece of burp cloth on her shoulder, rubbing her back gently after she breastfed her before handing her to the nanny to carry her on her back.

"Mummy, why don't we have a brother?" I asked one day. I was just a little over six then, playing with a blonde-haired Barbie doll dressed as a doctor or maybe an astronaut.

"Mummy, baby brova," three-year-old Sara echoed. She was my echo assistant at that age, spending all day repeating my sentences.

Umm'Hafsa laughed, "A brother? You girls want a brother?"

"Yes, a big brother," I said mindlessly. Having a big brother would be nice. It would be like having a mini-daddy to protect us and play with us.

"Big brovaa," my little echo squealed.

Brother.

Turns out, I had a brother even then. A half-brother. No, wait, I have many half-brothers. And one of them is Sadiq? My boyfriend is my brother?

No, that's impossible. There has to be a mix-up somewhere. There has to be a mistake. We don't even look alike. I have seen his sisters. Fatima is slim and tall with a high forehead. Hadiza is cute, light-skinned as well, a bit chubby, but also tall. The one that got married over the weekend, Madina, has ebony skin and... and I look nothing – absolutely nothing – like them.

Next to me, Daddy passes Umm'Hafsa a box of tissues from the lower level of the center table in the living room. She picks two or three squares as she thanks him, sniffing as she dabs her moist eyes.

"B – bro – brother?" my voice didn't sound like mine. "You know he has another uncle, Saifullah Ringim. I think he has a son Sadiq, too. Maybe...maybe that's the man you – maybe it's –" I am not really sure where I am going with this train of thought, but all I know is that there has to be a mistake.

"Saifullah Ringim has only one wife," Umm Hafsa reaches for my hand. "Isn't Abu – sorry, Sadiq – isn't Sadiq the one who lost his mother during childbirth? He lived with me for months when I was married to his father."

"But... but w –why ... how come you didn't recognize him?" Umm'Hafsa looks towards daddy like she needs help and I turn my attention to him too, trying to get him to understand my point. "No, daddy, think about it. There has to be a mistake. Mummy has met Sadiq multiple times. If she didn't recognize him, maybe it's a different Ringim. M–maybe it's not him," I feel my voice start to break as I fight tears.

Daddy sighs out loud like he is about to give a patient of his a really bad prognosis. "Hafsatu, lo –"

"No, it's a large family. Even on Instagram, there are like five Sadiq Ringims around the same age," I look at Umm'Hafsa with tears in my eyes, begging, silently pleading for her to say it's a mistake. Maybe there are a few abusive Ringim brothers.

"Hafsat, *shi ne*, it's him. We used to live in Ungwan Rimi... His sister who got married this weekend, isn't she Hajiya Mami's youngest daughter,

Madina?"

Oh my God.

That is what he calls his stepmother that lives in Kaduna. Hajiya Mami. But even that is such a common name in most Hausa households. Even one of Ilham's aunties is called Hajiya Mami.

She passes me the box of tissues and I realize I have tears streaming down my face. I ignore the box and reach for her hands, allowing myself to fall to the floor next to her feet as I bury my face in her lap. "Mummy, please. Please tell me it's not true."

"Bebi, I know, I know, I am devastated," she shushes me as she rubs my head, trying to wipe my tears that wouldn't stop.

My brother? How – No. Why? Of all the men I have dated all my life, why did I fall the hardest for my brother? I might have been on Umm'Hafsa's lap crying for ten minutes or thirty minutes. I am not sure. All I remember is hearing the call to prayer for *Zuhr*. When I stand up, assuring my parents that I will be fine, I decide that I'll perform ablution, pray and then call Sadiq. Their voices that carry their questions to my ears sound worried, but I keep nodding, even though what they are saying is not registering in my brain.

As I climb the stairs, I realize that I am angry. Not sure at whom, but I am angry. Maybe at Bashir, for being a cheat in the first place. If he was a decent boyfriend, I would have never fallen out of love with him. Then I start to blame myself for liking my ex-boyfriend's friend. Then I blame Sadiq, for ... I can't find anything to blame him for, so I blame his abusive father. He caused all of this. What kind of man hits a woman? A terrible man, that's who. One so bad that a woman was forced to hide her child's existence from him. That child was me. That woman is Umm'Hafsa. And that man... the abusive me... that man is …. He is my... No, I can't bring myself up to say it.

When I reach my room, I don't pray *Zuhr*. I crawl into bed and get under the covers. By the time, Umm'Hafsa comes to the room to check on me, my back is turned to the door, and I am laying still. I hear her whisper to someone, "she's asleep." And the door shuts quietly behind her.

Asleep. I can't see myself sleeping ever again.

I've kissed my brother. I've kissed him many times. We made plans for our home and our marriage, and our kids. Kids! That's like Mohammed and me thinking of having kids. Thinking of that triggers a nausea from deep in my belly and something knots and climbs up my throat.

I blame Sadiq's father for all of this. I don't even know what he looks like. I pull up my phone to google his name, to have a face I can direct my anger towards. As I spell out his name and hit the search button, many Ringims come up – some chieftains, some in the government, some in private businesses. I go back to the Google search and add 'late.'

Multiple online news outlets pop up reporting a plane crash in 2010 that claimed the lives of several dignitaries, including one Alhaji Aliyu Ringim. I start reading pages and pages of multiple condolences that come up tab after tab. I zoom into a picture of him. In the picture, he is wearing a white *babban riga* and a regular Hausa cap. He was a huge man. I use my fingers to zoom into his face, his graying hair, and wide-set eyes. He looks like someone else's father. An absolute stranger. He didn't have kind eyes with crinkles at the corner or a half smile, like the one I am used to seeing on daddy's face. I look at another picture. So this is the face of an abuser, the same man that broke Sadiq's arm.

Right then, Sadiq's face comes on my screen as his call interrupts.

Oh my God. What am I going to tell him?

I can't pick the call, but I am fixated on his picture on my screen. There is no resemblance between him and the man I saw seconds earlier but then again, there is no resemblance between me and the man either. I keep looking at Sadiq's picture as my phone rings nonstop – his smile, the thick, dark lines of his brows, his lips – until the ringing stops and his caller display picture disappears from my screen.

When his message comes in, my fingers hover before I finally open it: *B, Imran and Nasreen are gonna join us for games night.* Before I reply, another comes in: *Fa'iza suggested that we have it at their place. Can you tell Ilham it's not at Ranchers anymore? I can send the driver to pick you guys up.*

Fa'iza. The person who is supposed to be my neighbor, with our kids going to each other's birthday parties. We were supposed to be carpooling to school events and activities. Sadiq already has an interior decorator creating mood boards and room layouts for us to choose from for the house we both fell in love with. The one we thought our kids would grow in.

I have no idea how to deal with all of this. I am slowly coming apart. The confirmation that daddy isn't my father is the least heavy of all the revelations today because I have been mentally prepared for it. The disclosure, however, that Sadiq is… that my boyfriend is… who they say he is is sickening and absolutely unfair.

How am I going to tell him? Should I call him back? And say what?

Sadiq, I am… I am your sister?

SubhanAllah.

* * *

After *Asr*, the door to my room opens twice.

The first time, it's Mariya with my salad. With my voice muffled in my pillows, I tell her to take it away. If it stays in my room, it's just going into the garbage. I don't have an appetite. Can I even eat? Can I keep anything down? I remain unmoving in the same position, with my knees tucked below my chin and unopened notifications on my screen, on the phone that's now on silent.

The second time my door opens, I don't hear *sallama* or anything. I can tell from the slow squeak of the hinges that the door opens gently. The perfume that wafts in is floral, fruity almost. It is one of Umm'Hafsa's, but I know it isn't her. It doesn't have the undertones of her *humrah*. I wait for the door to close but when it does, the approaching footsteps tell me that the person didn't leave. They are light and unhurried. Aisha, maybe. I feel the weight of someone lighter dip on the bed. When thin arms circle my shoulders, I hear the chime of the charms on her bracelet. Our matching pandora charm bracelet with the inscription sisters on a silver heart that we've worn every day since her nineteenth birthday.

"Are you gonna be okay?" Sara whispers as she snuggles behind me.

I don't bother wiping the tears from my face. It's not like she can see them anyway. I pull her hand tighter towards me. "I – I don't think so." I answer honestly.

"Aww, Bebi." She holds me tighter and we remain in that position for a while, in silence. The only sound in the room is the central air conditioning from the floor vents, and I keep staring at the slightly moving drapes above the vents.

In this room months ago, Sara and I discovered that something was off with the DNA results we received. In this very room, we concluded that I was not adopted but that we shared a parent. I haven't spoken to her about any new discovery since then. I wonder how much she knows. She hasn't said more than two sentences to me all weekend. Can this be the reason why?

"How did you know?" I ask her eventually.

She remains quiet for a very long time. Then I hear her sniff and reply, "Professor Kershaw." Kershaw is one of her lecturers at the University; I have heard Sara complain about the grading rubric and expectations of this Professor Kershaw. She takes her hands off me. "I got obsessed with genomics all semester, I always saw her during her office hours, she analyzed the screenshots of the results – without our names of course – and confirmed that we share matrilineal DNA."

Matrilineal DNA. Umm'Hafsa. So she knows that daddy isn't my father and that we are half-siblings? How long has she known for? I remain quiet.

"Before exams, Fatima got tired of me making noise about my Senegalese roots, sending her new Senegalese music I found on YouTube and finally indulged me. She got the same test we did, just for bragging rights *fa. Like, wallahi*, we were just playing around…"

I go still as I turn around to face her, "Fatima Ringim?"

"It was the weirdest thing, Bebi. Like, one-half of my result and another half of her result made up yours. I thought I was going crazy."

"Does she know?"

"No, no, I never showed her your result. I just saved the screenshot she sent to me." She sighs, "Just after new year's, Professor Kershaw finally replied my inquiry. She said there was a chance that you were related to Fatima. She said it might be patrilineal relation."

I scoff. Frigging science.

Fatima, my sister's best friend is my step-sister. This is one big convoluted mess.

"I kept telling myself that a chance isn't confirmation, but it kept bugging me. When I got back from the gym on Friday and Mariya told me you had a big fight with Umm'Hafsa about your marriage and that you left the house upset, I – It was easy to assume the worst."

Mariya and her *gulma*! She is such a gossip. Nothing goes on in this house that she doesn't know, except when Umm'Hafsa specifically tells her not to come upstairs. I have seen her cleaning the same spot for hours when daddy and I are deep in conversation. The father I wish I share blood with.

"He – he used to beat Umm'Hafsa," I say to Sara about my biological father, my voice breaking. Our heads are on the same pillow as we face each other, teary-eyed. "My father.. he... he used to beat her." I can't imagine a man beating me, and yet my mother experienced that when she was even younger than me. Her thumb gently stops me from scratching my nails; only two fingers have color on them now. I have managed to pull off all the shellac gel from most of my nails. "I treated her with so much contempt. I was so so nasty to her, Sara, *baza ki gane ba*. I thought she cheated on daddy," I start crying again. "I stopped going to her room to greet her *fa*. Even when I get home, I just come straight here." The days that I saw her in the living room, my greetings were very flippant.

"It's okay, you didn't know," Sara hugs me again.

"No, you don't understand. I made her cry when she came to talk to me that day," I keep crying, and Sara joins me. "I made our mother cry."

"She loves you. I know she has already forgiven you..."

"Can you imagine breaking all these rules – ignoring *shariah* just to keep your child safe – and the child grows up to accuse you of something so ugly, of infidelity?"

"Hey. No need beating yourself like this. It's okay. *Daina kuka*, stop crying." She keeps consoling me until I stop crying, but I have a lot of things to cry about, including the things I am not talking about. Still, she stays, drying my tears. My sisters both take after daddy's kindness. But not me. How can I, with a man like my father?

Eventually, when I calm down, Sara asks, "have you told him?"

I can't even look at Sadiq right now or bear the sound of his voice. How does one make the switch from boyfriend – no, fiance – to brother, in less than six hours?

I sigh. It's a long, deep sigh filled with emotions I have no words for. Maybe I should spare him from this unbridled sadness, loss, shame, and mild disgust I am currently filled with. I love him enough to spare him from this feeling. I don't have to tell him the details. I can just break up with him. I'll tell him that I have decided to respect my parents' decision and that we should both move on.

Then, I will try to move on. I will try my very best.

Sadiq

2022

The evening starts with a lie.

I arrive late at Ahmad and Fa'iza's house. I can already hear Nasreen and Fa'iza laughing over the current round of 'Apples to Apples', which is a cleaner version of 'Cards Against Humanity'. It's a game we play whenever I visit Toronto. Imran hosts and sometimes, Fa'iza and Ahmad show up. Games night is always punctuated with dinner. Today, it's just six of us because when I told Assad that it was not going to be at Rancher's, he decided to skip it and Lily doesn't go anywhere without him. Or five of us rather, since I doubt Hafsatu will miraculously show up here on her own.

They are almost at the end of the game when I come in. Imran is laughing hysterically at the girls' answer submissions. To Fa'iza's side, Ahmad is shuffling his cards, looking for a card that would trump the current options on display. They all look up as I walk into their living room alone.

"Where's Hafsat?" Fa'iza asks as she places her drink back on the coaster, away from the multiple boxes of unopened games on the carpet.

"She sends her apologies. She's still a bit under the weather." I tell them the same lie I told everyone who asked at Madina's reception. Today, I can't tell them that I haven't been able to reach her for most of the day. It is very unlike Hafsat to pull a disappearing act, so I know there has to be a reasonable explanation. I just have to wait until she reaches out.

"Aww, *har yanzu*? Such a shame. I hope she feels better soonest."

Nasreen looks up from her cards, "I was really hoping I could meet her before we leave. I'm the only one who hasn't met her *fa yanzu*."

"Oh, she's like really sweet. And gorgeous," Faiza says.

"So I've heard." Nasreen shuffles her cards before dropping them on the floor in front of her. "*Toh, sai mun zo bikin kenan.* Until we come for the wedding then."

"When are you heading back?" I ask to change the topic.

"Tomorrow morning – spending a week in Paris, then back to the Six," Imran answers, "*Toh* can we eat now? *Dama* we were waiting for you guys. I'm famished."

All through the dinner chatter, I can't stop looking at my phone to see if she has replied to any of my messages. I have no such luck.

Ahmad leans towards me, "you should try the salmon, it's good."

"Ah, *na gode.* I never say no to salmon." I say as I use a spatula to place a fish cutlet on my plate. "Fa'iza did you make this?" I point at the table covered with three different entrees, appetizers and desserts.

"Ha! As much as I'd love to take credit for it, no I didn't. Oh that reminds me, Hasfat was asking about my cook. I sent her numbers of two that I interviewed before we decided to go with my current one. Did she get my message? She never replied."

I lift the glass of water to my mouth, drinking it just to buy myself some time.

"Oh, I'm sure she'll get back to you as soon as she sees it." I drop the glass back on the table and cut into a piece of glazed salmon.

After dinner, my phone beeps and my elation is cut short when I read Ilham's reply to my earlier inquiry: *She's not picking up my calls either.*

Interesting.

I text back: *Okay, thanks.*

Ilham played a role in me and Hafsat getting together. I don't even know if Hafsat herself knows just how much, but her friend was a huge help. My mind wanders to the day I was sitting with Ilham and Usman at the Nova restaurant on the main floor of Bellanova, the day after I gave her the DNA kit when we met at the gym. I had just joined her and Usman for brunch when we saw Bashir's car pull up and park a few meters away.

"Is that Bashir's car? I thought he was in Lagos." She slurped her drink through the straw as the door opened and a girl emerged from the driver's seat. She was alone and had boxes of takeout with her as she made her way upstairs.

"Wait, who's that girl?" Ilham asked Usman as she dropped her milkshake on the table.

He shrugged, "why are you asking me?"

She then looked at me. "Sadiq, who is the girl that just drove Bashir's car here?"

I looked back at my phone as I exited Hafsat's Instagram profile, and I answered her, "she's his girl." The anger in my voice was hidden under annoyance that I hoped would stop her from directing her questions my way.

Her mouth fell open, "his what? Oh, hell no." She got up as if to follow the girl toward the elevator but Usman stopped her, while I watched, amused.

"*Ina za ki?* Where are you going?"

"He's cheating on my friend." Her raised voice drew the attention of some patrons as they looked towards our table." Why won't you guys talk to him?"

"Because he's a grown ass man," I blurted out. And if he wants to fumble what he's got, I am more than happy to watch him do it.

Ilham looked disappointed at my answer and she turned to Usman. "Give me the key to the apartment."

"You know I can't do that. What do you want with it?"

"I'm gonna give it to Bebi. I need her to catch him red-handed."

"*Gaskiya ni ba ruwa na.* I don't want to get involved." Usman always looks the other way when things don't concern him – a good but cowardly trait.

"That means you're capable of doing the same." She stood up and started putting her phones in her bag, muttering something about birds that flocked together.

"You know I would never – Where are you going now? They haven't even brought out our food yet."

I was beginning to get bored, so I went back to scrolling through my phone. There was nothing new about Ilham and Usman fighting; they do that every three days.

"I'm going home."

"C'mon. I –"

"If I mean anything to you Usman, you will give me your key." Oh, she pulled the trump card. My attention went back to them.

He couldn't refuse her then and of course, as I watched him, he reached for his back pockets. "I left it upstairs."

The whole exchange was taking too long with no resolution. I brought out my keycard and tossed it on the table. "Give her mine. Just make sure she gets it as soon as possible." I chuckled at the thought of how it would play out. Maybe Hafsatu Gaya is not a doormat after all.

About an hour later, I saw her go up to Bashir's apartment on the sixteenth floor.

A quick chime gets my attention back to the game I just lost. Again. Even after dinner, Imran is still on a winning streak, Nasreen is demanding a rematch and Faiza is snuggled against Ahmad on the sofa as they share a drink from the same cup. I think they deliberately lost out early just to relax from the competition. My phone chimes and it's a message from Hafsat.

It's a breakup text.

* * *

The following day at noon, I get to H&I. I don't see her car parked outside but then again, if she is avoiding me, she will not let me know her whereabouts by having her car visible. I walk up the stairs until I get to the double unit. Between rows of ready-to-wear outfits and the carpeted sitting area decorated in yellow and green, the salesperson is helping two ladies who are paying for their purchases at the cash register. One of them nudges the other as I enter and they both whisper something. After a quick nod to the manager, who called me discreetly to let me know that Hafsat was in the premises after I gave him a little something to keep me posted, I enter the hallway through the door hidden by three golden mannequins on a draped stage.

The hallway is deserted, very different from how it was during her fashion show. The first door on the right leads to the tailors' space, where all her seamstresses, tailors and embroiderers work. I know because I've watched Hafsat go in there to find fabric pieces to glue to her sketch designs. The door opposite it leads to a staff room, where her salespersons eat lunch on their break.

Down the hallway is Ilham's office but before it, the closed door in front of me with no nameplate, position, or anything else to indicate her stake in this fashion house is Hafsat's office.

I push the door open and see her standing over her desk. In front of her is a mid-sized cardboard box, and she's filling it with her sketchbooks and laptop. She holds the framed picture of her and her stepfather as she looks up at me as I close the door, and our eyes meet.

She's in a long black dress and an unbuttoned blue jean jacket. She isn't crying, but she doesn't look great either. Her lips are dry, the circles around her eyes are prominent and the blue veil around her head is wrinkled, un-ironed. The bleak look in her eyes keeps me transfixed to the ground as I close the door behind me. I look around the office. The white walls are now devoid of their pin-up posters of models and enlarged covers of fashion magazines, except for one framed poster with the word CoCo on the wall behind her.

Her desk has also been cleared out; all that remains on it is her monitor display unit. I clear my throat, "are you going somewhere?"

She sighs as she places her graduation picture gently over the things in the brown cardboard box. "What are you doing here?" She avoids my eyes as she turns around to disconnect her charger and starts rolling it up.

"I wanna believe that that text message wasn't for me. But if it is, I wanna hear you say it to my face," I say slowly. She says nothing as she places the now folded charger in her collection of things, careful not to put it over the picture. Something is off. "Hafsat, a text message? You are breaking up with me over text? Don't I deserve the courtesy of a face-to-face?"

"Sorry, I sent a text message. I should have –" her voice trails off. She's still avoiding my eyes.

I slowly walk toward her, and she's looking away from me, at everything but me. "B, what's going on?" My voice is lowered.

"Exactly what my text said. I'm going to respect my parents' wishes."

"That is bullshit, Hafsat. You are lying to me," I move closer to her and notice that her breathing gets faster as she concentrates on closing the box.

"And where are you going with all these? Are you packing up the shop?"

"No, I'm just traveling for a few days. I –"

"You are leaving town? Wait, are your parents threatening you or forcing you to do this?"

She looks up at me for the first time since I walked in, "my parents have my best interest, Sadiq. They love me."

I scoff out loud, "what's this? Are you under surveillance? Are they tapping your phone, or something?" I look around the corners of the ceiling, half expecting to see cameras recording us because I can't understand this act she is putting on about respecting her parent's wishes all of a sudden. As I move closer, I reach for her face, forcing her to look at me. "Whatever it is, I can fix it, but I can't help us if you don't tell me what exactly is going on." My voice is calm and my speech is slow, but she does not respond. "What did your uncle say?"

Her eyes fill with tears and she shrugs out of my hold, "The only thing you can do for me right now is to inform your family that we have broken up because we're not going to be around for *gaisuwa*."

"The *gaisuwa* that's supposed to be next week? You know my uncles stayed back in Abuja and they did not return to Kano after the wedding so they can come to see your parents. And you are telling me this? Now?"

"I know, and I am sorry…"

"I asked you. I asked you before I went to Kaduna. I said, are you sure you are in this with me?" I keep my gaze on her. She keeps shaking her head as the tears start falling down her cheeks. "You said yes. You told me yes. So what has changed?"

She holds her palms to her face, crying. There's so much pain in her eyes, yet she seems so closed off, so out of reach. I know there's no amount of asking I can do to get her to be completely honest with me. There's more to this; I can tell from how she fidgets with her fingers and avoids my eyes.

"I'm sorry," she whimpers. I can barely hear her.

"That's not enough, Hafsat. Words mean something to me; *love* means something to me. When I told you I'm in this with you, I meant it. I didn't mean I'm only here for a good time, and I'll bail out when the going gets tough. Now I know it's not the same for you."

I'm about to turn around and leave, walk away from it all, but something about my words makes her cry even harder. I feel weak seeing her cry. I can't bear the way she buries her face in her palms as her shoulders shake in anguish. It actually hurts me to see her like this. All I can do is embrace her and let the downpour of her tears soak through my shirt. I can feel her silently screaming, suffocating with each breath she takes.

I want to tell her to stop crying and tell me to fix, but I can't find the words. So, I hold her for what feels like hours then I lift her hands to uncover her face. I see that her eyes are shut tight. "Why are you crying so much if this is what you say you want?" I ask.

"It's what I want," she manages to say in between sobs, even though she keeps her eyes closed like she can't bear to face reality.

So stubborn. How can the strong-willed quality I love about her be what tears us apart? "Then look me in the eye and tell me you don't love me anymore."

Her eyes remain shut.

"Tell me that between yesterday and today, you have fallen out of love and you don't want me as much as I want you. Tell me, and I'll never bother you."

My hands reach for her as my fingers stroke the soft skin of her chin, jaw and neck as if to remind her of how it feels when we are together. She opens her eyes slowly. Her breath quickens as my thumb traces her lips. She takes a step back, and I move forward, closing the distance she put between us. Her back presses against the wall and her head is next to the glass frame hanging on the wall.

"Hafsat." I'm helpless in my attempt to calm the silent war within her mind.

"Sadiq..." she starts. The creases in her forehead and her strangled whisper don't stop me from leaning down to kiss her. Breathing in her light scent – not a perfume – it was more like detergent from her clothes. Right before my lips touch hers, she turns her head away. "Please, don't."

I pause.

My desperation is quickly replaced by anger and it unfurls in me in the only way it knows how. It's like I am back in the gym, in front of my punching bag. It's all a blur and the pain is the only thing I feel as my fist connects to the wall next to Hafsat's head. At the same time, I hear the glass frame shatter as its broken pieces fall to the floor around us.

The look of shock and fear in her eyes doesn't stop the rage from erupting further. "Fuck!" I mutter, mostly to myself. I need to get out of here before I do something worse. I turn around and before I can open the door, it swings open, and Ilham rushes in.

"What was that?" she shouts, looking at me and then at Hafsat. Her eyes widen as they find my bloodied fist, the broken frame, and the glass splinters all over the floor as Hafsatu slowly slumps to the ground, crouching where we stood moments ago. Ilham hits both her fists on my chest, her eyes bewildered. "What did you do? Did you hit her?" She rushes over to console her best friend before I get a chance to reply.

Before I leave, I take one last look at the colossal mess our lives have disintegrated into – Hafsat Gaya crouched amidst the broken splinters of something that was once whole, her face buried in her hands as she cries uncontrollably, and I am the reason for it. I am the reason behind her tears. I, who promised never to hurt the people I love.

Yet, I almost punched her. She's the love of my life, and I almost physically hurt her.

I am my father's son, after all.

Zuwaira

2022

Retirement has its perks; living off my pension is better than I thought it would be.

Although I believed that when I finally stopped working, I would be able to sleep in as much as I wanted, that is not the case. I am always up a few minutes before *Fajr*, even before Ibrahim wakes up. On the days I am not fasting, I eat the first meal of the day with him at the breakfast nook in our bedroom. As soon as he leaves for work, instead of relaxing, reading a book, or watching some of the movies that my daughters recommend to me, I find other things to do because I am so used to being busy. I've been working since I turned twenty-four, except for when I was on maternity or annual leave when we go on our family trips. These days, I spend a lot of time fixing things around the house; first, I had the carpet in our living room changed to a soft brown colored one, then I got Ladidi to change the drapes in Mohammed's room. Eventually, I made it outdoors, getting a handyman to fix the cracks in the floor tiles. Last week, I contracted a cleaning company to come in and wash all the glass panes on the windows around the house. Our forever home. When we moved into this house eight years ago, it was a dream come true, a life we had worked hard towards for years for our children.

Now, Saratu and Aisha have returned to university, and the house is unbearably quiet during the day. I don't hear doors banging down the hallways or their laughter from their bedrooms. I miss the appetizers they normally bring to the table from their time in the kitchen recreating meals they see on shows on *The Food Network*. My youngest, Mohammed, is getting more serious with his evening football practices. Most days after *Asr*, he goes to a football field with one of his friends from school, and by the time the driver brings him back home, it is already time for *Maghrib*.

After we pray, we eat dinner in the living room together. On some days, Hafsatu joins us. Ever since the debacle from a few weeks ago, she has become a shadow of her previous self. I see her trying to make an effort by showing up for dinner with us, but something in her has been altered.

Sara made a family group chat on Whatsapp and added all our numbers. It makes it easier for me to send information once instead of multiple times to their individual numbers. Mohammed fills it up with funny videos from an app called Tiktok. Sara sends us links to papers she writes that make it into Academic Journals. Aisha sends pictures of her and her friends at school excursions and shopping activities. Ibrahim loves the family group chat; he comments on every single message and picture with long paragraphs he ends with, 'love, dad.' I always remind them to read Suratul Kahf on Fridays, and most of my Whatsapp messages to the family group are prayers and duas. But Hafsatu never sends any messages to the group. She just adds a small red heart to every single message. No replies, just the tiny heart every single time.

"Hafsatu, you didn't even step out of the house today," I say to her one evening as she drops the glass pitcher full of water on the bedside table next to Ibrahim's pillow. I fold my praying mat and sit on the bed to read Ibrahim's message giving me details about the 59th Annual Conference Of The Nigerian Medical Association he is attending in Ebonyi.

She leans against the dresser that has my vanity mirror. "I was going to go out *fa*, but then I slept off after *Asr* and only woke up when Mohammed came to show me his wound from football. Did you see it?"

"Another wound?" I overlook the way she expertly changes the topic the way she always does when we start having conversations that go close to

406

me asking about her feelings.

"Well, it's a small one, but he wears them like badges of honor," she replies.

I watch her, and even though she says she is okay, I can see in her eyes that she is far from okay. *"Komai lafiya dai ko? But is everything okay?"* I ask. I always ask.

She nods ardently, even before I finish my question.

Weeks later, I supervise my latest project, the repotting of most of our outdoor plants and the newest succulents I got from Flora Green House. The gardener, Ashir, works with me daily; I keep correcting his watering practices all day as my sunflowers are dying out. When Ibrahim returns one evening, he sees me in the backyard. I am standing by the pool's edge, watching Ashir scoop the debris from the surface with a long pool net.

"Ashe kina nan. I was wondering why you weren't picking up my calls." As he joins me, I lean into him for a hug, and he kisses my forehead.

"The phone is upstairs, my love. You're back early. Is everything okay?"

"There was nothing else for me to do at the hospital." Medela Hospital is Ibrahim's healthcare center located in Katampe extension. Since 2018, they have helped families through their fertility clinic, which specializes in IVF and other forms of assisted reproduction. Although during the pandemic, it became a major testing center for the coronavirus. "Do you want to go for a walk? We haven't stepped out together in a while."

A few minutes later, we are holding hands as we walk down the pavement of the quiet cul-de-sac lined with tall palm trees that bristle in the evening wind. Most houses on the street have heavy wrought iron or steel gates in black, white, or brown with exterior walls plastered in stone masonry or limestone decals. We walk past a house with the words 'EFCC KEEP OUT' written in big block letters dripping with red paint on its white walls. From what I hear, this is one of the many properties they seized from some corrupt politician on embezzlement charges. I wonder why they deface property like this. Don't they have removable tape they can use instead? And what is the use of the multiple padlocks they used to lock the gate, when one would suffice?

"Bebi wants to leave Abuja for her masters," Ibrahim tells me as we walk around a bend.

After he left for the hospital this morning, I had breakfast with Hafsatu, and she showed me the websites of two universities she was looking into. I was surprised to see that they were both in Canada. "I feel like she's running away. She chose the farthest possible option from home," I reply. It is clear that her heart isn't in Abuja anymore, not since her relationship with Sadiq ended. She doesn't even go out to see her friends anymore; she spends most nights in the game room sketching elaborate designs that end up torn in the garbage bin and sleeps in most of the day. "Have I ruined it for her?"

Ibrahim raises his hand to acknowledge a greeting from one of the guards outside our neighbor's house as we walk past it. "Ruined what, my love?"

"Happiness, love..." A chance for my daughter to find something I am lucky to have with my husband, something people spend their whole lives searching for. "What if that was her one chance at it?" The memory of Hafsatu breaking down in front of us still haunts me. Proud Hafsatu broke down. Will she ever get over that loss?

Ibrahim sighs. I know he sees it, too, the way the light has disappeared from our daughter's eyes, the way she stares into space when she doesn't know we are watching her, the loneliness she feels even when surrounded by family.

"She'll find her person in the future *insha Allah*. Sadiq was never meant for her."

Theirs was not a love story that was supposed to happen. It was an error, one I caused with my own two hands. A consequence of a choice I made years ago. All choices have consequences, and in trying to protect her, I made a choice that led to a very painful consequence – not just for me but for her. My Bebi.

"If I could go back in time –"

"What would you do? Stay until he killed you?"

"No, staying was never an option. But maybe I should have said the truth about my pregnancy, like you advised me to."

We are now walking past the gate of the Poland Embassy at the end of our street. We cross the road to start making our way back home, and as usual, Ibrahim switches sides with me, standing between me and the road.

"He would have taken her away. She would have grown up with stepmothers who wouldn't have cared about her."

"But at least she would have grown up knowing that – that – knowing that he is her brother." Yes, it would have pained me to live away from my child. To not be able to be with her every day – to not know what is going on with a child you gave birth to, a child you labored for – is like having your heart beating outside of your body, in someone else's hands, at someone else's mercy. Just thinking about it seems unbearable, but if I knew that that was the sacrifice I had to make to save my baby from the pain she is currently going through now, I would have made that sacrifice.

"Your heart could not bear leaving her with a man like that, and that's okay," Ibrahim reminds me. "If he was not abusive, I know you would have done exactly what the Qur'an says."

I shake my head. "Alhaji Isa was right. I should have just allowed what Allah willed to happen."

"If everything is preordained, then isn't the choice we made that day part of our fate? Is free will not part of an already written script that we unknowingly act out even in our rebellion?"

I sigh out loud as a white Audi slowly drives past us and turns toward the driveway of the house two gates from ours. Maybe this is what Allah willed. Maybe this is Hafsat's test of faith. Still, I don't feel any better. For the longest time, I felt like I had failed my test of faith, that maybe that pregnancy during my *iddah* was my test from God to see if I would obey His word. I disobeyed him. When Ibrahim took me on a pilgrimage for the first time, praying for forgiveness was all we did. Every time my forehead touched the ground in *sajdah,* and each time I raised my hands to the sky with baby Hafsat next to Ibrahim and me in the holy city of Mecca, I prayed for forgiveness.

"Do you regret anything?" I ask as we get closer to the house.

He has a slight smile on his face as he unscrews the bottle of water he brought from the house and hands it to me. "*Na gode*, thank you." I take a sip, and hand the bottle back to him.

"Regret what exactly?" he takes a much bigger gulp than mine.

I shrug, "anything... everything. Leaving Kaduna with me, the secret..." My voice trails off.

I would have gone to Lagos on my own if Ibrahim hadn't offered to help. Who knows what kind of life I would have found myself in, with my poor educational background? But maybe that would have been better; he would not have been dragged into this mess. My mess. But the thought of me living a life without him makes my throat start to close up, and I reach for the bottle again.

"If you're asking me if I regret taking you to Jos with me or giving Hafsat my name, the answer is no. It will always be no." He watches as I wipe my lips with the back of my hand. "If I were to go back in time and find myself at that same crossroad, I will still make the exact same choice. Do you want to know why?" I shake my head. He continues, "because you're the best thing that has ever happened in my life."

"Please don't make me cry."

"No, it's the truth. Without Allah and you, I wouldn't have everything I have now. Our family is my greatest gift from Allah, and I couldn't have done it without you."

I reach for his hand and hold it tightly in mine. He raises it to his lips and kisses it. As we approach the gates, the single pedestrian gate swings open, and we walk in.

"I think Canada will be good for her. *Kuma* we have never been there. It's an opportunity for us to visit when she's settled in."

"Did she say anything about your referral for counseling?" I ask after a few seconds.

He shakes his head no.

"Let's give her some more time." As we enter the quiet house, he asks, "and you? You can't drown yourself in house renovations. You need professional help, too."

I don't tell him, but our family secret is something I intend to carry to my grave. There is no counselor or therapist I can ever open up my heart to. It will do me no good.

Sadiq

When one of my uncles, Kawu Liman, calls to confirm that they are not going for the *gaisuwa* anymore. I answer in the affirmative, as I apologize for keeping them away from Kano for so long.

"*A'a ka bar wannan maganan*; dont worry about that," he says loudly. That has always been his manner of speaking, and I know that all the people around him at this given moment know what's going on in my private life. "*Dama* I said let me ask, *wai yar gidan waye ce yarinyan?*"

Yar gidan waye ce? I scoff quietly. In regular conversation, that means: whose daughter is she? However, it means a lot more in situations like marriage and engagements. When Hajiya Amina told my stepmother that I was getting engaged, that was one of her first questions. You could almost confuse it for simple interest, an innocent inquiry. Except it really wasn't. Who is her father? It's a loaded question for her to gauge how much importance she should accord the impending union. Her gifts to the bride-to-be will also match the answer. Is she from a high-status family deserving of high-end, quiet luxury brands, or were her parents struggling, or *nouveau riche*, better suited for the mass-market designer brands?

Like how my uncle now waits, breath bated, to hear the name of the family that dares to turn down a Ringim-Dankabo entourage. I never brag about family name, but it is a converted entourage. In the long history of marriages, I doubt my family has ever been turned down or refused at *gaisuwa*. Asking for a girl's hand was mostly just a formality, to give tradition the respect it demands, even though we know for a fact that the answer would always be yes, at least, for this family.

"She's Dr. Gaya's daughter," I answer.

He repeats the name a few times,s like he's trying to trigger a memory, "which of the Gayas? Mahmood Gaya?"

"No, Ibrahim Gaya."

"*Wai* Ibrahim Gaya," his voice gets faint as I hear him talk to someone in the background. The chatter continues for a few seconds, and his voice becomes clearer as he talks to me again.

"Is he the one who owns that hospital that had the original COVID test kits?"

"Medela Hospital? Yes, that's him." Now the migraine begins to set in; it is like the moment I allowed myself to think of her, my mind remains fixated on her.

"*Oho*, just forget about her."

Before we end the call, I tell him that she is already in my past. At least he is not as brusque as Uncle Dankabo when I broke the news to him. I met him at his former constituent office just before a closed-door meeting with some APC politicians. The scowl of disappointment directed at me didn't leave his face as he muttered, "*aikin banza*. Nonsense. So didn't you know her father was not in support all this while?"

Between the difficult conversation with Imran's father and hanging out with Usman at Ranchers, who acts like he doesn't know what I did to Hafsat at *H&I*, even though I know Ilham must have told him, I find myself on a downward spiral. It is masked by high productivity – hitting the gym twice a day, spending hours in meetings, and looking for things to fix on my quads.

I know it's only a matter of days or weeks, but I will eventually see her speeding past a red traffic light or grabbing lunch with someone when I am out. That is the problem with Abuja – we all move in the same circle.

I wonder when she will start dating again, and if that person would be someone I know. But why do I even care? She is free to date whomever she wants.

When Hajiya Amina calls and asks to see me, I pray *maghrib* at the mosque by the main gate before driving to the main house. The living room is filled with a few family members – two distant cousins and an aunt who have been in Asokoro since the wedding.

As I walk into Hajiya's private living room in the inner section of the main floor, hidden behind double doors, she looks up from the package on her lap; it's the one I brought from Kaduna.

"Ki tashi ki bamu waje, give me some privacy," she says to her help, who is crouched next to her, massaging her left leg as it sticks out at an odd angle on top of the red cushion on a low table.

I greet her and she waits until I sit down before speaking: "Your uncle called me to ask why you made him waste his time. He said he postponed his trip to Egypt to attend your *gaisuwa*. Sufyanu *fa*, that's my problem with him. He doesn't think about others. *Shi dai kullum* – his honor, his pride. Anyway, I gave him my mind. I asked him why he was not even worried about how you are feeling right now." The scowl on her face deepens as she speaks.

How much longer would this whole reaction from my family take before it dies down? My mind wanders again to Hafsat and the hole in the wall at her office. I should send her a cheque for the damages. Would she accept it?

Hajiya's voice brings me back. "Take a look at this. Do you recognize her?" She hands me a picture from the white office envelope. It's a faded picture of a woman; her torso is covered with the heavy damask fabric draped over her. Her eyebrows are straight, and her eyes are hooded, but the most distinct feature on her angular face is the bottom-heavy lip, a tell-tale family trait. In this picture, she is about twenty years younger than the pictures my father used to have of her in his study in London, but I recognize her instantly.

"Of course, Hajiya Uwa." In the picture, my grandmother is in her early forties, much younger than any of my memories of her, most of which were of her shielding me from my father's anger.

Hajiya Amina hands me another picture as I drop the one I am holding on the couch next to her.

"*Allah ya jikan* Hajiya Indo; may her soul rest in peace. That woman hated me so much," She says, looking at the picture of my great-aunt. "Do you remember when we were moving to Abuja, and she insisted you remain in Kaduna so that she can make sure you're not being maltreated by me," she hisses as though the memory of a fight from two decades ago is still fresh in her memory.

She keeps flipping through the pictures. Some were of my older siblings, some of her and my father looking like any normal couple, and most were taken at the family house in Kaduna. She stops at one picture. "Yauwaa!" she exclaims, dragging out the word like someone who has found something they have been looking for, "Where are my glasses?"

I point to the top of my head. She always has her reading glasses on top of hers, and she always looks for them every time she needs to read something.

She reaches for them, wears them, and squints at a picture, "Abubakar," she says quietly, "come closer."

Honestly, I don't care about the pictures she wants to put in the memorial album for my father; I don't even know why she needs my input. With some reluctance, I get up from my comfortable position on the sectional and sit on the chair next to her. Even as I take the picture she holds out to me, I grimace at his face. There he stands – smiling for the cameras the way he always did in public. It looks like a ribbon-cutting ceremony and next to him on his right is my oldest stepmother, Hajiya Babba. With a smirk of pride, she holds the scissors with him as he cuts. The other women aren't touching his hand like she is. They just stretch their hands toward the scissors. I recognize a much younger Hajiya Mami; she's the only one in a hijab and, of course, Hajiya Amina, her signature sunglasses tucked in front of her blouse, standing tall and proud among them all. She always stood out, even back then.

Then I see her.

For a minute, I think I am imagining things. I blink and look even harder. But she was still there.

Hafsat?

Why would she be in a faded sepia-toned picture from twenty-something years ago? I turn the picture and see a scribble in the corner, 'Kaduna 1998' written in fading blue ink. I turn the picture around again. She is a little skinnier, but with the same high cheekbones, the same sharp jaw, and almond-shaped eyes that looked straight at the camera, her pointed nose pronounced by the slight tilt of her oval face with full lips that form a shy smile close to dimples I have never seen on her.

Dimples?

"Who does she look like to you?" Hajiya Amina is peering at me through her rimless glasses with such great interest.

I squint at the picture in my hand as if it will give me a different view that will remove the resemblance. I clear my throat. "Who is she?"

Hajiya Amina sighs, "*Allah sarki*, God is great. You don't remember her? She was your father's fourth wife," she paused, then asked again, "who does she look like to you?"

Her answer to my question leaves me unsatisfied. From the similar fabric print they are all wearing, and how close they stand to my father, I can already deduce that they were all co-wives. So why haven't I seen her pictures before? I inspect the picture closely, and there is no denying that the resemblance is uncanny. Could this be...? No, it can't be.

"Hmm?" She urges me to answer, as if she needs me to validate something important.

"I feel like you're trying to say something."

"*Ba ta kama da Hafsatu?* Doesn't she look like Hafsatu? Or is it just me?" she pushes her glasses back to the top of her head. "No, I just want to know if you see it. *Ka san*, the day you brought her here, I said it. I said, "I know that face," but I couldn't remember from where and it bothered me so much for the longest time." She leans back into the chair with a satisfied look, like someone who has finally removed a long-buried thorn

416

from their heel. "I know that face. That is Zuwaira's face! When she left your father, it was like she dropped off the surface of the earth."

I feel the hair on my arms flare up. "Zuwaira?" I ask slowly. That is Umm'Hafsa's name. I know because Hafsat told me. Umm'Hafsa was married to my father before she married Dr. Gaya?

"When you told me Hafsat's parents withdrew their support, I added two plus two. I think it's because they realized who your father is. I'm sorry to say this but Zuwaira saw his worst side, so it made sense to me."

I badly want to agree with what she is saying, but I have been unable to get Hafsat's inexplicable behavior towards me out of my mind – how dispirited and crestfallen she appeared. It had to be something more than the fact that my father was abusive.

Something changed for Hafsat after her Uncle came from Kaduna. Is it possible that...? No, it can't be. Did she know something else?

"You know, there was a day I think I saw her at Yankari or maybe it was Fifth Chukker? I don't remember where. But it was on your birthday..." My stepmother was still recalling happenings from the past. When we were younger and still lived in Kaduna, I always looked forward to birthdays because Hajiya Amina did not just do celebrations at home with a cake, games, and guests. She threw the most elaborate parties for me, Fatima, and Hadiza. She used to take all my father's children, a few cousins, and the house helps on trips to Yankari, a wildlife game reserve in Bauchi, or Fifth Chukker in Kaduna. I still remember the blue 20-seater Mercedes Benz bus we always traveled in. We spent all weekend outside the booked Villas our family stayed in, going on Safari rides, learning to ride horses, and trying to stay afloat in the Wikki warm spring.

"...I can swear that she saw me too. But then she hurriedly went around a corner, like she was running away from me."

"Why would she run?"

The back of her hand hits her palm as she says she doesn't know, "I just wanted to say hello to her. We had developed some kind of friendship while she was still married to your father. I thought we left on good times and was actually happy to see her. Anyway, I saw her a few minutes with a man – maybe her husband, I don't know – and two or three children. They were leaving," she pauses, then adds, "*ko* she was ashamed *ne, oho.* I don't know."

Was it shame? Or was she hiding a secret?

Hafsat is not Dr. Gaya's daughter. That is something I know for a fact. If she was still my father's wife in 1998, and Hafsat was born in 1999... Does that make her... no, that's not possible. Does that mean Hafsat is my father's child?

My sister?

* * *

Two months later, I am sitting in Maher Zubin's office, thanks to a relapse after a three-year clean streak. I am back in my therapist's office for anger management and borderline depression – a diagnosis I don't exactly agree with. Maybe the anger issues, I can agree with that. After all, I have his features, his wealth, and clearly, his anger is also part of my inheritance. Something I thought was under control, but it turns out that the monster in me was only dormant.

The therapist's office has mostly stayed the same since the last time I was here. Maybe the semblance is supposed to evoke a feeling of safety for his patients. But it unnerves me – the bland-looking wallpaper, the dripping coffee machine, the fish tank at the corner.

"How are you doing these days, Abubakar?" The middle-aged man with a clean-shaven face taps his pen twice on his notepad as we start our weekly session. "How are you feeling with everything we discussed last session?"

It's like paying to be tortured mentally. I turn my head to the left and right as my neck cracks. I haven't been sleeping well; the pillows in my hotel room are softer than I like. My head always sinks right through the pillows, and I end up with this horrible neck pain all day. Even pain medications don't work anymore. "I still think it's messed up."

"What part of it?" He looks at me like he sees through me, and I wonder if he is trying to fit me into a box. Do I meet the criteria for certain issues? Is he profiling me? I wonder what psych evaluations he is currently putting me through. Abandonment issues? But people always leave, ever since I was a kid. Anger issues? Issues with the father figure in my life? He answers himself. "When I told you that it is a variation of the Oedipus complex?" He taps his pen again. Twice.

I grind my teeth, "yes, the complex – whatever you call it."

"Why do you disagree with it?" His face is expressionless; he's just watching me like I am a lab rat for him to test out his theories.

I tap my hands on my thigh. Twice. Mimicking him. "Like I said, it's messed up."

A few weeks ago, Maher presented a case – his words, not mine – for me to ponder upon. He wanted me to consider if my familial feeling for my father's ex-wife – who was like a mother to me decades ago – was why I sought Hafsat out.

Except I didn't seek her out. Our paths crossed, and I fell in love with her.

"If you feel so strongly about it, why don't you dissect it with me?" He makes a note in his padded book.

"There's no point to that. It's just a waste of time. I don't know if you remember me telling you last week that I had no recollection of what she – my father's ex wife looked like. It's been over twenty years."

His eyes twitch a few times as he listens to me. Maher has been my therapist since university, since the first time I got into a pub brawl while watching a football match in my first year. I had gotten a black eye that day, but the other guy had it worse with a broken nose and dislocated jaw.

"You said the dimple in the photograph triggered something in you. What would you call it?"

The damn dimple. I have always believed that my mother had dimples. But when I looked in my safe again, the sepia-toned pictures of my birth mother in there showed no dimples. When Hajiya Amina told me everything about how long I lived with Umm'Hafsa and how much she cared for me, it all started coming back to me. Painfully. Like the day I saw her on the floor unconscious. It felt like *Deja vu*. I ran out looking for help, scared out of my mind.

Still, I remain quiet. His voice drones on, "this is not the first time you have suppressed your memories Abubakar. We talked about this years ago."

Not true. I didn't talk to him about it. He probed and asked about it, but I didn't have much to say because I didn't remember much. My childhood speech therapist thought it would be good to get Maher to help with my memory distortions; I still don't think it's a problem. So I mix up some events? So what?

Memories are a prison one cannot escape from. Sometimes, to protect itself from unraveling, the mind would bury traumatic experiences in a part of the brain that gets forgotten over time, almost like it never happened. Except sometimes, subsequent trauma unearths the buried memories.

I groan as I sit forward in the chair and hold my head in my hands. I have been suffering from these on-and-off migraines since the last day I saw Hafsat. Or was it after my conversation with Hajiya Amina? And since then, I've been popping pain relief pills like mints.

"Your attraction to the young lady in question is based off a simple memory. Your subconsciousness recognized her without remembering why."

I scoff harder this time. Psychology is bullshit. I can't believe people make a living out of spewing this rubbish.

He has a knowing smile on face as he watches me disengage from the talk. "You said it yourself multiple times in the past weeks; you cared about her in ways you could not explain. When she cried, you could not stop yourself from trying to fix whatever the problem was."

I think back to the day she found Bashir cheating, the day she called me about a hypothetical question, the pictures that her ex threatened to leak. I think back to every single time she cried in front of me and something in me got unleashed. My brain floods me with memories of me wiping tears off my father's fourth wife's face while she cried silently in her flat in Kaduna. Now that my memories of her are back, I remember how unhappy she was. She cried a lot; she cried all the time.

I always gave her a toy – a yellow car or was it a red ball? I can't remember – but it always cheered her up the way she cheered me up when I came back from school crying after being bullied.

"That sounds like *Storge*, love towards a family member, that feeling to protect someone…" He continues.

Why is psychology still filled with Greek and Latin for words with a perfectly functional English alternative, yet somehow I can't stop thinking about it. When Hafsat was dating Bashir, I tried everything just to get her out of my mind. But it didn't work. Is that because she felt familiar to me? Safe? Am I believing this psych bullshit?

My mind lazily registers the sound of his continuous monologue "…but we live in such a hypersexual society today. It is easy to wrongly think of the fondness – the need to protect, the connection – as *Eros* or romantic love. Especially in your case, where you had no reason to imagine that she was your sister."

I groan again, this time louder than the last, as I scratch my two-week-old, outgrown beard.

My younger sister? I have had the most lustful thoughts about her, about us being together. It's been eight weeks, and my mind has been in the same state of turmoil since I left Abuja after I realized that this is the reason why she couldn't even bear to look me in the eye just twenty-four hours after we were all over each other.

She knows that I am her brother. That's the only thing that makes sense in this whole mess. Imagine if I had fucked my sister. How does one recover from that? Never.

I need more medication for my migraine. I should ask the pharmacy downstairs for something stronger. The wall clock in Maher's office is placed in a well-calculated position behind the patient's seat so that only he knows how many minutes are left during sessions. It doesn't stop me from turning my neck and glancing at the wall behind me. My head remains in that position for a while as I try to make sense of the branches pointing to numbers on the face of the simple white clock. It takes me longer than it should to know the time. I sigh out loud as I look back to him, "I think this is enough for today."

He is quiet for a short while, "if that is what you want." Then he adds quietly: "Abubakar, I can't help you from having another relapse, if you don't accept the trigger of this last episode."

Triggers. Episodes. I hate these words.

I stand up, but not before seeing how his lips form a disappointed line on his face. Is a therapist supposed to be so obviously judgmental? Or am I projecting my feelings onto him? Am I disappointed in myself?

"You can bill me for the whole hour, doc," I say as I open the door that I walked into eighteen minutes ago. I promise myself to cancel all future appointments as soon as I get something to stop my head from splitting.

I walk down the hallway to the elevator. *What are you running away from? You are Abubakar Sadiq. What are you running from?* As I press the button to call the elevator, Maher's voice keeps playing repeatedly in my head: "This is not the first time you have suppressed your memories. We talked about this years ago." That is the problem with many locks in a young child's head. You never know when the locks will burst open, threatening to bring the horrors that rendered a child speechless for years.

The elevator doors open, and I freeze. The memory surfaces as clear as day.

I can still see her vividly like she is right in front of me. The way she laid lifeless on the white tiles of the bathroom, the water from the broken pipe that was still flowing, the blood everywhere, her soaked dress heavy against her skin... I could not stop looking at her. There was a big red gnash on her face from her fall. She had run to the bathroom to hide from him during their fight when she slipped on the slippery tiles, falling backward into the bathroom sink. The white ceramic was scattered around her head like the pieces of a broken halo stuck in her hair. She was rushed out of the house on a stretcher that carried away her limp body, hands dangling from beneath the cloth that covered her. That was the last time I ever saw my mother. I heard him saying the doctors did their best, tried to save her and the unborn child. He said she went into labor, was rushed to the hospital, and died in childbirth. He lied.

I tried to say it that day, the first time I slept in my grandmother's flat when my mother didn't return from the hospital. Every time I tried to talk, I watched the scene unfold again, playing on a loop in my mind, from the pool of blood on the floor to the way her hands dangled lifelessly as she was taken out of her section late at night. I tried to tell my grandmother that it was his fault, that he caused it, but the words could not form. My lips wouldn't let the words come out. Or any other word for that matter.

Hafsatu

I am in my bedroom at the new apartment I signed a two-year lease for when I arrived in Vancouver. It's on the fifth floor of a high-rise apartment, near a small mall close to the university I go to. I spent my first few days furnishing it in minimalistic earthy tones with pieces I picked up from Ikea. I spend most evenings alone as it is hard to make new friends in a city so cold that I stay indoors when I don't have lectures.

After lectures and long hours at the Library all week, I do laundry and binge-watch reality shows on Netflix on the weekends. Today, I paused an episode of The Mole as my dryer beeps to bring out my clothes and fold them neatly into my brown woven laundry basket to take to the bedroom. I am closing my drawers when I see a Facetime call from Ilham. I set the basket on the messy bed, push one of the pillows aside and answer the call on my laptop.

Her face fills the screen and she has the biggest grin on her face. From the way the phone is moving, I can tell she's walking up the stairs. I recognize the artwork on the grey walls of her house.

"I was not sure if you would still be in the library, but I had to call," she says, doing a little dance with her shoulders. I hear her push the door to her room open and flip a switch as the room lights up in a brilliant yellow glare.

424

"I got back like thirty minutes ago," she knows that I was at the Library because I update my Snapchat a lot nowadays with details of my new academic life: my late nights in the Library (late being Maghrib, of course), pictures of the essays on my laptop with my student number hidden behind my Starbucks cup, my trips to Superstore to get groceries on Sundays, Shoppers Drugmart for flu medication. This is the coldest, loneliest place I have ever lived in all my life.

I watch as she removes her scarf and settles into her bed. "I've got something to show youuuu," she says as she raises her hands, wiggling her fingers at the screen. She is sporting a beautiful engagement ring.

I gasp as my eyes widen, "oh my God! You said yes?" I sit up properly as I pull the laptop closer to me. "I am soo happy!"

"I made him sweat a little, but yes. You can call me Mrs. Usman, if ya nasty," she tucks an invisible tendril of hair behind her ear.

"I have to start planning your bachelorette party." There has to be karaoke, that's for sure. What else should we do? Women's paintball, or maybe a pool party and spa retreat after? Ilham's bridal party cannot be anything but spectacular.

"Aww you're gonna do that for me?" she asks in pretend surprise.

"Of course! Or do you have another best friend? Let me know so I can eliminate her."

"Hahaa," her laughter is contagious, and I join her. "I love you. I can't wait to see you."

"So tell me everything. I want to know." I have been in my head so much these past few months that I didn't even know what was going on in other people's lives. Every time Ilham calls or texts, it is always about me – my feelings, how I'm doing – and we haven't really had a chance to catch up on her since I left Abuja. It makes me feel a little bad.

"Uff, Bebi I have so much," she raises her voice as she emphasizes again, "sooo much to tell you." Ilham is always a good storyteller. I already know this will be good, and the smile on my face is plastered as I adjust my position to listen to her.

"Love is pain," she starts dramatically.

"*Kuma dai*, why are you like this?"

"Usman, eh? Anyway let me start from the beginning. So, I don't know if you remember Mamman?"

"Mamman?" The name sounds familiar. I think he is a distant relation of hers. "Did I meet him in London?"

"Yesss, that one."

"Oh, okay," I say as I recall the tall, light-skinned but pompous man who graced our graduation with a ton of gifts for Ilham and for some reason, always started his sentences with, 'my work with the presidency...' It was definitely not as impressive as he thought that was.

"So, Mamman proposed to me a few months ago. It wasn't even a proposal. He literally came to tell Umma that he wants to marry me, and Umma was in support."

"Hmm, makes sense. Wasn't she the one who told him to come for your graduation?"

"Exactly! Anyways, I told Usman when we were hanging out in the evening –"

"Like you always do." I interrupt to tease.

She laughs, "yup, like we always do. So, I mentioned it to him. I was like, "Oh, by the way, Mamman proposed to me," she pauses for effect, and I raise my eyebrow, impatiently waiting to hear his reaction to the fact that the girl everyone knows he loves was going to marry another. "Usman said, "Oh, that's nice."

My jaw drops, "nooo, he didn't. Oh that's nice? What the hell?"

"Hmm, Bebi, I thought I was going to die. But I was a big girl about it. I was like, 'Yes, he did, and I don't know if I should say yes.'"

"You were even giving him another opportunity to redeem himself?" I ask. Ilham must really love Usman for her to even do that.

"Exactly!! Thank you, Bebi," she gestures wildly like my comment validated her thought process, "and he goes, 'you should say yes, he's a hotshot'."

I cover my mouth with my hands. I can't imagine what Ilham's face looked like at that moment. "What did you now say?"

"*Kinsan Allah*, I was going to call Umma right there and tell her that I accept so that he would hear, but I had to give him a piece of my mind, so as I stood up and said: "You're a coward, Usman and I hate that I love you. *Allah ya sawwake.*" And then I turned around and left. I left, Bebi," she starts laughing at what must have been a tough moment in her life… "I cried in my car, *ehn*. I didn't even realize I could cry that much."

"Aww, Ilhaaam." I wish I was in Abuja with her when this happened, if not for nothing, just to comfort her and be there for her like she was when I went through my heartbreak.

"He kept calling me and I kept rejecting his calls. *Na kai gida*, when I got home, I just started deleting our pictures, chats and everything."

This is the heartbreak Adda S was talking about, heartbroken over someone who was not even her boyfriend. They never defined it. I never defined my relationship with Sadiq either; we just eased into it.

"Long story short, Usman came the following morning and wouldn't leave until I came out to see him. He was like he can't let me go, he can't imagine his life with anyone else, blah blah."

"Aww, oh my God, okay. Now, I'm going to cry." My eyes even start tearing up. Usman knows Ilham better than anyone; he knows when she's upset and how to calm her down.

"Today, when he proposed, he told me that it was Sadiq who told him that he would regret it if he didn't act –"

My heart drops. It shouldn't have. But it did, just by hearing his name.

"I'm s – sorry. I shouldn't have said that. Are you okay?" Even Ilham doesn't know the real reason why I broke up with him she knew that I never wanted to talk about him.

I scoff loudly as I shake my head. "No, no, babe. I'm fine. Continue your story." But that's a lie. I can't even listen to what she is saying anymore. So is he still in Abuja? Has he moved on? What is he doing these days?

I haven't seen him since the incident at *H&I*. I wish I can say that I got over Sadiq the moment I heard that he is my… that we are related. I wish I can say that all my feelings for him got sucked out of my heart and magically disappeared, but that didn't happen. I waited for it to happen, but it didn't.

The days and weeks that followed the revelation were hell.

Then I got to the bottom of the barrel – my lowest point – the lowest point I have ever been in my life, mentally and emotionally. It was when I actually wished that my parents had died before telling me the truth about my paternity. That the secret died with them, that I never found out.

I hated them. I hated Umm'Hafsa for being the reason I was in this position. I hated daddy for his hand in it. That was when I knew I needed professional help and I finally accepted daddy's gentle nudges to go for counseling. We left for California a few weeks later, where his mentor Dr. Abba Aji, referred me for bi-weekly sessions with a counselor who helps people deal with grief and loss.

"So today, when he came, he brought a ring," Ilham says with a smile. "and a receipt."

"Receipt?" I give her my full attention again as I wonder if I heard her right.

"Yeah, he wanted me to see the date on the invoice. Can you believe he bought the ring in January?"

"Oh God, you guys are my favorite love story."

Well, Umm'Hafsa and daddy are my favorite love story, but now Ilham and Usman are up there too. Love that starts with friendship. They are both proof that your person is out there somewhere. It might not be who you hope or think it is, but that person is out there, waiting for you too.

Hafsatu

Edinburgh, December 2022

Heriot-Watt and Edinburgh have their Winter graduations a few days apart. While in Scotland, my sisters, Aisha and Sara, go for Fatima Ringim's graduation while I head out shopping with Mohammed, bonding after a few months of not seeing him.

Three days later, I'm in my dark grey tailored jumpsuit and white coat with Umm'Hafsa and daddy in the magnificent McEwan Hall. I cheer loudly for Sara, the first Biomedical Scientist in our family, who, like our mother, graduates with honors.

After the two-hour ceremony, we go outdoors to take more pictures. I excuse myself to use the restroom and when I come out, I see broad shoulders of a man in a navy blue wool blend coat, six foot tall, with dark waves in his short hair and his back turned to me. He looked like he was waiting for someone. As the bathroom door closes behind me, he turns around and our eyes meet.

Abubakar Sadiq Ringim.

"Hi." My hand instinctively reaches for the scarf wrapped around my head. I am surprised to see him after so long. Being away in Canada for my master's has completely removed me from Abuja's stratosphere.

"Hi," he answers as he puts his hands in the pockets of his dark pants. I see a hint of what looks like a smile on his face as we close the distance between us. He still wears the same cologne; I have a jacket that smells exactly like he does now in my closet in Abuja. It's the one he gave me the night he dropped me at home from the Gatsby party.

"How have you been?" I ask.

He nods slowly, "I'm good, Alhamdulillah. You?"

"I'm great. You know someone graduating?" It feels like a lifetime ago when we made plans to attend our sisters' graduation ceremonies together.

"No, I didn't attend the ceremony. I just dropped by because I was sure I'd see you here." He looks behind us and then back to my face, "you look great."

"Thank you," I say. *So do you*, but I didn't say that out loud. He knows he always looks good.

"I just wanted –"

"Did you just –" get here? I was gonna ask. We both chuckle at how we speak at the same time.

"Go ahead," he says with his right hand coming out of his pocket.

I shake my head slightly, "no, you first."

As he clears his throat, a serious look comes over his face, "I've been trying to reach out to you. I, um, wanted to apologize for what happened at your office. I–"

"No no. You don't have to apologize. It's okay."

"No, it's not okay, Hafsat, please let me do this."

I smile sadly as I listen to him. The crease between his brows furrows deeper as he concentrates on his words, "I um… I lashed out at you, and that was completely unacceptable; you didn't deserve that. Nobody deserves that. And I apologize. I wanna let you know that I'm back in therapy for anger management."

"That's great. I'm so proud of you," I say honestly. It is a considerable feat going to therapy. Acknowledging that you have a problem is one thing, but being strong enough to seek help is another. "And thank you for saying sorry. How's therapy been?"

A flicker of something I think looks like sadness crosses his face for about a second. "Very hard." Then he chuckles to himself, and for the first time in a long while, I see the crinkles around his eyes. "A lot of things came up. Things I buried for so long, you know..." he shrugs. "I guess I've learnt it's not enough to say I am not like... I'm not like our father. I actually have to do the work to not be him."

Our father. I open my mouth and close it. "You.. H – How did..?"

He is quiet for a few seconds and says, "A small part of me hoped you would correct me. I guess this the confirmation I needed." He chuckles sadly.

"When did you find out?"

He looks away as he answers. "A while back. Saw an old picture from the house in Kaduna. I saw Umm'Hafsa with Hajiya Amina... in 1998." There's a forlorn look on his face as his index finger touches the corner of his lip. "It explained everything about how you, why you –" his voice trails off.

A wave of sadness hits me all over again; I tried to spare him from finding out. "I – I'm sorry for how I handled thi – things at the end. But you can understand why now?"

He is quiet for a few seconds, and then he says, "I understand." We slowly start walking back towards the grounds, his hands back in his pockets and mine busy tugging one of my earlobes.

"When are you heading back to Abuja?"

"This evening, insha Allah," he looks at his wristwatch. "What about you?"

"I'm heading back to Vancouver in two days."

"You live there now?"

"Yes, I went back to school. Started my Masters in September." I needed something to occupy me.

"No kidding, that's great. Masters in what?" He asks slowly.

"Economics."

"What about *H&I*?"

"Oh, it's running itself now. I figured I don't need to be physically there 24-7 and Umm'Hafsa has always wanted me to go back to school. She's a big believer in education and women being able to fend for themselves..." after what she experienced with you – our – father. But I don't say that.

431

She believes a woman will not think twice about leaving an abusive relationship if she can stand on her own two feet financially. Financial independence is something she always hammers into the ears of my sisters and I. I didn't understand why before.

He nods as if he understands what I didn't say. "She did really well for herself. *Kinsan* I didn't even know she was Head Auditor at the Central Bank until someone mentioned it to me a few months ago."

"Retired," I correct him. "Yes, daddy was the reason she went back to school."

He remains quiet for a few seconds as we walk down the hallway lined with chatty graduates in their gowns and caps taking pictures in small groups.

His eyes soften as he looks at me, "Hafsat, I feel like you know this already, but I'm gonna say it anyway. If you ever need help with anything at all, you know I've got you, right?" His voice lowers as he adds, "I know the world will never understand the truth of the relationship between us, but I will always be here for you, okay?"

I nod. I know that, yet I can't think of anything that would warrant me reaching out to him for help, but it's good of him to offer.

I chuckle as I remember to give him an update on something I haven't shared with anyone yet. "Can you believe daddy knew before he heard me say it?"

Time shared together is a crazy thing; the way I talk to him about something without being specific, and he knows exactly what I am talking about: "He did?"

"*Wallahi fa*, he was there with her from the beginning; he knew. He helped her with everything."

He stares into space with his eyebrows raised like he is mulling over what I just said. "From the beginning? Wow, that is... something," he says slowly. "How did that make you feel?"

We have reached the doors leading out to the grounds. In the distance, my parents are deep in conversation with another family. I can tell they are Nigerian too, from their attire. Umm'Hafsa is holding onto daddy's arm and she looks up at him as he speaks.

How does that make me feel? I think about it for a while before replying, "it blows my mind, to be honest. I'm still in awe. It's crazy how he never wavered, *ya rike amana*, that's love."

Theirs is a love that has stood the test of time. It's the kind of love books are written about. Their love has taught me a lot. It has taught me self-love and self-acceptance. It taught me what to look for in a partner, to look for a man who's patient and kind. A man who understands the deen and doesn't use it as a means to oppress.

I have loved and lost, but I will never settle for just anyone until I find a man who makes me feel the way daddy makes Umm'Hafsa feel. Like royalty. Like I am the only one who matters. If I ever find someone like that, I will tell him everything about the man who loves my mother, *fisabilillah*, for the sake of Allah. The man who brought me up and loves me with his whole heart – because of the love he has for my mother.

The past year has allowed me to see my parents as human beings; we all make mistakes. We are all flawed. I ask myself what I would have done if it was me in my mum's situation. I know about my parent's humble beginnings. Imagine not having the privilege I have had my whole life - thanks to them. If I was in Umm'Hafsa's dire situation, an orphan up against the most influential man she had ever met, what choice would I have made at seventeen, barely eighteen?

I would have done the same thing. Or something worse. She is a better person than most, and for her love, I am thankful. Sometimes we forget that our parents are human. They were once just as young as we are, also trying to figure life out. We place them on pedestals, expecting nothing but perfection from them.

It took a while, but today, I am able to hold them in good grace; now I relate to my mother with the utmost respect and my father, with even more love than before. I understand that everything – *everything* they did – was done out of love, and that is my identity.

My name is Hafsatu Ibrahim Gaya; my family calls me Bebi, and I am proof of the love my parents share. A love that has stood the test of time.

About the Author

Fatima Bala is a lecturer, poet, and writer who lives on Vancouver Island with her husband, children, and a pet fish called Fishy. Her books have received starred reviews from *The Los Angeles Tribune, London Post, and New York Weekly*. She enjoys playing board games and her favorite ones are Scythe, Dead of Winter, and King of Tokyo.

She is a graduate of Algonquin College, Vancouver Island University, and Stanford, where she studied Tourism, Business Management, and International Women's Rights.

She can be reached on Instagram at @aka.fatima.bala.

Also by Fatima Bala

Broken

A story of imperfect love. Broken from the start; yet constant.

Fa'iza Mohammed grew up very sheltered as the youngest daughter of a conservative northern Nigerian family. Her otherwise sane life is thrust into turmoil when she finds herself falling for someone with a completely different set of values from hers.

Ahmad Babangida believes everything is a construct. Rules and society condition people to be sheep, and he goes out of his way to live his life on his terms. Attracted to Faiza from the very start, he soon realizes that they are probably better apart but when the lines between *halal* and *haram* start to blur, can they stay away from each other?

Printed in Great Britain
by Amazon

33739249R00253